P9-CEK-925

SLY
FOX

SLY FOX

A Dani Fox Novel

Jeanine Pirro

HYPERION

NEW YORK

Mass Market ISBN: 978-1-4013-1261-9

FIRST MASS MARKET EDITION

1   3   5   7   9   10   8   6   4   2

SUSTAINABLE FORESTRY INITIATIVE | Certified Sourcing
www.sfiprogram.org
SFI-00993

THIS LABEL APPLIES TO TEXT STOCK

Dedicated to my mother, Esther Ferris—
my backbone and the woman who taught me
to never remain silent in the face of injustice

A NOTE TO READERS

As an assistant district attorney, the first-ever woman elected county judge, and, later, District Attorney in Westchester County, New York, I have always fought for the underdog in a legal system that often favors the accused.

This book is fiction, and the events, incidents, and characters are imaginary or are used in a fictitious way. Nevertheless, much of this book was inspired by actual events and criminal cases that I personally prosecuted.

I'm using this fictional venue to give readers an intimate glimpse into what really happens inside and outside of courtrooms and to describe a time not long ago when women, children, and the elderly were treated as lesser citizens.

Helping victims has always been my calling. I don't want justice to be blind. I want her to see the victims, to feel their loss and their pain, and to make sure that those who are responsible for causing those losses and suffering are rightfully punished.

The great judge Learned Hand once wrote, "The spirit of liberty remembers that not even a sparrow falls to earth unheeded."

I see myself as a "sparrow catcher"—no matter how small or insignificant, the fallen sparrows in our society deserve to have their day in court and a champion determined to fight for their rights.

—*Jeanine Pirro*

CONTENTS

PART ONE

NOT ONE OF
THE BOYS

*A woman, a dog,
and a hickory tree.
The more you beat them,
the better they be.*

—*SIXTEENTH-CENTURY ENGLISH PROVERB*

Monday, Spring 1976

I WAS LATE.

It was because of my dark, naturally curly hair. The alarm at my bedside had gone off at six a.m. and I'd thrown on a pair of running shorts, a tie-dyed T-shirt, and done a three-mile jog, returning in plenty of time to get to work at the Westchester County Courthouse. But when I'd looked into the mirror while cooling down, I'd seen the face of Janis Joplin staring back at me after one of her whiskey-and-drug-fueled concerts. I'd been a sweaty disaster with an out-of-control mane. A shower and wash had only made it worse. I'd been forced to flop my head on my ironing board and iron my locks to get them under control.

I'd only run one red light—in my opinion it was set too long between changes anyway—before reaching the courthouse's parking lot at 8:10 a.m., where I slipped into a row of spaces reserved for courthouse workers.

My name is Dani Fox and I've been an assistant district attorney for about a year. At age twenty-five, I'm young for the job. But that is not unusual for me. I'd come into this world in a rush and had no intention of slowing down. I'm currently the only female assistant district attorney in Westchester County. One hundred ten male lawyers and me.

Westchester County was America's first real suburb. It's just north of New York City and the Long Island Sound. Many of our residents commute to work in Manhattan each day. They used to live in the city but they moved here to start families. What many of them didn't leave behind was their New York attitudes. Our county is the second richest in the state. Only Manhattan's got more money. And our wealthier and more sophisticated residents aren't shy about letting you know that if you're a public servant, you work for them. Because of our county's close ties to Manhattan, there are challenges here that are a bit different from those that a prosecutor in Topeka faces. I'm not saying the district attorney in Kansas doesn't feel the same pressures as Carlton Whitaker III, our district attorney, whenever he's prosecuting a headline-breaking case.

But to quote *The Great Gatsby*'s Nick Carraway, "The rich are different from you and me."

Mostly, because they have more money.

And with their money, they can hire fleets of Manhattan's finest lawyers to make the forty-five-minute drive along the Henry Hudson Parkway north to White Plains in a cavalcade of black limos to rescue them.

There's another side to Westchester County as well. The landscape is dotted with lower-income neighborhoods where blue-collar workers struggle to pay bills and kids grow up on mean streets. In these areas a drug called cocaine is exerting a deadly grip.

Justice in Westchester County is dispensed to the rich and the poor alike in our new nineteen-story courthouse, one of the tallest buildings in White Plains. It was the first project in a massive urban renewal program approved in the 1960s that has pretty much destroyed the original village-like character of our community. It's fitting that the stark design of our courthouse is called Brutalist architecture. That refers to the building's concrete-and-stucco exterior and its strikingly repetitive angular design with rows of identical windows. But I also think that tag describes how some of the masses who flow through its doors are treated. We call it the Criminal Justice System, giving the creeps top billing. I think it should be the Victims' Justice System. If I sound a bit touchy about all of this, it's because I am. Only, I prefer to call it passion. I don't like it when the meek are preyed upon. The Bible may say the meek are going to inherit the earth, but until God reaches down and signs over the deed, it's my job as a prosecutor to protect them.

I've never wanted to be anything other than a prosecutor. Even as a kid when I was watching Perry Mason on television, I'd root for Mason's district attorney rival, Hamilton Burger, hoping that he would win at least one case. After a while, you had to wonder how Burger kept getting reelected, given that every time Mason defended a client, it turned out that the D.A.'s office had been bamboozled and was trying to convict the wrong guy. I especially enjoyed how the guilty leaped up in court and confessed. That doesn't happen in real courtrooms—particularly if there is a defense attorney within reach.

Even though I am an assistant D.A., I haven't officially been given a chance to try any bad guys in court. That's because I'm assigned to our office's equivalent of Siberia. All the male lawyers who were hired at the same time as I was were immediately sent to the criminal courts division to prosecute cases. But D.A. Carlton Whitaker III, in his infinite wisdom, assigned me to the appeals bureau. He doesn't believe a woman has the killer, go-for-the-jugular instinct that you need to win in court. One day I am going to prove him wrong.

Whitaker, my boss, can actually be a pretty decent guy. He's just part of an old boys' network that thinks a woman's place is in the kitchen or the bedroom but certainly not trying cases in the hallowed halls of justice. When he hired me, he said he really didn't have a choice. He had to meet a quota; or, as he put it, "I was forced to find a girl lawyer somewhere." So much for being magna cum laude, Phi Beta Kappa, and on Law Review at Albany Law.

I spend my days reading court transcripts of trials that some male attorney prosecuted. Once convicted, the guilty of course have the right to appeal, and it's up to me to review what happened during their trials and explain to an appellate court why the guilty got exactly what they had coming to them.

What I do is important, but I want to get into a courtroom to try a case so badly I can barely stand it.

As I hurried across the parking lot on this bright sunny morning, up the sidewalk toward the courthouse's door, I spotted Westchester County judge Michael Morano a few steps ahead of me. I actually didn't see his face. Rather it was the back of his head that gave him away. A tall, thin man, Judge Morano had bushy salt-and-pepper hair divided equally on either side of his head with a bald streak down the center that reminded me of a bowling alley. I'd encountered him many times in the courthouse hallways but we'd never been formally introduced. At age sixty-three, he was one of our county's most senior judges and was known for his cracker-jack legal mind and disagreeable temperament. He wasn't a happy man. Behind his robe, everyone called him "Miserable Morano" or "Misery" for short. In addition to his distinctive hair, he had massive bushy eyebrows that moved when he spoke, making it appear as if he had two woolly caterpillars doing push-ups on his forehead.

I entered the courthouse behind him and by chance stepped into the same elevator. There we were, just the two of us, with him looking straight ahead. I decided I wasn't going to let his gruff reputation intimidate me.

"Good morning, Judge Morano," I said cheerfully.

He gave me a puzzled look. "Young lady, do I know you?"

"I'm Dani Fox, an assistant district attorney."

He replied with an ambiguous grunt.

As the door opened to his floor, I said, "I hope someday to prosecute a case in your courtroom."

He glanced at me with contempt and said, "It's unlikely, my dear. I handle serious matters."

As soon as the elevator door closed, I made a sour face and repeated in a snickering voice: *"It's unlikely, my dear. I handle serious matters."* What an arrogant jerk, I thought.

I don't deal regularly with police detectives, which is why I was surprised when I arrived at my cubicle and found White Plains police detective Tommy O'Brien sitting in my chair, talking on my phone with his feet propped up and his well-worn shoes resting on my desk.

Just as I hadn't been properly introduced to Judge Morano, I'd never been introduced to O'Brien. But I'd read transcripts of testimony in the appellate division that he'd given in dozens of high-profile criminal cases and seen him in the halls. He was a street-smart cop who—how should I put this—didn't have a high opinion of lawyers. Or to be blunt, the guy was an "old school" Irish cop.

He certainly looked the part. Although only in his early fifties, O'Brien looked older. Tired. Twice divorced, he had a watermelon belly that draped over the two-inch-wide brown belt that kept his J. C. Penney black slacks in place. He was wearing a shabby navy blazer, a white shirt with its frayed collar unbuttoned, and an ugly maroon tie that he'd undoubtedly gotten as a Christmas present in an office exchange. There was a bald spot inching its way forward from the back of his huge skull and his once-bright red hair was now specked with gray. He had a toothpick protruding from the corner of his lips. He was one of those men who could use the term "doll" or "honey" or "gal" and not realize how archaic it sounded.

When I'd first arrived at Albany Law School, the female students used the term "FEK" when they talked about men who were like Detective O'Brien. When I finally asked what the acronym meant, they said it was not a compliment. It referred to these men's Neanderthal outlook. Whenever they encountered something new, they tried to fuck it, eat it, or kill it.

The only male figure in my life of that generation was my father, Leo, and he wasn't anything like that. Dad was kind, humble, and he loved to laugh. But the older women warned me that I would be encountering a lot of FEKs once I became a lawyer, regardless of whether I went to work in a high-priced law firm or chose the public route.

O'Brien showed no sign of removing his ample posterior from my office chair, but he did lift his feet from my desk and leaned forward, jabbing a manila envelope at me as if it were a knife—all the while continuing the conversation that he was having on my phone.

Placing my leather briefcase, a gift from my mother, on the industrial-grade white tile floor, I accepted his packet and shot him a glare that was meant to say: "Okay, Detective, I'll look inside your envelope, but get your butt the hell out of my chair."

O'Brien either didn't get my social cue or didn't care. From his comments into the phone, it sounded as if he was speaking to a woman.

Still waiting in front of my own desk, I slipped open the envelope and removed a handful of eight-by-ten glossy, color photographs. The pictures showed a woman's face. Her eyes were swollen shut, her nose seemed broken, her lips were puffed out, her jaw was askew, and her cheeks were varying shades of black and blue. From the photographs, I estimated she was in her twenties, although her appearance had been so brutalized that I couldn't be certain. Several more photographs showed there were no visible marks on the rest of her body, which meant her attacker had focused exclusively on her face.

Whoever did this wanted to make her ugly and remind her every day when she looked into her mirror that he'd done it. This was a crime of emotion. Why would a stranger beat her so savagely? This attack must have been personal. Someone she knew had done this to her.

Having finally finished his conversation, O'Brien put down the phone receiver and nodded toward the packet of photos. "He worked her over good this time," he announced, without identifying who "he" was, but implying that "he" had delivered this sort of beating before.

Nor did O'Brien vacate my chair.

I asked: "Who's 'he'?"

"Her husband, Rudy Hitchins," O'Brien replied. "She's Mary Margaret Hitchins, age twenty-four. Tends bar, or did until yesterday, at O'Toole's, down on Mamaroneck Avenue."

O'Toole's was a favorite watering hole for cops but I'd never been there. I'd never been invited.

O'Brien said, "Rudy's a raging asshole—a jealous prick and he don't like cops. Mary Margaret, well, she is—or was—a real looker before he decided to rearrange her face."

I slipped the photographs back into the envelope and pointed out the obvious: "Detective, you're sitting in my chair."

O'Brien gave me a look-over, running his eyes from my knees to my face, all the while twirling the toothpick in his mouth with his right thumb and forefinger. He didn't say anything and I thought this practiced scrutiny was probably an intimidation tool that he used whenever he was interviewing a suspect or a witness. Reluctantly, he rose from my chair.

I edged by him and sat down. I noticed that in addition to using my phone, chair, and desk, he'd eaten all the candy in a bowl near the phone. Sweets are one of my vices. Thankfully, I have a metabolism that lets me satisfy my taste for chocolate yet weigh in at 105 pounds at five feet four inches.

Now he was the one standing at the side of my desk. "A few

of the regulars at O'Toole's wanted to deal with Rudy on our own. But the prick would only take it out on her later if he got what he deserved and he's the sort of asshole who'd hire a lawyer and go after our badges if we taught him a lesson. Besides, he's not really the type who can be educated." He paused and then added, "There's a few other complications, too."

"Complications?"

"Mary Margaret is knocked up and rumor is it's not his kid. That's what pissed him off."

"So who's the real father?"

O'Brien shrugged, indicating that it wasn't really important. But I was quiet for a moment and that awkward silence apparently loosened his tongue. "I guess the father could be a cop. Mary Margaret, well, she's a flirt at the bar, makes lots of tips that way."

"A cop got her pregnant?"

"I'm not saying that. The kid's probably Hitchins's, okay? But, like I said, she's a popular girl at the bar—if you catch my drift. And if the kid is a cop's and the cop is married . . ." His voice trailed off.

"Why are you showing me these photographs?"

"Because you're the only gal who works here. We figure this is a female thing."

"No," I said firmly. "It's not a female thing, Detective. It's an assault thing. Rudy Hitchins should be put in jail for what he did to her. But he hasn't broken any laws here because it's not against the law in New York for a man to beat his wife—we both know that. Especially if he accuses her of cheating on him and getting pregnant by another man."

O'Brien said, "Hold on, Counselor. No one is talking about filing criminal charges here. Me and the boys, we just thought maybe you could go talk to her in the hospital and tell her to leave town, maybe start over someplace new. Just get away from Rudy because of her situation with the baby and all."

"What?" I said incredulously. "You want *her* to leave town because *he* beat her?"

"Hey, let's get real here. It's not like she's got a lot of options. You're from the D.A.'s office so she might listen to you, especially if you told her it'd just be better for everyone if she left White Plains and had her baby."

I hesitated, not certain I should ask the next question, but since he wanted my help, I needed to know what I was getting into. "Detective, why do you know so much about Rudy and Mary Margaret Hitchins? This baby, it isn't yours, is it?"

A look of anger washed over O'Brien's face. I'd clearly hit a nerve.

"No," he snapped. "I didn't fuck this broad. I know Rudy because I've busted his ass a half-dozen times. And I've talked to her at the bar. She's a sweet kid. That's it."

"Okay, so tell me about Hitchins."

During the next several minutes, O'Brien described how Hitchins had grown up poor in a White Plains neighborhood and moved quickly through juvenile correctional facilities into adult ones. At age thirty, Hitchins's most recent arrest was for an afternoon robbery at a White Plains jewelry store on Mamaroneck Avenue. Along with three thugs, Hitchins had burst into the store in broad daylight. Three of the robbers had smashed the glass display cases with hammers, scooping up diamond rings, precious jewels, and watches. The fourth had held the owner and clerks at gunpoint. For some bizarre macho reason, three of the robbers had not been wearing masks. But the fourth had concealed his face. Detectives had identified and arrested the three without masks. But the masked gunman—who they were certain was Hitchins—had slipped through their hands.

"Hitchins is a murderer waiting to strike—if he hasn't

already done one," O'Brien said casually. "The punk can't stay out of trouble. Meanwhile, Mary Margaret needs to get out of town. She might not be so lucky next time."

Lucky? I thought. He nearly beat *her* to death and she's lucky?

O'Brien said, "She's over at White Plains Hospital in Intensive Care if you want to pay her a visit. Me and the guys, well, we'd appreciate it."

He started to leave.

"Wait," I said, holding up the envelope with the grisly photos.

Removing his toothpick, O'Brien glanced over his shoulder at me and said, "Keep 'em. Tell Mary Margaret when you see her—the guys down at the bar are thinking of her."

2

ALTHOUGH NO ONE IN MY OFFICE had given me permission to get involved, I made up an excuse, ducked out the door, and headed to the White Plains Hospital at 41 East Post Road. I drive a British green Triumph TR6 sports car. It was my first splurge after I got hired and had a regular paycheck. On such a beautiful morning, I would have been tempted to put the top down, but after being forced to iron my hair that morning, there was no way I was going to take that chance.

I'd bought my car at an English import dealership but it had taken me two trips to find the right one—not the car, but the right salesman. The first one tried to steer me toward a white MGB, explaining that Triumphs were considered masculine because the TR6 came with a six-cylinder engine, as opposed to the standard four in an MGB. The boxy shape of the Triumph screamed male, he warned, especially when compared to the soft curves of the MGB. Hearing that had ended our discussion. I actually drove thirty miles over the Tappan Zee Bridge to a different dealership to buy my Triumph. I hate when men pigeonhole women.

You can blame my father for my taste in sports cars. Leo was a salesman by trade and a car buff by choice. He especially admired sleek European race cars. Dad died of cancer not long after I was hired as an assistant district attorney and one of my deepest regrets is that he never got a chance to watch me prosecute a defendant in court.

As I was walking to the hospital entrance, a car came to a screeching stop, nearly hitting me. I looked, assuming someone in it was injured. But the driver stepped nonchalantly from one of the ugliest vehicles that I'd ever seen. He'd clearly customized his 1973 Chevrolet Monte Carlo. Half of its roof was covered with white vinyl and the car's body had been spray painted a brilliant gold and then flecked with silver. The wheels were chrome. You might have expected to see it on a seedy Times Square side street being driven by a pimp, but not here in White Plains.

The car's owner seemed equally out of place. Recent issues of movie magazines had published photographs of John Travolta's upcoming release called *Saturday Night Fever* and the driver was clearly mimicking the actor's disco-dancing character. The top buttons of his black silk shirt were undone, exposing his dark chest hair. He was wearing a white three-piece suit, white leather shoes, and had a half-dozen gold chains dangling from his neck. As he shut the door, he leaned down to speak through the open window to a woman with bottle-blond hair.

"If the cops bug you, tell 'em I'm coming right out," he said as he left the Monte Carlo parked next to a No Parking sign. He began walking toward me and the hospital's entrance, but something caught his eye. It was a nearby trash can that contained a ditched bouquet of spring flowers. Snatching up the drooping flowers, he plucked off a few dead petals and headed inside.

I followed and walked to the receptionist's desk while Disco Man and his bouquet marched to an elevator.

"Can you tell me if Mary Margaret Hitchins is still in ICU?" I asked the receptionist, a fresh-faced candy striper.

She said, "Mrs. Hitchins was moved into a private room last night. It's on the fifth floor, room five-o-five."

The elevator doors announced my arrival on the fifth floor with a loud *ding*. I stepped onto a gray tile floor with pink and green specks and was immediately hit with the strong smell of antiseptic. A plastic sign attached to a pale green wall pointed me to the nurses' station, where a uniformed woman wearing a name tag that read Susan RN was working. When she glanced up from a medical chart, I said, "Hi, I'm from the district attorney's office and need to speak to Mary Margaret Hitchins—if she's up to seeing visitors."

Before Susan RN could reply, an angry male voice yelled: "Go to hell! Both of you!" It was followed by the sound of cracking glass.

Nurse Susan darted down the corridor with me in pursuit. As we reached the doorway to Room 505, Disco Man burst out into the hallway, almost smacking into Nurse Susan. Red-faced, he stomped to the elevator without acknowledging us.

We rushed into the room.

An older woman was hovering near a hospital bed where a young woman was lying. The patient's face was a mask of bandages. An IV bag hung next to her left arm and an electronic monitor tracked her vital signs with flashing yellow, green, and blue lights. I guessed this was Mary Margaret Hitchins and noticed that her swollen eyes, visible through a slit in the white gauze covering her face, were closed. She was either asleep or unconscious.

Addressing Nurse Susan, the older woman said, "I don't want that animal allowed in here again! He's got no right after what he did to my baby girl."

I put the woman at about forty-two, a real beanpole, standing at least five feet ten in flats. Only she seemed even taller because she'd teased her dyed black hair into a B-52 beehive—a popular hairdo fifteen years ago. Although she wasn't that old, her face was a road map of wrinkles and her husky voice suggested she was at least a two-pack-a-day smoker. This, I assumed, was Mary Margaret's mother.

Judging from the yelling, profanity, and shattered water glass on the room's floor, I further assumed that Disco Man's visit had gone poorly. The discarded bouquet that he'd so lovingly plucked from the trash can was scattered on the tiles, too.

Two plus two told me that Disco Man was Rudy Hitchins.

Nurse Susan said, "I'll get someone to come clean this mess," as she stepped gingerly over the broken glass after quickly checking the IV and vital-signs monitor connected to Mary Margaret. Satisfied, she slipped by me out the door. The older woman noticed me and asked: "Who are you?"

"My name is Dani Fox. I'm an assistant district attorney from the Westchester County district attorney's office. I've come to speak to Mary Margaret."

The woman replied, "She can't speak to no one right now because of what that bastard done to her face. He broke her jaw."

I asked, "And you are?"

"I'm Rebecca Finn. Her mother."

I looked again at Mary Margaret's eyes. She seemed oblivious.

Mrs. Finn said, "They drugged her up with painkillers. She's out of it. Thank God! He busted her nose this time and then he has the nerve to come in here with flowers like he cares about her. I ain't stupid." She hesitated and then asked, "My daughter's not in any trouble, is she?"

"Oh no," I replied.

"Then why are you here? Do you know my daughter?"

I explained that Mary Margaret was well liked at O'Toole's

pub, especially by the police. "A detective asked me to look in on her."

Mrs. Finn said, "She's pregnant, you know."

I faked a surprised look. "This isn't the first time that he's beat her, is it?"

A flash of suspicion appeared in Mrs. Finn's eyes. I couldn't tell if she wanted to be cautious because she was speaking to a prosecutor or if she was afraid she might say something that might anger Rudy Hitchins. Hoping to reassure her, I said, "I don't think Rudy Hitchins should get away with this. He should be in jail. But we don't have laws in New York yet that protect women from this sort of brutality."

"Damn shame," she replied.

"I came to speak to your daughter about her plans, after she's discharged. There are women's shelters here and in Manhattan especially for battered women, or maybe she could go somewhere on the Jersey shore where it's peaceful so she could have her baby and escape her problems for a while."

"She's only got one problem—that prick who hit her!"

"Do you have relatives living out of town where she could stay?"

Mrs. Finn shook her head, indicating no. "She's not going to run away and hide. Our family's been in White Plains for generations."

I noticed tears forming in her eyes. "I just wish her father was alive. He'd put Rudy Hitchins in a hospital bed right next to this one—if he didn't kill him first."

"I know you're angry but vigilante justice isn't the answer."

She looked at me and snapped, "Oh, it ain't, is it? Then what is? This happening like this? If the law don't protect you, then you got to take it in your own hands. This never would have happened if my Harry were here. He'd make short work of that bastard."

I replied, "That's why we need to make it a crime for men to hit their wives like this."

"His wife?" Mrs. Finn asked.

"Yes, isn't your daughter married to Rudy Hitchins?"

"Hell no! She isn't married to that son of a bitch."

"Doesn't she use his last name?" I asked, surprised.

"Oh that. It don't mean nothing. She began calling herself Hitchins the first time he got her pregnant a year ago. She didn't want anyone to think her baby was a bastard. But she had a miscarriage and, well, she just kept telling everyone that Hitchins was her last name, but them two never got married."

"Are you absolutely certain? You're one hundred percent sure they didn't visit a justice of the peace in Atlantic City or fly off to Las Vegas and get married without telling you?"

"Look, I'd know if my only daughter was married, wouldn't I?"

I broke into a smile. "Mrs. Finn, I don't know what others might have told you, but New York State does not recognize common-law marriages. Do you understand what this means?"

She shook her head, indicating no.

"It means Rudy Hitchins was not beating up his wife. It means he doesn't get a free pass."

She still seemed confused.

"Because they aren't married, Rudy Hitchins can be charged with a felony and put in jail."

"Well, he should be in jail." She paused and whispered: "He didn't just beat her, you know. There's more."

"Oh no."

"He comes home and is pissed off from the moment he walks through the goddamn front door, of course. Excuse my French. He starts yelling at her, accusing her of being a whore, claiming it's not his baby. When she tells him it's his, he slaps her and calls her a lying whore. Then that sick son of a bitch pushes her down on her knees, unzips his pants, and pulls out his dick and tells her to, well, you're a woman, you know what he wants her to do."

Without waiting for me to respond, she continued, "When my daughter refused to suck his dick, again, excuse my French, well, that's when he started beating her, and after he's nearly killed her, he pulls down her pants and screws her."

I took a deep breath and tried to get past the vision of a violent rape. I looked at Mary Margaret, remembering that her mother had just mentioned that Hitchins had cracked her jaw, and asked, "How do you know these details? Can Mary Margaret talk? When did she tell you this?"

Rebecca Finn looked at me and I could see embarrassment in her eyes. "This ain't the first time he's done this, that's how. Only he don't usually beat her so bad. I also talked to Mrs. Latham."

"Who?"

"She's the one who called the cops. She lives upstairs next to Mary Margaret and that bastard. Them walls in them apartments are like paper. She heard everything—them yelling— plus Mrs. Latham is a real busybody. You can bet she had her ear pressed up against the walls as soon as she heard him hollering."

"The rape? You said that happened before, but how do you know he did it this time?" It was the prosecutor in me kicking in. I was already forming a case against Hitchins in my mind.

"After Mrs. Latham heard Hitchins leave the apartment, slamming the door behind him and stomping down the hall, she looks out to make sure he's really gone and then she hurries over because she's scared my Mary Margaret is dead. She has a key to their place in case one of them gets locked out. She opens the door and sees Mary Margaret lying half-naked on the floor. Mrs. Latham called me and we pulled up Mary Margaret's panties and pants before the cops got there because we didn't want the police to see her all exposed that way."

As she stood next to the bed, she gently caressed her daughter's right arm. Rebecca Finn said, "I'll testify against the bastard. I'll tell the jury what he did to my baby girl."

"I'm afraid you can't do that, Mrs. Finn," I said quietly.

"Why not? She's my daughter."

"Anything Mrs. Latham told you would be considered hearsay and not admissible and I wouldn't be allowed by a judge to ask you about the other times that Hitchins beat Mary Margaret. The court considers that information prejudicial and a violation of a defendant's right to a fair trial."

"His rights? What about her rights?"

Trying to soothe her, I said, "If Mrs. Latham is willing to testify, I can ask her about what she saw and heard that night. But the truth is, I really can't do much unless your daughter is willing to file a criminal complaint against Hitchins and testify in court. If she isn't willing, he's going to get away with this."

I was speaking to Rebecca Finn and had moved closer to the hospital bed so that we could talk without people in the hallway overhearing us. I hadn't noticed that Mary Margaret had opened her eyes. Nor had I seen her slowly inching her hand toward my right arm. Without warning, she grabbed my wrist with such force that I jumped. She tugged on it, indicating that she wanted me to bend down close to her face.

Between clenched teeth in her wired jaw, she whispered, "Make him pay for what he did. I'll testify."

3

T HE FIRST CALL I MADE WHEN I RE-
turned to my office was to White Plains police detective Tommy O'Brien. He was not at the station but
one of his fellow detectives gave me O'Brien's beeper number
and he returned my call minutes later from a pay phone.

"Mary Margaret and Rudy Hitchins are not married," I
proclaimed. "They lived together, but never officially tied the
knot."

"Yeah, so," O'Brien replied, clearly unimpressed.

"So? It means we can file felony criminal assault charges
against him."

O'Brien was quiet.

After a few moments, I asked, "You still there, Detective?"

"I didn't send you to the hospital to see her because I want
to arrest Rudy Hitchins," O'Brien replied, clearly irked. "I
sent you there to tell her to leave town for her own safety."

The superior tone in his voice irritated me. He didn't have
the authority to send me anywhere. "Listen, Detective, whether
you like it or not, a crime has been committed. You're a cop.
Mary Margaret is a victim. And I'm an assistant district attorney. It's that simple."

"Okay, Counselor, you think it's really that simple—a
crime's been committed, I'm a cop, you're a prosecutor, he's a
perp? Well, let me explain a few facts of life to you, sweetheart.
Right now, Mary Margaret is pissed. She wants that son of a

bitch in jail. But he's going to come around with flowers and apologize in a few days, if he hasn't already. And when she gets out of that hospital, he's going to be waiting for her in his car to take her home. Where else is she going to go? She lives with him, remember? She's pregnant so she's going to lose that bartending job at O'Toole's because no one wants a knocked-up broad serving them. And Mary Margaret ain't like you. She don't have a fancy law degree to fall back on and she don't have any job skills, so you tell me, Counselor, what's she going to do, being that she's pregnant, homeless, and out of work?"

Continuing, he said, "I'll tell you what she's going to do because I've seen it a hundred times. She's going to keep her trap shut—until one day when she can't stand it no more. On that day, he's going to come home drunk and start hitting her again. And that's when she's finally going to fight back and whop him in the head with a frying pan. But all that is going to do is piss him off even more. And now he's going to be so furious that he's not going to put her in a hospital, he's going to put her in the ground. And nothing is going to happen because some slick defense attorney will claim he was just defending himself."

God, I thought. This is more complicated than I had imagined. And yet there was something about this incident that made me believe it could turn out differently.

"I know you've done this a long time, Detective, and you know more than me. But when I was at the hospital, I saw Rudy Hitchins and he was with another woman, a blonde. He's cheating on Mary Margaret. He might not want her back. Besides, shouldn't we let Mary Margaret make the final decision? She's the victim."

He didn't answer. "Detective, there's something more. He not only beat her, he raped her."

I thought that might sway O'Brien but it only seemed to make him more reticent.

"What the hell?" he said. "I didn't read anything about that in the original officer's report."

"That's because the neighbor who found Mary Margaret pulled her pants up before the police arrived."

"Are you telling me that you not only want to charge this prick with assaulting his longtime girlfriend but also with raping her, too, even though they were living together, sleeping together, and there's no mention of rape in the original report? Do you have any idea what's going to happen if we charge him with rape? You're going to be laughed out of the courtroom. You can't rape some broad who's living with you and passing herself off as your wife."

"I disagree. Rape is about control, domination—not sex."

"And where did you hear that, young lady? Some sociology course or at some women's rally on a fancy-dancy college campus? You need to get real, Counselor. You might get him on assault—if you're really, really lucky. But toss in rape? Hell, you'll never get this case out of a grand jury. They'll think you're bonkers!"

Sadly, I suspected he was right. "Okay, forget the rape charge for right now."

"No. Forever."

Neither of us spoke for a moment and then he said, "Listen. You're a good kid, okay. But do you realize what you're stepping into here? You're going to be putting this victim in even more danger by going after that prick. What do you think Rudy Hitchins is going to do if I bust his ass? He's going after her."

"I'll get a temporary order of protection keeping him away from her. She wants me to file charges. If you'll help me, we can do this. We can get him for felony assault."

O'Brien was still hesitant. "Okay, Counselor," he finally said. "Let's assume I go along with your harebrained scheme and arrest this prick. Are you telling me your boss is going to allow you to try Rudy Hitchins in criminal court or is he just going to send this case over to family court?"

"He's got to file charges in criminal court," I said. "Family courts don't have jurisdiction over couples who are not married, only couples who are married. That's the law."

"That may be the law, Counselor, but you and I both know that anytime there is a fight between two people who are living together in this county, the cops, prosecutors, and judges consider the case a domestic issue and that means they get sent to family court for touchy-feely counseling. That may not be the letter of the law, but it's what always happens."

"If you can get Mary Margaret to swear out a complaint against Hitchins for first-degree assault, I'll do my job and make sure this gets into criminal court, where it belongs."

O'Brien considered my offer silently for several moments. Finally, he said, "Well, you got moxie, I'll give you that, Counselor. Okay, I'll go out on a limb here and have a chat with Mary Margaret and if she wants to file criminal charges, I'll arrest Rudy Hitchins for assault. I don't mind getting laughed at at the station. But you're playing with fire, Counselor. You'll end up with more than egg on your face if we blow this. And Mary Margaret will be putting herself in real danger. He's not the sort who forgets and forgives. He's the sort who gets even."

There were a million responses that shot through my mind. I knew O'Brien was right. If I managed to get D.A. Whitaker to prosecute this case in criminal court—where it belonged—and not shuffle it over to family court and then I flubbed it, I'd never get out of the appeals bureau—ever. And that was assuming I'd be able to keep my job. I also knew Rudy Hitchins would want revenge. Was I ready for what he might do? Was Mary Margaret ready?

I didn't want to think about it.

Instead of admitting my fears, I replied with a smart-ass comment.

"Egg on your face? Frying pans? Really, Detective, if we're going to work together, you've got to move out of the kitchen and into the brave new world."

"Not a chance, Counselor," O'Brien replied in a deadpan voice. "I like it fine in the world we're in right now."

4

W ESTCHESTER COUNTY DISTRICT
Attorney Carlton Whitaker III liked to refer to
himself as a "hands-off" manager who gave the
assistant district attorneys in our office the freedom to work
without second-guessing their actions or peering over their
Brooks Brothers–clad shoulders. What that really meant was
that Whitaker spent most afternoons at the Westchester Country Club in nearby Harrison playing golf and kissing up to the
club's elite. There were plenty of prestigious posteriors worth
smooching. Howard Hughes used to play at the club's links,
along with Ed Sullivan. Just getting through the country club's
front door was rumored to cost as much as $100,000 in mem-
bership initiation fees. The fact that D.A. Whitaker, whose
annual salary topped out at $65,000, was a member raised eye-
brows in the courthouse, especially after it was revealed that
his membership fee had been waived. But Whitaker was willing
to risk possible public criticism in order to hobnob with the
likes of *Tonight Show* host Johnny Carson, comedian Jackie
Gleason, and boxer Gene Tunney. It was the ultimate old boys'
club perk.

In New York, district attorneys are elected every four
years, which is why my boss spent time schmoozing at the
country club. But Whitaker was no dope. Whenever a high-
profile prosecution surfaced, he jumped in to claim the head-
lines. While Whitaker was a capable prosecutor, the real legal

strategist in our office was an immaculately dressed fellow who could always be seen seated next to Whitaker at the prosecutor's table or standing behind him at press conferences.

Paul Pisani was the most successful assistant district attorney in the history of Westchester County. It had been years since Pisani had lost a criminal prosecution. Even his most hated rivals referred to him as "Mr. Invincible."

The two men had much in common. Both were handsome and razor smart. But there was one glaring difference. D.A. Whitaker rarely permitted the public to peek behind his well-crafted public mask. Paul Pisani didn't give a damn about public opinion. If anything, he viewed the public with contempt. He was vain, condescending, and arrogant—except when he appeared in the courtroom. Pisani put his ego in check and transformed himself into whatever was necessary to win the hearts of jurors. He was especially brilliant when it came to interpreting the law and he knew how to lead jurors exactly where he wanted them to go. His opening and closing statements were delivered in eloquent bursts, aimed directly at the heart of the defense counsel's case and the unlucky defendant who'd come into Pisani's gun sights.

Together, Whitaker and Pisani ran an efficient operation. Whitaker glad-handed the Westchester County power brokers and kept the public happy with his glowing news reports about his office's successes while Pisani made sure the bad guys were sent up the river to Sing Sing. The third member of the triumvirate was Mark Steinberg, who was Whitaker's chief of staff. Although he was an assistant district attorney, Steinberg had never tried a case. Rather, he oversaw the day-to-day operations, paying particular attention to anything that could impact his boss's political well-being. Steinberg's stress level was at its highest at reelection time. He handled the media, political polls, campaign management, and fund-raising.

With Whitaker serving as the public face, Pisani as the legal

mastermind, and Steinberg running daily operations and overseeing politics, the D.A.'s office performed much like a well-
oiled machine.

On paper, the prosecution of criminals in Westchester
seemed straightforward. After the police made an arrest, the
accused was taken before a judge for arraignment, advised of
charges, told to get himself an attorney, and had a bail hearing.
If the accused couldn't post bond, he was remanded to jail.
Next came a preliminary hearing at which the state was required to show it had sufficient evidence to seek an indictment
from a grand jury. All grand jury hearings were secret, but if
its members agreed that the prosecution had a solid case, the
accused was bound over for trial. Next came a series of pretrial
maneuvers by both sides that eventually led to a trial.

At least, that's how the legal system was supposed to work.
What really happened was quite different. As soon as someone was arrested, charged, and got a defense attorney, that
lawyer and a prosecutor from our office would begin wran-
gling. Ninety percent of all criminal cases filed in Westchester
County would never make it to an actual trial. Deals would be
cut at some point in the process. These plea negotiations were
exercises in bluster, horse-trading, and strong-arming and had
more in common with the give-and-take that happens each
day on used-car lots rather than with our blind, lovely Lady
Justice.

Detective O'Brien had promised me that he'd get the criminal justice process started by interviewing Mary Margaret,
doing a background investigation of her and Hitchins, and
collecting sufficient evidence to arrest Hitchins on first-degree
assault. But I knew O'Brien was a realist and he'd find a reason
to drag his feet until he heard through the grapevine that D.A.
Whitaker or Steinberg had agreed to let me move forward with
my plan. O'Brien wasn't going too far out on a limb for me

without glancing over his back to see if anyone was firing up a chain saw.

The next step was to convince either Steinberg, who oversaw our office, or D.A. Whitaker that prosecuting Hitchins in criminal court was a good idea. I decided to focus on Whitaker. What would make our golf-playing D.A. want to charge Hitchins with a felony?

The answer seemed obvious. Whitaker was a publicity hound. That was the key. There was nothing especially newsworthy about the Hitchins case. I suspected there were plenty of men who slapped around women in Westchester. But the political and social climate in our country was clearly shifting. While it was not illegal in New York for a husband to hit his wife, there was a movement afoot to draft legislation that would make spouse abuse a crime. Women were gaining more political power. More and more unmarried couples were living together. And the legal system was being dragged into the social fray. A few years earlier, Michelle Triola had filed a lawsuit against actor Lee Marvin claiming that she was entitled to "palimony" because they had lived together even though they weren't married. The media seemed fascinated by the changes in traditional male and female roles. If I could convince Whitaker that prosecuting Hitchins as a criminal could get him on the front page of the *White Plains Daily* and help him politically with women voters, he might sign on.

I had an idea. Not long after I'd been hired, Will Harris, a reporter at the *White Plains Daily*, had telephoned me. He'd wanted to write a feature story about me since I was the first female assistant D.A.

I'd turned him down because I already knew that I was going to face resentment from male prosecutors and I didn't need the additional grief. I hadn't even bothered to mention it to Whitaker or Steinberg.

If I could get an appointment directly with Whitaker, I could tell him that Harris was interested in writing a story about women and the legal system. I could tell him that having me prosecute Hitchins as a criminal would give reporter Harris a terrific news angle. D.A. Whitaker could tell the public on page one how concerned he was about battered women in our county and that message would surely help him win the female vote in his upcoming reelection in November this year.

The trick was getting to Whitaker. And that meant I had to find a way to get around Steinberg. Our office was all about chain of command.

I picked up my phone and called Steinberg's office. His secretary, Patti DeVries, answered. Our office had a strict policy when it came to addressing fellow employees. Everyone was required to call secretaries by their last name. The same was true about the male lawyers. But for some reason, which no one had ever bothered to explain, the secretaries and male attorneys usually called me by my first name and didn't think anything of it.

"Hi, Mrs. DeVries," I said. "This is Dani."

I liked Patti DeVries. She had been a real pal when I was hired. I'd been shunned at noontime by my male counterparts. Not one of them had invited me to lunch—not even now. It might sound trivial, but their fraternity-brat tactics hurt my feelings. Of course, I'd refused to show it. Instead, I'd begun brown-bagging it, pretending I was too busy at work to take a break. And then one afternoon Patti DeVries had waltzed into our office and she'd spotted me eating a tuna sandwich at my desk. She'd invited me to join her and the other women for lunch.

The male attorneys thought it was hilarious that I had been relegated to eat with secretaries. But what their testosterone-drenched brains hadn't realized was that my lunches with the secretaries quickly paid off. Any jealousy that the women felt toward me because I outranked them had vanished. I got to know them as peers and they got to know me. I asked them for advice about things that they talked about—mostly men, but also where to shop, office politics, and family problems. They began watching my back. Best of all, there was no better way to keep track of the latest gossip than by lunching with the girls. Nothing, and I mean nothing, escapes the eyes and ears of a good executive secretary. If a married judge groped his clerk, I heard about it. If a defense attorney had a drinking problem, I heard about it. There was only one secretary who stayed aloof from the rest of us. She was Hillary Potts, the personal secretary of our boss, Whitaker. I suspected she thought she was better than the other secretaries and me, too.

"I need a favor," I told Patti on the phone. "Can you tell me when Mr. Steinberg is not going to be in his office?"

"Don't you mean when is he going to be here?"

"No," I replied. "I want to know when he will definitely *not* be in the building."

Patti chuckled. "Well, hon, he has a dental appointment tomorrow morning. He's taking the entire day off to get his wisdom teeth removed."

I avoided making a crack about Steinberg and wisdom. Instead, I said, "Isn't he a bit old for that?"

"Apparently not," she replied. "They're impacted. Actually, he's going to be out for two days—at least. Why do you want to know?"

"I'll tell you tomorrow at lunch, okay? I'm buying."

"Oh, this should be good, especially if you're buying."

We hung up, and for a second I thought about Patti DeVries and the other secretaries who worked in the courthouse. She'd gone directly from high school to a local two-year program for secretaries and had been hired by the county. Because she wasn't a college graduate and was married to a blue-collar worker, the lawyers in our office looked down on her. But she was a fast learner, and after a year as Steinberg's secretary, she knew more about how to navigate the county court system than any of the lawyers. Our office would have become paralyzed without her and the other secretaries, although their paychecks certainly didn't reflect that.

5

HILLARY POTTS, A STRIKING, BUT stern-looking woman in her fifties, always maintained a formal air at her desk directly next to the double doors that opened into D.A. Whitaker's massive office. She was more than his personal secretary. She was a gatekeeper. No one got in to see him without first getting by her. No one.

When I arrived first thing the next morning in Whitaker's office, Miss Potts made it clear that she was in no mood for chitchat. Instead, she focused on a letter that she was typing until she got a call on her intercom from the Boss.

"District Attorney Carlton Whitaker III will see you now," she announced solemnly as if I were being presented to the Queen of England. She opened one of the doors that led into his office.

As I approached the doorway, I recognized the voice of Paul Pisani, Westchester County's "Mr. Invincible," coming from inside. I had heard that Pisani made it a practice to meet most mornings with Whitaker to review that day's court docket. I stepped inside just as Pisani was lowering a porcelain coffee mug from his lips.

"Jesus Christ," Pisani declared, "why can't our cops make some goddamn decent drug arrests? Rudy Giuliani began going after drug dealers three years ago and look where it's gotten him. He's a goddamn associate deputy attorney in the

Justice Department going after mobsters now just like Bobby
Kennedy did in the sixties. Mark my word, Giuliani has a
bright political career ahead of him in New York and he's only
half the prosecutor that I am. Don't we have any gangsters
around here we can arrest? What the hell's wrong with our
cops?"

Apparently, Whitaker had heard Pisani's refrain before because he shot me a "here we go again" look. Pisani also glanced
over his shoulder at me and I felt an immediate sense of dread.
We'd never formally met, but I certainly knew him by reputation for being a formidable prosecutor, a complete snob, and a
notorious philanderer. The secretaries in our office had warned
me about Pisani and his endless flirtations. Rumor was that
Pisani had tried to bed every attractive woman whom he'd
encountered in the courthouse—and some unattractive ones,
too! I'd been told that he hadn't found any of them as fascinat-
ing as he found himself.

In our courthouse almost every lawyer and judge had a last
name that ended in a vowel. Even so, Pisani stood out. He had
graduated from Phillips Exeter and Harvard Law. He was also
the only assistant district attorney in Westchester who'd ever
walked into a courtroom dressed in a London Savile Row suit.

The secretaries had also tipped me off about Whitaker and
his insecurities and ego. Shortly after he was elected, he'd
spent thousands having contractors remove walls in the suite
of rooms that included the D.A.'s office so it was now the
equivalent of three offices remodeled into one. The additional
space at one end had been made into a massive conference area
with a table large enough to seat sixteen. On the opposite side
of his expanded domain, he'd installed a lounge area with
leather sofas and chairs clustered around a wooden coffee table. Directly in the center of the room was a hand-carved ma-
hogany desk from the 1800s that was rumored to have once
been owned by one of New York's robber barons. Whitaker,

who was in his midsixties, had a fondness for antiques and had found a way to purchase the desk with public funds when the desk showed up at an estate sale on the Hudson. A Waterbury school clock, another antique that he'd secured, was hanging on the wall to his left. Its noisy pendulum had been intentionally stopped because Whitaker had found the tick-tocking distracting. The clock was the only decoration in the room. All of the remaining wall space was taken up either with framed photographs or documents. The photos were eight-by-tens of Whitaker shaking hands with local, state, and national politicians or celebrities. The framed documents were certificates, honors, and awards that he had received. It was a museum of egomania.

Pisani was seated directly in front of Whitaker's massive desk in one of two red leather chairs. I nodded politely to Pisani as I walked across the thick carpet. I could feel both men's eyes giving me the once-over. It seemed to take forever to reach the empty chair next to Pisani. I did not sit down but rather remained standing until Whitaker acknowledged me.

That was not something he apparently was in a hurry to do.

Seeing them together reminded me of the 1969 movie *Butch Cassidy and the Sundance Kid*. The older Whitaker would have been cast as Paul Newman while Pisani would be an Italian version of Robert Redford.

As always, "Mr. Invincible" was stylishly dressed and not a single piece of his slicked-back black hair was out of place. He was in his midforties and had a strong jaw and beautiful steel-gray eyes.

Some fifteen years older, District Attorney Whitaker did not have as impressive a legal pedigree as his younger impresario, which was why, I suspected, the D.A. had furnished his office with the antique remnants of the once powerful and had covered his walls with reminders that he was someone of importance. He'd graduated from Fordham University Law

School and returned to White Plains, where he'd used his physician father's social connections to open his own successful legal practice while immersing himself in local politics. Like Pisani, Whitaker dressed well, but not so well that his constituents would be resentful. Both men could feel at ease on the ninth hole at the country club. But only Whitaker could shed his jacket, roll up his sleeves, and drink mugs of draft beer with the cops and blue collars at O'Toole's well into the night.

After a few intentionally awkward seconds, Whitaker said, "Miss Fox, you told my secretary that it was urgent for you to see me. Something about a potential news story and big case. What's it about?"

As I started to answer, Pisani interrupted. "I'd like another cup of coffee, wouldn't you, Carlton? Can you fetch us some, Ms. Fox?" He nodded toward a silver urn in the office's northwest corner, yet another antique, and held out his white mug. I didn't move. What a pig, I thought. I was a prosecutor, not his personal waitress. I made eye contact with Whitaker and much to my disgust, he slowly hoisted up his empty mug, too. I noticed that Whitaker's had the words THE BOSS emblazoned on it in gold leafing. I thought both of those mugs should have had the word PRICK on them.

"No problem," I said flatly.

"I take two lumps," Whitaker said.

"I take mine any way I can get it," Pisani added.

How about with some added spit? I thought.

I had brought the manila envelope with me that contained photographs of Mary Margaret's beaten face. As I reached toward Whitaker's outstretched hand to retrieve his coffee mug, I handed him the envelope. Then I turned and took Pisani's mug with the most disingenuous smile that I'd ever flashed anyone.

When I returned from pouring the two men's coffees, Whitaker was examining the photos.

"Mr. Whitaker, I wanted you to see these photographs so

you would know what sort of defendant we're dealing with here."

"Defendant?" Whitaker asked. "Has someone already been charged with this beating?"

"Well, not yet," I said, correcting myself. "The victim is Mary Margaret Finn, a local White Plains girl, and the man who did this to her is her boyfriend, Rudy Hitchins."

Pisani said, "Would this be the same Rudy Hitchins who got a free pass a few weeks ago on an armed robbery charge? A 'smash and grab' at a jewelers on Mamaroneck Avenue?"

"Yes, sir," I replied, genuinely impressed that Pisani remembered.

Because Whitaker wasn't familiar with the case, Pisani briefed him. "Mr. Hitchins and his criminal associates were arrested but the charge against him was dismissed. They burst in the store, smashed the glass display cases with hammers, grabbed as much as they could carry, and then ran outside. Not real inventive, but efficient. The case wasn't that interesting, but I remember it because I've been watching this Hitchins character."

"Why?" Whitaker asked.

"He's got potential." Pisani laughed. "He's a wannabe gangster. He does work occasionally for Nicholas Persico's crew."

"He works for the Butcher? Persico?" Whitaker asked, clearly impressed.

"Excuse me," I said. "I'm afraid I'm not following any of this."

Pisani sounded irritated but looked pleased to show off his knowledge. "Persico is a member of the Genovese crime family. We've been after him for years."

"Why did you call him the Butcher?"

"'Cause he runs a family-owned butcher shop in Yonkers and he likes to use a butcher knife when he tortures his victims."

Growing suddenly impatient, Whitaker asked me, "What's so important about this Hitchins character that you needed to see me? He sounds like small potatoes and this sounds like a family court matter, not a big case."

I quickly explained that Mary Margaret and Rudy Hitchins were not married. I added that she was pregnant with his baby and that he'd put her in the ICU. Following Detective O'Brien's advice, I said nothing about how Hitchins had raped Mary Margaret.

Whitaker said, "Get to the point, young lady."

"Since they aren't married, I'd like to prosecute him in criminal court on first-degree assault charges. Family court lacks jurisdiction. I want him to go to jail for what he did—and Detective Tom O'Brien agrees with me, sir."

Out of the corner of my eye, I noticed Pisani smirk. Mentioning O'Brien's name had been a mistake. It made it appear as if I wasn't strong enough on my own to handle this—that I'd been be prompted by O'Brien.

Whitaker asked, "Miss Fox, aren't you assigned to the appeals bureau?"

"Yes, sir."

"The last time I checked, attorneys assigned to the appeals bureau don't try criminal cases, or has someone changed my office policy without telling me?"

Pisani smirked again. He was enjoying this.

"Sir, I'd like to prosecute this case, just the same. It's important to me."

Whitaker glanced at Pisani, who decided to join the conversation. "Ms. Fox, what makes you think *you* can prosecute a case if you've never tried one before?"

I turned my head so I was looking directly at Pisani. "But I have tried cases in court, Mr. Pisani. Actually, I've tried thirteen misdemeanor jury cases in Westchester County."

"Ms. Fox," Pisani said, "each morning when I come to work, I review all the criminal matters this office has prosecuted in county court and in our other forty-three jurisdictions in Westchester County. I do the same before I go home each night, and I have never read your name as the assistant district attorney of record on a single criminal case."

"That's correct, sir. The cases I prosecuted were all night cases assigned to other assistant district attorneys. The men couldn't keep up so I helped them out."

"The men in this office couldn't keep it up, so you helped them? You gave them a hand?" Pisani asked, making yet another sexual entendre. "And who gave you permission to do this? Does your division chief know?"

Whitaker interrupted. "Are you saying you volunteered to take other attorneys' night court cases?"

"That's correct, sir. Most were DWIs but there were also assaults and burglaries reduced to misdemeanors at the local court level."

"And were any of these defendants represented by counsel or did you simply work out plea deals?"

"All of the accused in the thirteen cases that I tried were represented by legal counsel. They had defense attorneys."

"Really," Pisani sniffed, lifting an eyebrow as a clear sign of his skepticism. "And how many of these thirteen cases did you actually win?"

"All of them."

Whitaker liked my response. "So what you're telling us, Miss Fox, is that you tried the cases but your colleagues claimed credit for it on the paperwork?"

I thought he might be trying to get me to criticize my coworkers, something I was not going to do. "Whether or not my fellow assistant district attorneys gave me credit on the paperwork is something you'd have to ask them. I've never bothered to check. But I showed up in night court and I did my job as a prosecutor. That's why I am confident I could prosecute Rudy Hitchins and win."

I couldn't tell if Whitaker was impressed or amused by my reply, but Pisani was neither. He said, "Ms. Fox, you didn't lose a single case that you prosecuted? Is that correct?" It suddenly sounded as if he were interrogating me on the witness stand. And, in fact, he was interrogating me.

"That's right, sir."

"Tell me, Ms. Fox, how does someone in the appeals bureau who came to us without any trial experience win every case she has ever tried? Are you claiming to be some sort of legal prodigy?"

Again my eyes locked with his. "No, sir, but I had an excellent teacher and I am absolutely certain that you, yourself, would call him a prodigy. In fact, you might describe him as a genius in the courtroom."

"At Albany Law School?" he replied dismissively. "I hardly think so!"

"No, sir, to the best of my knowledge, he's never taught at a law school."

"Then who is this genius?"

"You. My teacher was you."

Whitaker laughed out loud.

I explained that I had studied every major transcript of criminal cases that Pisani had tried in the past five years in Westchester County. I'd read every opening statement that he'd given, every direct examination that he'd performed, every cross-examination, and every closing argument.

"That's the fucking funniest thing I've heard all morning," Whitaker said, adding, "She's right about one thing. You would describe yourself as a legal genius."

The D.A. laughed again.

Pisani wasn't amused. "If you have studied my cases,

Ms. Fox, then you'll have no problem telling me about the Billy Prescott murder?"

"I'm assuming you're referring to the defense's charge that your star witness—a teenage boy with a long juvenile record—had admitted under oath during questioning that he'd originally lied to the police."

Pisani didn't answer. He wasn't going to help me prove that I was telling the truth.

"In your closing argument, you told jurors that if the police locked up every witness who had held back information or had lied to them when they were first interrogated, the jails and prisons would be overrun with frightened and foolish witnesses who'd merely panicked and had become confused during questioning."

I knew I was right and so did Pisani.

Whitaker glanced at his watch and said, "Okay, let's cut to the chase here. I've got an afternoon tee-time. What makes you think the victim—who is pregnant—is going to testify against him?"

"It appears that Hitchins already has a new girlfriend. When Mary Margaret hears that, he's not going to be able to sweet-talk her into dropping charges—especially after what he's done to her face."

"Hell hath no fury like a woman scorned," Whitaker said. "I get that. What else you got?"

I sensed it was time to test my scheme. "A reporter named Will Harris from the *White Plains Daily* wanted to write a feature story about me when I was first hired as an assistant district attorney. Of course, I refused. But I thought this case might be a good chance for your administration to show how concerned it was about domestic violence. Having a woman prosecutor handle it would make the news even more unique."

Whitaker rocked back in his chair, considering my idea.

"My, my," Pisani said with a mix of sarcasm and hint of

admiration. "You certainly have figured out all of the angles here, haven't you, Ms. Fox?"

I sat there waiting, waiting, waiting.

Finally, Whitaker spoke. "Here's the deal. I'll let you try this case in criminal court rather than shuffling it off to family court for some couples counseling. You can charge this Hitchins character with first-degree assault. And I'll let you prosecute it. But you cannot, and I just said *cannot*, talk to that reporter. You tell him that you can't discuss the case because it's a pending legal matter. I want him to talk to me and only me at this stage. Is that perfectly clear?"

I couldn't believe what I was hearing. He was giving me exactly what I wanted.

Pisani, who clearly couldn't let this matter drop without making a comment, said, "Well, well, well. Congratulations, Ms. Fox. Bravo. It seems you have gotten what you came in here for, but there is one angle that I think you may have overlooked."

"What's that, Mr. Pisani?"

"The fact that you're probably going to lose. This is not a simpleminded DWI prosecution; your objective is to put a man in jail for an alleged crime that, as I'm sure you know, is not a violation of the law if a couple is married in New York."

"But Hitchins and the victim aren't married."

Pisani replied, "Yes, you said that. But they were living together, she is pregnant with his baby, and apparently she was using his last name."

I wondered how Pisani knew that, since I had not mentioned it. And then I remembered that the words MARY MARGARET HITCHINS were written in large black letters on the back of the eight-by-ten-inch photographs that I'd handed Whitaker earlier. Clearly, Pisani had seen her name.

"You can go now, Miss Fox," Whitaker said, "but I want

you to keep Mark Steinberg informed of everything you do and you are not—not—to talk to that reporter. Got that?"

"Yes, sir."

Having mentioned Steinberg's name, Whitaker suddenly looked a bit puzzled and said aloud, "Where the hell is my chief of staff? Miss Potts said he wasn't around today. I'll want to talk to him about this Hitchins matter."

I volunteered, with a slight smile, "I understand he's at the dentist."

Whitaker shot me a curious look.

Pisani said, "Carlton, you'd better keep an eye on this one. She's one sly fox."

I began walking toward the door but Pisani wasn't finished. "Ms. Fox, have you heard that old saying: 'Every female in a relationship needs to be taken with a grain of *assault.*'"

As I exited the office, I thought: I really should have spit in their coffee mugs.

6

D ETECTIVE TOMMY O'BRIEN AN-
swered my telephone call in his well-practiced
growl: "Homicide. O'Brien."

"Detective, this is Assistant District Attorney Dani Fox.
The district attorney has agreed to move forward and file
criminal charges against Rudy Hitchins for assaulting Mary
Margaret."

O'Brien didn't immediately respond so I continued: "I'm
assuming you did a routine background check of the criminal
files and complaints?"

"Yeah, yeah, nothing surprising in them."

"And you went to the hospital and took the victim's sworn
statement and she is still willing to testify against Rudy
Hitchins—am I correct?"

"Yeah, yeah, sure. I talked to her and her mother, too, and
they want to nail that prick. But let's back up. You said Whitaker is okay with you prosecuting Hitchins in criminal court?"

"That's right. We're prosecuting Hitchins the same as we
would if he had beaten a man on the street."

"Well, I'll be goddamned."

"Detective, there are a few things I'd like to get squared
away before you arrest Rudy Hitchins."

"Such as what, Counselor?"

"I've already prepared the necessary filing to get an order
of protection to keep Hitchins away from Mary Margaret. I'd

also like to know if you can arrange for a police officer to accompany Mary Margaret's mother when she goes to Hitchins's apartment to collect her daughter's belongings while she's still recuperating in the hospital."

"That's not going to happen."

"Why not?" I replied, my voice rising. "I don't believe it's safe for Mary Margaret or her mother to go anywhere near Rudy Hitchins. I'm sorry, but I'm going to have to insist on the police doing this."

"You're going to insist, huh? Hold on, Counselor. The reason why her mother won't have to go through the apartment is because when I talked to Rebecca Finn in the hospital, I found out that Hitchins don't own the apartment. That bastard don't even pay rent. The mother owns it. Mrs. Finn inherited the whole apartment building after her old man kicked off. It's four units. Mary Margaret lives in a second-floor unit next to an old lady named Sarah Latham. There's another tenant, an old man who lives on the bottom floor in a unit, and then Rebecca Finn lives in the other ground-floor apartment. The building is over on Canfield Avenue. Now, here's the kick in the ass. You're going to love this. Rudy Hitchins is still living there, but he's got a new girlfriend, a broad named Gloria Lucinda, and she's staying there with him. He's with this blond bimbo while Mary Margaret's still in the hospital."

I thought about telling O'Brien that I'd already discovered that Hitchins had a girlfriend, having seen them at the hospital. But I certainly hadn't known the two of them were now sharing Mary Margaret's apartment—and bed.

"How do you know they're living there?"

"Hitchins told the old lady next door that the blonde was his sister visiting from Chicago, but old lady Latham heard moans at nighttime coming through the walls—not the kind that a brother and sister should be making. She called Mary Margaret's mother at the hospital to tattle. Them walls must be thin."

"Or," I joked, "Gloria Lucinda is quite a moaner."

"Why, Miss Fox, I didn't know you had a sense of humor."

I ignored him.

O'Brien said, "Either way, Rudy Hitchins's not scared about nothing if he's moved his girlfriend into an apartment he don't even own with Rebecca Finn living downstairs."

I thought, *You're right*.

Actually, I was pleased that Rebecca Finn owned the apartment building. O'Brien had warned me that most battered women were afraid of complaining about how they were being beaten because they had no place to go. Mary Margaret was going to be an exception. She'd be able to move home after O'Brien arrested Hitchins and tossed Gloria Lucinda out onto the street. This was working out perfectly.

"I need to speak to Mary Margaret one more time at the hospital before you arrest Hitchins," I said. "I'm going over there as soon as I hang up the phone."

Sounding enthused, O'Brien said, "Okay, Counselor, you did your part, I'll do mine. I'll arrest that prick."

But our conversation wasn't finished. "I have a favor to ask, Detective. I want to be there when you arrest him. I want to slap that protective order in his hands and watch his face. I want him to know that a woman is going to prosecute him in court for what he did to another woman."

Once again, O'Brien was quiet for a moment. This time, I suspected he was smiling on the other end of the phone line. "You know what, Counselor? I'm beginning to think you clang when you walk."

"What?"

"It means you got balls, little sister. Big brass ones!"

A S I DROVE TO WHITE PLAINS HOSPI-
tal, I asked myself: Why would a woman stay with
someone who beat her? Rebecca Finn had told me
this was not the first time that Rudy Hitchins had brutalized
Mary Margaret. If her own mother owned the apartment where
the couple lived, then why hadn't Mary Margaret kicked him
out the first time that he'd struck her? I didn't get it.

Mrs. Finn looked exhausted when I walked into hospital
room 505. She was seated in a chair, standing guard at Mary
Margaret's bedside, but as I entered the room, she didn't look
up. I noticed both of them had their eyes closed. I touched
Mrs. Finn gently on her arm.

"Mrs. Finn, you look like you could use a break."

Rubbing her eyes, she said, "I would like to go home and
clean up a bit. I need some cigarettes, too. Damn hospital gift
shop refuses to sell them."

"I need to talk to Mary Margaret if she is up to it, and I'd be
happy to stay here until you get back."

Rising from her chair, Mrs. Finn said, "That would be great,
honey. Actually, Mary Margaret was doing much better this
morning. Her mouth is wired shut so she's hard to understand,
but once you get used to it, you can make out most of the
words. I'll wake her." She reached over and touched her daughter's hand. Leaning down, she said, "Mary Margaret, that lady
from the D.A.'s office is here. She needs to talk to you."

I watched as Mary Margaret's eyes popped open. With a grimace, she pushed herself upward on her pillows. I heard her whisper through clenched teeth. "Okay, Ma. You going to be here?"

"Naw," Mrs. Finn replied. "You don't need me. I'm going for smokes. But I'll be back in an hour. You two have a nice talk."

With that, she left the room. I sat down in the chair that Mrs. Finn had been using and told Mary Margaret about the D.A.'s decision to have Rudy Hitchins arrested on a first-degree assault charge. Next, I explained the process and how I would get a protective order to keep him away from her. I felt she might be more comfortable talking if she knew a bit about me. After all, I was about to ask her to share intimate details about her relationship with Hitchins, so I decided to build some rapport with her by telling her a bit about myself.

I took a few minutes to cover such basic information as where I grew up and went to college. She listened and asked questions, which was good because I used those moments to get accustomed to her clenched-teeth responses. I'd just finished telling her about how I'd grown up in Elmira, New York, with one sister and had moved to White Plains immediately after I'd finished law school, when she asked, "Miss Fox, do you have a boyfriend?"

"Yes, his name is Bob and he's in medical school in Albany."

"Do you see him often?"

"We try to get together every other weekend. It's been tough lately. But we're committed."

"Is he cute?"

"He's a hunk. Brown hair, long legs, great build. It was magic from the start."

"I'm glad. I thought Rudy was one of the sexiest men I'd ever met."

"Tell me about him and your relationship."

"Okay, but first, I want to hear just a little bit more about Bob. How'd you meet?"

"I was still in high school, working weekends at a combination dairy and café that was attached to a creamery where they made ice cream and other milk products."

"Like an ice-cream shop?"

"Yes, but we also sold sandwiches, and because it was on a main highway outside Elmira, a lot of truckers used to stop in."

"You were a waitress, like me at O'Toole's? Truckers, they come on to you, right?"

"I was pretty young and naive. I didn't really know sometimes what they were saying. Anyway, Bob's parents owned a farm and he used to bring milk into the creamery and I thought he was adorable, so one day, when he was unloading his truck, I made sure to walk by and he said hello. We've been a couple ever since. He was my first and is my only love."

"You going to marry him?"

"If he asks after he finishes medical school. He hasn't given me a ring, but he gave me a pig."

"A pig?" She tried to laugh but it came out more as a giggle through her wired jaw.

"Yes, from his farm. I loved the book *Charlotte's Web* and he gave me a piglet named Wilbur."

"I don't read much. But I'm glad you are in love. I thought Rudy loved me when we first met. He made me feel so special."

In her guttural monotone, she described how they had met four years earlier in a Manhattan nightclub. They'd bumped into each other at the bar.

"He came on strong, but I liked that."

"When did you become a couple?"

"We clicked from that first night. But we kept seeing other people for about a month. That's when I first saw his temper."

"Tell me what happened."

"We were in the same nightclub and a guy I used to date came over to talk to me. Rudy totally ignored him but I gave him a hug when he left. When we went outside to leave, Rudy accused me of disrespecting him. We were walking next to each other when he suddenly grabbed me and started choking me. He choked me to the point he lifted me off the ground, and I was trying to scramble with my feet to get some type of footing because I started seeing stars. I felt like I was about to lose my breath and pass out. I started to fight at him to break him off of me. I swung at him but missed. That's when he released me and slapped me across the face. That was the first time he ever hit me. He said, 'You're my girl now. You don't talk to and hug other men.'" She paused and then whispered, "That's how I found out we were only dating each other from that point on."

"Why didn't you run away from him at that point?" I knew that would be a question that jurors would wonder and I did, too.

"'Cause I felt it was my fault. I mean, I'd hugged that guy and that's what made Rudy angry. The next day after he choked me, he apologized. He was really, really sorry. He told me he was afraid that I was going to leave him and he even broke down and cried. It was so, so sweet. He went right out that same morning and he brought me flowers—not just a dozen, neither, he bought me sixteen red roses and a big box of chocolate-covered cherries. The next day, he done the same thing. He did it every day for a week and I said, 'Rudy, you're spoiling me. I'm going to get fat if I eat all this candy.' He swore he would never lay a hand on me again, never. We'd been drinking that night, too, and, I thought, 'I shouldn't have hugged that guy. I was wrong to do that. And Rudy is just a very passionate guy.' The truth was that I liked that he was jealous. It meant he cared about me. I was his girl, no one else's."

"Were there other times when he hit you?"

Mary Margaret's already quiet voice grew even quieter. "Not in the beginning. I mean for weeks—maybe two—everything was great. But then he got mad at me again and it would happen. But by then, it was too late 'cause I was in love with him. And every time he did it, he would apologize and be really sweet and I'd forgive him. I told myself, 'I got to stop making him angry,' and I was sure it wouldn't happen again."

She seemed to be growing tired so I decided to focus on the sort of questions that I might ask her during a trial rather than questioning her more about why she'd put up with him for four years.

"Can you describe a typical incident?"

"Rudy liked to drink, especially on weekends, and he'd come home drunk and he always wanted sex. If I was drunk maybe I would've been okay with it, you know. But when he was drunk, he got rough, and if I tried to stop him, he'd get mean. He'd slap me around and hold me down. One time he tied me to our bed and left me there naked for an entire day. He'd rip my blouse off, too, if he were drunk. He liked that— getting all tough with me. One night I decided to fight back, well, not really fight back, but just tell him to stop when he grabbed me. I dug a fingernail into him."

"That was brave of you."

"And stupid. He went crazy. He slapped me and then he said he was going to teach me a lesson. He's really strong and he grabbed my arms and held them above my head with his left hand. Then with his right hand, he pulled down my panties and that's when he—"

She hesitated. I said, "That's when he forced you to have sex?"

"Yes. I started crying because it wasn't love, it was rape, but that only seemed to make him more turned on. That was the first time he did that to me, and the next day, he laughed about it and said, 'You liked it, baby, and you know it. You just don't want to admit it. Deep down, you're a dirty little whore.' "

"How often did that happen—forced sex?"

"Too many times."

I gently squeezed her hand. "I'm so sorry." Putting my prosecutor's hat back on, I asked, "Did he ever tell you what he thought of women in general?"

"Oh yeah, he said a woman was good for two things, having sex and cooking, and I didn't know how to cook very well. Then he said I wasn't very good in bed, either, because I didn't like to do things he wanted me to do. He told me no one else would want to be with someone like me because I was frigid and stupid. I never finished high school. He brought that up a lot. And he told me I was getting fat and that I smelled bad when we had sex."

In a gentle voice, I said, "Mary Margaret, jurors are going to wonder why you stayed with him for four years when he treated you like that."

Tears began to form in her eyes and she whispered, "I loved him and I thought he loved me. Once he came into O'Toole's when I was working and he heard this customer tell me I had a really nice ass. Rudy went outside and waited for him to leave. When the guy came out into the parking lot, Rudy hit him with a tire iron and beat the crap out of him. I'd never had anyone do something like that for me. He told me I was special and he'd always take care of me. I knew he had a nice, sweet side. And I kept thinking, 'Why can't I get that Rudy back? What am I doing wrong?' When I got pregnant the first time, he was so happy. I thought, 'This is great. We'll be a family.' Then I had the miscarriage and he told me that I couldn't even do that right—have a baby. I was too stupid for even that. I thought he was right. I keep thinking if I could only do things right, then the old Rudy would love me."

"Did you ever consider leaving him?"

"Yes, after the miscarriage, things got so bad, I thought we should break up."

"But you didn't leave."

"I was too scared."

"Of him?"

"Yes, I was scared of him but that wasn't the only reason. I hadn't been able to make him happy. I kept doing everything wrong so I didn't think anyone else would want me. Then I got pregnant again and I thought, 'He was happy the first time. A baby will make him happy again.'"

Mary Margaret gingerly moved her right hand to her belly.

"Did it make him happy?"

"No. He seemed to lose interest in me and I learned he was cheating on me with that other woman."

Ah, I thought, *she knows about Gloria Lucinda.*

She looked emotionally spent, so I said, "You've done great. You'll make a fantastic witness. When we get into court, I probably won't be able to ask you much about those other times he raped and beat you."

"Why?"

"It's not allowed generally, but I can ask you about the Friday night when he put you in the hospital. That should be enough."

"I talked to Detective O'Brien about that night. He has it all in his report now."

I nodded. "We can talk more about that later, but for now, we've done enough." I gave her a tissue and she wiped her eyes with her right hand.

"You're going to put him in jail, right?"

"I'm going to do my best."

She looked scared. "You got to do it," she said, squeezing my hand hard. "If you don't, he'll kill me."

AN HOUR LATER, O'BRIEN AND I WERE sitting on the front seat of an unmarked Ford police cruiser parked less than a hundred feet from the entrance to O'Toole's bar. We were waiting for Rudy Hitchins to surface. I'd assumed we'd simply drive over to the apartment house on Canfield Avenue that Rebecca Finn owned and arrest him, but O'Brien had insisted on waiting here. In my hand was a temporary order of protection signed by a judge that prohibited Hitchins from coming within five hundred feet of Mary Margaret and the apartment that they'd once shared. I checked my watch and it was 4:45 p.m. The evening traffic was beginning to back up as weary workers made their trek home through downtown White Plains.

"Why do you think Hitchins is going to show up here? Isn't this the last place he'd want to show his face?" I asked.

Detective O'Brien, with his ever-present toothpick held firmly on the right side of his mouth, said, "Oh, he'll come here."

I noticed a sudden glint in his eyes. "You a betting girl?" he asked. "I'll bet you a ten-spot Hitchins shows up here."

I shook my head. "No thanks." He seemed too confident for me to bite.

"C'mon," he prodded. "I thought you had balls. Look, I'll make it even sweeter. If he don't show up in the next fifteen minutes, I'll give you fifty bucks. If he does, then you owe me only ten. He shows in fifteen minutes or you win."

I could hear my father's voice screaming in my head—"Watch out! You're being suckered!"—but I said, "Okay, I'll take those odds."

O'Brien grinned and part of me was glad. Even if I lost the bet, he seemed to be warming up to me. Or so I thought. His smile could also be part of a con.

I checked my wristwatch again and as I was raising my head, O'Brien said, "There he is and he's got that blond broad with him."

I glanced out the sedan's front windshield at O'Toole's, but didn't see Hitchins or Gloria Lucinda. I looked at O'Brien and saw that he was looking into the car's rearview mirror. As I swung my neck to check behind us, Rudy Hitchins and his girlfriend strutted by my car door on the sidewalk next to where we were parked. I reached for the door handle, but O'Brien gently took my left arm and said, "Not yet! Wait for him to actually go into the bar."

I didn't understand, but figured O'Brien had a reason. As soon as the couple stepped into O'Toole's, O'Brien barked, "C'mon, Counselor." He shot out the driver's door and I scrambled from the passenger side. We walked briskly toward the bar's solid wooden door. Like many drinking establishments in White Plains, the bar's front windows were tinted so you couldn't see the patrons inside. It was a throwback to the times when drinking alcohol was taboo and barflies didn't want their neighbors spotting them knocking down shots of Jack Daniel's.

When we reached the bar's entrance, O'Brien again gently touched my arm, forcing me to stop. "Wait," he commanded.

At that moment, the door swung open and Rudy Hitchins stepped outside with his new lover. They stepped forward and almost walked into us.

"Hitchins!" O'Brien growled.

Hitchins had been preoccupied, but now he saw the plain-clothes detective.

"You're under arrest."

"For what?" If he was intimidated, he wasn't showing it.

"For assaulting Mary Margaret Finn!" I answered before O'Brien could.

The sound of my voice seemed to surprise both men, as well as Hitchins's girlfriend.

"Who the hell are you?"

Suddenly time seemed to slow down. I'd been so intent on confronting Hitchins that I'd not noticed that three men had slipped silently out of the bar and were now standing directly behind Hitchins and his girlfriend. Without warning, one of these men slammed his right fist into Hitchins's right side while another hit him on the left side of his head with a pocket-size blackjack. Hitchins hit the concrete sidewalk hard from the blows and immediately began to reach inside his blue windbreaker. Before he could grab whatever he was going for, O'Brien stomped his right foot against Hitchins's wrist, pinning it to his chest.

Hitchins hollered in pain.

Two of the men behind Hitchins dropped to their knees. One pinned Hitchins's shoulders against the sidewalk while the other began hitting him repeatedly in his face. All this time, O'Brien kept his foot firmly on top of Hitchins's wrist and chest. I could hear Hitchins's nose crack. Blood spurted from his nostrils. The man hitting him landed at least six hard punches. I had never seen such brutality.

Without warning, Hitchins's girlfriend lunged at me. I'd never been physically attacked, either, but I instinctively reeled back to avoid the bright red fingernails that were targeted at my face. As I was back stepping, one of the men grabbed Lucinda's arm and expertly twisted it back behind her.

In a well-practiced move, he slapped a pair of handcuffs on her wrists.

It dawned on me that these men were off-duty White Plains police officers who'd been inside the bar and had come outside to assist O'Brien. Obviously, he'd tipped them. As she was handcuffed, Lucinda began shrieking obscenities. The officer slapped her with his open hand and said, "Shut the fuck up!"

"Don't hit her!" I yelled. This was getting out of control.

The officer glared at me.

O'Brien removed his foot from Hitchins's wrist, bent down, and flipped open Hitchins's windbreaker. A small-caliber handgun was tucked into his waistband. O'Brien snatched it as the other officers lifted Hitchins to his feet and handcuffed his hands behind him. Blood was flowing from his broken nose.

"Now we got some other charges to file against you, tough guy," O'Brien said. "Resisting arrest, attempting to assault a police officer, not to mention a gun charge." He glanced at the pistol, rolling it over in his hand. It was a cheap Saturday night special. "What were you going to do, if you'd gotten that?"

Snorting out blood, Hitchins said, "Fuck you and fuck your bitch, too!"

The officer who had been slugging Hitchins released his grip while his partner instinctively tightened his hold on Hitchins's handcuffed wrists, keeping him from moving. The first officer punched Hitchins in his gut. Like a trained boxer, the officer followed that sucker punch with a left jab and then got another shot in with a right to Hitchins's abdomen. Leaning back, the officer lowered his right shoulder and delivered an upper cut that hit Hitchins in his jaw with such force that it lifted his feet from the sidewalk.

"Wow," the officer holding Hitchins's wrists said admiringly. "That must have hurt. Carl—have you been working out?"

I was stunned and afraid that Carl—I had no idea what his last name was—would continue punching Hitchins to the point that the attack might jeopardize my trial. I shouted, "I'm from the district attorney's office and I have a court order here that says you can't get anywhere near Mary Margaret Finn until this order is lifted by a judge. Do you understand what I've just said?"

Everyone stared at me. Hitchins could barely hold his head up. He didn't say a word, but Lucinda did.

"Why would Rudy want to see that skank Mary Margaret again?"

"Yeah, especially when he's got a prize like you waiting in his bed," I responded.

The cops, including O'Brien, burst out laughing. He handed the Saturday night special that he'd taken from Hitchins to Carl.

"Take this and that piece of shit to the car."

But Carl wasn't finished. He took the handgun and then swung the pistol upward, smacking the gun's metal grip against the side of Hitchins's head. The prisoner's entire body went limp.

"That's for Mary Margaret," Carl declared.

This arrest seemed personal to him and I wondered if he might be the cop responsible for getting Mary Margaret pregnant—if she was carrying someone else's baby.

"Give him another pop," an officer chimed in.

"No! Stop this, right now!" I shouted. My cry surprised them and me, too. "That's enough!"

The officers looked at me and then at O'Brien. He took a step toward Hitchins, and for a moment, I was afraid O'Brien was going to join in the beating. Instead, he pulled Hitchins's wallet from the pocket of his windbreaker and began rifling through it. He plucked a folded piece of green paper from the billfold and then returned the wallet to Hitchins's pocket.

Turning, he handed me the paper and said, "This is Mary Margaret's paycheck. Her boss leaves O'Toole's at five o'clock and hands the paychecks out just before he goes home."

That was how O'Brien had known Hitchins would be coming to the bar before five o'clock.

"You might want to give it to Mary Margaret. She needs it more than he does."

The off-duty officers dragged Hitchins and his girlfriend to our unmarked police car, where they were shoved into its rear seat. As soon as the car door was slammed shut, Lucinda became hysterical.

O'Brien was unfazed but I was shaken by what I'd witnessed. The arrest was nothing like I thought it would be.

"You owe me ten bucks, Counselor," he said.

M Y MOTHER, ESTHER, IS A CLASSIC beauty with huge brown eyes, great cheekbones, raven hair, and a fit figure that hasn't changed since the first time I noticed her as a woman, not just as my mother. I remember thinking she was more attractive than most other moms. You certainly never caught her in public wearing hair curlers the size of orange juice cans or stirrup stretch pants.

Unlike my girlfriends, who rebelled as teens and fell into the much-hyped generation gap, my young feet stayed on solid family ground. In fact, Mom was one of my heroes, and the bond between us became even stronger after my father died from cancer.

Of course, we didn't agree on everything. What mothers and daughters do? But I trusted my mother more than anyone. She was my muse. Part of the reason why is because of her past. Even though my mom was born in New York, strangers often assume she is a recent immigrant because of her accent and exotic looks. She is of Lebanese descent and it shows in her olive skin. Her beauty masks an inner toughness that was forged from necessity. My mother's childhood was not easy. The reason was my grandfather Charles, who had been both cantankerous and charismatic.

He was a Lebanese immigrant who believed my grand-mother's single purpose in life was to provide him with a male heir to whom he could leave his fortune. Instead, she gave birth to four daughters. Wanting a son, he divorced her and sent his daughters—including Mom—to Lebanon so he could search for a new wife to bear him a son.

Mom and her three sisters lived in Beirut with an uncle who was wealthy and influential. He treated them well but considered them liabilities. After all, they were girls, and in the 1930s, women were reared to be subservient to men. Even young boys had more social prominence. The male-dominated culture drilled into my mother's head that, at best, she was a second-class citizen.

Back in the United States, my grandfather quickly found a second wife who promptly gave him two sons.

Our story could have ended there—with my mother banished to Lebanon and my grandfather going happily on with his life in the United States. But fate intervened. When the Japanese attacked Pearl Harbor, my grandfather enlisted in the navy, and while at sea, he met a young sailor who was a second-generation Lebanese American. One night my grandfather mentioned that he had four daughters living in Beirut. One of them, he said, was especially beautiful. After the war ended, this young man went to Lebanon to see for himself. As soon as he set his eyes on my mother, he was smitten. They eloped.

At least that is what I was told as a child.

Although my grandfather had abandoned my mother, he invited the newlyweds to live with him in Elmira until they could find a house. He also offered my father a job at a prosperous business that my grandfather had started. By the time I was born, my mother and grandfather had reconciled, and I spent my childhood in a happy, loving home.

My mother's past shaped her character, and after she returned to the United States, she never allowed anyone to treat her as a second-class citizen—not even my grandfather. She also became adamant that I would get an education. She didn't want me dependent on a man for my well-being. She used to tell me: "Luck is for the lazy. You must work to achieve, and because you're a woman, you must work three times as hard as any man."

Despite all attempts by her father, her uncle, and what was then the Lebanese culture to crush her independent spirit, Mom was a woman with iron-strong self-esteem. She demanded to be treated with respect and she treated others likewise.

While she was incredibly independent, she also honored old traditions. She ran our house, reared me, and took special pride in her cooking. The first plate that was prepared always went directly to my father, who sat at the head of our table.

I wanted to talk to my mother about what I'd witnessed outside O'Toole's pub, so I drove to the ranch-style house that she'd bought in White Plains after my father died.

She swung open the front door as I pulled into her driveway, having tuned her ear to the sound of my TR6. We went immediately to her kitchen, where we did all of our serious talking. Earlier that morning, she had cut daffodils, the first of the season to bloom in her garden, and arranged them in a vase on the Formica-topped kitchen table.

Knowing that I had an insatiable sweet tooth, Mom said, "I'm almost ready to take some ma'amoul from the oven. You can add the sugar."

Mom knew ma'amoul was my favorite Middle Eastern pastry. It was made of dough with pistachios tucked inside, and the more powdered sugar sprinkled on it, the better.

Her baked ma'amoul filled the kitchen with a pleasant aroma, causing me to think of my father. He loved my mom's ma'amoul and baklava. I envisioned my father sitting at the table, drinking a cup of *ahweh*, a strong, thick Arabic-style coffee. My parents were both extremely patriotic Americans, but like so many children of immigrant parents, they also paid homage to their heritage.

As I started to sprinkle sugar over the fresh ma'amoul, Mom asked if I was thirsty.

"Do you have any Dr Pepper?" I replied. She frowned. My mother didn't care for carbonated drinks and she especially didn't like them served with ma'amoul.

"How about a glass of milk? Or coffee."

"I'd really rather have a Dr Pepper. I brought several bottles over last week. They should be in the back of the refrigerator on the second shelf—unless you drank them."

She knew I was teasing her and reluctantly fished a Dr Pepper from the refrigerator and handed me a bottle opener.

I served her the first of the powdered ma'amoul after she had sat down at the kitchen table, and she poured herself a cup of fresh coffee.

"I need advice, Mom." I picked up a pastry and took a bite. The taste was delicious. "I've gotten involved in something."

I quickly explained about Hitchins and how he'd beaten and raped Mary Margaret. I told how I'd gotten Whitaker to file criminal charges against Hitchins. I then recounted the brutality that I'd witnessed outside O'Toole's.

I ended my story by saying, "When I get to work tomorrow, I know O'Brien will want Hitchins charged with resisting arrest and a long list of other criminal charges. But the police never gave him a chance to resist. That police officer named Carl threw the first punch and pistol-whipped Hitchins after he was handcuffed."

"This Rudy Hitchins, he had a gun?" she asked me.

"Yes."

"Perhaps this Carl person knew this and felt he had no choice but to strike him first. This Hitchins sounds like a violent man. You choose a life of crime and you pay a price."

"There's no question he is vicious. I can understand why they might have attacked him first. The truth is that I wanted to smack him, too, for what he did to Mary Margaret. As you said, he is a criminal. He deserves what he got. But do the police have a right to hit him after he has been handcuffed and disarmed, and then accuse him of attacking them?"

My mother took a sip of her coffee and asked, "Have you told Detective O'Brien that you disagree with what happened?"

"No."

"If you have a problem with this detective, you must tell him now. Otherwise, your silence is the same as approval and eventually becomes the norm and no one questions it."

My mother took another sip of coffee and added, "You also need to wipe your lips. You have powdered sugar on them."

10

O'BRIEN'S ARREST PAPERWORK FOR Hitchins was waiting on my desk when I reported to work the next morning. As I had anticipated, a slew of new charges had been lodged against him, including resisting arrest, criminal possession of a weapon, and assaulting a police officer. The only thing missing was a littering charge from the blood that he'd left behind on the sidewalk.

I telephoned O'Brien, who sounded uncharacteristically pleased to hear from me. His tone did an immediate 180-degree spin after I told him that I was not comfortable pursuing any of the new charges that he'd sent over.

"Not comfortable?" he snarled, mimicking me. "What the hell does that mean?"

"It means that I am not going into court and lying."

My blunt answer got an immediate and angry response.

"Lying? You're accusing me of lying? What the hell are you talking about?"

"I know what I saw. Hitchins never had a chance to resist arrest because your guys threw the first punch. And after he was handcuffed—well, do I really have to go into details here? You and I both know what happened."

"And what's that, Counselor? What exactly do you believe you saw yesterday outside O'Toole's?"

"Your buddy Carl used Hitchins as a punching bag after he

was handcuffed and smacked him in the side of his head with a pistol grip."

For a moment, O'Brien didn't respond, and then he asked, "And tell me, Counselor, who owned that little Saturday night special? The one Carl—excuse me, Detective Carl Jones— allegedly used to hit poor Rudy Hitchins in the head after he was cuffed?"

"It was his. You took it away from him."

In one of the coldest voices that I've ever heard, O'Brien said, "That's right. Don't you dare tell me how to do my job."

Without raising my voice, I replied, "Don't you tell me how to do my job, either. I'm going to try the assault charge but I'm not going to file these new charges because they aren't true."

"Not true? I know three White Plains police officers who will each testify that Rudy Hitchins attacked first. They'll also testify that no one put a finger on him after he was handcuffed. Not one finger. You might want to think about that. You also might want to think about whose side you're on here."

It was his final sentence that stung the most. Although O'Brien was twice my age and had years of experience on the street, I was not going to have him lecture me. "I know whose side I'm on. Listen, I became an assistant district attorney to prosecute criminals. I'll work harder than anyone in this office to get a conviction. But I'm not closing my eyes for you or anyone else just because you're a cop. I don't work that way. You give me a good case and I'll try the hell out of it and pro- tect your back eight days a week. But I don't go for what I saw yesterday. I don't lie for anyone. You think I'm giving Rudy Hitchins a pass here but you're wrong. I'm giving your friend Carl a pass. The real question is why did you put me in this position? Whose side are you on, Detective?"

O'Brien slammed down the receiver.

Well, I thought, at least I took Mom's advice. O'Brien definitely knew how I felt. I'd drawn a line.

Fifteen minutes later, my phone rang.

"Hello?"

"District Attorney Carlton Whitaker III would like to speak to you," Hillary Potts announced, summoning me to his office.

As I made my way, I tried to predict what might be happening. I couldn't imagine O'Brien had stormed over from the White Plains police station in person to complain. First of all, the district attorney would never have met directly with the detective because both of them would have been usurping the bureaucratic chain of command. O'Brien would first need to complain to his direct supervisor, who then would talk to the chief of police, who then would decide if he wanted to complain to the district attorney. The chief and D.A. were bureaucratic equals.

I wondered if O'Brien had been so angry that he'd orchestrated all this in a mere fifteen minutes.

A queasy feeling began churning in my stomach. I'm generally not the nervous type but I sensed this was not going to be a pleasant encounter.

Hillary Potts looked stern, as always, when I arrived. She motioned toward a chair and said, "Let me see if he's available." She called him on her intercom and then quietly opened one of the doors for me to enter his office, saying, "The district attorney will see you now."

I expected to be greeted by an angry Whitaker, but the D.A. was all smiles when I entered his cavernous chamber. I gave the room a quick once-over, half expecting to see O'Brien and the police chief, but the only other person in the room was Paul Pisani.

Damn, I thought. Does this guy ever do anything else but hang out in the boss's office?

As soon as Miss Potts shut the door behind me, Whitaker said, "Take a seat, Miss Fox, and tell us how the Rudy Hitchins prosecution is going."

Was Whitaker playing dumb? If he was, so would I.

Trying to appear relaxed, I said, "Actually, sir, it's going really well. I just interviewed Mary Margaret and she'll make a great witness."

"Good, glad to hear it. Now, what the hell is this nonsense about you not filing additional charges against Hitchins after he resisted arrest and assaulted White Plains police officers?" His smile was gone. His voice had turned ugly.

Wow, I thought, O'Brien really had pulled strings.

"Sir, I don't believe we need these new charges to successfully prosecute Rudy Hitchins for first-degree assault."

"Oh," he said in a mocking voice. "Miss Dani Fox, who has never officially tried a criminal case in Westchester County, has decided that it's perfectly okay to resist arrest and assault White Plains police officers now. She's decided that those charges don't matter because she's already charged this suspect with beating up his girlfriend and that's enough."

Without giving me a chance to explain, Whitaker continued: "You realize the police are on *our* side, don't you, Miss Fox? You understand that when a criminal resists arrest and assaults an officer, the police really don't like that. And when a prosecutor decides to blow off those charges, it doesn't sit well with the officers who were in danger or with the chief of police. You do understand that, right?"

He was lecturing me much like a kindergarten teacher speaking to a five-year-old. Once again, Whitaker didn't let me answer. "Now, Miss Fox, I realize how eager you are to go to trial on this case, but let me give you a quick lesson on how justice works here in Westchester County and in every other prosecutor's office in our glorious nation—just in case you missed this crucial bit of illumination in Albany Law School.

The police charge a suspect with as many serious felonies as possible each and every time they make an arrest. A prosecutor then uses those charges as leverage to negotiate the best plea bargain for the public good. This avoids wasting taxpayers' hard-earned money on frivolous and expensive trials and also eliminates the chances of a jury of complete fools releasing someone to the streets who needs to be locked up." He paused, apparently to give me time for this to soak in, and then said in a ridiculing voice, "*Am I making this simple enough for you, my dear?*"

My dear? Who did he think he was, my mother? I really was going to have to find a coffee mug with the word PRICK printed on it. Keeping my temper in check, I replied, "Yes, you are."

With his voice still dripping with sarcasm, Whitaker said, "Well then, Miss Fox, perhaps you can explain to me why I just got a call from a very angry White Plains chief of police telling me that you are being a real—" Whitaker caught himself midsentence and said, "How can I put this more delicately?"

He glanced at Pisani, who was clearly enjoying my dressing-down.

"Perhaps you can substitute the word 'witch,'" Pisani volunteered.

Whitaker nodded. "Let's just say, the chief of police feels you are showing a certain lack of esprit de corps."

"Sir, I was standing there when they arrested Rudy Hitchins. I saw what happened."

I hoped my reply would be enough for Whitaker to understand why I didn't want to move forward on the extra counts. I was trying to warn him that O'Brien hadn't told his boss the real story and that his boss hadn't told the police chief the entire truth about what really had gone down outside O'Toole's. I hoped my admission—that I had been there when Hitchins had been arrested—would be enough for Whitaker to read between the lines. But judging from the expression on his face, Whitaker was used to reading unlined paper.

He said, "If you were at the scene, then you realize how serious these charges are and why the White Plains police are furious and want them filed against Mr. Hitchins."

Okay, I thought, I'm going to throw out another bone. "Sir, as I just mentioned, I was there. I saw what happened and I would not ever want to be in a position in court where our office might be embarrassed." I paused and said, *"How can I put this more delicately?* Let's just say 'questionable criminal charges.'"

Out of the corner of my eye, I saw Pisani smirk. He apparently found my response entertaining.

This time Whitaker got it. Being a politician first and district attorney second, his survival instincts kicked in. He understood that I was warning him. Something had happened during the arrest that he really didn't need to know and didn't want to know, especially if it could come back and bite him later on the campaign trail.

The district attorney leaned back and thought about what I'd just hinted. After a moment, he said, "Miss Fox, why are you making this so difficult? It doesn't need to be. It's the police who will be describing what happened on the witness stand if they get called to testify. And if the defendant claims he was the victim of, let's say, alleged police misconduct, then it would be up to a jury to decide who's lying. It has nothing to do with you."

His comment surprised me. "Sir, I realize the easiest thing for our office to do is to charge Rudy Hitchins with resisting arrest and assaulting a police officer. It would make the police happy and the additional charges would give us more legal pressure to apply. I'm sure we could then plea-bargain this matter. We would win. But as an officer of the court, I cannot in good conscience file those charges."

"Your good conscience?" Whitaker howled in a condescending voice. "What the hell did they teach you at Albany Law? I don't give a rat's ass about your conscience. No one does. You're a prosecutor—an assistant district attorney—not a priest. Just do your job and park your conscience outside the courtroom door. Do you think the attorney defending Rudy Hitchins has trouble sleeping at night because he knows his client is guilty of turning his girlfriend's face into a meatball? Your job is simple here, Miss Fox. You bring bad people to justice. The cops arrest them and bring them to us. We prosecute them. If they don't want to plea-bargain, then a judge or jury decides their fate. None of this should have anything to do with your conscience."

"With all due respect, sir, I disagree. I believe my conscience does matter in a courtroom. It matters a great deal."

At this point, Pisani decided to interject himself into our conversation. "Ms. Fox, I'm curious. Why do you believe your conscience matters?"

"Because my conscience is why I became a prosecutor. And I don't plan on checking it at the door when I go in to a trial."

Pisani, who apparently felt this was amusing, said, "Can you elaborate on that, Ms. Fox? I'd like to hear more and I'm sure District Attorney Whitaker would as well."

He was baiting me and I realized I was going toe-to-toe with both of them. How smart was that, especially since Whitaker could fire me on the spot?

"I think of this office as a moral battleground. I believe there is a war being waged here between good and evil every day. We are the good guys. Our job is to protect the victims and make certain that the victims—not the criminals—have their day in court."

"Interesting," Pisani said. "A battle between good and evil. I find that very noble. And romantic. Please continue. I'm actually getting excited."

"No one asks to be a victim," I said. "No one asks to be preyed upon. A woman could be going about her normal routine when bang, like a thunderbolt, a criminal wreaks havoc. She comes to us for help. That's our job. Helping those who have been victimized. But we don't do our jobs by getting down in the gutter and acting like the very people we are putting on trial. We do what it takes to convict them, but we do it by upholding the sanctity of the law, not with dirty tricks, fists, and billy clubs. We don't do it by accusing people of crimes that they did not commit, no matter how horrible those criminals are."

Pisani slowly began clapping. He was ridiculing me. "Ms. Fox, you told me that I was your mentor. So let me give you some mentoring advice. This courtroom is not a battlefield. It's a back-alley street fight. We do not compete on a level playing field. Our glorious U.S. Supreme Court under Justice Earl Warren gave the criminal an upper hand, an unfair advantage — a knife when we must fight with only our bare hands. To counter that, we should use every advantage we have to win."

Pisani continued, "Because of your inexperience and naïveté, there is a practical matter that you're overlooking here. The moment Hitchins's defense attorney discovers our office is not going to pursue these new counts against his client, he is going to wonder why. It is not unusual for our office to file additional charges after someone is arrested. But to drop charges of resisting arrest and assault on a police officer is a clear sign of dissension within the ranks. It's a sign of weakness and he is going to exploit that fracture if he can."

I knew Pisani had faced hundreds of defense attorneys. He'd prosecuted hundreds of scumbags like Hitchins. By contrast, I'd tried thirteen cases in night court.

"A good defense attorney," Pisani said, "is going to accuse the cops of beating up his client. He's going to find a way to tell jurors that you refused to file charges because you knew what the cops did was wrong. He's going to make the police look like vigilantes with badges and he's going to cast a shadow over this office. If you don't file these charges, it's possible that you're going to hand a defense attorney and his dirt-ball client the reasonable doubt that he needs to get Rudy Hitchins off. Because unlike you, a defense attorney has no conscience. Absolutely none. In fact, it is his legal duty to prepare a logical defense and what that translates into is that a good defense attorney is going to make up any fiction that he wishes—anything, no matter how ridiculous—to sway a jury. If he believes telling jurors that aliens came down in a spaceship and little green men jumped out and beat Mary Margaret, then, by God, that's what he'll tell the jury. Are you prepared for that? Are you prepared to look Mary Margaret Finn in the eyes and tell her that you blew it because of your conscience? Are you willing to let Rudy Hitchins go free, when this office could have charged him with not just beating her up but a half-dozen other felony charges?"

Now that Pisani had softened me up, Whitaker moved in for the kill. "You're creating a real shit storm here, young lady—all because of your 'conscience.' I'm glad that you have such a flowery view of our justice system. But it is not a moral battleground. What we have here is more of a production line. Victims come in. We're flooded with cases. The quicker we prosecute one, the sooner we can help someone else. The more we win, the sounder the public sleeps at night because there are fewer dirtbags on the streets. Shit storms aren't good for production lines."

As strange as it sounds, I suddenly had newfound respect for our district attorney. He and Pisani made the choice seem incredibly simple. If I played along and did what everyone wanted me to do—if I closed my eyes to what I had seen—and filed the trumped-up charges that O'Brien had sent over, then the system would run smoothly. The production line would keep moving. Faced with assault and resisting arrest, Hitchins and his attorney would cave. They'd cut a deal. The fact that Hitchins was beaten and pistol-whipped while he was handcuffed—facts that could result in very bad press for the police—would never be mentioned and, even if the defense raised it, who would believe him?

"Look," Pisani said, "file the extra charges and then offer to dismiss them in return for Hitchins pleading to assault. That way you'll win without the risk of a trial and your conscience will be clean. We get what we want and Hitchins gets what he deserves. Case closed."

It sounded so simple. But for some reason, it stuck in my throat.

"Sir," I said firmly, addressing Whitaker. "I don't want this turning into a shit storm and I'm not a bitch regardless of what the chief of police told you. All I want to do is my job. I want to put Rudy Hitchins on trial. But if you decide to remove me from this case and have someone else handle it, that's your call. But I will not file additional charges just to keep the production line moving."

Whitaker glared at me. "Miss Fox," he said coldly, "I would have replaced you the moment that I got the call from the chief. But I've already given an interview to Will Harris at the White Plains newspaper about this case. I bragged about how our office was going to go after this schmuck in criminal court and how this matter had been brought to my attention by the first female assistant district attorney in our county's history. I talked about the importance of women's rights. So you tell me, Miss Fox, how would it look if I suddenly replaced you?"

Clearly frustrated, Whitaker made one more attempt. "If you take this case to trial, there's a chance you're going to lose it. Have you thought about that? How will that help anyone? But if you get Hitchins to plea-bargain, then it's perfect. This office wins. You win. Hitchins goes to jail. The newspaper reports that our office is cracking down on abuse. The public is happy. Why can't you just be a team player here? Why are you conjuring up this internal drama? Do you honestly believe Hitchins is the first punk slapped around a little by the police?"

I didn't respond, and in my silence, he knew that I wasn't going to change my mind, so like the skilled politician that he was, Whitaker offered me a way out. He gave me a chance to please everyone.

"You could withdraw from this case. Voluntarily. Then your conscience would be clear, there wouldn't be any hard feelings between the police and this office. Mr. Pisani here could negotiate a plea bargain. We'd drop the additional charges in return for Hitchins pleading guilty to beating up Mary Margaret Finn. Justice would be served."

"And what would I tell Will Harris at the newspaper when he calls and asks me why I dropped the case?" I countered.

Whitaker didn't hesitate. "First of all you never—ever—talk to the press. I do. Got that?"

Pisani jumped in. "Here's what you could tell him. You could tell him it's a woman thing. You know, that time of the month. You're too emotional. You didn't feel up to handling the case. Trust me, he'd understand."

I sat there in stone silence for nearly a minute. Whitaker and Pisani both probably thought I was pondering their suggestion. But I was actually fighting the urge to reach over and throttle Pisani. It took me a moment to get the image out of my mind of my hands around his neck and squeezing. I said, "I have no intention of resigning voluntarily from this prosecution."

Whitaker twisted his neck as if he was trying to exorcise

some pain from it. "Okay, Miss Fox, we're going to do this your way. The hard way. But you need to grow up and ditch this misty-eyed view that you have of our criminal justice system. The hard-core reality is that we live in a dark world here, a murky world. So let this be your first lesson. If this thing blows up in our faces, especially mine, then this will be both your first official case as an assistant district attorney and your last."

He waved his hand, dismissing me, but as I started to leave, he couldn't resist throwing one more barb my way.

"When you go out the door, take a look at whose name is on it. It's mine. Not yours!"

The next morning the *White Plains Daily* published on the front page a photograph of District Attorney Carlton Whitaker III looking stern behind his desk. The headline read: "D.A. Whitaker Champions Women's Rights."

My phone immediately started to ring with calls from reporters and women's groups. I referred them all to Whitaker's office.

11

THE OLD OBSERVATION THAT PET owners choose dogs and cats that resemble them applied to Rudy Hitchins's choice in lawyers as well. Alexander Dominic was a familiar face in the White Plains courthouse and quite a sight. He could have easily hired himself out as a department-store Santa Claus without needing any extra pillows around his ample waist. He stood only five feet six but appeared taller because he wore his dyed brown hair in an Elvis pompadour. Adding to the illusion were the two-inch heels on his two-tone, square-toed, blue-and-white stacked-heel shoes. The upper lace portion of the shoe was white, the remainder was blue, and there was a white strip between the shoe's leather and its built-up blue soles. A chain-smoker of unfiltered Camels, he preferred polyester leisure suits when he worked in his combination apartment/office that he rented above a pharmacy in one of White Plains's rougher neighborhoods. His favorite leisure suit was lime green. He wore its light jacket over a spinach-green open-necked shirt with a four-inch-wide collar. At age fifty-five, Dominic thought of himself as the William Kunstler of White Plains, but he had none of that radical lawyer's brilliance or his oratory skills. Dominic was exactly what he appeared to be—a low-rent bottom-feeder who would proudly defend anyone who could scrape together his forty-five-dollar-per-hour fee. It didn't matter if the defendant was a repeat child molester, streetwalker,

cop killer, or drug pusher. If you needed a lawyer, Dominic
was eager to become your mouthpiece, apologist, and loyal
lapdog.

Normally, a defense attorney wants to delay going to court
as long as possible. There is no advantage in rushing a client to
judgment, especially one as guilty as Rudy Hitchins. Delays
allow the defense to plot a plausible explanation for why the
accused is innocent, even though he'd been identified by a
half-dozen witnesses fleeing from a convenience-store robbery or had plowed the family station wagon into a lamp pole
at two a.m. so inebriated that he couldn't say his own name
coherently. Delays give both sides time to posture and rack up
billable hours.

But any interest Dominic had in stalling waned after he
read the *White Plains Daily* article about how Rudy Hitchins
had become a test case and also learned at the police station
that I had refused to move forward on the additional resisting
charges.

All this was heady stuff for Alexander Dominic Esq., opening his eyes to a real opportunity. If he was lucky, he could get
his name and photograph in the newspaper, too.

And publicity, even bad publicity, was good for his business.

For those reasons, when Dominic made his first official appearance in court in the matter of the *People of the State of
New York v. Rudolph Hitchins, aka Rudy Hitchins*, the pudgy
defense attorney announced that he wanted to get his client's
case fast-tracked. What he actually said was more grandiose,
which was his modus operandi.

"Your Honor," Dominic declared loudly, "an innocent
man such as my client shouldn't have to spend one day longer
than necessary with these ugly and false charges hanging over
his head and clouding his future."

His speech nearly made me gag. The only future Hitchins

had waiting for him was a 6-by-6 cell. I was seated at the prosecutor's table entirely by myself. Because of my dustup with Detective O'Brien, my boss had decided to hide out at the Westchester Country Club's ninth hole. The courtroom was half-filled mostly with other attorneys and their clients, since this was merely a hearing to set a possible trial date. I glanced back and saw a man furiously taking notes. I assumed that he was Will Harris, covering the arraignment for a follow-up story.

Judge Michael Morano, who was well familiar with Alexander Dominic and his sad-sack clientele, couldn't help himself from smirking at the defense attorney's remarks, knowing full well that the idea of Dominic actually representing an innocent client was mind-boggling.

From a prosecutor's point of view, I saw no reason to delay. In fact, I welcomed it. In his haste, Dominic had overlooked an important fact about the victim. Mary Margaret was pregnant and had such severe injuries that it would take months for them to heal. When Judge Morano scheduled the case to be heard in five months, I was elated. My victim would be on the verge of giving birth and having a pregnant victim testify about being beaten would have an emotional impact on jurors.

Dominic thanked the judge for speeding up the trial and declared in a voice loud enough for our local reporter to hear, "Your Honor, I'm not even sure I will need to call a single witness because these charges are so groundless." Just the same, Judge Morano set aside two days on his judicial calendar for the trial. The good judge then announced that he wanted to see both of us in his chambers, an office directly behind the courtroom. Dominic waddled in behind Judge Morano with me bringing up the rear, but I stopped short in the doorway of his chambers. Judge Morano had removed his heavy black robe and fired up a thick cigar. Dominic had taken this gesture to mean that he could light an unfiltered Camel.

Judge Morano noted that I had hesitated and said, "I'm going to need you all the way in here so we can close the door."

"Judge, I have asthma. I'm allergic to smoke."

"Oh," he responded in what, at first, sounded like a concerned voice. He glanced at Dominic, who began puffing madly, trying to get as much nicotine into his lungs as possible before the judge told him to put it out.

But rather than lowering his foul-smelling cigar, Judge Morano took a long, slow, and apparently satisfying pull on it, causing the dark ashes at its tip to burn red. He smiled and said, "Well, that's a real shame, dear. Now get in here so I can talk to you both."

Reluctantly, I took another step inside his office and closed the door behind me. I was standing at the outer edge of a Spartan room that had clearly been furnished by the lowest government bidder. The walls were lined with metal shelves that contained leather-bound volumes of New York State's penal law, most of which appeared as if they had never been opened. There were no family photographs, no legal degrees, no plants, no paintings. The place reeked of cigar smoke and coffee. The tiles on the floor were covered with layer upon layer of wax, which made them look yellow, not white.

Judge Morano looked directly at me and said, "When I first met you in the courthouse elevator, young lady, I told you my courtroom was for serious crimes, so why are you cluttering up my docket with this bullshit?"

Without waiting for me to respond, he said, "This is a marital dispute; the case should be in family court, not here." I explained to the judge that although the parties shared the same last name they were never married. Under Section 812 of New York's Family Court Act, an unmarried couple could not appear in family court. Judges do not like being lectured about the law, and judging by his irked look, Judge Morano, in particular, didn't appreciate it. Turning his attention to

Dominic, the judge demanded, "Why hasn't this matter been plea-bargained?"

Dominic shrugged his shoulders, did his best to look bewildered, and nodded in my direction, much like a schoolboy escaping blame. "Your Honor, I told her the defense is willing to plead to a misdemeanor, but she won't negotiate."

Both men looked at me.

"Your client savagely beat Mary Margaret Finn, putting her into the hospital with life-threatening injuries. We're not going to reduce this attack to a misdemeanor."

"Let's cut through the crap," Judge Morano said. "I saw the newspaper article about how you and District Attorney Whitaker are hoping to make this matter into some sort of women's liberation case. And I don't like it at all. Politics have no place in my courtroom and my courtroom is not a test laboratory or a platform for political theater. How many times do I have to tell you, Miss Fox, my court deals with real crimes?"

"Your Honor, the reason this matter is in your court is because it is a real crime."

Judge Morano apparently didn't like my answer, because he rested his cigar in the ceramic ashtray that was perched atop a stack of yellow legal files on his cluttered metal desk and said, "I would strongly urge both of you to reach some sort of agreement before the trial date so we are not wasting the taxpayers' hard-earned money and taking me away from more important cases. Am I making myself clear?"

"Judge," said Dominic, "I'm all about making a deal. It's her."

"Yes, I can see that," the judge said, fetching his cigar from the ashtray. I noticed his caterpillar eyebrows were starting to pump up and down nervously as if they were in Marine boot camp doing push-ups.

"Judge," Dominic said, breaking the momentary silence. "If I may, there's something else."

"What's that? Don't you think you've wasted enough of my time today?"

"My client is in jail; he was unable to post bond—a bond that was unreasonably high given the minor nature of this matter." He hesitated for a bit of dramatic effect and then added, "His incarceration is beginning to have an impact on his livelihood and ability to pay bills."

Because Judge Morano was already upset with me, I bit my tongue, but pictured the "livelihood" that Hitchins would be earning on the streets. The image of a terrified woman having her purse snatched and being beaten with a clenched fist popped into my head.

I'd been standing with my back pressed against the closed chamber's door to keep myself as far away from the two human chimneys in front of me, but now I stepped forward. "Your Honor, the reason the bond was set at five thousand dollars was because of the ongoing threat that Mr. Dominic's client poses to the victim of his attack."

Judge Morano addressed Dominic: "Why hasn't your client gotten a bondsman to release him?"

Dominic made another of his well-schooled, blank looks.

"The reason why a bondsman doesn't want to mess with Mr. Dominic's client," I piped in, "is because he has a reputation for not paying his debts and using violence to keep people from collecting them."

The dumbfounded expression on Dominic's face turned into one of fake outrage, but before he could speak, Judge Morano said, "I've issued a temporary order of protection instructing Rudy Hitchins to stay away from the alleged victim. Ergo, I'm going to release your client on his own personal recognizance."

"What?" I exclaimed, stepping even closer. Leaning down, I put both of my palms on the judge's desk and bent forward to address him. "Your Honor, this man is dangerous. There's no telling what he'll do to the victim."

Judge Morano looked with disdain at my hands on his desk and I quickly removed them. He leaned back in his seat with a smug smile and said, "Young lady, if you are so concerned about your client's welfare, then I strongly suggest that you and Mr. Dominic step outside my chambers and reach a resolution."

He blew a mouthful of stale smoke directly at my face and said, "Mr. Dominic's client will be released this afternoon. We're done here."

As soon as I returned to my office, I thought about who I needed to call for help. I could think of only one name so I mentally prepared myself for a big slice of humble pie and dialed O'Brien's number.

"O'Brien here."

"Detective," I said, mustering up my courage. "This is—"

"I know who it is, Counselor. I recognize your voice. I'm a detective, remember? Why the hell are you calling me?"

"Judge Morano is going to release Rudy Hitchins this afternoon on his own recognizance."

"What? Why didn't you stop him?"

"I tried. But he wouldn't listen. I'm afraid Hitchins is going to do something to Mary Margaret. She's still in the hospital and I—"

O'Brien interrupted: "Well, well, well, what do we have here?"

I could smell the humble pie heading toward my lips.

"So Judge Morano is freeing Hitchins because the good judge doesn't think that piece of pond scum is a threat. Oh, but then, you didn't think that either, did you, Counselor?"

I resisted the urge to reply. More pie was clearly coming my way.

O'Brien said, "Do you need to hear me say it? Do I need to tell you how this would not be happening if you had done what every other goddamn assistant district attorney in White Plains would have done when I brought you those additional charges?" Raising his voice, he said, "It could have been so easy. And now you call me for help. You got some balls!"

I thought about reminding him that we'd already discussed my lower anatomy during our first meeting when he'd been impressed that I was willing to prosecute the Hitchins case. But when you are eating humble pie, it's best to keep such thoughts to yourself.

"I realize you're angry with me, but I'm worried. I really—"

In the middle of my sentence, Detective O'Brien cut me off.

"I'll see if I can get someone to watch Hitchins. I doubt he'll do anything as long as she's in the hospital."

"Thank—"

He hung up on me.

12

I DROVE DIRECTLY TO THE HOSPITAL TO tell Mary Margaret and her mother that Judge Morano was going to release Rudy Hitchins, but I assured them that Detective O'Brien had promised to have the cops keep an eye on him. Mrs. Finn told me that O'Brien had already stopped at the hospital and briefed them.

Feeling somewhat relieved, I drove home. I live in a simple bungalow-style home less than two miles from my mom's place. She helped me buy it after my father died and we decided to move here from Elmira. I wanted my own place to live, even though she would have loved for me to live with her. Besides, it wasn't like I lived alone. I had Wilbur, my pet pig, for company.

Wilbur is a Vietnamese pot belly, a breed of domesticated pig that obviously originated in Vietnam. As far as pigs go, he's considerably smaller than most and about the size of a large-breed dog. Just the same, Wilbur had grown up to weigh 110 pounds and stand eighteen inches high. He has upright ears, a straight tail, and a swayed back because his big belly drops within inches of the ground. His favorite foods are apples and peanut butter, and he is always hungry. I keep him in a pen in my backyard. He waits at the pen's gate for me every night when I get off work. I let him loose and, much like a dog, he follows me into the house.

People think of pigs as being dumb and dirty, but they're

intelligent and clean animals that can be house-trained. Just the same, I keep Wilbur sealed off in my kitchen. He has a large mat there that he likes to burrow under at night; he actually made a good watchdog—as long as the burglar didn't arrive with food.

I parked my Triumph in the driveway and went immediately to the backyard to break the bad news to Wilbur.

"Sorry, but it's my turn to drive to Albany to meet Bob this weekend."

I paid a neighbor boy to feed Wilbur on the weekends when I was traveling so I knew Wilbur would be fine. Just the same, when he grunted, I felt guilty leaving him in his pen. As I was unlocking the back door, I heard the kitchen phone ring.

"Hello?"

"Hey, beautiful," I heard Bob say.

"Hi. I was just outside saying good-bye to Wilbur. I'll pack and hit the road, so I'll get to your apartment just before eight o'clock. Where are you taking me to dinner?"

"I got bad news, honey. I'm jammed and really need the entire weekend to study. I want to see you, but this is just one of those weekends."

It seemed we'd had a lot of them lately between his studies and my work.

"I understand, but I've had a really rough week and I need to escape from here."

He asked me to tell him what had happened so I filled him in on the Hitchins case. Because Bob and I have been sweethearts since we were in high school, I knew he wouldn't be putting off seeing me unless he had a good reason.

"What if I drove up just for tonight?" I volunteered. "I promise I'll leave first thing in the morning." God, I was sounding desperate.

"I'd love that normally, but I'm really buried here with work. I've got a study group tonight. I just can't take the time, sweetheart. I really can't. The pressure is on, just like when you were in law school. Remember?"

I did. I remembered the pressure that I had put on myself to graduate at the top of my class. Could I expect anything less from him?

"Okay, Wilbur and I will spend the night here. But you should know, he's a poor substitute."

"I hope so!" Bob said.

"Call me tomorrow, please, just for a few seconds. I just want to hear your voice," I said.

"Why don't you go to church with your mom? She'd like that."

"Maybe I will. But call, please." I missed him.

We ended the call, as we always did, by saying each how much we loved the other.

As I was hanging up the phone, I thought about my third year in law school when I had been under pressure and the two of us had managed to sneak away on Christmas Eve for a much-needed break. We'd driven home to Elmira a day earlier to check in with our folks, but then escaped to Bob's grandfather's farm. His family leased the 120 acres to a tenant farmer but kept the main farmhouse for a private getaway.

SNOWFLAKES WERE BLOWING and the evening moon cast a blue hue over the white-blanketed earth. Icicles were hanging from trees. We rode in Bob's Jeep Wrangler through rolling hills where his grandparents had once raised crops, grown apples, and herded livestock. Because it was still a working farm, there were chickens, cows, horses, and pigs in the huge barn near the main house. Their tenant lived in a more modest house about a mile from the main one.

I loved coming to the farm. As we burst through drifts of snow on the gravel road, we laughed in pure joy. I reached over and touched Bob's right leg with anticipation of our night ahead. Bob Dylan, Bob's favorite singer, was playing on the radio: "Girl from the North Country." It was a mellow, sweet song whose lines described a snowflake storm, frozen rivers, howling winds, and the need for the singer's lover to keep warm. I'm sure Bob was thinking about me as he sang along in a deep voice. Although I smiled appreciatively, the song reminded me of my mom and her never-ending concern for dressing me warm and protecting me from winter's colds and sniffles. It also made me a bit sad that I would miss Christmas Eve dinner with her. But Bob and I would reconnect on Christmas Day with our families and relatives to attend mass.

"I see the farmhouse, Dani."

I looked through the wet windshield and spotted the lights coming from the old two-story wood-framed house. Bob had called ahead and the tenant had turned the lights on for us.

"I've brought along a great bottle of red wine," Bob said.

"You won't need to get me drunk, Doc. I'm a sure thing tonight."

Bob downshifted and rolled right up to the front porch. The ignition was barely off when he wrapped his arms around me and pulled my body into his. His kiss was wet, warm, and longing. It was going to be another great night.

I lugged the basket of precooked turkey, yams, brown gravy, mashed potatoes, and cranberries from the back of the Jeep while Bob hurried inside to start a fire.

"I hope you cooked as good as last year," Bob called.

"Do I ever let you down?"

I was lying. Mom had actually cooked everything earlier in the day.

Inside, we kicked off our boots and I put the food in the oven to warm. By the time I emerged from the kitchen, Bob had poured two tall goblets full of wine and there was a beautiful blaze in the fireplace. He motioned me to join him and

I could feel the fire's warmth on my legs as we stood before the hearth.

"Here's lookin' at you, kid," he mimicked, raising his glass.

"Okay, Doctor Bogart, right back at you."

We were so eager to pull off each other's clothing that we barely had time for our first sip.

"Don't you want to eat first?" I asked.

"Hell no, don't you dare go anywhere." We fell to our knees in front of the stonework. He whispered into my ear how much I meant to him and I did the same as we fumbled with each other's shirts. As I undid his buttons, he slipped his hands up the back of my white turtleneck sweater and un-snapped my bra. I tugged his shirt out of his jeans and off his toned body. I kissed his face, his neck, his chest, and moved down to his stomach as he pulled my top off.

His mouth was warm and radiating with love. He undid my pants buckle and unzipped me. With my corduroys off, I leaned back in my white bikini underpants. He stood and I admired his beautiful chest and shoulders as he undid his jeans, slid them to the ground—no underwear! God was he hot.

I fell to my back and he slid my panties off. He kissed my foot, then my inner thigh. I pulled him up on me and looked into his eyes. He told me that he loved me and I knew he meant it. In an instant, everything was smooth, slow, and deep. I was building and he read my excitement. He moved deeper and faster as I wrapped my legs around him.

"Come with me," he said.

"Now?"

"Yes, please now, now, now!" He exploded inside me and we both gasped in pleasure.

After, we continued to hold and kiss each other, completely unaware of time. He left me briefly only to toss more wood into the fireplace and pull a heavy blanket over us. He ran his tongue over my breast and moved his hand across my hips.

"What about dinner?" I asked.

"Fuck it," he said. We made love again and drifted off to sleep. Dinner would wait.

I LOVED BEING WITH BOB that Christmas Eve. And there was no doubt in my mind that Bob loved me. I let out a sigh and walked to the backyard where I opened the door to Wilbur's pen. With an excited squeal, he waddled toward the house.

13

O

N A FRIDAY, THREE WEEKS AFTER
she'd been attacked, Mary Margaret was discharged
and I drove to Canfield Avenue to check on her.
The flat-roofed apartment building that her mother owned
had a dingy yellow-brick facade. Hitchins's name was still taped
to one of the four mailboxes hanging near the entryway. Another belonged to Mrs. Latham, the snoopy tenant who lived
next door on the second floor. I'd telephoned Mrs. Finn before
leaving my office and she'd told me that her daughter would
be recuperating with her, so I pushed a buzzer next to APT.
1 on a ground-floor unit and waited. Rebecca cracked the door
a few inches. She had one of those hotel-type chains, but if she
thought that flimsy contraption would keep out someone as
violent as Hitchins, she was wrong.

"Come in," she said, smiling. "Mary Margaret is resting but
I'll get her."

She left me standing in a dimly lit living room with badly
faded wallpaper decorated with red and white roses the size of
pumpkins and the stench of stale cigarettes. The white shades
on the two front windows were closed. Beneath my feet was a
well-worn Oriental rug with smudges left from fallen ashes.
Mrs. Finn had a tan Naugahyde couch and two vinyl easy
chairs positioned around the rug's edges. All of the furniture
faced a console television that had a rabbit-ear antenna poking
up from behind it and family photographs displayed on its

veneer top. The largest was a wedding shot of a much younger Rebecca and her beaming late husband, Harry. I didn't notice anything unusual about her apartment until I looked into the kitchen and saw a barber's chair anchored to the tile floor where most renters would have placed a breakfast table.

Hanging from the chair's arm was a long gray strap used to sharpen straight razors. I suddenly felt nauseated. It wasn't the musty air. It was a memory.

"YOU GIRLS ARE GOING to be punished," Father George McCleary said as he slapped a razor strap against the open palm of his pudgy left hand. "Don't you realize God watches you every moment? He writes your names in his book of good deeds and bad deeds and today you're in the bad book."

I was only ten, a skinny girl in a plaid skirt and green blazer, the school uniform at Saints Peter and Paul in Elmira. My two best friends, Amy Johnson and Susan O'Brien, were standing next to me at attention. A few minutes earlier we'd been giggling inside a school bathroom using a match to light a cigarette that Amy had pinched from her father's pack of unfiltered Camels. Amy assured us that she had smoked before, but when she inhaled, she began coughing so loudly that she'd drawn the attention of Sister Sarah McGill, the hallway monitor. Amy was in the midst of passing the cigarette to me when Sister Sarah burst in, confiscated the cigarette, and marched us to Father McCleary's office.

I knew Father McCleary was a chain-smoker. I'd seen him puffing away. But that didn't stop him from giving us a stern lecture about smoking at school. All the while, he waved a twenty-inch-long razor strap, which he used for spankings, in front of our wide eyes. Without warning, he slapped the strap down onto his desktop, causing a loud *WHACK*. I jumped.

Susan burst into tears and Amy soon joined her. Father Mc-Cleary appeared satisfied until he noticed there were no tears streaming from my eyes.

"Dani Fox, step forward, turn around, bend over, and touch your toes."

I didn't move. "My mother and father don't believe in spanking," I declared.

Father McCleary squinted over the half-glasses perched on his nose. "Is that so, young lady. Well, your parents aren't here, are they? Now you do as you were told or you'll get a double dose for being insolent."

With a chorus of sobs coming from my pals, I took one step forward and turned around as ordered. I was now looking directly into my terrified friends' faces.

"Grab your ankles."

I bent forward and took hold of my white socks.

He swung the strap quickly and with such force that I fell forward onto the wooden floor. There wasn't time to soften my fall with my arms. As I began pushing myself up, I realized my underwear was wet and my face burned with embarrassment. But I did not cry.

"You want another?" he asked.

"No, Father," I said softly as I took my spot next to my friends.

He raised the strap over his head as if he were going to swing it again and took a step toward the three of us. Susan and Amy shrieked and covered their faces with their hands.

"Let this be a lesson to the three of you!"

He lowered the strap. "I am calling your parents and I will strongly suggest they punish you when you get home."

That was the first and the last time that anyone had ever struck me. Obviously, that incident didn't compare to what Mary Margaret had endured. Yet it was burned into my memory and I could still feel the humiliation, helplessness, and anger of that moment when I had no control and another person hurt me.

MARY MARGARET SHUFFLED into the apartment living room wearing a terry cloth pale blue bathrobe. She still had bandages covering her face, and because her mouth was wired shut, she couldn't speak loudly. Mrs. Finn walked behind her as she inched forward and settled into one of the easy chairs.

"I saw you looking at Harry's barber chair," Mrs. Finn said. "He used to cut hair at night here. My Harry, if there was a way to earn an extra buck, he was on it. Our families were Irish, but he had a bit of Scotch in him, too, and I don't mean the liquor."

She laughed, took a seat on the sofa next to me, and fired up a cigarette.

I asked, "How are you feeling?"

"Better," Mary Margaret replied.

"My mother made you some baklava," I said, handing Mrs. Finn a paper plate covered with wax paper. "Have you ever had it?"

Neither had.

"It's a sticky pastry. It goes great with coffee."

"I'm sure we will enjoy it, dear, please thank her," Mrs. Finn said, taking the plate into the kitchen. "Of course, Mary Margaret can't eat solid food yet."

I felt myself blushing. I'd not thought of that.

"Has Rudy Hitchins tried to contact you—either by phone or coming here?"

"No," Mary Margaret said. "We heard he's living with that whore."

"Gloria Lucinda," Mrs. Finn volunteered, returning from the kitchen. "But don't you worry. He'll soon be doing to her

what he did to my baby girl. Then she'll see what kind of bastard he is."

We spoke about Hitchins for several moments and then I
got to the point of my visit. "You were understandably angry
and upset while you were in the hospital. Now that you're
home, I need to know if you are having any second thoughts
about moving forward with this case."

Mary Margaret shook her head.

"When will that bastard be put on trial?" Mrs. Finn asked.
"When can we get him locked up again, this time for good?"

I gave them a rudimentary outline of how the process
worked and explained that Judge Morano had put the case on
his docket five months from now.

"Five months is expedited?" Mary Margaret asked.

"Yes."

"That's about when she's having her baby," Mrs. Finn said.

"I want jurors to see you pregnant in court," I said.

"That's smart," Mrs. Finn replied.

"How's the pregnancy going?"

"I wish I'd miscarry. I already hate it."

"Them's just your emotions, honey," Mrs. Finn said. "Hor-
mones. You're tired."

I took that as a cue to leave. "I'd better go."

Mary Margaret asked, "You told me about your boyfriend.
Bob, right? How's that going?"

"We're both still busy. I didn't get to see him over the
weekend. But we're fine."

"Listen, honey, absence don't make the heart grow fonder,"
Mrs. Finn said. "It makes men look at other women."

"Mother," Mary Margaret said, "she told me about Bob in
the hospital. They've been together since high school. He's her
first love. It's romantic."

"It should be," said Mrs. Finn. "You take my Harry. It was

sparks from the moment I saw him. I'm not ashamed to say we gave our bed a good pounding."

"Mother, please!"

"There's no shame in it. We're all girls here. Many a night we'd sit in this room, having coffee and a smoke afterward, and he'd say, 'Rebecca, you're the sugar in my cup.' Now that's how it's supposed to be. I told Mary Margaret that. But no, she never listened. She took up with that no-good Rudy Hitchins. And look what happened."

Mary Margaret gave her mother an angry look as I stood and moved toward the door.

14

I WAS SLEEPING SO SOUNDLY WHEN THE telephone rang that I thought it was part of my dream. Fumbling for the receiver, I said, "Hello?" The light on the nightstand clock showed it was just after four a.m.

"This is Dispatcher Henderson at the Elmsford P.D.," a male voice announced. "I'm trying to reach Danny Fox."

"Yes."

"Can you get him on the line?"

"I'm Dani Fox."

"Sorry, ma'am. But I need to talk to Mr. Fox. A Detective O'Brien told me to notify Assistant D.A. Danny Fox. Is he available?"

"There is no Mr. Fox. The only male in this house is a pot-bellied pig and he's not talking right now. What's O'Brien want?"

"Urr, ah, um, well, we've got an emergency west of Elmsford near the interstate and I was told by O'Brien to get Danny Fox out there ASAP. Here's directions." I grabbed some dark chocolate on the way out the door.

It was only a five-minute drive to Elmsford at this predawn hour, but it took another ten minutes to find the rural road that the dispatcher had described. I'd traveled about a mile down it when I came upon an Elmsford police car blocking my path.

"Sorry, lady, but you've got to turn around," he said.

"There's a crime scene up ahead and it's going to be a while before this road opens again."

"I'm from the D.A.'s office."

"Sure you are."

I fished out my credentials.

"I didn't know they had girl prosecutors in Westchester," he said. "You'll find the detectives up the road."

A few minutes later, I arrived at a spot where three cars were parked side by side across the road with their headlights on. Their beams cast a spotlight on four men standing in front of them. I didn't see O'Brien.

"I'm Assistant District Attorney Dani—"

"We know who you are," one of them said gruffly. "O'Brien's in the woods. He wants you out there." He nodded to his right but didn't offer any additional information.

"What's this about?"

"Go see for yourself," he snapped, handing me a flashlight. "About a hundred yards through the trees."

I took his flashlight and walked into the pines that edged both sides of the road. The ground was flat and soft here because it was covered with pine needles. The trees shot up as if they were a giant fence. I shined the flashlight to my left and then swung it to my right. Every damn tree looked the same. I stopped and listened, but didn't hear anything except my own rushed breathing. Was I lost? I had no idea where I was going, but I continued forward, fighting a growing sense of alarm.

I moved quietly across the needles. I continued going straight, and in another five minutes, I heard voices, and in another twenty feet, I emerged into a clearing where I could see beams from other flashlights. I shined my light toward them and spotted O'Brien along with three other figures about thirty yards in front of me. One of the men was Carl, the detective who'd beaten Hitchins on the sidewalk outside O'Toole's.

They reacted to my flashlight by shining their lights at me, temporarily blinding me.

Unlike the barren ground in the woods, the clearing was covered with knee-high grass that was swaying in a morning breeze. I heard O'Brien tell someone to "walk away, Detective Jones" and then I heard another man utter a profanity. I realized it was Carl who was now breaking away from the threesome.

"What's going on?" I asked when I reached O'Brien. I shined my flashlight at his face and he glanced down, pointing his beam into the tall grass at his feet.

A bloody Mary Margaret was sprawled naked in the grass.

"One shot in her head," O'Brien said. "Another directly into her heart. Her clothes are over there." He swung his light to his right where her terry cloth bathrobe and her flannel pajamas had been tossed.

I felt horrible. The last dead person I'd seen was my father. Complications from cancer had killed him and ravaged his once-strong body. But he'd looked peaceful dressed in his best suit in his casket at his funeral, as if he were sleeping. Mary Margaret's empty eyes stared blankly ahead. Her face was frozen in a groan with her mouth gaping open. Her lips were twisted in a grotesque position. I'd seen plenty of autopsy photos of murder victims, but this was so much more real. This was someone I knew. Someone whom I had just been speaking to a few hours earlier. I had to turn my head to catch a breath of air.

"Hitchins must have brought her here," O'Brien said. "Forced her to strip, probably to humiliate her or maybe make her beg for her life. Maybe he just wanted a last fuck. Who knows? I figure he got them after they'd gone to bed."

"Them?"

"He killed Mrs. Finn, too. We got officers at the apartment.

They found her in her bedroom with her throat slit. He must have broken in, killed her, and then surprised Mary Margaret and brought her out here."

My revulsion turned into anger. Daughter and mother murdered.

"The baby?"

"No heartbeat."

I turned my face back toward him, then peered down again at Mary Margaret's nude corpse. Three lives ended at Rudy Hitchins's hands.

"Why'd he have to do this?" I asked.

"You're the big expert," O'Brien replied mockingly. "Power. Control. What did all those Ivy League experts tell you about men like him?"

Before I could respond, a voice coming from behind O'Brien said, "It's your fault." Detective Jones was returning.

"I told you to walk away," O'Brien said.

"She needs to hear it. We could've put that son of a bitch in prison but she had to do it her way."

"Bullshit," O'Brien said. "The guy was a walking time bomb. It was only a matter of time."

"You keep telling yourself that," Jones replied, directing his comments more at me than O'Brien. "If it helps you sleep at night, you believe it. But take a good, hard look at what he did to her. 'Cause no matter what your friend here says, in my book, lady, you and that fucking judge who turned him loose are as much responsible as Hitchins is."

I said, "You're blaming me? I'm the one who wanted to put him in jail. Or is it because I refused to prosecute him on trumped-up charges? You called me here to make me feel guilty?"

"We called you because you always follow the rules," Jones said snidely. It was standard procedure for an assistant district attorney to be called to the scene of every homicide. Because

I worked in the appeals bureau, however, I wasn't on the list and had never been called before.

"Mary Margaret was your case," O'Brien said.

Jones added, "We called you because she was your responsibility."

"What about you? I thought you had someone watching Hitchins."

"They thought he was with his girlfriend," Jones said.

"Enough of the blame game," O'Brien said. "Pisani is personally coming out here. This case is too big for you now."

I could feel my face turning red. But he was right. This was a triple homicide and Pisani would be all over it. He wouldn't want me as a partner. Still, I would ask. I owed Mary Margaret, her mother, and her unborn child that much. I'd promised to put Hitchins in jail.

"I was talking to Mary Margaret and her mom a few hours ago," I said. "In their apartment."

"Then you're damn lucky he didn't nab you, too," O'Brien said. "You could still be a target. It would be best if you stayed out of sight this weekend until we get Hitchins. Is there somewhere safe you can go?"

Safe? I wasn't sure if he was worried about Hitchins coming after me or Jones and his buddies from O'Toole's.

"I'm not hiding. I want to talk to Whitaker about this case."

"It would be better," O'Brien said, "if you just went somewhere and let this situation play itself out a little. By Monday, the dust will settle, and if we're lucky, Rudy Hitchins will no longer be a problem."

From his tone, it didn't sound as if he was talking about an arrest.

"Don't you get it?" Jones snapped. "This isn't your problem anymore. You've done enough damage. Now why don't you just get lost?"

"Let me know where you're going to be," O'Brien said.

"Why? So you can have your officers watch me like they did her?"

Before he could answer, I said, "I'll go to my mom's place." But as soon as I said it, I knew that was a mistake. Hitchins had just killed Mary Margaret's mother, and I didn't want him murdering mine, too.

"I'll go out of town. Albany. A friend."

"Then get the hell out of here," Jones said.

I glanced at Mary Margaret, whispered, "I'm sorry," and walked toward the woods. I was so preoccupied that I'd gone about a hundred feet before I realized I had no idea if I was headed in the right direction. I stopped and turned off my flashlight. I thought I might be able to see the headlights from the squad cars parked on the dirt road. Like a lighthouse, they could guide me in. But everything was pitch-black.

Just as I was about to turn on my flashlight, I heard a sound and saw a sliver from a flashlight cutting through the woods about sixty feet to my left. I started to call out but suddenly caught myself. What if it was Rudy Hitchins? Like an arsonist who lingers at a fire to watch the carnage that he'd caused, was Hitchins still prowling the woods? The flashlight beam moved quicker as the figure picked up speed. He seemed in a rush. I stayed frozen, not sure how to react. I couldn't make out a face.

As soon as the figure disappeared in the darkness, I began walking without my flashlight. "Ouch." Something had pricked my calf. I flipped on my light and saw that I'd wandered into a patch of thorny vines. I was bleeding. Damn it.

Dani, I told myself, stay focused. The road is minutes away. Don't let your imagination run wild. I never knew how frightening a forest could be. Maneuvering around the thorns, I continued walking, and in another thirty feet, I finally emerged from the pines. The three police cars were about a hundred yards north of me. When I reached them, I didn't bother to speak to the officers. There was another car parked next to mine and I assumed it belonged to Pisani. That must have been who'd passed by me in the woods—not Hitchins.

As I was unlocking my car, one of the officers yelled, "Hey, did you see those two guys from your office in the woods?"

Two guys? I'd only seen a lone man. I yelled over to the cops, "Did you get their names?"

"Yeah, it was Paul Pisani and your D.A. They came personally."

I walked over and explained that I had just seen an unknown man in the woods.

"Did you arrest him?" one of them said, laughing.

"You might want to see who it was."

"Okay, sure, we'll get right on that," another said.

Idiots. I got into my car and drove away. When I got to the interstate, I finally released my emotions. Tears filled my eyes, forcing me to pull over. I opened the car door and vomited.

15

I HURRIEDLY PACKED A SUITCASE WHEN I got home and headed for Albany. The Saturday-morning sun had risen by the time I reached the apartment building where Bob lived adjacent to the medical school campus. I pushed the button that connected to the intercom in his apartment. When there was no response, I punched it again and again. I checked and it was a few minutes after eight a.m. Where was he?

I decided to drive to a pay phone, but as I was walking across the parking lot to my car, I heard his familiar laugh and spun around. Bob was coming up the sidewalk with a drop-dead gorgeous blonde walking next to him.

"Bob," I called. "Bob."

I waved and he saw me. He said something to the woman and the two of them came to me.

"I thought you weren't coming until next weekend," Bob said.

"Change of plans. Something horrible has happened."

Bob said, "This is Linda, a friend from my study group."

She stuck out her hand. "Bob and I are coming back from an all-night study session at the medical library. We stopped for coffee and bagels."

I shook her hand and she said, "I got to run and get some sleep."

Watching her walk away, I felt jealous. She had killer long

legs, a confident gait, and long locks that bounced on her shoulders with each step.

"What's wrong? Is it your mom?"

I said, "Hold me, tight." He wrapped his arms around me and I put my face against his chest and whispered, "I may have gotten two people and an unborn baby killed. That case I told you about."

He pushed me back so he could see my face and said, "How? I'm sure it's not your fault."

As we walked to his apartment, I recounted what had happened. Once inside, he said, "I don't have any Dr Peppers left from your last visit, but I can get you coffee."

He started toward the kitchen.

"What I want is for you to come back here and hold me."

Bob hugged me tight. "I'm sure everything is going to be okay," he said, patting my back.

"The cops hate me. They blame me."

"Well, I can kind of see why."

"What?" I said, clearly hurt.

"I mean, I understand why they are upset, but they certainly can't hold you responsible, especially since they dropped the ball when they were supposed to be watching Hitchins."

"You think I should have filed those bogus charges?"

"Dani, you're exhausted and emotionally upset. You've just been through a horrific incident. Let's get you into bed. You'll feel better after you get some sleep."

He led me into his bedroom, where I stripped down to my bra and panties and climbed under the covers. "Aren't you joining me?" I asked. "I thought you guys were up all night."

"We were and I'm exhausted. But the coffee I just drank is giving me a buzz. I want to make a few notes and take a shower. Then I'll join you."

I curled up in a fetal position. I was disappointed. I wanted to feel him holding me. I wanted to have him spoon with me and feel the warmth of his body and feel loved. I also wanted to get that image of Mary Margaret out of my mind.

"Don't take long," I said.

"Okay." He bent down and kissed my forehead.

"Bob, I should have done something to protect them."

"Think about something else."

When I woke up, it was late afternoon. Bob was snoring next to me in bed. For a brief moment, I felt happy, and then I remembered what had happened during the past twenty-four hours.

16

T HE BANNER HEADLINE ON THE *White Plains Daily*'s Sunday edition screamed in all capital letters: KILLER MURDERS THREE. A sub-head on the page added: Mother, Daughter, Unborn Baby Dead: Boyfriend Suspected. The newspaper published a large photo of Mary Margaret and Mrs. Finn standing next to each other in happier times at what appeared to be an amusement park. A second photo showed a body covered with a white sheet being pushed into the back of a medical examiner's van. In a sensational account, reporter Will Harris told readers that Charleston Taylor, an Elmsford-area farmer, had been doing his early-morning chores when he'd heard a woman screaming from a clearing not far from his barn. "I've done enough rabbit shooting to recognize the sound of gunshots and that's what I heard next. Two of 'em." Alarmed, Taylor called the police.

Harris quoted White Plains police chief Harvey Cutler stating that Rudy Hitchins was "a person of interest." Hitchins's mug shot was published inside the newspaper where the story jumped from page one. The paper also published a photograph of Chief Cutler and D.A. Whitaker standing outside the court-house holding a Saturday press conference.

Whitaker was quoted liberally, explaining how his office had been in the midst of prosecuting Hitchins with felony as-sault because of his earlier attack on Mary Margaret. He further noted that Hitchins had been freed from jail by Judge Morano despite strong protests from the D.A.'s office. "My staff was actively going after this man in an extremely violent domestic case," Whitaker declared. "In some communities, domestic violence is ignored, but not here, especially not while I'm the district attorney. I only wish Judge Morano had been as alarmed as we were." There was no love lost between Whitaker and Judge Morano.

In the final paragraphs of the news story, Harris identified me as the prosecutor who had been overseeing the Hitchins case.

I'd read the Sunday paper as soon as I returned home from Bob's apartment in Albany. After my weekend respite, I was eager to return to work. I needed to talk to Whitaker about teaming me with Pisani once Hitchins was arrested. But when I got to work in the morning, Steinberg told me that Whitaker had decided I needed to take "a few extra days off."

"I want to help," I protested.

"Look, Dani," Steinberg said, "the cops are still angry and Will Harris has been fishing around for a story. He's asking to interview you. We don't want you talking to him right now, especially while Hitchins is loose. No reason to make you a target."

Was that really the case, or did Steinberg simply want to keep me out of the limelight so Whitaker could bask in it? The reason hardly mattered. I was being told to stay scarce and I didn't like it. For two days, I was like a caged animal at my house until Wednesday when I decided to attend a funeral mass at St. Mary's Assumption Catholic Church for Mary Margaret and her mother.

As I approached the church, I spotted two television news trucks in the parking lot. Reporters were interviewing mourners, so I kept driving and parked my car on a side street. I waited until the mass had begun before discreetly slipping into the sanctuary through a side door. About two hundred attendees had come to pay their last respects. The church could hold as many as a thousand, so only the pews in the front were full. I took a seat in the back. From my vantage point, I could see the backs of the heads of Police Chief Cutler, D.A. Whitaker, and Paul Pisani sitting in the front row. Our mayor and a slew of candidates running for election in November for various Westchester County posts were seated close by them. Several pews were filled with uniformed police officers, a testament to how popular Mary Margaret had been at O'Toole's.

I exited the church several minutes before the mass ended, hoping to avoid attention, but as soon as I stepped outside, someone called my name.

"Ms. Fox, Ms. Fox."

The man approaching me had a runner's slender build. He stood about six feet tall, was in his late twenties, and had a mop of brown hair that needed to be trimmed. He was wearing a dark blazer, a white collared shirt that had its top button undone, and gray pants that were too long in the cuff. I noticed his trousers were frayed in the back where he'd stepped on them.

"I'm Will Harris with the *Daily*—the reporter who telephoned you after you were first hired—and I wondered if I could speak to you now."

"Now's not a good time. Besides, I can't talk to the media unless my boss okays it in advance."

"Sure, I understand, but you're an important part of the Rudy Hitchins story. The only reason Whitaker filed felony assault charges against him was because of you. Otherwise, none of this would have happened."

I couldn't believe he was blaming me for the murders. I spun around and began walking.

"Wait, wait," Harris called. "That didn't come out right. I didn't mean the murders were your fault. What I said was supposed to be a compliment—that no one really cared about domestic violence around here until you were hired."

"For a man who makes his living with words, Mr. Harris, you seem to choose them poorly. You need to speak to Mr. Whitaker."

I turned my back to him and started toward my car.

"I'll run it by Whitaker," he yelled.

Hoping to avoid other reporters, I picked up my pace. I was just about to my car when I noticed its right rear tire was flat. The left rear tire was flat, too. Hurrying forward, I saw both front tires were flat. Obviously, someone was sending me a not-too-subtle message.

A car moved slowly up the street and then stopped next to me. Its tinted windows and the antennas sticking from its trunk meant it was an unmarked police cruiser. The driver lowered the passenger window.

"Need a lift, Counselor?" O'Brien asked. He reached across the seat, grabbed the interior latch, and shoved open the passenger door. "The two of us need to talk."

O'BRIEN DROVE TO A GREASY SPOON on the fringes of White Plains that only cops and truck drivers would patronize. Given the warm reception he received from Ellen, our busty, middle-aged waitress, it was a favorite.

"I'll take my usual," he announced.

"That's one chicken-fried steak, piled with French fries smothered in white cream gravy," Ellen revealed with delight as she scribbled on a notepad. "And what would you like, dear?"

"Do you serve salads?"

"Only when I have to!" She chuckled.

"They serve food here that sticks to your ribs," O'Brien said.

"And your arteries," I replied. "Surely you can fix me some sort of salad in the kitchen."

Ellen gave me a disappointed look and then waddled away.

"I heard the boys were playing a little rough with you," O'Brien said. "So when I saw you duck out of the church, I followed you. I've already called a tow truck. The driver will pump up your tires and drop off your car at your house. I gave him the address. No harm done."

"No harm?"

"The boys just let the air out. They didn't puncture your tires."

For that I was supposed to feel grateful?

"Where's Rudy Hitchins?" I asked.

"His girlfriend claims he fled south, which makes us think that he probably headed to Canada. We have contacted U.S. Customs and also the Mounties."

"I think he's still here."

"Oh, so now you're a detective?"

"The other night in the woods, I saw a man. I couldn't tell who he was. But he was hurrying through the woods, all alone. I know it wasn't Pisani and Whitaker."

"This guy—did you see him right after you left the clearing?"

"Yeah, I did."

O'Brien grinned. "That was me. I was looking for you. I thought you might get lost. Obviously, you didn't."

Ellen brought coffee and a Dr Pepper.

"How do you drink that stuff?" O'Brien asked. But he didn't wait for me to reply. Instead, he said, "I'm gonna tell you a story. My old man worked as a correctional officer all his life at Attica. Ten of his pals died during the big riot there in nineteen seventy-one."

"Was he hurt?"

"Naw, he'd retired a month before. But he watched the riot on TV and he wished like hell that he'd been part of it. He was angry as hell that the state lost control to the inmates. A few weeks later, he died unexpectedly."

"A heart attack?"

"Him? Naw. Not sure he even had a heart. It was retirement that killed him. He wasn't cut out to sit at home."

O'Brien didn't seem too upset about his father's death.

Ellen arrived with food and the plate she plopped down in front of O'Brien was gigantic. He tucked a paper napkin in his collar and cut into the battered steak. "What you got to understand is that my father didn't have anything in his life but his job. At Attica, he was a somebody who could crack heads and push people around. After he retired, he was just another retired schmuck."

He took a sip of coffee and a huge bite. "Now to the point of my story. At Attica, whenever a new hire showed up, the other officers would test him. They'd wait for an inmate to go nuts. When inmates did, most would throw soapy water on the cell floor to make it slippery. They'd rub butter all over themselves for the same reason, and finally they'd break off a mop handle to use as a weapon. They'd scream at the officers, challenging them to come into the cell. That's how they did it back then."

"That's awful."

"Are you kidding? My old man loved it. Four or five officers would gather outside the cell and they'd talk about how they were going to rush in and tackle the inmate. Meanwhile, the inmate would back as far as he could against the cell's rear wall and then the officers would pop open that cell door. Only the old-timers would always hesitate to make sure the new guy went through first."

O'Brien paused to take another bite. "Do you know why they wanted the new guy to go first?"

I shrugged. I wasn't in the mood for guessing games.

"Because they wanted to see what he was made of. Was he going to hold his mud and fight or was he going to run? The ones who got scared—the older officers would let that inmate whup on him for a while because they knew he was a coward and they wanted him to get injured or scared enough that he'd quit. But the ones who went toe-to-toe with that inmate—as soon as the others saw that, they'd race in and kick the shit out of that prisoner."

I nodded.

O'Brien said, "What you got to understand, Counselor, is you're being tested—especially because you're a skirt."

He pointed a gravy-smeared fork at me. "There are three types of people. The wolves: people like Hitchins. The sheep: the good, law-abiding folks in our communities who have nine-to-five jobs, nice families, and go to church each Sunday. And the shepherds: the cops, correctional officers, state troopers, deputies, and, yes, even the prosecutors. We're the only thing standing between the wolves and the sheep."

"I get it."

"I'm not sure you do get it, Counselor. When you refused to back up Jones and his buddies outside O'Toole's, that made you suspect. They don't know if they can trust you. Now that Hitchins has killed Mary Margaret and her mother, well, some of the guys are blaming you. So they're testing you to see if you're going to run back to Whitaker and cry. They're watching to see if you are going to complain to our chief. Or maybe you'll even quit."

"I'm not going to run away because someone let the air out of my tires. But you've got to understand. I don't break rules. Most things are black and white to me. There's not much gray."

"How old are you?"

"Why's that matter? Okay, I'm twenty-five. How old are you?"

"More than double that, but I still remember how I thought I knew everything at your age. I lost that in the streets. You'll learn. The streets wear you down and pretty soon those black-and-white rules start to bend. After a while, the streets take over your life, just like Attica took over my old man's life. It begins when you stop feeling like you're off the clock. No matter what, your mind is on the streets, even when you're at home with the kids and wife having dinner. Your mind is thinking about that homicide you just saw, thinking about those punks who are beating up some lady for pocket change. Watching television, playing cards with a neighbor, going to church and singing 'Glory Glory, Hallelujah'—all that normal shit most people do suddenly bores the hell out of you. You become addicted to the adrenaline, the danger. All you think about is the streets. Pretty soon the only friends you got are other cops because they're the only ones who understand the streets. You got more in common with your partner than your wife. The streets will strip you of your idealism, Counselor. In a few months, you won't be so black and white. If you last."

He swallowed a big wad of French fries that he'd stabbed. "Consider these murders your wake-up call."

"Do you blame me for what happened?"

"Hell no! You did the right thing going after that prick. How were you to know he was going to kill her and her old lady? You can't go around blaming yourself every time someone else goes crazy."

"That's not what Carl Jones thinks."

"You shouldn't care what he thinks. If anyone should feel guilty, it's him. He's more responsible for Mary Margaret's death than you."

I suspected O'Brien was telling me that it was Detective Jones who had gotten Mary Margaret pregnant.

"Anyway," he continued, "all you can do is learn from this."

"Learn what?"

"Learn what I just told you. That being black and white don't always work. Sometimes you got to bend the rules."

I'd hardly taken a bite from what was supposed to be a salad—a few pieces of lettuce, a tomato, and some mushrooms— but he'd finished the steak and most of the fries. He waved to Ellen to refill his coffee and made no pretense about averting his eyes from her ample posterior when she walked away.

Apparently done with his lecture, he asked, "So how come your parents gave you a boy's name? I figured your name was Danielle, but I ran a background check on you."

"You ran a background check on me?"

"Yeah, so," he responded in a matter-of-fact voice.

"That's illegal, isn't it?"

"I'm a cop. I was looking for your address. Don't be naive."

"My first name is Dani. It's not short for anything. My grandparents came from Lebanon. My parents chose it because of its meaning."

"Oh yeah, what's that?"

"Judge or judgment."

"Well, they got that right. You're definitely judgmental."

I wasn't certain he meant it as a compliment.

"How about Fox? Where's that come from? I thought all they had in Lebanon was camels and sand."

"No one could pronounce my grandfather's name when he arrived at Ellis Island. Some immigration official thought it would be funny to change it to Fox."

I decided to turn the tables. "Since I didn't run a background check on you, what's your story? Why did you get divorced—twice?"

"I wasn't very good at marriage."

"Let me guess, your wives didn't understand you. They didn't understand the streets?" I said mockingly.

"Actually, they *did* understand me. That's why they left. Both of them realized they'd never be as important to me as the guys who backed me up each day at work. Even a prick like Jones. Every birthday, anniversary, holiday—I was like a caged animal at home. I'm not the type who remembers anniversaries or goes to kids' school talent shows."

"You got kids?"

"Yeah, two. Don't see them."

"Too busy?"

"They don't like having me around. One's in high school and the other is married. Putting me and their mothers in the same room ain't good."

O'Brien pushed his plate away, finished his coffee, and inserted a new toothpick between his lips. "What I'm trying to explain to you, Counselor, is that guys like me and Jones, we don't have nothing much in our lives but this. We don't have no one but each other. And when someone new comes in and pisses on our turf, it doesn't go well."

Continuing, he said, "Speaking of taking a piss, I need to use the little boys' room. You still owe me ten bucks from our bet, so you pay the check and leave Ellen a good tip. I don't want her thinking I stiffed her. I'll meet you at the car. This little talk ain't done, but the next part needs to be said in private."

The bill was $5.75. The diner didn't charge cops for their food, Ellen told me. I left her a ten. I paid my debt.

18

O'BRIEN WAS WAITING IMPATIENTLY behind the steering wheel when I got to the cruiser. Pulling into the street, he asked: "You know who Mark Steinberg is, right?"

"I'd better. He's our chief of staff."

"But do you know who Kieran McMichael is?"

"No. Don't have a clue." I really didn't like him playing these guessing games. "Look, if you got something to tell me, just spit it out, okay?"

O'Brien slid the toothpick in his mouth from one side to the other, a sign that I assumed meant he was irked. "Kieran McMichael works for a large political consulting firm. Every four weeks, he and Steinberg meet with your boss in the D.A.'s office to discuss the latest polling numbers."

"It's spring. The November election is still months away."

"McMichael does polling year-round. If you know which way a parade is going, it's easy to jump out front and be the bandleader."

That was a good one, I thought.

"The reason," O'Brien said, "these early polls are important is because they're real polls—ones that truly reflect the attitudes of voters."

"I thought all polls did."

"Naw, it don't work like that. When it gets closer to Election Day, McMichael will change his polling technique. He'll do what is called a 'push poll,' which is a poll that is intentionally designed to create favorable results. Those doctored results will be leaked to reporters to help Whitaker's campaign. But right now, Whitaker is interested only in real data."

I was impressed with O'Brien's political savvy and also curious how he knew what was going on in the D.A.'s inner sanctum.

"A few weeks ago," he said, "McMichael told your boss something that he didn't want to hear."

"How do you know what goes on in Whitaker's office?"

"That don't matter, okay? I'm trying to help you, so listen instead of asking questions."

I sat quiet.

"For the first time in Whitaker's political career, he is losing ground with voters and not just any voters. He is losing ground with registered women voters. Men love him, but women are drifting away to his opponent. That's because his challenger is targeting women and seniors."

"When did you say McMichael's polls first started showing Whitaker losing ground?"

O'Brien smiled. "Ah, now you're beginning to get it, aren't you? He found out he was losing ground with women about the same time that you waltzed into his office and asked if you could file felony charges against Rudy Hitchins."

Suddenly, I did get it. The reason why Whitaker had let me prosecute Hitchins in criminal court was politics.

"Your boss wanted to see how women and senior citizens would react when you charged Hitchins. In fact, I've been told that McMichael ran a special poll after Will Harris wrote that Hitchins was being indicted. You remember that story, right?"

I did. "What'd the polls show?"

"His numbers with women jumped." O'Brien jammed his palm into the car's horn, blasting the driver stopped in front of him who wasn't moving quickly enough when a stoplight changed to green. "Would you like to guess who paid a special visit to the D.A.'s office on Monday afternoon? It was McMichael armed with yet another special poll that he'd conducted after the chief and Whitaker held their press conference about the homicides. It showed Whitaker's numbers had jumped even more with women. That, my dear, is why you saw Whitaker and the chief and the mayor all perched on the front row today during that mass."

"Why are you telling me this?"

"Because when we met you told me you wanted to do something about domestic violence."

"I do."

"Then seize the moment."

O'Brien stopped at the curb outside my house, where my Triumph, with inflated tires, was now parked in the driveway. "Told you there was no harm."

19

M Y OFFICE PHONE WAS RINGING when I came to work Thursday, even though it was fifteen minutes before eight a.m. when we officially opened.

"Miss Fox, this is Miss Hillary Potts, calling from District Attorney Carlton Whitaker's office."

I swear Potts was the tightest-wound secretary in the entire courthouse—and also the most unapproachable. I'd bent over backward trying to befriend her and had gotten nowhere.

"Yes?" I replied.

"Mr. Whitaker would like to see you. He, Mr. Steinberg, and Mr. Pisani will be speaking to you."

An unsmiling Miss Potts greeted me a few moments later, but she kept me waiting in the outer office while she went inside to alert her bosses.

"You can come in now," she announced when she returned, opening the door for me.

Steinberg and Pisani were sitting across from Whitaker, who was sitting at his desk. There were only two chairs, and since both of them were occupied and no one offered me a seat, I stood awkwardly among the triumvirate.

"Are you feeling okay, Miss Fox?" Whitaker asked, sounding concerned.

"Yes, of course, sir."

"Good, good. I know you had developed a friendship with

the homicide victims so you'll be happy to know the chief has his best detectives searching for Hitchins."

"When they catch him," Pisani added, "I'll convict him and get him locked up for life. It'll be a slam dunk."

"Damn right," said Steinberg.

It sounded as if I had entered a boys' locker room before a big game.

"The reason," Whitaker continued, "I've called you in here this morning is because I've decided to transfer you out of the appeals bureau into the trial division. Congratulations, Miss Fox. You're one of the boys now." He stood and stretched out his hand to shake mine. "Mr. Steinberg and Mr. Pisani will fill you in later today on your new duties."

"Thank you, sir," I said. "Will one of my new assignments be helping Mr. Pisani prosecute Hitchins after he's caught?"

"Whoa," Whitaker said. "Slow down."

Pisani jumped in. "Ms. Fox, you still have not prosecuted a jury case—at least not one under your own name. You don't go from night court to a triple murder."

"Even if it's a 'slam dunk'?" I asked.

"Mr. Pisani and I will be prosecuting the Hitchins matter together," Whitaker said. "I have a different role for you."

PART TWO

A SERIOUS MATTER

There are only about twenty murders a year in London and not all are serious—some are just husbands killing their wives.

—*COMMANDER G. H. HATHERILL,
SCOTLAND YARD, 1954*

20

"WHAT EXACTLY DO YOU CALL that?" Will Harris asked after I gave the woman behind the deli counter my order. It was noon Monday and we were inside Ruth's Deli down the street from the Westchester County Courthouse. An hour after welcoming me to the trial division, Whitaker had given a thumbs-up to me being interviewed by Harris. The reporter had suggested today's lunch and had even offered to pay.

"The girls in the office call this 'cat food,'" I said. "It's dry tuna—definitely no mayo—hot peppers with vinegar on whole wheat bread. Along with a Dr Pepper, it's what I have nearly every day."

"The girls? Aren't you the only female A.D.A.?"

"Yes, but I like to eat with the secretaries. We're friends."

"Interesting," Harris said, writing on his notepad.

"That really makes me nervous, having you writing down stuff like that. What does what I eat and who I eat with have to do with domestic violence?"

"You're the subject of my story. Details such as these will make it more colorful."

I handed him a sheet of statistics that I'd compiled over the weekend. "Here's what your story should be about."

We had moved to a Formica-covered table for two in the back of the deli. Harris glanced at the statistics. "One in four women will be the victim of domestic violence during her lifetime. Domestic violence is the most common source of injury to women, more than car accidents. As many as four thousand women a year are killed during domestic violence incidents." He folded up the sheet and put it in his coat pocket. He was wearing the same blazer that I'd seen him in at Mary Margaret's funeral mass, along with a light blue shirt, no tie, and gray slacks. His hair still needed trimming, but he looked handsome. "This is great stuff," he said, "but I'm not writing a college term paper. 'Dear Abby' is the most-read feature in a newspaper because readers love to hear about other people and their problems."

"I thought you were going to write a serious article."

"Domestic violence is serious. But statistics are boring. I want to put a human face on the issue, the face of a crusader who's going after Rudy Hitchins and men like him." He shot me a smile and added, "And you have a pretty face."

"Thanks, but flattery isn't going to change my direction. I'd rather focus on how many women in our county are being beaten every day by the very men who say they love them."

"What if I promise to work some of these statistics into the story? Will you tell me more about you so I can personalize it?"

Before I could respond, he said, "Let's start with me asking you if Hitchins is the first wife-beater who you went after."

"No, he's the first one I prosecuted, but there was an earlier incident that had a huge impact on me. It was the very first case that I was assigned when I reported to work in the appeals division. The victim was twenty-five years old and her name was Debbie."

Harris began writing.

Continuing, I said, "Debbie was a beautiful young woman. She had two kids and she had a husband who beat her. One day, she disappeared with the kids. She ran away and got a job as a waitress and started going back to school. She was getting her life on track until her husband tracked her down and hired a kid—a seventeen-year-old punk—to kill Debbie. That kid stabbed her twenty-one times. You could see the slashes on her arms where she'd fought back. The husband paid that kid a thousand dollars so he could go buy himself a used motorcycle. I'd never seen such horrific autopsy and crime scene photos. Blood was splattered everywhere. But the most disgusting photo was the mug shot of her husband in the file. He was smirking. Grinning like he was proud of what he'd done. I worked my tail off on that appeal to keep the husband and that punk in jail and even argued the case in the appellate division before a panel of judges. I won. In fact, that case made legal precedent. But what I did came too late for Debbie."

"How old did you say she was?"

"She was my age—twenty-five—and she had everything to live for and some controlling man took it away and laughed about it. Who are these monsters who beat women? Who are they? What right do they have to shoot, stab, and brutalize women and then feel so at ease, so protected, so entitled to take their lives, as if these women aren't human beings. They're chattel? And why isn't anyone doing anything to stop them?"

"That's what I'm after," Harris said, encouraging me. "Your anger, your passion. Is Debbie one of the reasons why you decided to go after Hitchins?"

"Actually, she was. A White Plains detective showed me photographs of Mary Margaret immediately after she'd been beaten by Rudy Hitchins. When I looked at them—she reminded me of Debbie. Only Debbie was dead. Her photos were marked in big bright letters: AUTOPSY. The photos of Mary Margaret were marked with the word 'EVIDENCE.' I thought that if I didn't do anything to punish Rudy Hitchins, I'd soon be looking at a new set of photos of Mary Margaret with the word 'AUTOPSY' on them."

"And that's exactly what happened."

"Yes," I said softly. "I thought I could prevent Hitchins from hurting her and now some people think I'm responsible. That I should have stayed out of it."

"Someone like Carl Jones?"

"I'm not going to say who."

Harris stopped writing. "Look, I know about the cops and the charges you refused to pursue."

"Are you putting that in your story?"

"No, it's water under the bridge."

"Thanks."

"Look, I admire what you are trying to do. But tell me something, is there more to your story?"

"What do you mean?"

"Do you have a boyfriend? Has he ever abused you?"

"I do have a boyfriend, and no, he has never raised his hand to me, and he better not!"

"What if he did?"

"Bob wouldn't do that, but if he hit me, I would file assault charges against him."

"Even if you loved him and you had been together for years?"

"Mr. Harris, if a man loves a woman, he doesn't beat her. Because that's not love. That's abuse and control."

"Is it really that simple?"

"Can I tell you something off the record?" I asked.

"Sure."

"I mean it. Can I trust you to keep this private, just between us?"

"You have my word."

"I have lots of relatives and we always gather at Thanksgiving for dinner. Growing up, I was especially close to my cousin Monica, who was a couple of years older than me. She always included me when she and her friends shopped in Elmira or went to a movie—even their pajama parties. When she was sixteen, Monica fell in love with Gary and I thought it was magical. But a year later, she got pregnant. Abortion wasn't an option in our family and she and Gary didn't want to put the baby up for adoption. My aunt and uncle opposed them getting married, so they eloped and moved to Canada. Even though they were estranged from her parents, my mom invited her and Gary to our family Thanksgiving. I remember how excited I was when I saw Gary's old pickup pull up in front of our house. When the doorbell rang, I flew to open it and what I saw left a scar on my heart. Monica stood there with little Gary Jr. in her arms. She was pregnant again and her right eye was swollen shut. It was black and blue and so was her right cheek. Her lip was cut and looked like it had been stitched. Gary was nowhere in sight."

Harris said, "How did your family react?"

"Monica told everyone that she had been in a car accident, but my mom knew better and I was suspicious because they only had that old pickup and it was fine and Gary wasn't with her. That afternoon, Monica and I had a chance to talk privately and she broke down and told me that Gary had lost his job, he'd started drinking, and he blamed her for ruining his teenage years. He wished that they'd had an abortion and never married. She told me that the first slap was over a meal he didn't like. It was followed by progressively worse beatings. I told her to go to the police, but she said, 'I love him, and besides, it's my fault. If I hadn't gotten pregnant, we both would have gone to college. He would have gotten a good job and not started drinking. Besides, I'm pregnant again and who'll want me?'"

Harris interrupted. "How old were you when this happened?"

"I had just turned seventeen." Continuing, I said, "Monica stayed for the night and everyone was told that she was in a car accident and was lucky to be alive. Only Mom and I knew. My mom tried that night to get her to move in with us and leave Gary, but she left for Canada the next morning. A few months later, I was in college and my mom called and said Monica had miscarried when she was rushed to the hospital one night after Gary had beaten her. Of course, she told doctors that she had slipped and fallen."

"Are they still together?"

"Yes, they are but she no longer stays in contact with us. He has cut her off from us."

"I see, so you know personally what it is like to have domestic violence in your family."

"That's right. I wanted you to know that, but I don't want it in the papers."

I stopped to buy Junior Mints on the way back to work. With everything going on, I felt like I deserved a box or two.

21

"I MADE A MISTAKE THIS AFTERNOON," I told Wilbur, who was brushing up against my leg while I stood at the sink in my kitchen slicing apples for him. He grunted, and for a moment, I suspected he actually was listening and not simply urging me to hurry up with his dinner. "I told a reporter about Gary and Monica. Oh God, Mom is going to kill me if he writes about them. Even if he doesn't use their names but describes them as relatives, I'm going to be in real trouble."

Wilbur grunted again.

I debated calling Mom and telling her what had happened, but I didn't. Instead, I called Bob in Albany and listened as he gently reprimanded me for being so trusting—especially of reporters. That night I hardly slept.

Just before six a.m., I jumped out of bed and slipped on my jogging pants, sweatshirt, and running shoes and headed out the door to a neighborhood grocery that carried the *White Plains Daily*. My photograph—a picture provided by the D.A.'s office—was just under the fold. The headline read: "Feisty Female Prosecutor Fights Abusers."

In the first paragraph, Harris described how I had filed felony charges against Rudy Hitchins. He quoted me calling Hitchins a "controlling, abusive coward." I quickly scanned the remainder of the story for some mention of my cousin and her husband. They were not mentioned. Harris had kept his word. Our talk had been off the record. I breathed a sigh of relief.

My kitchen phone was ringing when I got home. Mom, I thought. Who else would call me so early in the morning? But when I picked up the phone, a male voice said, "Dani Fox?"

I didn't recognize the voice.

"Yes, this is Dani Fox."

"You fucking bitch! We'll see who's a coward."

The line went dead.

Had the caller been an angry husband or had I just heard from a furious Rudy Hitchins? I called the White Plains police and left word for Detective O'Brien to contact me as soon as he got to work.

22

M Y OFFICE PHONE DIDN'T STOP ringing. Most callers were women who thanked me for condemning domestic violence. A few asked for help. The director of the White Plains women's shelter telephoned to tell me that the federal government was awarding grants to local prosecutors who wanted to prosecute domestic violence cases. The money was coming from the LEAA, an acronym for the Law Enforcement Assistance Administration. Three years earlier, the LEAA had caused a national uproar by announcing it would not award any federal funds to local police departments unless they dropped height requirements for new applicants. The cops had started using minimum-height rules to avoid hiring women as officers. The LEAA's stipulation put a stop to it.

"You should apply for a grant," the director urged. I listened intently as she told me more about the process.

Shortly before ten a.m., O'Brien returned my call. When I told him about my early anonymous caller, he said, "Probably some prick who slaps around his wife and didn't like you implying he was a coward. The detectives handling the case still believe Hitchins is hiding in Canada, and the last time I checked, the *White Plains Daily* isn't circulated there. Just the same, it might be a good idea if you made one of those out-of-town trips this weekend that you like to take."

I'd not mentioned Bob or my sojourns to Albany to O'Brien

and I wondered how he knew, but I didn't want to give him
the satisfaction of asking. When I didn't respond, O'Brien said,
"Oh yeah, I heard Whitaker's polling numbers are on an upswing. I'm sure he loved today's story."

As soon as I placed down the receiver, my phone rang.

"This is Miss Hillary Potts calling. Mr. Whitaker would
like you to come to his office at eleven a.m. sharp."

I grabbed some candy and hurried upstairs only to have
Miss Potts keep me waiting in the outer office for a few minutes until it was precisely eleven. When I was allowed to enter
his office, Whitaker was all grins. "Great story today, Miss
Fox," he said while seated at his massive desk. "Bravo!" I'd
made a point of mentioning to Will Harris how supportive
Whitaker had been in prosecuting Hitchins and the reporter
had included several quotes that flattered my boss.

Mark Steinberg was sitting across from Whitaker and he
added a quick "Congratulations."

"I'm so pleased," Whitaker said, "that I'd like you to begin
speaking to women's groups about domestic violence. Make it
a top priority, at least for now."

I said, "You mean—between now and the November elections?"

Whitaker gave me a startled look.

I thought, If you want me to help you win reelection, then
I want something in return. Otherwise, you might simply forget about domestic violence cases after the ballots are tallied.

"Mr. Whitaker," I said. "The LEAA is awarding federal
grants to a handful of prosecutors to create Domestic Violence
Units, specifically to go after married men who beat their
wives. I'd like to apply for a grant—especially since you are
asking me to speak out about domestic violence."

Whitaker leaned back in his chair and looked at me suspi-
ciously. "Why, Miss Fox, are you seeking a quid pro quo here?"

"I simply want to help our community, and the LEAA

grant seems like an excellent opportunity to address domestic violence."

"My, my," Whitaker said, "I *am* going to have to keep an eye on you when it comes to politics."

Steinberg asked, "Do we really need a separate unit to prosecute domestic violence?"

"Judging from the calls that I've been getting, we certainly do," I replied.

"Shall I assume," Whitaker asked, "that you would want to run this unit if you were fortunate enough to get a grant?"

"That would make sense, sir, wouldn't it?" I asked in my most innocent voice.

"Yes, I guess it would," he said appreciatively. "Okay, Miss Fox, you can apply for an LEAA grant. Give it your best shot. Meanwhile, I'll expect you to begin speaking to as many groups as possible. I think it will be a good deal for both of us."

23

I LEFT WORK EARLY SO I COULD GET HOME and fix dinner for Bob's weekend visit. It was his turn to drive down from Albany. Because of conflicts in our schedules, three weeks had passed since we'd last gotten together and I was eager to tell him about my meeting with Whitaker.

I decided to fix a traditional Lebanese meal beginning with *mezze*, the Middle Eastern equivalent to French hors d'oeuvres. I was fixing baba ghanousch, a dip from cooked pureed eggplant. My main course would be a lamb casserole that I would serve with rice and a fresh salad that I planned to season heavily with olive oil, garlic, salt, and lemon. *Marcook*, a flat, fire-baked bread would round out our main course. For dessert, I prepared a milk-based custard.

I got everything going, then jumped into the shower, worked on my hair, and slipped into a sexy short dress and red pumps. Everything was ready and I was eager for our romantic evening to begin. As if on cue, Bob arrived armed with a bottle of champagne. He gave me a long hug and said, "Your mom read the newspaper story to me first thing this morning on the telephone before I went to class. She's very proud of you and so am I."

He kissed me passionately. I loved that my mom and Bob got along so well.

While I was bringing out the baba ghanousch, I told him about the LEAA grant.

"It's great to see you so excited about this," Bob said.

I intentionally didn't ask him about medical school. The last time that we'd talked, he'd mentioned that he'd been thinking about his residency. I'd always assumed he would do it at one of Manhattan's premier hospitals. But he'd talked about going west, possibly to Colorado or California, neither of which made sense since both of our families lived in New York. Besides, I had my career here. We had argued, which was rare for us. I didn't want to get into a disagreement tonight. I wanted to have a magical evening, much like the one we'd enjoyed on Christmas Eve years ago at his grandfather's farm.

"Where's Wilbur?" Bob asked.

I nodded toward the back door and Bob went out to see him. By the time he returned, I had the candles lit on the dining-room table and the champagne on ice.

"Here's to us!" he said, popping the cork.

"And our fabulous future together," I added.

I put down my flute and wrapped my arms around him. He kissed my forehead and I looked upward so he could kiss my lips. This is just what I need, I thought.

And at that very moment, the phone rang.

"You need to answer that?" he asked.

"Not a chance."

But the caller didn't hang up. The damn phone just kept ringing. Bob said, "It's okay, really. Obviously, someone really wants to talk to you."

I hurried into the kitchen and grabbed the wall phone. "What do you want?" I snapped.

"Are you always this brash?" Mark Steinberg asked.

"Ur, sorry, Mr. Steinberg, I'm busy right now."

"In a few minutes," Steinberg said, "you're going to receive a call from Mr. Whitaker, who is going to tell you some exciting news. I wanted to call ahead to make sure you're available."

"I'll be here. What's this about?"

"Just pick up your phone and, Miss Fox, I wouldn't sound so angry when you answer."

I walked into the dining room, where Bob had taken his seat at the table. The romantic spell had been broken—at least for the moment. I offered him some baba ghanousch, saying, "I hope you like this."

"If you made it, I'm sure I will." But when he tasted it, he got an awful look on his face. "I guess I'm not really much for eggplant. Sorry."

I put the dip aside and brought my casserole out from the oven. I prepared him a plate and he politely waited for me to sit down with my plate before he tried the lamb.

"Now, Dani, this is great," he announced approvingly.

"No more eggplant. I promise. Next time hummus. Chick-peas will be more to your liking."

He laughed. I loved his smile and I was beginning to relax when the phone rang.

"I'm sorry," I said, shooting him a puppy dog look, "but this is my boss calling and I really have to take it."

"Sure," he said. "I understand."

I stepped into the kitchen and grabbed my phone. "Hello."

"Miss Fox," Whitaker said, "I've got great news for you. You're going to be getting a call in a few minutes from the governor's office in Albany."

Whitaker explained that the governor was appointing a task force to help draft legislation that would give battered women the option of filing criminal charges against their husbands rather than having the case automatically go into family court.

"It should be obvious why he wants you," Whitaker said. "The Hitchins case made all the papers and the story in today's paper caught his eye. He called me after he read it and I told him that you were my liaison with women's shelters."

"Thank you, Mr. Whitaker."

"Listen, there's a condition. I don't want you to tell anyone—not a single soul about this. The governor's office will make the announcement at the state capitol in a day or two about who's on the task force. I'm having Steinberg coordinate it with Albany so we can have our own White Plains press conference. Steinberg will work out the details but it will be in my office and, naturally, I'll do the talking. You'll be there, of course."

"Of course."

"So keep your mouth closed because if word gets out before the governor makes his announcement, I can promise that you'll be dropped from the task force. Got it?"

"Yes, sir!"

I floated back into the dining room and discovered that Bob had finished his plate. The call had taken ten minutes.

"Must be good news," he said.

I nodded and said, "Unfortunately, it's all hush-hush. So I can't talk about it." I sat down to my cold casserole.

"Now you really got me interested. A murder? A scandal?"

"I can't talk about it. I promised."

He looked hurt.

I said, "Have you heard from your parents lately? How are things in Elmira?"

Bob started telling me about his mom and a new project at the farm, but all I could think about was the task force. I'd never been called by a governor. Bob knew me well enough to know that my mind was miles away.

"You haven't heard a word I've said."

"Sorry. It's just these phone calls. Work. It's very distracting."

Rising, he walked to my chair and said, "I know a way to get your mind off your job." He looked toward my bedroom and pulled my chair back from the table so I could stand.

"What about dessert?" I asked.

He kissed me hard. "Afterwards."

The phone rang.

"I don't care if there's been a double homicide," he said. "Let someone else get it. I want you to myself right now."

He leaned down to kiss me again and I could feel the intensity in his lips.

"I'm sorry, Bob. I can't explain it. But this is an extremely important call. I really have no choice."

"Okay, but make it short."

I darted into the kitchen, took a deep breath, and answered.

"Is this Dani Fox?" a male voice said.

"Yes, Governor," I replied proudly.

"This isn't the governor," the voice said. "I'm his chief assistant, Benjamin Baker, but I am calling on his behalf. Before the governor calls you, he wants me to ask you a few questions. That okay with you?"

"Oh, sure."

"It's background stuff that we ask all political appointees when we put them on a task force. That way no one gets embarrassed later on. Now, tell me when and where you were born."

I thought: All this for a task force?

One by one, I answered his questions. A half hour later, I hung up and walked out into the dining room, where Bob was patiently waiting.

"This never happens," I said. "It's just tonight. I've got to take these calls and I'm sworn to secrecy, but trust me, it is very important to my work."

I put my arms around him and gave him a kiss. But I could tell he was irritated. I took his hand and started toward my bedroom when the kitchen phone rang again.

"Bob, I promise this is the last call of the night. I can't tell you who is calling, but I must answer it. Just hang on one more minute."

I dashed back into the kitchen and answered with a cheery hello.

I expected to hear the governor's voice. What I heard was Mom.

"I just made baklava. Want to join me for dessert?"

"Bob's here. I've got to go."

"Oh, please tell him hello for me."

I started to respond when I heard my front door open and shut. I looked into the dining room. Bob was gone. I couldn't believe it. He had never walked out on me before and I'd never walked out on him, either.

"Mom, I can't talk now. Good-bye."

I started after Bob, hoping to catch him, but when I got to the door, he'd already started his car. I felt hurt. I'd told him the calls were important and he'd just gotten here. Was he really going to drive all the way back to Albany because of the phone calls?

I started out to stop him, but as I stepped over the threshold, I heard the kitchen phone ring. Bob started backing his car down the drive. The phone rang again and then a third time.

I hesitated and then hurried back inside to answer.

"Miss Fox," a woman's voice said, "please hold for the governor."

24

I TELEPHONED BOB THE NEXT MORNING, but there was no answer at his apartment. I thought about driving to Albany to salvage our romantic weekend, but the director of the women's shelter dropped by my house unexpectedly with the forms that I needed to apply for the LEAA grant. She warned me that the deadline was only days away and the application was massive. When she offered to help, I invited in and we spent all of Saturday and most of Sunday completing the application. During breaks, I called Bob's apartment, but he either wasn't there or wasn't answering.

The next few days were a whirlwind. The governor announced that he was appointing me to a special legislative task force and Whitaker held a press conference. He did all the talking but I was suddenly in demand as a speaker at various county women's groups. The task force took whatever time I had after work. I did manage to finally speak to Bob and he apologized for leaving at the exact same moment that I was trying to apologize to him for being preoccupied with the phone calls. His final days of school and my career, we agreed, were making it rough on our relationship. But I knew everything would be fine once he chose a hospital for his residency and the attention that I was now drawing dissipated. We'd been together nearly nine years. We could certainly weather a few rough weeks of being apart.

Our task force drafted a new statute and the governor

rammed it through the state legislature just before the November elections. My boss won handily with strong support from women voters.

Everyone assumed there would be a stampede of battered women charging their husbands with abuse now that we had given them the right to have their abusers arrested. But we didn't even see a trickle at our office. Women didn't seem to be asking us to pursue cases against their abusers.

It didn't take me long to pinpoint why. Despite our new law, the forty-three police departments in Westchester County were still treating domestic violence as "family disputes." Every cop wanted to be Dirty Harry, not a social worker with a badge. I worked with women's groups to get the local American Civil Liberties Union to announce a civil rights lawsuit against the police in all forty-three departments unless they began enforcing the new law. I made sure that Will Harris at the *White Plains Daily* heard about the ACLU filing. His story, "Local Cops Face Possible Suit," got everyone's attention, especially after he quoted me saying, "I believe battered women should have every weapon at their disposal to guarantee justice is done. If that means suing the police, then they should do it."

The police chiefs were furious but public pressure was on my side and they had no choice but to back down. I was learning how to work the system.

None of my fellow assistant D.A.s wanted to pursue domestic violence cases, either. Like the cops, they were interested in only "real criminals"—murderers, rapists, and burglars. I reminded them that Rudy Hitchins was a murderer and that domestic violence was a serious crime. A few agreed to prosecute cases against husbands who were beating their wives, but things were not happening fast enough, and now that Whitaker was safe for another four years, his interest in domestic violence was beginning to wane.

And then a miracle happened. Whitaker called me into his office and told me that Westchester County had been selected for an LEAA grant.

"Do you know what other counties got grants?" I asked.

"Philadelphia, Miami-Dade County, and Santa Barbara, California. That's it. I want to hold a press conference this afternoon to announce that you will be creating and running our new Domestic Violence Unit."

As soon as I got back to my desk, I called Bob's apartment to share the news. But there was no answer. I called Mom instead. We not only had a new law on the books, but I now was going to get federal funds to give that law teeth. It was the beginning of a new dawn in women's rights and I was excited to be playing a role in it.

25

I HIT THE GROUND RUNNING. WHITAKER arranged for space in the annex across the street from the Westchester County Courthouse. I wanted abused women to feel welcome, so I designed our lobby to look like a living room, not a sterile, cold office. Steinberg nearly wet his pants when I added playpens. Many battered women who brought complaints to police or religious leaders were told by these men that they didn't have any options but to stay in their relationships. I thought women would be more comfortable talking to women, so I hired Lucy, Eunice, and Anne Marie as domestic violence aides.

Through the courthouse grapevine, I heard the cops and male assistant D.A.s refer to us as the "Tit Patrol" and "Panty Brigade." Paul Pisani was taking great delight in ridiculing us, especially me. I didn't let the other cynics bother me, but I was angry about "Mr. Invincible." The more I heard about him, the more I hated him. I knew he was personally responsible for causing two marriages to break up. He seemed to enjoy using his charm to seduce married female employees whom he then dumped after they had blurted out to their husbands that they'd fallen for someone new. It takes two to tango, but he seemed to delight in targeting emotionally vulnerable women, bedding them, and then tossing them aside like used tissues.

With the threat of an ACLU civil rights suit hanging over their heads, the police begrudgingly began making arrests when a battered wife complained and Harris wrote a sensational story about the upswing in domestic violence prosecutions. He was unabashed in his support for our new unit, and soon we were being inundated with women from Scarsdale to Bedford asking for help. Finally, the dam had burst! When it came to abuse, social status and fat wallets didn't count.

While Lucy, Eunice, and Anne Marie did a fantastic job interviewing women, when they confronted the abusers, the men either ignored them or worse. These men didn't believe anyone had a right to tell them how to treat their wives. I learned quickly that most of our new clients didn't want their husbands in jail. They just wanted them to stop hitting them. We came up with a ploy. When a battered woman came in, we warned her husband that he would be arrested and charged with a crime if he didn't agree to counseling sessions. I had stationery printed with **DOMESTIC VIOLENCE UNIT, WESTCHESTER DISTRICT ATTORNEY'S OFFICE** emblazoned across the top in bold, impressive letters, in English and Spanish. Whenever a woman came to our office, we issued her a letter on our stationery that declared: "This woman and her children are under the protection of the Domestic Violence Unit of Westchester County . . ." We told our clients that they needed to show the letters to their husbands and also the police if they were called. Actually, the letters had no legal clout. Only a judge could issue an order of protection. The letters scared some abusers and infuriated others, but they also helped identify true victims to the police. We were slowly making our criminal justice system respond.

Judges were another problem. Time and again, I'd walk into a courtroom and a judge would bark at me, "Why don't you get a real case, Miss Fox?" Or they'd throw the case out with an admonishment to stop wasting the court's time. One judge told a married woman with a black eye and a swollen jaw that she didn't belong in his courtroom. "You need to go to family court," he said. I had to remind him that a battered woman had additional rights under the new law. Even when we got a case to trial, jurors would openly ask during jury selection, "What did she do to make him so mad that he beat her?"

I also discovered that many of our clients were flawed. They had poor self-esteem, and many had drug and alcohol problems. When a badly bruised Janet Cummings arrived in our office and told us that the police had refused to arrest her husband, I got angry. I called the White Plains police officer who'd responded to the call and demanded to know why he hadn't done anything.

"Her husband beat her within an inch of her life," I said.

"You know, she's a drunk," the officer responded. "She falls down a lot."

"Come off it! What kind of fall leaves welts and bruises under your arms or on the backs of your legs? What kind of a fall leaves choke marks around a woman's neck?"

I got Cummings to press criminal charges against her husband, but when I tried to get her into a shelter, the director said Cummings wasn't welcome because she was, indeed, an alcoholic. No one wanted her. On the day her case was called in court, she was nowhere to be found. She finally arrived, intoxicated, two hours late. The furious judge dismissed the case and admonished me for wasting his time.

I was angry at Cummings until I realized that she drank because she was miserable. Her husband threatened to strangle and burn her. But she was too emotionally crippled to save herself and I didn't have the resources to help her.

Each case taught me more. Each case helped me sharpen my skills.

We'd been open about a month when Maya Lopez, a petite, soft-spoken woman in her early thirties with faint bruises, came to see us. She said her husband, Juan, often came home drunk and beat her. She endured his brutality until he started hitting their ten-year-old son. The morning she asked for help, she had put their son on a flight to Puerto Rico to live with his grandmother and then took a bus to our office.

"Juan is going to kill me for sending our son away."

"We can move you into a women's shelter where you'll be safe," I told her. "I'll have him arrested, but you'll have to swear out a complaint and agree to testify against him."

A horrified look filled Maya's face. "No, no, no, he will kill me if I do that."

"We can get an order of protection from a judge. You can't let this man brutalize you and your son."

Despite my pleadings, Maya was simply too scared. Juan had her under a controlling spell. I felt frustrated. I couldn't help her if she didn't want to help herself. Before she left, I wrote my home number on the back of a business card and gave it to her.

"Your husband has no reason to stop unless you get the police involved."

After she was gone, I tried to focus on my work, but I was worried about her. I didn't want a repeat of the Hitchins/Mary Margaret tragedy, so I called the police in Yonkers where Maya lived with Juan. Unfortunately, I hadn't been able to develop a relationship with the Yonkers police chief and he wasn't around, so I spoke to one of his deputies.

"There's a woman in Yonkers, her name is Maya Lopez, and she's the victim of domestic violence. Her husband beats her and I'm worried that he is going to seriously hurt her. She put their son on a flight to Puerto Rico this morning because the husband began beating him as well."

"She swear out a complaint with your office?" he asked.

"We're working on that. I'm calling to see if you could you have one of your officers swing by their apartment to check on her."

"We don't have enough manpower to do that. Especially not for a domestic. I don't know how things are in White Plains, but in Yonkers, we can't babysit every woman who gets backhanded by her husband."

"Listen," I said in an irked voice, "I'm not talking about someone being slapped. This guy may kill her."

"Well, if you're that damn worried, maybe you should drive down here and check on her yourself," he said, hanging up.

I was restless all night. The next morning, Anne Marie hurried into my office. "It's Maya," she announced. "You won't believe what he's done to her!"

"Is she okay?" I asked, shooting up from my desk.

"She's in our lobby. I'll bring her into your office."

Maya appeared with two black eyes and swollen lips. I was angry, but not horrified. I had seen much worse.

"Juan was angry because I sent our son away. He said I had no right to take his son. I showed him your card and told him he couldn't treat me like a dog."

"Good for you!"

She shook her head and said, "No, it was not good for me."

Anne Marie said, "Maya, show Miss Fox what he did to you."

There was more? I thought.

Maya pulled up her blouse, revealing a large strip of bloody gauze across her abdomen. She gingerly removed it. Just under her bra, her husband had carved his name—JUAN—with a paring knife. The red cuts were ugly jagged lines.

"Anne Marie's taking you to a doctor right now," I said. "And you're going to a shelter. I'm having Juan arrested."

"No, no. I shouldn't have sent our boy away."

"Bullshit! Maya, your husband beats you. He cut his name into your skin. We need you to go into a safe house before he harms you again. I'm getting him arrested."

"But he'll lose his job. How will we pay our bills?"

"I'll get you help. This man doesn't love you. Someone who loves you doesn't cut his name into your flesh."

"He gets jealous. But that's because he does love me. Maybe you can talk to him first. Tell him to stop. Please, just talk to him first."

It was the same rationalization I'd heard from Mary Margaret and a dozen other abused women. I told Anne Marie to take Maya to the emergency room and then to a Yonkers women's shelter. The moment they were gone, I called the police. As I was dialing, I heard the sounds of a commotion coming from our lobby. I dashed out to see what was wrong and nearly collided with a huge Hispanic man who weighed at least 285 pounds and stood well over six feet tall.

"You the bitch who gave my wife this card?" he yelled, holding up the business card that I'd given Maya the day before.

"Juan Lopez?" I asked.

The fact that I didn't appear intimidated surprised him.

"Stay away from my wife," he said, poking a finger at my nose. "You've got no right to interfere between me and her. This is family!"

"Sir, I have every right to interfere when you beat your wife and cut your name into her abdomen. I can put you in jail right now for what you did to her, and if you ever touch her again, I'll—"

Juan cut me off. "Look," he hollered. He dropped both of his massive arms to his side and grabbed his untucked shirt, which he raised with his hands, exposing his fat belly. The word "MAYA" was carved into his skin.

"You don't know nothing. I cut us because we love each other. This shit is family, not you."

Lowering his shirt, he said, "No one tells me what I can and can't do when it comes to my wife and kid. Stay the fuck out of my family's business."

"Mr. Lopez, I'm calling the police!"

He looked at me with menacing eyes and said, "You ain't taking Maya from me. She's mine!" He headed toward the exit as I raced back to my office phone.

One of our workers called the Yonkers shelter where Anne Marie was taking Maya.

"Maya's not here," the shelter's director said. "She left a few minutes after Anne Marie dropped her off. She was too scared to stay."

No one knew where Maya had gone, but I suspected it was back to be with her abusive husband. That was the last place she should go.

I telephoned O'Brien. "Please call someone you know at the Yonkers P.D.," I pleaded. "I want Juan arrested, but they aren't taking me seriously."

A half hour later, O'Brien called back. A Yonkers policeman had stopped at the apartment that the Lopezes rented but no one had answered.

It was late when I got home that night, and Wilbur made it clear when I brought him inside the kitchen that he didn't like waiting for his dinner. I generally fixed something for both of us at the same time. If you think dogs can be persistent beggars, you've never had a pot-bellied pig at your feet.

I was putting the final touches on my pasta salad and Wilbur's bowl of apples and pig pellets when I heard the sound of breaking glass and car tires squealing. I stopped what I was doing and quietly moved to the front of the house. Nothing seemed amiss until I noticed slivers of glass sprinkled across my hardwood floor beneath my front window. I walked closer for a better look, and what I saw made me instantly drop to the floor.

There was a bullet hole in the front window about the size of my pinkie. Someone had shot into my house, and for all that I knew, the car I'd heard squealing away had left the shooter lurking outside.

Keeping low, I pulled the drapes and duck-walked to a light switch. I turned off the light in the room, making it completely dark. Rising next to a window, I peeked outside. I didn't see anything suspicious.

Suddenly, I remembered I hadn't locked my front door, so I immediately crawled to it and threw the dead bolt. That's when I remembered that I'd brought in Wilbur through the back door and not dead bolted it, either. Wilbur looked up from his bowl as I rushed past him in the kitchen. For the first time since I'd gotten him, I thought about how a Doberman might have been a better choice.

I didn't own a handgun. I didn't even have a baseball bat in the house. The only weapon close was a knife. Wilbur gave me a nervous glance and grunted when I grabbed it.

I dialed the police and waited with the knife in my hand while Wilbur happily gobbled his dinner. A uniformed officer arrived within minutes, followed by O'Brien. The detective looked at the bullet hole in the window and followed the trajectory to my dining room wall where the slug was embedded.

"I'll have forensics dig it out," he explained.

"I'm sure glad I was in the kitchen."

O'Brien noticed Wilbur. "What's a pig doing in your kitchen?"

"Wilbur is my pet."

"Fox, you're one kooky broad. Don't you know, you eat pigs, not feed them."

Obviously, O'Brien and Wilbur were not going to become pals.

"Any idea who took a shot at you?" O'Brien asked.

"I think it was Juan Lopez."

"The guy from Yonkers who likes to cut names in his wife's belly?"

"And also his own belly."

"I'll station an officer outside your house tonight."

"Don't bother. I'm not spending the night here. I'm going to my mom's."

"How about the pig?" O'Brien asked. He glanced at Wilbur and went "Oink, oink."

Wilbur grunted and walked past O'Brien to his bed for a nap.

"You need to get yourself a handgun," O'Brien said. "I should have insisted on it after Hitchins murdered Mary Margaret."

"How do you know I don't already have one?"

"If you had one, you'd still be carrying it or it would be on your coffee table or in the kitchen. I saw a knife next to the sink. That's what you grabbed, am I right?"

"Yes, Detective."

"Let me ask you something, Counselor. You ever cut up a chicken?"

"Of course I've cut chicken."

"Then you know what it's like to cut through meat and bones. You really think you got it in you to stick a knife into a man and feel that blade cutting through the flesh and muscles, ripping into his organs and hitting his bones? Knives are personal."

The thought of it turned my stomach.

"We're going to get you a gun," he continued. "Pulling a trigger is easy. Besides, chances are Juan Lopez would have taken that knife away from you and carved something on your belly."

I couldn't tell if he was trying to scare me or was just being honest.

"Get your stuff together," O'Brien said. "I'll have an officer drive you over to your mom's."

"What about my car?"

"Leave it. That way if the shooter comes back, he'll think you're here. I'm going to have an officer watch your place. Besides, someone needs to guard that pig."

He chuckled but I don't think Wilbur found it funny.

I dumped most of my salad into Wilbur's bowl and took it and him out to his pen while O'Brien stood watch. After collecting a few personal items, I was ready to leave for Mom's. The patrolman driving me had gone only a few blocks when the radio in his squad car cracked with O'Brien's voice.

"Change of plans. I just got a call from Yonkers. I need you to drive Miss Fox to this address. I'm heading there now." He gave the officer instructions. We took the Cross Westchester Expressway to the Saw Mill Parkway and didn't speak the entire twenty-five-minute drive. I spied O'Brien's unmarked car parked next to two Yonkers cop cars on Hamilton Avenue. An officer from the Yonkers fourth precinct was standing guard on the front stoop of a row house that had been converted into apartments. He yelled inside an open door of a ground-level apartment to O'Brien, announcing my arrival.

"You found Maya?" I asked, rushing to the entrance.

"Yes, but there's no sign of Juan."

O'Brien was standing in the doorway, blocking my path.

"Well, let me talk to her," I said impatiently.

"Dani. She's dead. He killed her."

"She's dead?"

I felt like I was caught in a recurring nightmare, only this time the victim was not named Mary Margaret. How could this be happening again?

"I want to see her."

O'Brien bit down hard on the toothpick in his mouth. "Not sure that's a great idea, Counselor."

"Where's her body?"

O'Brien stepped out of my way so I could enter the tiny

apartment's living room, where a Yonkers officer was writing on a notepad.

"The woman," I said, "where is she?" He glanced at me and then at O'Brien, who said, "It's okay, she's a lady assistant D.A."

The Yonkers officer pointed toward the kitchen.

O'Brien said, "Dani, you really don't need to see this. He stuffed her in the oven."

I froze.

"He shot her first," O'Brien said, walking up next to me. "So she probably was dead when he turned it on." I knew he was sugarcoating it. Something in my gut told me that Juan had put her in that oven while she was still alive. He wanted to punish her, to torture her for disobeying him.

I walked into the efficiency kitchen and was hit by a putrid smell that caused me to gag. The oven door was open. Thankfully she was not inside. The medical examiner had put Maya's body on a stretcher under a white cover. The outline showed that she was still in a cramped position.

"I want to look at her. I want to see what that bastard did."

"Why?" O'Brien asked.

"Because if I ever have a moment of weakness when I might feel sorry for one of these sick sons of bitches, I want to remember Maya and what she looked like."

O'Brien didn't react. "Show me!" I said.

He lifted the sheet.

What I saw turned my stomach, but I refused to look away from the burned woman curled in front of me. Her entire face was burned. Most of her body had been in the open oven for several hours.

"You need to go to your mom's now," O'Brien said. We walked outside together. I took a deep breath but I couldn't get the smell of burned flesh out of my nostrils. I wondered if

I ever would. All I could think about was the last time that I had seen Maya. She'd had such a desperate look in her eyes.

I asked O'Brien: "Do you ever get used to this?"

"No—and you better not. You just put it in a spot of your mind that you don't visit often. But you feed off it. Feed off the anger. Our job is to protect the sheep—remember?"

"I failed her. Just like I failed Mary Margaret. They were counting on me and I let them down and they died."

"Counselor," O'Brien said in a gruff voice that surprised me, "you need to get over yourself. Do you really think that you're responsible for what Rudy Hitchins and Juan Lopez did to these women? Do you think that this sort of brutality hasn't been going on for years? The only one responsible is the bastard who did the killing."

I looked at him and said softly, "Thanks for being here."

"That's what partners are for," he said.

I WENT DIRECTLY TO Whitaker's office when I got to work and told Miss Potts that I needed to see him immediately. O'Brien had already tipped him off about Maya Lopez, so I was ushered into his office without having to wait.

"Are you okay?" he asked, genuinely concerned. "Do you need a few days off?"

"No. I want to catch that bastard and being in our office is probably safer than being on the street."

"Okay, I agree."

"We need protection in our unit—security like you have here at the courthouse. We can't risk having an abusive husband simply walk in and attack someone."

"I'll talk to the court officers."

"No, I don't want court officers. We need an investigator assigned to our unit, someone who can arrest a Juan Lopez on the spot when he carves his name into his wife's belly."

"You want a White Plains cop assigned to your unit?"

"I don't want any cop. I want O'Brien."

"What do you have against O'Brien?" he said, but I didn't laugh and he realized this wasn't the time for jokes.

"I need a detective," I said, "who takes what we do seriously. Who doesn't think we're a joke!"

"I know you've been through a lot, but do you really think a veteran homicide detective who's been on the force for decades is going to voluntarily transfer from the White Plains P.D. into the Domestic Violence Unit?"

"Yes, if you hire him as a D.A. investigator, he will. We'll get an experienced cop who understands what we do."

"I'll talk to the chief."

"Do it today," I said in a harsh tone that surprised even me.

26

I WANTED TO ESCAPE FROM WHITE PLAINS and the ghosts of Mary Margaret and Maya Lopez. I needed a break, and although it wasn't one of our scheduled weekends to visit each other, I decided on Friday afternoon to drive to Albany to pay a surprise visit to Bob. I wanted him to wrap his arms around me and tell me that I wasn't to blame for all the bad happenings in my life. I wanted him to tell me that everything would be fine—the police would arrest Juan Lopez and I would prosecute him. I wanted him to tell me that all the pain and guilt I was feeling would go away.

I also felt as if I had been neglecting Bob. The calls between us had become rushed. He was busy studying. I was busy working. The events in our lives had taken priority. I was scheduled to work Saturday and Sunday as the duty assistant district attorney "on call" for that weekend, but after Maya's murder, Steinberg took me off the rotation.

The drive to Albany seemed longer than usual simply because I couldn't wait to get there. When I finally reached the parking lot at Bob's apartment, I felt a tremendous sense of relief. It was a few minutes after nine p.m. A young couple was walking out the door, so instead of buzzing Bob and asking him to come open the building's secure front door, I ducked by them and headed up the stairs to his apartment. I was grinning widely when I knocked on his door.

But no one answered. I assumed he was with his study

group. Fortunately, I had a key. I decided to go inside and make myself useful by cooking spaghetti for us with olive oil and garlic. Bob always kept boxes of pasta in his cupboards. I'd select a nice wine, too.

I stepped inside and heard music coming from the living room. "Bob?" I called. No one replied. I entered the living room and noticed that a delivery box with half a pizza still in it was on the coffee table, along with two wineglasses and several medical books and study papers. Why were there two glasses? My heart began pounding hard when I heard a sound coming from his bedroom. I walked down a short hallway and opened the door. That's when time stopped.

Bob was lying naked on his bed with his back resting against the headboard and his eyes closed. There was a naked woman with her back to me giving him a blow job. His hands were on the sides of her head holding her blond hair, guiding her up and down, and he was so engrossed in the moment that he didn't realize that I had caught them. Although I could not see her face, I remembered that long hair and her slender figure from when I had seen Bob and her a few weeks ago walking to his apartment from what they said had been an "all-night study session." It was his "study partner," Linda.

"You bastard!" I shrieked.

Bob's eyes popped open. "Dani!"

Linda raised her head and looked at me.

I ran from his apartment, slamming the door behind me. I was driving my Triumph from the lot when I saw Bob running from the building's entrance wearing only his pants.

"Dani, wait!" he yelled.

I pressed harder on the accelerator. How could he have done this to us—to me? We'd been together nine years! Hadn't those years and all of our dreams and secrets meant anything to him?

I drove down Route 17 and went west as if I were on

autopilot. I couldn't believe he had betrayed me. Was she pret-
tier? Smarter? All of my insecurities bubbled to the surface.
Why hadn't I tried harder? What warning signs had I missed?
Why? Why? Why?

Those "whys" were only followed by more questions.
How long had Bob and Linda been doing this? Had they
spent the night at her apartment when I first met them coming
from having bagels and coffee? Is that why he had insisted on
taking a shower before joining me in bed that day? Is that why
he had fallen asleep rather than holding me—because he was
exhausted from his night with her? I was torturing myself but
I couldn't stop it.

I got to Mom's just after midnight and ran up to her front
door. She'd heard my car as soon as I'd turned onto her block
and was waiting.

"What's wrong, honey?" she asked when she saw my tear-
stained face.

I flew into her arms sobbing. "It's Bob. I caught him with
another woman."

"Oh no!" she said, hugging me. "I'm so, so sorry."

She took me into her kitchen, fixed me warm milk, and
asked if I'd eaten. I hadn't but couldn't stomach food. I talked.
She listened. We sat there for two hours with me talking and her
trying her best to comfort me. Mostly she simply listened as I
went over and over again my most recent conversations with
Bob. What had I done wrong? Why had he cheated on me? Am
I not pretty enough, Mom? When I was so exhausted that I
couldn't say another word, she led me into her bedroom, and
we climbed under the flannel sheets and held each other.

"We'll talk more in the morning," she said. I cried myself to
sleep in Mom's arms, as if I were still her little girl.

When I awoke at noon and opened my eyes, I thought it
had been a bad dream. But then I saw that I was at my mother's and I knew better. I began crying again and didn't want to

get out of bed. My tears turned to anger. How could Linda have done this to me? Had she seduced Bob? That bitch! She knew we were a couple. How dare she! Mom eventually came into the bedroom and insisted that I get up.

"I made breakfast. Put this robe on."

I followed her into the kitchen. I sat at the table with my head in my hands. "My heart is broken. I feel so betrayed."

"Do you still love him?"

"Of course, but how can I love someone who is fucking another woman?"

"Dani, your language, please!"

"Mom, what should I do?"

"You will stay here this weekend and you will cry today and be depressed. But tomorrow, I'm going to take you out somewhere special, and when we are done with my surprise, you will go home Sunday night with your heart heavy but your head held high. Your father and I gave you a strong sense of values. There's right and there's wrong. People make mistakes. You forgive them. But you don't forget what they've done to you or ignore it. You're grieving now because the love that you had has died. But you will go on with your life and meet someone else, and someday you will be grateful that you found out early about Bob and did not marry him."

I heard her words but only half believed them. The "whys" were still nagging at me. I spent most of Saturday in bed. Sunday, Mom came into the room at ten a.m. and ordered me to get dressed.

"I want you to come with me," she said.

"I really don't feel like going out."

"Don't ruin my surprise."

I threw on a pair of jeans, blouse, and coat and followed her out to her car. Ten minutes later, we arrived at the parking lot at Bergdorf Goodman, the most exclusive department store in White Plains.

"Shopping, Mom? Really? My heart is breaking and you want to take me shopping? Is that your solution?"

"What we are going to do today is more than shopping," she said. "We're going to get you off to a fresh start, Dani."

I didn't know what to say.

Continuing, Mom said, "Dani, you're a professional woman now. You're no longer in college or law school. You run a Domestic Violence Unit and you are speaking to women's groups and prosecuting cases in court. This is a good time for you to change your appearance and outlook."

"It's a horrible time, Mom."

"Please, dear. Just come with me."

I reluctantly followed her into the store, where she took me to the cosmetics counter and introduced me to Jane Criswell, who I quickly learned was my mother's personal beauty consultant. Jane took one look at my puffy eyes and gasped, "Oh my."

I was too emotionally spent to argue with them, so I followed Jane into a private area of the store and sat in a chair while she began applying makeup to my face. Before I knew it, I was telling her about Bob, and Jane was telling me about men who had broken her heart. She was on husband three: Charlie. If her stories were supposed to give me hope, they didn't. But they were funny. As she spoke, she talked about skin color, texture, the application of base makeup, eyeliner, rouge, and a host of other cosmetic tricks. When I was finally handed a mirror, I was shocked. My plain face had been transformed into something more exotic through Jane's skilled hand.

Next, Jane and Mom patiently led me through the store in search of a new wardrobe. Because I was operating in a male-dominated arena, we decided I always needed to wear business suits to be taken seriously. This was especially true because I was young. But there had to be a feminine touch; otherwise when I appeared in court, jurors might think I was harsh and icy. Getting just the right look wasn't easy, but Jane helped me find several suits in navy pinstripes, gray, and beige. My favorite part was the shoe department. We bought two pairs of Charles Jourdan high-heel pumps, one in black and one in beige. Even I couldn't believe how much better my legs looked in a three-inch pump.

By the time we finished, it was late afternoon and Mom and I went to dinner at one of her favorite restaurants.

"See," Mom said, "that wasn't so bad, was it?"

I didn't want to admit it, but actually it had been nice. I'd needed a bit of pampering.

"Thank you, Mom, but clothing and all this makeup is superficial. I am who I am. The clothes don't define me. And whether I wear rouge or not shouldn't define me, either. I shouldn't have to doll myself up simply to please men or get their attention."

"That's right, dear, but what we did today wasn't about pleasing men or letting clothes define you. The reason I took you shopping is because I want you to feel good about yourself and to leave the past behind you. Forget Bob and get a fresh start. You're not the young, naive girl who fell in love with him back in Elmira. You're a mature and sophisticated professional woman. Your new clothes simply show that better than your old outfits."

The bags of clothing that I'd bought at Bergdorf Goodman barely fit in my car when we got back to Mom's house. We hugged and I thanked her for providing me with a safe place to grieve. When I got home, there was a letter taped to the front door of my house with my name on it. I knew from the writing that it was from Bob.

Was he apologizing? Did he want me to take him back? Had he understood how he had ripped out my heart? I read his note while standing on the porch.

Bob wrote that he was sorry that I had caught him and

Linda in bed. He'd wanted to tell me about her for several weeks, but hadn't known how to do it without hurting me. He and Linda had not meant to fall in love. It simply had happened. He had fought it as long as he could, he wrote. "But we can't control who we fall in love with. That's part of the beauty of love." He went on to write that he would always cherish the time that we had spent together and he even cited our Christmas Eve date at his grandfather's farm as an example of how he would always "love" me. But he now was deeply in love with Linda. Someday, he hoped we would be friends. He ended his note by writing that I deserved someone better than him.

I crumpled his letter in my hand. At least his last sentence had been truthful.

I did deserve someone better than him.

PART THREE

IN THE RING

---

*Justice is blind; but, fortunately for
the sake of the welfare of society,
she can often see through
the bandage.*

—ANONYMOUS

27

"**W**OW! WHAT HAPPENED TO YOU? I mean, you look sensational!"

That confused compliment came from Will Harris, who was standing in the doorway of my office. It was Monday morning and Harris had been sent by his editor to write a feature story about our unit and the dangers that women faced when they filed criminal charges against their husband. The paper's reporter had written a story that weekend about Maya Lopez's murder.

"So what's with the new look?" he asked.

"I decided to make some changes."

"Well, you look fabulous."

He flopped down in a chair and we spent the next half hour talking about the Domestic Violence Unit. Next, Anne Marie took him on a tour and drove him to a women's shelter where we'd arranged for him to interview a victim of domestic violence.

I had just begun doing paperwork when another figure appeared in my doorway.

"Why are you so gussied up?" Detective O'Brien asked.

Gussied up? Did people still use that idiom?

I ignored his question and asked, "What brings you here?"

"The chief told me that I could transfer here, if I wanted."

"So do you want?"

"Let's go for a ride. I got a couple of conditions and I need you to go somewhere with me."

When we got inside his unmarked squad car, O'Brien said, "I got two conditions. First, I want my own office, so if being around all you broads all day gets under my skin, I'll have somewhere to retreat."

"I agree," I said, adding, "I think all of us would like somewhere in our office for you to go when you're not needed."

He chuckled and said, "Second condition. If we're going to be partners, you got to start carrying a gun."

Actually, I'd already considered the idea, especially now that Juan Lopez was on the loose.

Ten minutes later, we were standing before a glass counter in O'Brien's favorite gun shop. I chose a .38-caliber police model Smith & Wesson revolver. As an assistant district attorney, getting a full carry permit for a concealed weapon was not a problem. I tried it out in the shop's indoor shooting range. It was therapeutic. At first, I pictured the male targets as Juan Lopez. But when I had fired a shot low and it struck the silhouette in the genital area, I pictured Bob.

While I liked the Smith & Wesson, it was a bit bulky and heavy in my purse. The gun dealer recommended that I buy a second handgun, a Smith & Wesson Model 19, a .357-caliber snub-nosed airweight that had more kick but with its smaller barrel was easier to hide. He suggested I keep the larger .38 next to my bed at night and never go anywhere without the .357 snub-nose in my purse.

After I had spent a good hour testing the guns by firing at targets, O'Brien drove me back to work.

"Does this mean you're going to join us?" I asked him.

"I can start tomorrow, assuming you have my office ready. In fact, I already have a case for you to take on."

"What's the case?"

"A young girl. I'll bring her in tomorrow."

Neither of us spoke for a moment, and then I said, "Thank you, O'Brien, for agreeing to help us at the unit and for taking me to the gun shop."

"Dani," he said in a serious tone, "there's something I need to tell you. We got a ballistics report back from that bullet that was recovered from your wall—the one that someone shot at you."

"Did it match the gun that Juan Lopez used to shoot Maya?"

"No," O'Brien said. "Actually, it matched the bullet that ended Mary Margaret's life. Rudy Hitchins isn't in Canada. He's still here somewhere, and obviously, he's out for revenge."

THE NEXT MORNING when I walked into the center, Anne Marie greeted me with a huge grin, making a buzzing noise as if she were a bee. The other women in the office did the same, making it sound as if we all worked in a beehive.

"What's going on?" I asked.

Anne Marie said, "You haven't read this morning's paper, have you? Will Harris wrote his article about us." She handed me a copy so I could read his front-page story.

Assistant District Attorney Dani Fox is a snappy dresser with a great pair of legs, a lush mop of curly black hair, scarlet nails painted to match her bee-stung lips and a penchant for ankle bracelets—a real looker. She's also a smart, impassioned advocate for battered women . . .

I'd never read the term "bee-stung lips" before. When I was in grammar school, other kids used to call them "fat lips." Now, apparently they were an attribute.

Anne Marie said, "It looks as if Will Harris might have a crush on you."

I carried the paper into my office so I could read the rest in private. I'd just finished when O'Brien ducked his head through my door and said, "Miss Fox, there's someone I'd like you to meet."

Standing next to him was one of the prettiest teenagers I've ever seen. She had long black hair that fell past her shoulders, olive skin, and big eyes. Although she was at least five feet nine, I guessed she only weighed about 120 pounds.

O'Brien said, "This is Carmen Gonzales."

"Pleased to meet you, Miss Fox," she said. Despite her adult appearance, her voice was that of a child's.

O'Brien had invited Anne Marie to join us, and as soon as all three of them were seated across from my desk, he began.

"Carmen's father is currently locked up in the Metropolitan Correctional Center on charges that he distributed cocaine and laundered drug money at a high-end jewelry shop that he owned in Manhattan. His name is Carlos Gonzales and he's a White Plains resident."

He looked at Carmen and said, "Now that her father's in jail, Carmen wants to tell you what he's been doing to her for some time now."

"What did your father do?" I asked.

"He raped me," she said, casting her eyes toward the floor.

"Don't be ashamed," I said. "You didn't do anything wrong if he raped you. Why don't you start at the beginning?"

"The first time he did it?"

"Yes, but would you like something to drink first? Water—a soda?"

She shook her head, indicating no. With her eyes still locked on the floor, she began. "The first time he did it was a month after my stepmother died. My father—he called me into my parents' bedroom. I'd just had my fourteenth birthday—that was two years ago. My father had photos of my dead stepmother spread out over his bed and he was snorting cocaine.

I'd seen him use it before. We'd all hide when he got high because he'd get mean. He had a shotgun on the bed, too. At first, I thought he was going to kill himself. Or me. I was really, really afraid."

Her voice cracked and Anne Marie quickly offered her a tissue. I picked up the ever-present candy dish that I kept on my desk and offered her some Junior Mints. When I was nervous or upset, I immediately reached for dark chocolate and found it comforting. She thanked me but refused.

"My father told me to sit on the corner of the bed and I did. I was in my pajamas. He put cocaine in his nose and then he grabbed the shotgun and he ran into the bathroom and slammed the door. I thought, 'Oh my God, he's going to shoot himself.' I didn't know what to do, so I just sat there trembling. After about twenty minutes, he opened the door and he came out. I could tell from his eyes that he was really high and angry at me. I didn't know why because I hadn't done nothing wrong. I'd just been sitting there."

She began to cry.

"Take your time," O'Brien said.

She looked up from the chair at me. "My father told me, 'I could have killed myself in there. I could've blown off my head. But you didn't do nothing. You don't care about me. You didn't care about your mother, neither. You only care about yourself.'"

Her voice dropped to a whisper. "My father took off his belt and he hit me across my back. It stung and I screamed. He said a good daughter would have come into the bathroom to check on him. A good daughter would have tried to stop him. But I didn't care about him. I didn't try to stop him. I wasn't a good daughter. He said that's why he hit me. That's why he was going to beat me. He whipped me again with his belt and I fell on the floor on my stomach and tried to protect my head with my hands because he just kept hitting me with his belt. It hurt so much. I kept thinking, 'Why is he doing this? It can't be happening.' I was screaming and that made him even madder. He yelled, 'You want something to cry about? I'll give you something to cry about!' He hit me so many times that my back began bleeding and I was begging him to stop, but he just kept hitting me."

The only sound in the room except for her voice was the noise of Anne Marie's pen on her notepad.

"My father told me to go into his bathroom and take a shower because my back was bleeding. He said I was a dirty, rotten whore who didn't care about anyone. I ran into the bathroom, and while the water was running, I cried and cried because I knew he couldn't hear me. I stayed in there as long as I could. I didn't know what else to do. Then I thought maybe the cocaine had worn off and maybe he'd fallen asleep and maybe I could get back to my room if I was real quiet. I dried off but I couldn't put my pajamas on because they were bloody. I looked in the mirror and my back was covered with bruises and welts. I wrapped myself in two towels and opened the door. But he was waiting for me on the bed and he told me to come over to the bed. That's when it happened."

I said, "That's when he raped you?"

She nodded.

"I just looked at the ceiling. I didn't make noise because he told me that I could not cry, that I had no right to cry, but I was crying inside."

"How many times did he sexually assault you that night?"

She held up three fingers. "When he was done, he told me I was sleeping in his bed from now on. He said, 'Your stepmother slept here so now you have to sleep here.' The next day he told me to put on my stepmother's clothes. He told me I wasn't going back to school ever again. He told me I was the family's new mother and I had to take care of the younger kids. When he left for work at the jewelry store, he told me to clean the house and get dinner ready for him when he came home. I wanted to run away, but I didn't know where to go and I didn't want to leave my little brothers and sister behind. He said he would kill me or them if I said anything. That night, after I put the other kids to bed he took me into the bedroom and he told me to take cocaine with him. I didn't want to so he began hitting me with his belt. When he got tired of hitting me, he made me take the cocaine in my nose and he put cocaine on his penis. He said it would make him like Superman. Then he raped me again two times that night. It was awful. I wanted to die. I wanted him to kill me."

"Did you tell anyone?"

"No, I kept thinking someone would realize something was wrong. I kept thinking someone would stop him. My father made me dress in my stepmother's evening clothes and he took me out at night. He'd take me to bars and tell people I was his girlfriend. No one said anything, even people who knew I was his daughter. They laughed and said it was great that he was spending time with me. Then I got pregnant."

"Your father got you pregnant?"

"Yes. When he found out, he was so mad. He beat me with the belt. I think he was trying to kill the baby. But it didn't work so he took me to one of those clinics. He went with me and paid to have it done."

"How long ago was that?"

"Three months ago. He went with me when they did it. Not long after that, he met a woman. His new girlfriend. She was a lingerie model. He told me I could go back to my room after she moved in with us. He told me that if I ever said anything about what he'd done to me, he would kill me and kill my brothers and sister."

I said to O'Brien, "Detective, I'd like you to step outside for a moment." As soon as he did, I said, "I want you to show me your back, where he whipped you with his belt."

Carmen stood up and took off her shirt, unsnapped her bra, and turned around.

Anne Marie let out a gasp.

The teen's back was a road map of raised scar tissue, hundreds of linear slash marks.

"Thank you. You can put your shirt back on."

Seeing Carmen's scars substantiated her story. But we would need to do much more investigation to justify charges of forcible rape, sodomy, unlawful imprisonment, incest, and child endangerment—all potential counts that I was mulling over.

"Carmen, do you understand that if we file criminal charges against your father, you'll have to testify against him in a courtroom?"

"Yes, Detective O'Brien already told me."

"Are you going to be able to look him directly in the eyes and tell twelve jurors the same story that you just told us?"

"I think so."

I didn't want to frighten her, but I also knew a defense attorney was going to be relentless when she testified.

"You can't think so. You have to *know* so."

For the first time since she'd entered my office, I saw fire in her big brown eyes.

"Yes, I will tell them."

Addressing Anne Marie, I said, "Take Carmen into your office and get color photos of the scars." I turned to Carmen and asked, "Are you hungry?" It was nearly noon.

"Yes. I didn't have any breakfast."

"Anne Marie, get Carmen something to eat, too."

"Maybe I could get something to take back to Hector, my brother. He and I are living with my mom's best friend."

"Anne Marie will do it."

O'Brien returned as soon as Carmen and Anne Marie left.

"What kind of sick son of a bitch does this to his own

daughter?" I asked. "What can you tell me about Carlos Gonzales?"

O'Brien removed the toothpick from between his lips and said, "Carlos is a real piece of work. The Feds got a drug case against him in Manhattan. He's never been busted before and his arrest came as a real surprise to the Hispanic community."

O'Brien said Carlos had come to America from Bogotá, Colombia, when he was a small child and had become a naturalized citizen. Through hard work, he'd learned the jewelry business and had eventually opened a high-end outlet in Manhattan's Inwood neighborhood. He'd married his first wife, Rosita, and they'd settled in White Plains, where she gave birth to Carmen. Two years later, she'd died while having their second child, Hector. Carlos, meanwhile, soon emerged as a powerful political figure in Westchester County's Spanish-speaking communities. He attended church each Sunday, donated to Latino charities, and was president of the local Hispanic business council. He donated money from his store to buy sporting equipment for a local youth center. His second wife, Benita Archuleta, was from a respected Manhattan family, which owned more than a dozen profitable bodegas. She bore him two more children, Angel and Adolpho. According to a police report, Benita had committed suicide a few days before Christmas two years ago. Carlos's newest love interest was Maria Hildago. She'd moved into the family house in White Plains about two weeks before the FBI arrested Carlos on charges that he was distributing drugs through his jewelry business.

I said, "So in public, he's an upstanding, pull-yourself-up-by-the-bootstraps immigrant success story and Hispanic leader. In private, he's distributing drugs, using cocaine, and beating and raping his own daughter."

"That's Carlos. He thinks he's slick."

"Where are the kids?"

"Carmen and Hector moved in with Yolanda Torres, in New Rochelle. Yolanda was their mother—Rosita's—best friend. Angel and Adolpho are living with their grandmother."

"Anything else I should know? What about the suicide—the stepmother?"

"You mean Carlos's second wife, Benita. The medical examiner listed it as a suicide, but it was odd."

"Why's that?"

"Benita had a clean-cut reputation, came from a good family, and was popular. Then she OD'd right before Christmas on cocaine. According to the report, all the kids were in the house the night it happened, including Carmen."

"Maybe she had secrets just like Carlos."

28

IT'S HARD FOR DEFENSE ATTORNEYS TO counter physical evidence. The scars on Carmen's back proved she had been beaten. She'd also had an abortion—something I needed to confirm. Just the same, a good defense attorney would try to create reasonable doubt in jurors' minds. Who had delivered those blows? Who had gotten her pregnant?

The truth? That didn't matter—not to a defense attorney. It was someone else's problem. When you were hired as a defense lawyer, the goal was acquittal, not truth. Ask a defense attorney how he slept at night and you always got the same answer. If the state did its job, then the guilty would be deservingly punished. There wouldn't be any reasonable doubt. Jurors would know instantly who was guilty and who wasn't. It wasn't up to the defense to determine who had committed a murder. That was the state's job. The defense was responsible for making certain the innocent were not railroaded.

It all sounded noble. But it rarely was. Most defense attorneys knew their clients were guilty as hell. But that didn't stop them from cooking up stories and blaming others for crimes that they knew their clients had committed.

I wanted to corroborate Carmen's story, so while O'Brien and Anne Marie began interviewing neighbors, relatives, and the other Gonzales children, I hopped on a train into Manhattan. Normally, I would have had a police officer drive me, but

I didn't want to call attention to myself because of where I was going.

Carmen had said her father had taken her to a women's clinic on East 60th Street for an abortion. Obviously, I could subpoena the doctor who worked there, but I thought he might talk more freely to me if I showed up in person. I also had Carmen sign a legal release authorizing me to read her medical charts.

It was a three-block walk from the subway station to the concrete high-rise that housed the women's clinic. As I neared the address, I spotted a couple accosting a teenage girl and an older woman. They appeared to be a mother and daughter.

"Don't kill your baby!" a middle-aged man in a worn dark suit hollered at the teen. The equally middle-aged woman with him tried to force pamphlets into their hands. The antiabortion activists kept maneuvering themselves in front of the pair, momentarily blocking their path.

"Leave us alone!" the mother finally yelled. "This is none of your business." Grabbing her daughter's hand, she pulled the terrified teen into the building.

The activists noticed me and pounced, like hawks swooping down on an unsuspecting prey.

"Give up your baby for adoption," the man pleaded. "Don't murder your child."

The woman thrust a pamphlet toward me. The cover had a color photograph of a fetus discarded in a trash can under the words: "HUMAN GARBAGE."

"We can take you to a safe place where people can help you with your baby," the woman said. "They can find someone to adopt your child. You don't have to commit murder."

"Sorry," I said, "but I'm not pregnant. I'm an assistant district attorney and I'm curious. How long have you been outside this clinic doing this?"

I wondered if Carmen and Carlos had encountered this pair three months earlier.

Both took a step away from me. "We have a legal right to do this," the man declared. "It's our constitutional right. We have lawyers, too, you know."

"I simply asked you a question."

"We're not talking to you!" the woman exclaimed. "We're not breaking any laws. We're good, churchgoing, God-fearing people. Instead of bothering us, you should be arresting those doctors in there." They retreated.

The waiting room on the eighth floor was depressing. ABORTION CAN BE LONELY was written on a wall poster. The Eagles hit "Hotel California" was playing over a loudspeaker in the ceiling. There were about a dozen molded red plastic chairs with chrome legs along with two worn sofas. A dusty plastic fern was sitting in a corner and a warning sign that said No Smoking was posted nearby. A chipped wood veneer coffee table in the center of the room was covered with thumbed-through magazines and brochures about sexually transmitted diseases and birth control. I counted four women, in addition to the mother and daughter whom I'd seen outside. All were young, age twenty-two or under, I guessed. Two had boyfriends with them. The other two had girlfriends. A black trash can in the corner was filled with the antiabortion pamphlets that the activists outside had been distributing. At the far end of the oblong room was a metal door that could be opened only by a receptionist who was perched behind a thick window, much like a bank teller. I slipped a business card through a slot in the Plexiglas. The receptionist, a tired-looking woman in her fifties, eyeballed me. Standing, she walked to the right, disappearing from my sight. About a minute later, a thirty-something woman wearing a medical gown with a tie-dyed surgical cap came into view. I heard a loud *thunk* coming from inside the metal door, and the woman in the surgical outfit stuck her head out of the door and said, "C'mon in."

I followed her to an office that was barely big enough for a metal desk, office chair, and two uncomfortable-looking metal folding chairs.

"I'm Doctor Joyce Cox," she said, immediately firing up a cigarette. "What's this about, Ms. Fox?"

I'd expected a male doctor. Dr. Cox was thin with closely cropped black hair. Her fingernails were cut short and not painted. Even though she was not wearing makeup, there was a natural rose tint in her cheeks.

"I'm investigating a rape," I explained. "I believe the girl's father brought her here for an abortion."

"Let's be clear," Dr. Cox said. "I don't do 'abortions.' I do 'procedures.' And I don't kill babies no matter what those screwballs outside claim. I remove unwanted 'tissues.'"

"I'm not here to judge you or debate you. I'm fully aware of the Supreme Court's nineteen seventy-three decision in *Roe v. Wade* that confirmed a woman's right to self-determination." I took the medical release that Carmen had signed and handed it to her. "I've been authorized by Carmen to discuss any medical procedures that she may have undergone here."

Dr. Cox scanned the sheet. "Confidentiality is important to us," she said. "As you can imagine, our clients want to keep their records private. I need to make a call."

She dialed a number that was taped to her desk phone and asked for someone named Sandra. Dr. Cox explained over the phone who I was and read Sandra the medical release word for word. I could tell from Dr. Cox's end of the conversation that Sandra was a lawyer who apparently wasn't too happy with any of this, but after she asked if the release had been signed by a witness (it had) and was notarized (it was), she instructed Dr. Cox to ask me a question.

"If I don't comply, are you going to subpoena these records?" Dr. Cox asked.

I was getting tired of this rigmarole, so I reached over and took the phone out of Dr. Cox's hand and said, "Sandra, I'm an assistant district attorney dealing with a rape case. Of course, I can subpoena your records and also make Doctor Cox testify, but at this juncture, I'm mostly fact seeking, so if you want to do this the easy way, then you'll inform the doctor to cooperate."

Without waiting for Sandra to respond, I handed the phone back to Dr. Cox, who spent the next several moments answering questions with one-word grunts such as "huh," "yep," "okay," and "sure."

When she finally hung up, she said, "I'll be happy to answer your questions."

I asked, "Do you remember Carmen Gonzales?"

"We see about sixty women a day here. I don't remember names. The women who come here don't come to make friends and chitchat. But I think I remember the woman who you're speaking about. Did she have black hair, young, Latino, and rather striking—could be a model?"

"That's her. How come you remember her?"

Dr. Cox took a very long drag on her cigarette, which she then smashed in a black ceramic ash tray.

"Great question. We do have lots of women come in, but in the two years I've worked at this clinic, there has been only one girl who came in with her father—that's the girl you're asking about. That's why I remember her. Girls come in with their girlfriends or boyfriends—if the guy is decent enough to show up—and we get lots of mothers who bring in daughters. But no girl—no one—ever comes with a father. Except her."

She walked from her desk to the door and called down to the receptionist in the booth. When the aide came to see what she wanted, Dr. Cox gave her the medical release. "Make a copy of this for our file and bring this girl's records to me."

Returning to her desk chair, Dr. Cox said, "You're going to be disappointed if you think our records are going to help you. All that's in them is a photo, basic information provided by the client, and my medical notes about the procedure. We simply do our job and send them home."

"There are no follow-up calls, no visits by social workers, no detailed interviews?"

"Ms. Fox," Dr. Cox replied, "most of our patients never want to see or hear from us again. We explain the procedure, they sign the paperwork, and that's it. Four to five hours tops and they're gone. If we knocked on their doors later, some of these women would be mortified. Maybe they're married and don't want another mouth to feed. Maybe they're cheating. Maybe they're single. Maybe they're unmarried teens. I'm not their therapist."

"Was there anything about Carmen Gonzales that was different—besides her father being with her?"

Dr. Cox paused and then said, "I remember the father insisted on staying with his daughter during the entire procedure. He wouldn't leave her alone, not for a second. Sometimes we have mothers do that, but I thought it was odd that a father would want to be in the room when we did the actual procedure."

It was coming together just as I had suspected. Carlos had not been worried about Carmen's health. He had been exercising total control to keep her from revealing the multiple rapes and scars.

"Did she appear frightened of her father?" I asked.

With an exasperated look, Dr. Cox said, "How would I know? Most of the teenage girls who come here are emotional wrecks. All I can tell you is that he didn't hold her hand or try to comfort her. He seemed angry, suspicious, but I didn't find that out of character given that he was the father. My first impression was that her boyfriend had gotten her pregnant. He mentioned that his wife had died. Suicide, he said. But then I did get a little bit suspicious."

"Why?"

"He did all the talking for her. It's not my job to speculate but it just seemed odd to me."

I wasn't going to let her off the hook that easy. "Did you suspect incest?"

"Like I said, I just thought it was odd behavior for a father."

"But not odd enough to call anyone?"

Dr. Cox gave me an icy stare as her assistant walked in with a thin file folder. Dr. Cox opened it, withdrew a Polaroid picture, and handed it to me.

Carmen Gonzales seemed distraught. Her eyes looked frightened. Yet even without makeup and with uncombed hair, she remained striking.

Dr. Cox said, "She's the one I remember."

I quickly read the five pages in her file. She'd been given blood and urine tests at 9:45 a.m. to confirm she was pregnant and had met with a counselor who questioned her about why she wanted an abortion. According to the counselor's notes, Carlos Gonzales had been present during questioning. Two hours later, after Dr. Cox had been satisfied that Carmen was in her first trimester, she authorized the procedure. With her father at her side, Carmen had been taken into a room and asked if she wanted to be asleep or awake. She'd chosen to be knocked out. Even then, Carlos refused to leave. The sixteen-year-old had been given an intravenous injection of Brevital and her legs had been put in stirrups, just as if she were about to give birth. The actual abortion had taken only two minutes. Her body had discharged the fetus without complication. The clinic had charged her father $150, which he'd paid in cash. Father and daughter had departed before four p.m. That was it.

"Is there any way to tell who the father of the fetus was?" I asked.

"No, we don't keep removed tissues," Dr. Cox replied. "Are you going to subpoena me if you file a rape charge?"

I was truthful. "Probably." The medical records should have been enough, but sometimes testimony has more impact, especially if I asked Dr. Cox about Carlos Gonzales's dominating presence.

"Look, if you call me, can you at least not ask me to reveal my home address? These zealots outside are always trying to discover where I live. I've had to move four times since I took this job. They follow me almost every night. They put out flyers with my picture on them calling me a Baby Killer. Neighbors always like living next to a doctor, but not one who does procedures."

"Why do you do this then?"

"Ms. Fox," she replied, "do you think Carmen Gonzales was raped by her father?"

"Absolutely. Multiple times."

"And if I had not removed that tissue from her, and a baby had been born, a baby of incest, a baby of rape, with a brutalized teenage mother and an incestuous father, what sort of life would that baby have?"

Not waiting for my reply, she said, "I don't think every piece of tissue needs to become an unwanted and unloved baby. Now let me ask you a question."

"That's fair," I said.

"You a Catholic?"

"Actually, I am."

"A third of the women who come here are Catholic. They're going against their church's adamant position by coming here. That same church forbids contraception. Those anti-abortionists outside claim the Bible is against abortion. But sometimes I wonder how many of them actually have read the Bible or understand it."

She lit another cigarette and said, "You familiar with Deuteronomy, chapter twenty-three, verse one, Ms. Fox?"

"No, I think the nuns skipped over that one when I was in school."

"It says a man with smashed testicles and a cut-off penis shouldn't be allowed inside a church." She blew out a puff of smoke. "I'd like to see priests standing at the front doors checking that out. My point is there's lots of stuff in the Bible that doesn't make sense. No one should judge me or what I do."

Standing, she said, "Don't call me as a witness unless you really need me. The receptionist will let you out. I have a procedure to do."

29

T HE NEW YORK FIELD OFFICE OF THE
FBI is located on the twenty-third floor at 26 Federal
Plaza in Manhattan and is one of three field offices
overseen by an assistant FBI director rather than a Special
Agent in Charge. That's because New York, Los Angeles, and
Washington, D.C., are the largest of the bureau's fifty-six field
operations.

O'Brien had arranged a meeting for us with Jack Longhorn, the Special Agent in Charge of the Carlos Gonzales case.

I'd not had many dealings with the FBI. But I knew the
bureau was in flux. The FBI's director in Washington, D.C.,
was on the verge of being canned. A new president had been
elected and he wanted to appoint his own director. O'Brien
had told me that rumors were rampant inside law enforcement
that the New York FBI office was going to be gutted. That
meant Agent Longhorn was in a tenuous position. "You're
only as good as your last big arrest," O'Brien explained. "That
means Longhorn might be under pressure to make the Gonzales case into something bigger than it actually is so he can impress his bosses in Washington, D.C., and get a promotion
rather than a transfer. Word is that he's gunning for the top
job, running the office."

We'd asked for the meeting to exchange information since
the FBI already had Gonzales locked up at Metropolitan Correctional Center. I felt obligated to tell Agent Longhorn that

I was about to indict Carlos Gonzales on abuse charges. I didn't want to get into a jurisdictional dispute with the bureau.

During our ride, O'Brien offered me a tip. When it came to sharing information—the FBI was all for it—*at least when it came to the bureau getting information*. But the FBI was never forthcoming in its dealings with local cops. It always kept its cards close to its vest. It was the biggest nonsecret in law enforcement—the FBI felt superior.

O'Brien had me convinced that our encounter with Longhorn was going to be adversarial. But when we entered his office, he welcomed us as if we were long-lost relatives. Lanky and in his late thirties, Longhorn had a thick southern drawl that he'd acquired in his native Ardmore, Oklahoma. He also prided himself on his folksy chatter.

"I'm having a cup of joe," he said. "Would you like one? It's fresh." He brought a glass coffeepot from a sideboard over to his desk, where he filled two Styrofoam cups. Smiling, he said, "Now, Detective O'Brien and Miss Fox, how can the bureau be of service to you today?"

"We've come to talk about Carlos Gonzales," I explained. "I plan to have a Westchester grand jury indict him on twenty-two counts of rape, sodomy, incest, and physical abuse of his teenage daughter."

"Whew," Longhorn responded, blowing air through his lips. "Little lady, did you just say twenty-two counts?"

"Yes, all involving his teenage daughter."

"Well, I'll be danged," Longhorn said. "Crimes, like chickens, always come home to roost."

What, exactly, any of this had to do with chickens was beyond me, but I smiled and said, "I wanted to coordinate our efforts. I know you have first shot at him and I don't want our prosecution to get in your way on the drug charges."

Agent Longhorn thought about that for a few moments and then said, "You're right. Our case does take priority, but we're still putting it together." He paused, as if he were in deep thought, and then said, "You know what, Miss Fox, I've got an idea. Let's say you indict him on those charges. Then he's got us to worry about and you, too. He's going to feel even more pressure. You know what they say about pressure?" He smiled, revealing a row of perfectly formed teeth. "It makes eggs crack."

I was not a fan of Longhorn's folksy wit. The moment he mentioned putting pressure on Gonzales, I suspected he was thinking about offering the accused a plea bargain. "Mr. Longhorn, you're not thinking about cutting a deal with Carlos Gonzales, are you?"

Longhorn gave me a pained look. "Miss Fox," he said sternly, "let me tell you a bit about the kind of animal we're dealing with here. But first, I need you to promise what we say in this room stays in this room, because I'm going to share bureau intel with you. You okay with that?"

"Of course."

"In 1975, a well-known drug dealer in the town of Medellín, Colombia, was murdered by his up-and-coming rival, Manuel Rodriquez. We believe Rodriquez is slowly taking control of all drug trafficking in Colombia and is hoping to form a cartel to distribute cocaine inside the United States."

He handed me a file marked FBI/INTEL. "Take a few moments and read this," he suggested.

The file contained a detailed report about Rodriquez and how he was smuggling thousands of pounds of cocaine from Colombia into southern Florida via Panama. He had a fleet of planes and helicopters at his disposal. The report described Rodriquez as a ruthless smuggler who was known to either bribe or murder anyone who got in his way, whether they were police officers, judges, or politicians.

Longhorn said, "Our sources have told us that Rodriquez wants to expand into New York. We know that Carlos Gonzales was selling cocaine out of his jewelry shop. If we can show that Gonzales was in cahoots with Rodriquez, well, that would make our case against Mr. Gonzales rather important now, wouldn't it?"

"What do you mean?"

"I mean, we wouldn't just be dealing with a little old neighborhood drug pusher now, would we? We'd be dealing with a possible New York City cocaine connection right to the Colombian cartel of Manuel Rodriquez."

"So how do you want to proceed? How can we both go after Carlos Gonzales without stepping on each other's toes?"

Leaning forward, Longhorn asked, "Miss Fox, you ever heard 'You can't make cookies if you don't have the dough'? We're still piecing together our cases, still collecting the dough, so if you want to hold Carlos Gonzales's feet to the fire, then light your match. You take that slick bastard down and then we'll come in and finish him off."

At this point, Longhorn actually winked at me. It wasn't a sexual wink. It was more like the sort of wink that fraternity brothers might give each other because they both knew a secret handshake. I interpreted his wink to mean: You can trust me and I can trust you, Miss Fox. We're on the same team.

Still, I wanted to make sure I understood exactly what he was saying. "If I move forward with my case, you won't object to Gonzales being tried in White Plains before your try him here in federal court?"

Longhorn placed his coffee mug down on his desk. "My fellow agents make fun of me because of my homespun sayings, but, I swear, I can't help myself sometimes. Miss Fox, an old horse gets you where you're going, only the ride takes longer."

I gave him a puzzled look.

"What that means is that you go ahead, and after you get him convicted, we'll prosecute him in federal court."

He'd just given me what I wanted—the first shot at Gonzales.

"That sounds great!" I said, beaming.

Longhorn stood up, stuck out his hand, and gave me a firm shake. "Glad we're together on this, young lady. I'm sorry but I have another appointment, but if you need anything from my office, anything at all, why you just give me a holler."

O'Brien didn't say a word as we rode down the elevator and exited the Manhattan skyscraper. As we walked toward a parking garage on Broadway, I asked him why he was so quiet.

"I don't trust Longhorn."

"Why not?"

"Dani, I've been dealing with these Hoover boys for a long time, and I'm telling you, they come at you with big smiles, big 'happy to meet you' grins—but you can't trust them. It's not until after they slap you on the back, you realize they've just stuck a knife in you."

"What about that INTEL file he showed me that says Rodriquez might be moving into New York? You don't believe Gonzales could be the cartel's contact here?"

"It could all be bullshit," he said. "I told you that Agent Longhorn was on the hot seat to come up with a big case to impress the brass in Washington. Did anything in that INTEL report actually say the Colombian cartel was moving into New York?"

Now that he mentioned it, there wasn't any specific mention in the report about Rodriquez moving drugs into the city. Only Longhorn had suggested that connection.

"I got friends at the NYPD," O'Brien continued, "and they tell me that the mob still controls all the drugs moving in and out of this city. Rodriquez and his cartel may be big in Miami, but if they want to do business here, they're either going to have to cut a deal with the five families, in which case the NYPD Organized Crime Task Force would know about it, or they're going to have to muscle in. And if that were to happen, we'd all know about it because we'd have a bunch of dead Colombians and Italians showing up on the streets."

"You think Longhorn just lied to us?"

"I'll play nice, okay? I'll just say he might have been exaggerating. He might be hoping to make Carlos Gonzales into a big witness, a huge catch, just to impress his new bosses."

The idea that an FBI agent would exaggerate the importance of a case to win political favor with his bosses seemed completely foreign to me. Prosecuting criminals was supposed to be about justice, not promotions.

"Personally," O'Brien said, "I hope he was full of bullshit."

"Why?" I asked, surprised.

"Because one thing that INTEL report said that was accurate is that Manuel Rodriquez is a stone-cold killer. He doesn't care who he murders—cops, judges, prosecutors—and if Carlos Gonzales is in bed with the Colombian cartel, then he could be much more than a pervert who rapes his own kid. He could have important and very dangerous connections."

30

I THOUGHT DISTRICT ATTORNEY WHITA-
ker was going to have an orgasm when O'Brien and I
briefed him about Carlos Gonzales. His face lit up as
soon as I explained that Carmen was a sixteen-year-old beauty
whose father had beaten her, repeatedly raped her, and then
dressed her in her dead stepmother's clothing and paraded her
around Manhattan nightclubs as his girlfriend. Whitaker knew
that Carlos Gonzales had been a mover and shaker in the
White Plains Hispanic community up until his arrest on drug-
smuggling charges. The additional charges of sexual depravity
that we planned to file against him were sure to make this
case—as only O'Brien could put it—a "tabloid editor's wet
dream."

Whitaker had Steinberg begin contacting news outlets. Usually, Steinberg notified only local television, radio, and newspaper reporters in Westchester County when we were about to
announce a big indictment. But Steinberg sent word to the *New
York Post*, *Daily News*, all the supermarket tabloids, and even
the Old Gray Lady herself—the *New York Times*.

The day before the press conference, Steinberg held a practice dress rehearsal with Hillary Potts playing the role of a
reporter asking questions.

When Whitaker's big moment arrived, he handled the
media masterfully, hitting all the right points, delivering clever
thirty-second sound bites that were sure to make the evening

broadcast. As for me, I stood quietly behind him watching five TV news crews jockeying for the best angle. Strangely, Paul Pisani was nowhere to be seen, which was a huge relief to me. Given his massive ego and "Mr. Invincible" reputation, I'd expected him to muscle into the case.

The indictment did not identify the teenage victim by name, and because state law prohibits publication of either the name or a picture of a rape victim, she was never identified in the papers.

Everyone in my office gathered together at five o'clock to watch the local news broadcast, and when I appeared on the screen, all the girls and even O'Brien cheered. The room became quiet when the anchorman announced that Gonzales had hired a defense attorney. Alexander Dominic's fat face suddenly appeared on the screen. "My client is innocent," Dominic declared.

I couldn't believe that Gonzales had hired the same bottom-feeding lawyer who had represented Rudy Hitchins as his defense attorney. My only guess was that no one else in White Plains would defend him.

"I'll be damned," O'Brien said, breaking into a smile. "This should be a cakewalk against a putz like Dominic."

The next morning, Gonzales was brought to the Westchester courthouse for the first of numerous court appearances and I got to lay my eyes on him for the first time. I half expected him to look like a Hollywood gangster. In the movies evil people look evil. But the Carlos Gonzales who strutted into court was a handsome, articulate, well-groomed, physically fit, middle-aged man with a charming dimple in his chin and a quick smile. He came across as a confident businessman, and I could tell from his cocky attitude that he wasn't worried about his daughter's accusations—nor was he afraid of me.

In the coming weeks, O'Brien and I worked furiously to prepare Carmen and our other witnesses. We wanted our case to be airtight. Even though Carmen was a teenager, she was amazingly poised. The only witness who made us nervous was Yolanda Torres. When I first met her, Torres reeked of alcohol and the first question out of her mouth was whether I was going to pay her for testifying and for letting Carmen and her brother stay in her apartment.

As we got closer and closer to a trial date, I began feeling a funny vibe. Dominic wasn't filing the sort of pretrial motions that defense lawyers generally filed; in fact, he wasn't really doing anything to help his client. There were no endless motions seeking delays, no requests for a change of venue because of pretrial publicity, and when O'Brien checked the jail logs, he discovered that Dominic was not even visiting his client. Something was up.

I became even more suspicious when Dominic didn't make any effort to contact me about a possible plea deal. Even for a lawyer as inept as Dominic, this was simply weird.

Three days before the trial, my suspicions proved true.

During what was supposed to be a routine hearing, Dominic suddenly announced that he was withdrawing as the lead defense attorney. As I watched in disbelief, Neal Kent, a well-known defense attorney from the Manhattan firm of Hart, Hammerman and Kent, approached the court and announced that he would defend Gonzales.

Kent was one of the best criminal defense attorneys in New York. *New York* magazine also had identified him as one of the city's most eligible bachelors. He had an impeccable legal background, having graduated from Columbia University Law School and gone directly to work in the New York County District Attorney's Office. After handling a series of sensational prosecutions, Kent had jumped sides by becoming a defense attorney. His clientele came exclusively from Wall Street and Park Avenue. If a trophy wife was accused of murdering her elderly rich husband, Kent got a call. If an investment banker got drunk in the Hamptons and drove his Lincoln into a local kid riding a bicycle, killing him, Kent got a call.

The stakes in the Gonzales case suddenly were raised. Rather than facing a pushover, I would now be going against one of Manhattan's shrewdest attorneys.

This was no longer a "cakewalk."

31

I FELT A BUTTERFLY RUSH WHEN THE trial of Carlos Gonzales finally began. On the morning when I was scheduled to give my opening statement, I arrived several hours early and went to sit alone in the courtroom. I wanted to practice without anyone hearing me. I imagined what it would be like in a few hours, the drama and the horror that would unfold in that courtroom.

This was where I had always wanted to be.

I looked at where the judge would be seated. The words In God We Trust were etched on the wall. The judge would be seated behind a raised desk, known as the bench, made of highly polished rosewood. The New York State and County of Westchester flags were on the left of the judge's chair. Old Glory was hanging, slightly higher, from a pole on the right. The Great Seal of New York was bolted on the wall directly behind the bench. Its dark blue seal had a shield in its center being supported on each side by a female. One of the women was Liberty and her left foot was firmly planted on a gold crown, a symbolic act that showed New Yorkers had freed themselves from British rule. The other woman was Justice, a symbol of impartiality and fairness. Her eyes were covered with a blindfold and she held a sword in one hand and a scale in the other. Beneath the two women's feet was a white slash with the state motto: *Excelsior*, Latin for Ever Upward.

As I gazed at the great seal, I felt a sense of irony and des-

tiny. Liberty and Justice were both represented in the courtroom by women. Yet there was not a single woman judge in
the entire courthouse. Not one, and I was the only woman
prosecutor trying cases. Good enough for display on the great
seal, but not yet equal for an actual courtroom.

The witness stand was next to the bench and there were
desks for the court clerk and court reporter directly in front of
it. The jury box was on the judge's left.

A waist-high barrier called "the bar" divided the room into
two parts. The spectators sat in the gallery. The other side was
where the judge, court officials, jurors, the prosecution, the
defense, and the accused were seated. This was known as "the
well." It was extremely disrespectful for anyone who was not
a court employee to "traverse the well" without the judge's
permission. What that meant was that you were not allowed to
walk around the well and especially not permitted to approach
the judge without being invited. The judge and court officials
entered directly into the well through a separate door. The jurors entered through a completely different door near the jury
box. And the attorneys came into the courtroom along with
everyone else through a door that led into the gallery. The
term "passing the bar" literally meant that the attorneys had to
pass through the bar to enter the well and do business before
the judge.

The prosecutor's table faced the judge and was closest to the
jury box on my right. The defense sat to my left. I walked to
the podium where I would be delivering my statement, took a
deep breath, and began reciting it. I had memorized it the night
before. When I finished, I took a deep breath and left the room.
I was ready for combat.

At precisely nine a.m., the bailiff Ronald Maselli announced
in a booming voice that the County Court for the County of
Westchester for the State of New York was now in session
with the Honorable Sheldon Williams presiding. Everyone

rose from the room's hard wooden benches. His honor entered wearing a heavy black robe.

My mom was sitting directly behind me in the gallery, having come to watch her daughter's first big trial. I spotted Will Harris among a cadre of news reporters seated on the benches. Because of the notoriety of the trial, the bailiff had held a lottery for the other seats. Courthouses attract an odd menagerie. I'd spotted two regulars who'd won coveted seats. One was a middle-aged gentleman dressed elegantly in a white linen suit. In court, he could be seen taking copious notes, and when he had first appeared, a rumor spread through the building that he was a famed New York writer doing research for a new book. But he wasn't and no one had a clue why he was such a prodigious notetaker. The other regular was known simply as the "knitting lady." She would sit in court with a bag of yarn and nickel-plated knitting needles. While keeping her eyes focused on the real-life melodrama unfolding before her, her fingers would furiously twist, spinning out untold numbers of brightly colored sweaters and scarves.

I'd sequestered Carmen and my other witnesses down the hallway from the courtroom.

"Please be seated," Bailiff Maselli declared after Judge Williams had entered and plopped into his chair. Williams had not looked at any of us, but had instead immediately gone to work on a stack of official-looking papers that his court clerk had carefully left on the bench before he'd entered. With a fountain pen, he began signing them. Out of the corner of his mouth, he said, "Representing the People of the State of New York is Assistant District Attorney Dani Fox." That was my cue to stand and face the gallery, as was the custom in New York. I immediately heard several whispers. Spectators were both unaccustomed and surprised to see a woman prosecutor. Without looking up, Judge Williams said, "Representing the defendant is Mr. Neal Kent." The handsome Kent stood and turned to face the spectators.

The court clerk read the charges against Gonzales, and after she finished, Judge Williams finally took his nose out of his papers and asked, "Miss Fox, are the People ready?"

Rising to my feet, I replied, "The People are ready." I walked to the podium that faced the jury box. I was wearing one of my new conservative pinstriped navy suits and had my hair pulled back. I had chosen the black pumps that accentuated my legs and made me appear taller and more imposing. Or at least I thought so.

Although Gonzales was in jail facing drug-trafficking charges, he appeared before jurors dressed in a tailored three-piece suit and crisp white shirt. I was not permitted to tell jurors anything about the U.S. Attorney's pending charges because that would have unfairly prejudiced the defendant. The only crime that mattered was the one for which Gonzales was on trial. For all they knew, the accused was a churchgoing, apple-pie-eating, naturalized citizen who had come here to claim his piece of the American dream.

My job was to crack that facade and expose him as the monster he was.

"It is my obligation to make an opening statement to you. I welcome the opportunity to describe for you what facts the People intend to elicit in this case. An opening statement is like the table of contents of a book. The state uses it to outline the substance of the case in its skeletal form. The actual pages of this book will be written by the various witnesses who take the stand and testify and by the exhibits which are introduced into evidence."

I paused to catch my breath and then continued. "There are many kinds of betrayal. A citizen can betray his country. A husband can betray his marriage vows by committing adultery.

A businessman can defraud his partners. A friend can lie to a friend. But there is no betrayal as ugly, cruel, and vicious as a father raping his daughter. That is the ultimate betrayal. The defendant in this case, Carlos Gonzales, sexually abused his daughter beginning at the tender age of fourteen for his own perverse sexual pleasure. The evidence will show that he routinely and regularly beat her with his belt until her skin was broken and bleeding. Then he raped and sodomized her. He did not do this once, or twice, or even three times. It became a sadistic nightly ritual, an exercise in cruelty."

I turned and looked directly at Gonzales. I wanted the jurors to realize that I was not afraid to accuse him directly to his face. "You will hear evidence that *this man* degraded his daughter in ways that even animals don't do. After he'd raped her, after he'd beaten her with his belt until she was bleeding, lacking even strength to scream, he showed her no mercy. Remember that when you are reviewing the evidence during your deliberations, when the defense is asking you for mercy."

Having finished, I walked back to my chair and got a thumbs-up from my beaming mom.

Neal Kent looked every bit like the successful Manhattan lawyer that he was when he addressed the jurors. Clean shaven, naturally blond, he came across as a patriarch in a thousand-dollar Italian suit and five-hundred-dollar shoes. Like me, he did not refer to a single note.

"My client," Kent declared in a confident voice, "doesn't want your compassion. What he wants is justice. What he wants is for you to know that he did not sexually abuse his daughter as the state has charged. He is not a rapist. He did not whip her. He is a good father. A respected businessman, a self-made man who came to our country with nothing, worked hard, and made something of his life."

He hesitated for dramatic purposes and then said in a sad voice, "I'm sure you are asking yourselves, well, if Mr. Gonzales is innocent, why he is charged with these horrific crimes—offenses that I am now telling you that he did not commit?" Kent glanced over at me and then returned his gaze to the jury. "The prosecution just told you that this trial is about betrayal. Ms. Fox is right. It is about betrayal. Only it is not Carlos Gonzales who betrayed his daughter Carmen. It is his daughter who is betraying his love, his devotion, and the years and years that he fed, clothed, supported, and loved her. William Shakespeare said more than three hundred years ago in *King Lear*, 'How sharper than a serpent's tooth it is to have a thankless child.' Carlos Gonzales is the victim of a serpent here. His own daughter. We will show that Mr. Gonzales was the victim of a failed extortion attempt. This is not a case of incest and rape. It is a sad tale about revenge, greed, and a psychologically impaired teenager who needs professional mental help."

I looked at the jury and had a pained thought: All it would take is one. One shred of reasonable doubt and we would lose.

32

M Y FIRST WITNESS WAS DR. THEO-
dore Campbell, a Harvard Medical School–
educated physician with an impeccable reputation.
At my request, the gray-haired, bespectacled sixty-five-year-old
doctor had given Carmen a complete physical.

"Doctor Campbell, are you licensed to practice medicine in
the State of New York?"

"Yes, and I am board certified as well."

"What is your medical specialty, Doctor Campbell?"

"Dermatology, but I later returned to Harvard and became
a forensic dermatologist. There are only about a dozen of us in
the country."

"What does a forensic dermatologist do?"

"We're skin specialists. Many people do not realize that the
human skin is the biggest organ of the body. I've been trained
to detect and identify what sorts of instruments have been
used to make marks and wounds to the skin."

"What did you find when you examined Carmen Gonzales?"

"This young woman's skin showed signs of deep scarring—
caused by what we call 'open wounds,' especially on her back
and buttocks. There was also evidence of scars that had been
caused by 'penetration wounds.'"

"What's the difference between open and penetration
wounds?"

"We divide wounds to the skin into two types: open and

closed. Open wounds are incisions or incised wounds, caused by a clean, sharp-edged object such as a knife or a razor. A laceration is an irregular tearlike wound caused by some blunt trauma; they can be linear—regular—or stellate—irregular. The terms 'incision' and 'laceration' are often misused. In addition to incisions and lacerations, there are other types of open wounds, such as abrasions, where the topmost layer of the skin—the epidermis—is scraped off. There are also puncture wounds, caused when something goes into your skin. And, of course, there are gunshot wounds and penetration wounds. All of these are open wounds because they open the skin. An example of a closed wound would be a contusion, more commonly called a bruise, and hematomas, caused by damage to a blood vessel under the skin."

I wasn't sure whether jurors were following Dr. Campbell's lecture but that didn't concern me. He sounded exactly like the Harvard-trained expert that he was. Picking up a half-dozen color photographs that Dr. Campbell had taken of Carmen's back and buttocks, I said, "Your Honor, with your permission, I'd like to have these photographs marked for identification."

His court officer stepped forward and carried the photographs from my hand to Judge Williams. Meanwhile, I handed an identical stack to Neal Kent to examine.

Judge Williams was in his early thirties and had been on the bench less than a year, having just been elected in November. He'd practiced mostly civil litigation and I knew this was his first sex-abuse trial. He scanned the photographs and said, "Counsel, approach the bench."

Introducing photographs of wounds was routine in criminal cases, so I wasn't certain why Judge Williams needed to speak to Kent and me. Keeping his voice low, Judge Williams said, "I'm not going to allow you to introduce these photos. They're so graphic they'll prejudice and inflame the jurors."

I was dumbstruck. Every prosecutor knew that judges

sometimes refused to allow gruesome autopsy photographs to be shown to jurors. But I had a legal right to submit these photographs as evidence.

"Your Honor," I said, "these are not autopsy photographs. They're crucial to our case."

Just to make sure Judge Williams understood, I cited the Court of Appeals case of *People v. Pobiner*, which clearly showed that my photos could be admitted. In fact, I would have been derelict as a prosecutor if I hadn't asked for them to be entered.

"Ms. Fox," Judge Williams replied, "I find these photographs too graphic and therefore they are prejudicial and I am not going to allow them as evidence in *my* courtroom."

"With all due respect, there is no legal basis for your decision. In fact, your decision is contrary to the law. Photographs may only be excluded if their sole purpose is to arouse the emotions of the jury and prejudice the jury, and that is not the case here. This physical evidence simply corroborates the testimonial evidence."

If Judge Williams had been irritated before, now he was angry. "Don't lecture me on the law, young lady. I've made my ruling and I'm not changing it. Now let's proceed."

"But your ruling is wrong. This is basic stuff."

"Do you want me to hold you in contempt, Ms. Fox?" he snapped, his face starting to turn red. It seemed he was so keenly aware of his lack of experience that his ego demanded he substitute his power for his incompetence.

"No, I want you to follow the law."

For a moment, Judge Williams didn't speak and I thought, My God! He's going to do it! He's going to hold me in contempt! But the inexperienced jurist regained his composure and said, "My ruling stands. Period. No photos. Move on."

"Your Honor, I am at least entitled to mark them for identification subject to later connection."

Begrudgingly, he granted that rudimentary request.

As we returned to our respective seats, Kent whispered in a sarcastic voice, "You got some real winners as judges out here!" But I wasn't smiling. All I could think about was how ridiculous it was that a lawyer who didn't understand basic evidentiary procedures in a criminal courtroom had gotten himself elected as a judge in Westchester County. *Asshole.*

I put the graphic photos faceup on my desk, hoping jurors could see the top one from their seats. I returned to questioning Dr. Campbell.

"Doctor Campbell, please describe what you saw on Carmen Gonzales's back and buttocks when you examined her."

"This young woman had been struck multiple times with an object. In my opinion, she had been whipped repeatedly over a several-month period."

"I object," Kent said. "Doctor Campbell is not an expert on whipping."

"Overruled," Judge Williams said. "He's a forensic dermatologist. I imagine he knows a lot about whipping."

I could hear a few spectators giggling, which caused Judge Williams to look even more peeved at me.

"Besides scars caused by whipping," I said, "you testified there were penetration wounds, is that correct?"

"That's correct. She had some tiny puncture wounds. Based on my analysis, I determined she had been beaten with a leather belt. The distance between the cuts on her skin suggested a belt that was thirty-eight millimeters, which is slightly larger than one and half inches, a standard size for men's belts. The scars caused by puncture wounds that I observed were consistent with a belt buckle, which left an imprint that you could see with the naked eye."

"To a reasonable degree of medical certainty, how would you rate the scars that you observed?"

"Rate?" he replied. "I'm not certain what you mean."

"What I am asking is, how badly had Carmen Gonzales been beaten in comparison to other victims whom you've examined?"

"I've examined more than two hundred victims of whippings as a forensic dermatologist and the scars on this young woman are the worst I've seen. I would say—to a reasonable degree of medical certainty, based on my experience—that a doctor would have to have lived during the early eighteen hundreds when slavery was prevalent to have seen an equal amount of scarring."

I held up a clear plastic bag that contained a man's brown leather belt, marked the belt for identification, and announced that I wanted to enter it into evidence. Judge Williams approved and Kent didn't object, so I handed it to Dr. Campbell, who opened the bag and carefully examined the leather belt.

"Have you seen this belt before?" I asked him.

Dr. Campbell said yes and testified that based on tests in his lab the belt was consistent in size with the scars that he found on Carmen's back. I thanked him and sat down.

Much to my surprise, defense attorney Kent didn't spend much time cross-examining Dr. Campbell. He asked a few simple questions, including how many hundreds of thousands of one-and-a-half-inch belts were manufactured, who would have used the belt, and even assuming there was beating, was there any way to determine if it had been consensual.

My next witness was from the chief medical examiner's office and an expert in serology, or the type and characteristics of blood. He testified that he'd found blood traces on the belt, the one I'd introduced as evidence, that were consistent with Carmen Gonzales's blood type. Once again, Kent asked him only a few routine questions.

If you weren't an attorney, you might not have noticed. But I was getting the strange sense that Kent was merely going through the motions of putting on a defense. He certainly was not the aggressive defense attorney that I'd read about in the flattering *New York* magazine cover story.

Next up for the state was Detective O'Brien, who testified that he had searched Carlos Gonzales's bedroom and had found the belt, which was now in evidence, in the closet.

When it was Kent's turn to cross-examine, he asked O'Brien: "Was the belt hidden or could anyone have used it?"

"Anyone could have used it."

That was all Kent asked, and again, I wondered why he appeared to be pulling his punches.

Having introduced evidence that established Carmen had been whipped, that her scars had been caused by a belt, and that her blood had been found on a belt hanging in her father's closet, I turned to the rape charges.

Dr. Joyce Cox took the witness stand reluctantly, and when I turned my head and looked into the spectators' gallery, I recognized the two antiabortion protestors from outside her clinic. They had won seats in the courtroom and were taking notes.

Through a series of questions, I had Dr. Cox describe how Gonzales had brought Carmen into the clinic for a "procedure" and how he'd refused to leave her side even when she was under anesthetic.

"Did you see Carmen Gonzales's back or buttocks while she was in the clinic?" I asked.

"No, I did not. Mr. Gonzales said his daughter was very modest and she kept her upper body covered at all times during the procedure."

Kent took more time than he had earlier with my witnesses when he interrogated Dr. Cox. He began by asking her to state her credentials and her home address for the record. He knew what he was doing and so did she. In the gallery, the antiabortion couple were poised to jot down the address. I objected, stating that her business address should be sufficient. Judge "Amateur" actually agreed.

Kent walked Dr. Cox through each step of an abortion, at times clearly baiting her. Eventually, he got around to Carmen.

"Doctor Cox, you testified earlier that you've never had a father bring his daughter in for an abortion, is that correct?"

"What I said was that I had never had a father bring his daughter in for a procedure."

"Ah, yes, a procedure. Were you aware that Mr. Gonzales was a widower?"

"Yes, he mentioned that Carmen's stepmother had died recently and her own mother had died when giving birth to a son."

"Wouldn't that explain why he brought her into the clinic?"

I objected. "Calls for speculation."

Judge Williams agreed and sustained my objection.

"Did you ask him or did you know anything about his relationship with his daughter?" Kent asked.

"No, I did notice though that he never let her open her mouth."

"Are you saying he put a gag on her?"

Some spectators chuckled.

"No, I mean he did all the talking."

Kent said, "So as far as you know, Carmen Gonzales might have asked her father to go with her because she needed him there, isn't that correct? She might have asked him to speak for her because she was too shy and reserved to speak for herself, isn't that correct?"

"I object," I said. "Speculative."

"Sustained."

"I'll rephrase," Kent said. "Doctor Cox, did you ask Mr. Gonzales if his daughter had asked him to come with her?"

"No. All I can testify to is that he brought her there and did the talking."

A smiling Kent sat down.

My next two witnesses were two bartenders who worked in nightclubs where Carlos Gonzales had taken Carmen on "dates." Both testified that Carlos had introduced her as his girlfriend. Kent didn't bother cross-examining either man.

It was now time for me to call Carmen Gonzales.

33

T O GET A CONVICTION, JURORS HAD
to believe Carmen. I had Anne Marie take her shopping the day before the trial. She appeared in court
wearing a baggy, high-necked dress with long sleeves that completely concealed her curves. She wore flats. Style was imma-
terial. I wanted Carmen to look even younger than her sixteen
years. She wore no makeup and her hair was in a ponytail to
diminish her natural sexuality.

I couldn't have asked for a better performance. Carmen's
eyes filled with tears as she described in graphic terms how her
father had called her into his bedroom after her stepmother's
suicide and beaten her so viciously that she'd been forced to
shower to wash away the blood. She'd then described the multiple rapes.

In her childlike voice, she recounted how she'd closed her
eyes while her father was raping her and had thought about
her favorite children's book, *The Velveteen Rabbit*, by Margery
Williams.

"My stepmother used to read it to me."

"Why *The Velveteen Rabbit*?"

"Because in the story the stuffed rabbit thinks he is real but
he isn't. When my father was on top of me, I pretended I was
a doll and what was happening was not real. I know it sounds
dumb, but I would imagine it really wasn't happening. That he
was doing these things to a doll."

"Were you afraid of your father?"

"My stepbrother and stepsister were too young to know what was going on. But my brother, Hector, knew, only he was so terrified and only twelve years old so there was nothing he could do. He could hear me being beaten and screaming. Hector told me that he would cry and cover his head with his pillow. When my father was at work, we would talk about how wonderful it would be if he had died instead of our stepmother. Hector even talked about getting a shotgun and shooting him."

I gingerly asked Carmen to describe her trip to the clinic. "My father was so angry when he discovered I was pregnant. He wanted to kill the baby. He punched me several times in my stomach, and when that didn't work, he took me to that place for an abortion."

I kept her on the witness stand nearly two hours and felt confident that Carmen had come across as truthful.

Kent began his cross-examination by asking: "Did your father ever hit you when your stepmother was still alive?"

"Not with his belt. He spanked us, but he didn't whip me until after she died."

"Why didn't you tell anyone he was supposedly beating you?"

"My father said he would hurt my brother."

"Is it your testimony that you never told anyone that he was doing these terrible things to you over and over again, night after night?"

"I was afraid to."

"That's not what I asked," Kent said. "Did you tell anyone— even at school?"

"I told Detective O'Brien after my father was arrested and in jail, but that was it."

Kent said, "Judge, I'd like a sidebar."

Judge Williams waved us forward and Kent said in a low voice, "I would like you to declare a mistrial."

"Why?" the judge asked.

"This witness has just poisoned the jurors' minds by testifying that her father was arrested and in jail when she first contacted Detective O'Brien. They'll naturally conclude that my client has been charged with additional crimes."

I felt a sense of panic. Judge Williams had already ignored the law when he wouldn't let me introduce photos of Carmen's scars. I certainly didn't think there was a reversible error in what Carmen had just testified but I'd lost all confidence in his judgment. "Your Honor," I said, "Mr. Kent opened the door by asking the witness why she finally told O'Brien she was being molested. At best, this is a harmless error. For all the jury knows, the defendant could have been in jail for a traffic citation."

Judge Williams pondered for a moment and then said, "I'm not going to declare a mistrial. Let's keep going." I breathed a sigh of relief. At least Judge Williams had gotten this ruling right.

Back at the podium, a clearly disappointed Kent gave Carmen a stern look and said, "You just testified that you didn't tell anyone about this alleged abuse—except for Detective O'Brien. Are you aware that you can be charged with perjury if you lie on the witness stand?"

An instant look of fear swept across Carmen's face. "I didn't lie. I didn't tell anyone."

"Isn't it true that you told your deceased mother's best friend, Yolanda Torres?"

Carmen looked surprised and so did I. This was news to me and, I assumed, O'Brien.

"I forgot," Carmen said softly. "The first time it happened. The first time he raped me. I went to see Yolanda because I thought I could confide in her. I thought she would help me, but she didn't do nothing."

"She didn't believe you?"

"No, she was drunk and said it wasn't her problem." Looking up at Judge Williams, Carmen said, "I didn't mean to lie. I forgot. Honest."

"Okay," Kent said loudly, "let's get to the bottom of what really happened here. Are you now telling this court—and remember you can be charged with perjury for lying—that you had a conversation with Yolanda Torres about your father?"

"I went to see her. I asked for her help."

"So you were lying a minute ago?"

I said, "I object, asked and answered."

"Sustained. Move on, Mr. Kent."

But the damage was done. A badly ashamed Carmen was staring at the floor, embarrassed.

Kent said, "Did you and Yolanda Torres discuss extorting money from him?"

"I never said I wanted money. I wanted her to tell him to stop hurting me."

"Did you and Yolanda Torres ever discuss how you could get money from him by accusing him of rape?"

"No, no, no," Carmen said, beginning to panic. "You're twisting my words. I never said I wanted any money. I wanted him to leave me alone."

"You're not answering my question. Did either of you have a conversation about making your father pay you?"

Carmen was quiet for a moment. I knew her well enough to know that she was trying to choose her words carefully, but I suspected some jurors saw her hesitancy as a sign that she was being coy.

"I told her," she said, "that he was beating me with his belt and having sex with me. I asked her to make him stop. I never asked for any money."

"Did Yolanda Torres say to you, 'I'll make him pay?' or something like that?"

"I don't remember. I just remember she was drunk."

"You don't remember or you don't want to remember?"

"I object," I said. "He's badgering the witness."

Kent said, "I'll withdraw the question. Isn't it true that Yolanda Torres demanded sixty thousand dollars in cash from your father? Otherwise, she said the two of you would go to the police and accuse him of raping and beating you."

Carmen looked stunned. "No. I never asked her to say that. She was drunk. She said she would talk to him. I don't know what she said. I don't know anything about any money."

"So now you are changing your testimony once again. Now you're telling us that Yolanda Torres said she would talk to him and did agree to help you, is that correct?"

"Yes, I mean, no. She told me later that she'd talked to him. But she never told me about asking him for money."

"Ms. Gonzales," Kent said, sounding frustrated, "isn't it true that you and Torres dreamed up this entire plot because you wanted money to buy nice things—a car, clothes, jewelry?"

"I never did any of that."

"Just like you didn't tell anyone—except Detective O'Brien—about these alleged attacks," Kent said in a disgusted voice.

Before Carmen could reply, he said, "Isn't it true that we're here today because you and Yolanda Torres wanted sixty thousand dollars, and when he wouldn't pay you, you told Detective O'Brien that your father was whipping and raping you—just like the two of you had threatened?"

I started to object, but before I could, Carmen looked directly at Kent and said with chilling certainty, "We're here because my father raped me. He beat me with his belt. I don't know anything about money."

Kent sighed, suggesting that he didn't believe her and moved on.

"When did you become sexually active?"

"I object, Your Honor," I said. "This witness was raped by her father. Whether or not she was or is now sexually active has no bearing whatsoever on these charges."

I knew that when someone young is sexually abused, especially by a parent, a common reaction can be inappropriate sexual behavior. But Carmen's sex life, if any, was not relevant to the issue before the jury. The New York Rape Shield law guaranteed that.

"Overruled," Judge Williams said. "Answer the question, young lady."

Carmen glared at her father at the defense table. She understood where this was going and that he was the source. He responded with a smug smile.

"My father raped me," Carmen said. "That was my first sexual experience."

I thought, Good for you.

Kent said, "And when was your second sexual experience? And the others that followed?"

I objected, but Carmen answered over me, "That would have been when he raped me the second time and the third and fourth and fifth."

Kent had underestimated Carmen as a witness. Her answers were alarming.

Trying to regain control, Kent said, "Didn't your father catch you when you were thirteen with a boy in the house fondling your breasts?"

Rising, I said, "Your Honor, really. How is this relevant?"

Judge Williams said, "I'm inclined to agree. If you have a point, you need to make it."

"I do have a point," Kent said. "Ms. Gonzales, isn't it true that you recently had sexual intercourse with four different teenage boys on the same night in a car parked less than a block away from your house and that your father caught you?"

Holding up his notepad, Kent added: "If you'd like, I can read you their names."

I immediately objected. "What does this have to do with her being raped by her father?"

Surprisingly, Judge Williams agreed. "You don't have to answer that question. The jury will disregard the last question."

But from the looks on their faces, I knew Kent had gotten his point across. He was victimizing Carmen again. I looked at her sitting in the witness chair. She had started to tear up.

"Isn't it true," Kent asked, "that your father took you to the abortion clinic after one of your many boyfriends got you pregnant?"

Standing, I said, "Your Honor, if Mr. Kent wishes to give testimony, then perhaps he should be sworn in."

Carmen's voice broke in. "It was his baby. My father's. He raped me."

Kent cut her off. "Yes, yes, we've heard all that. But no one really can be sure of that."

"He's not letting her finish her answers," I argued.

"I'll move on, Your Honor."

Changing subjects, Kent asked, "Ms. Gonzales, have you ever cut yourself on purpose?"

"What?"

"Have you ever cut yourself with a knife or intentionally beaten yourself?"

"No."

With that, Kent said, "I'm done with this witness—for now."

During my cross-examination, I tried to repair the damage that Kent had caused. Through my questions, I clarified that Carmen had never asked Yolanda for money or to extort money from Carlos. I also got her to testify that she had not engaged with sex with anyone but her father until after her abortion.

Just the same, I knew Kent had planted seeds of doubt in jurors' minds.

I had to find a way to counter that—or we would lose.

34

AFTER CARMEN STEPPED DOWN, Judge Williams adjourned court for the day. I walked with her outside the courtroom and, with help from O'Brien, shielded her from a mob of reporters. While they were not going to print her name, that didn't mean they didn't want to pepper her with questions. When we were safely across the street and in my office at the Domestic Violence Unit, O'Brien left us to run an errand and I gave Carmen a big hug.

"You did a wonderful job, Carmen."

"He made me sound like a whore."

She began crying. The emotion poured out of her and I held her for several minutes as if she were my daughter.

"You're a beautiful young woman. I don't know how you survived what your father did to you. I can't imagine having my mother die in childbirth and having a stepmother who killed herself."

Carmen looked up at me through her tears and said, "My stepmother—Benita—she didn't kill herself. My father murdered her."

"What? The police report said she died from an overdose of cocaine."

"Benita never used drugs. He forced her to take it. She didn't kill herself. I was there. The night she died, my stepmom had fixed meatloaf for dinner and he threw his plate on the floor and yelled, 'This fucking shit again?' He grabbed her by the hair and we kids—we all ran into our rooms and hid. You could hear him whipping her with his belt and him say, 'I'm going to keep hitting you, you fucking bitch, until you start bleeding.'"

She sniffled and wiped her eyes. "My father came to my bedroom later that night. He woke me up and told me Benita was sick. I went with him into their bedroom and she was lying on the bed, not moving. He'd hurt her bad. He told me she needed a glass of milk from the kitchen, so I got her one and then he sent me back to bed. A few hours later, he woke me up again and said, 'Something's wrong with your stepmom.' He took me into the room and she was lying there. She was dead. He told me to get my brother and I did. He had us clean up the room. He told us to tell the police that we were a happy family and that's what we did when the police came. He told them she'd killed herself. But I never believed it. He did something to her."

I started to ask her why she'd never told anyone but stopped myself. Who would have believed her?

My office phone rang. It was O'Brien calling. "I just talked to Yolanda Torres. She denies ever trying to extort money from Carlos. Claims Kent made up the whole story about the sixty thousand dollars."

"What sort of witness would she make if I call her?"

"Awful. She said she's been sober for a month, but I smelled booze on her breath and she's in no shape to take on Kent."

"Then there's no way I can show the jury that Kent's theory was bullshit?"

"None that I can think of," O'Brien said.

35

I RESTED MY CASE THE NEXT MORNING.
It was now Kent's turn to mount a defense. His first
witness was Dr. Simon Rothman, a clinical psychiatrist
who specialized in treating adolescents. After establishing
Dr. Rothman's credentials, Kent asked him to describe a practice called "cutting."

"It's a form of self-injury we often see in young girls. Injur-
ing yourself on purpose by making scratches or cuts on your
body with a sharp object—enough to break the skin and make
it bleed."

"Why would someone cut themselves?"

"It's not only cutting; sometimes young girls burn themselves, too. It's hard to understand why people cut themselves
on purpose but we believe it's a way some people try to cope
with the pain of strong emotions, intense pressure, or upset-
ting relationship problems. They may be dealing with feelings
that seem too difficult to bear or a bad situation they think
they can't change."

"So someone who cuts herself could be seeking temporary
relief or a thrill or even seeking attention?"

"Not a thrill and certainly not for attention. Most cutters
hide their wounds from everyone. People don't usually intend
to hurt themselves permanently when they cut. And they
don't usually mean to keep cutting once they start. But both
can happen."

"Does cutting mean a person is trying to commit suicide?" Kent asked.

"No. Cutting is usually a person's attempt at feeling better, not ending it all. It's usually because of emotional problems and pain that lie behind their desire to self-harm, not the cutting itself, and it can become a habit-forming, compulsive behavior, meaning that the more a person does it, the more he or she feels the need to do it. The brain starts to connect the false sense of relief from bad feelings to the act of cutting and it actually craves this relief the next time tension builds."

"Is it possible a young woman might begin cutting herself if she suffered a traumatic loss—such as rejection by her own mother and then the suicide of her stepmother?" Kent asked.

"Those could be two very plausible reasons that might cause a young girl to begin harming herself."

"Doctor Rothman, you talked about cutting. Where do most girls cut themselves?"

"On their wrists, arms, legs, and bellies."

Satisfied, Kent said he had no more questions.

Standing, I said, "Your Honor, I move to have the doctor's testimony stricken from the record on the grounds that it is not relevant to this case. Carmen Gonzales denied ever cutting herself. Her cuts are on her back. The defense has not produced any evidence that shows Carmen is a cutter or that cutters somehow injure their backs."

"Of course Carmen Gonzales has denied she is a cutter," Kent responded. "What would you expect her to say?"

Judge Williams considered our argument—for about a half second—before announcing that he was leaving the testimony in. As before, it was clear to me that the judge had just issued another incorrect ruling. He was better at ignoring the law than he was at interpreting it.

Kent next called Amanda Jones. She was a painfully thin woman in her early twenties, dressed modestly in a long-sleeved blouse and knee-length skirt, who was a patient of Dr. Rothman's. He quickly led her through a series of questions that established she had started cutting herself at age thirteen after her mother had died. She'd initially claimed the family cat had scratched her when people noticed marks on her arms.

Once again, I sat there wondering how this woman's testimony was relevant. I kept waiting for Judge Williams to reach the same conclusion. But he sat there seemingly engrossed in what the witness was saying.

Kent said, "Ms. Jones, did you do most of your cutting on your arms?"

"Yes, and thighs."

"Please show the jurors your arms."

Now I was just plain angry. Judge Williams had kept me from introducing photographs of Carmen's back that clearly proved she had been beaten. But he was about to let this witness, who never should have been allowed to testify, whose case was not before this jury, reveal her cut arms for jurors. I started to object but suddenly stopped myself in midsentence.

Judge Williams noticed and said, "Ms. Fox, do you have something to say?" He told the witness to wait—since Amanda had started unbuttoning her shirtsleeves. Looking at me, he said, "Were you about to raise an objection?"

I wasn't certain if he was taunting me or if he had finally come to his senses and recognized that he was allowing testimony into this case that was so irrelevant that it violated fundamental criminal procedure.

Much to his surprise, I said, "No, Your Honor. I'm not going to object."

Looking confused, Judge Williams said, "Okay, then let's proceed."

Amanda Jones rolled up both of her sleeves and held up her forearms for the jurors to see. The skin from her wrists to her elbows was a railroad track of healed slices.

"And you did this to yourself, correct?" Kent asked.

"Yes. I realize it seems odd but it made me feel better when I cut myself."

I did not bother cross-examining her but it wasn't because I was ignoring what had just happened.

In fact, Neal Kent had just walked into my trap.

36

A FTER A SHORT BREAK, COURT RE-convened and the question on everyone's mind was: Would Kent put his client on the stand? The jurors would expect Gonzales to defend himself. But Kent also knew putting his client on the stand was risky. I was itching to grill him about the beatings, the rapes, dressing his daughter in her stepmother's clothing, taking his underage daughter into night-clubs, introducing her as his girlfriend.

Kent had turned the spotlight off Gonzales and shone it on Carmen. It was a classic defense strategy—put the victim on trial. He'd questioned her credibility. He'd suggested to jurors that Yolanda Torres had tried to blackmail his client. Kent had planted the seed that Carmen was promiscuous, hoping it would bear fruit in the jury deliberation room. Finally, he'd suggested that Carmen had beaten herself with her father's belt because she was secretly a cutter.

"The defense rests," Kent announced. Putting Gonzales on the stand was apparently not worth the risk.

Judge Williams asked Gonzales if he knew he had a consti-tutional right to testify. "Yes, Your Honor," Gonzales declared. It was the first time the jurors had heard him speak. In a very articulate and clear voice he stated, "I will not testify," and he added in an arrogant tone, "I'm innocent."

After dispensing with a few procedural matters, Judge Wil-liams asked if I intended to call any rebuttal witnesses.

"The state wishes to recall Carmen Gonzales."

All eyes turned to the back of the gallery when she entered for a second round. She was reminded that she was under oath and sat down. I'd prepared her during the short court break for what was about to happen. I'd also had her change her outfit. She was now wearing a blouse and skirt.

"Ms. Gonzales," I said, "please stand, remove your blouse, and show the jury your back."

"What?" Kent exclaimed. "I object."

"Wait just a minute," Judge Williams said. "Don't you do anything yet."

Looking angry, he called Kent and me to the bench.

"Ms. Fox, what makes you think I'm going to let you show this girl's scars to the jury after I've already ruled that you can't show them photographs of her back?"

"Your Honor," I said sweetly, "you allowed Amanda Jones to show the cuts on her arms. The defense wants jurors to believe my client is a cutter just like Amanda Jones. You allowed that evidence even though there was no proven connection. If you allowed Ms. Jones to show her cuts, then common sense, let alone legitimate legal rebuttal, demands that I be allowed to have Ms. Gonzales show the jurors the scars on her back for comparison."

"You can't have her topless in court," Kent said.

"She's not going to be topless," I replied. "She's wearing a bathing suit top under her blouse. No one will see anything you can't see at the beach."

"Your Honor, she's turning your court into a circus sideshow."

"What's good for the goose is good for the gander."

I had Judge Williams trapped and he knew it. His face turned scarlet. With an exasperated look, the novice jurist said, "Proceed."

Returning to the podium, I said, "Ms. Gonzales, the defense

has hypothesized that you used your father's belt to whip yourself because of a mental illness that makes it pleasurable for you to cut and harm yourself. Did you whip yourself?"

"No. My father whipped me."

"Please show us your back."

Carmen stood and removed her blouse. As she turned, a wave of revulsion swept across the jurors' faces. Carmen continued rotating so spectators could see the myriad scars on her back. Finally, she finished a full circle and Judge Williams got a good look.

I watched Kent. At that moment, I think he knew he'd lost the case. The only person who wasn't horrified by what we all saw was Carlos Gonzales, the man who'd beaten her. He showed not a shred of remorse.

I had no more questions for Carmen and Kent didn't, either. There were no surprises in either of our closing arguments. In fact, I felt that Kent's argument was rather flat. An hour later, the jurors returned with a verdict. On the twenty-two counts of rape in the first degree, sodomy, assault, and incest: Gonzales was found guilty. Guilty of every charge.

Feeling triumphant, I looked over at the defense table. Much to my surprise, neither Kent nor his client appeared upset. In fact, Carlos Gonzales was whispering to a smiling Kent. Gonzales was not acting like a defendant who'd just been found guilty of crimes that would send him to prison for a minimum of twenty-five years.

Something wasn't right. I could feel it. But I didn't have a clue what it could be.

37

"I'M TAKING YOU OUT TO LITTLE ITALY for a big Italian dinner," O'Brien announced as we exited the courtroom. "We can take Carmen and her kid brother, too. Hell, let's invite your mom to go with us."

"You paying?" I asked.

"I know a place run by an ex-cop in lower Manhattan. Hell, he won't charge any of us. That's the best part of the deal."

It sounded like a fun evening, but I wasn't sure I was up for it emotionally. Preparing for the trial had kept me so busy that I'd not had time to fixate on my breakup with Bob. But now that I had convicted Gonzales, I realized that I really didn't have anyone special in my life to share it with, except for my mother and colleagues. I'd not heard from Bob, and even if I had, I would not have responded. Still, I felt as if there were a hole in my heart.

"C'mon," O'Brien said. "Stop being so uptight!"

At that moment, Mom came up to us, and before I could say anything, O'Brien invited her to join us.

"It does sound like fun," Mom said. "And Dani could use a night out. Of course we'll go."

"Great. I not only get to celebrate with Ms. Fox, I get to buy her foxy mother dinner, too." I suddenly realized that O'Brien was actually flirting with my mom. "I can sure see where your daughter gets her looks."

I smiled. It felt good.

Mom said, "I'm calling a car service to drive us into Manhattan."

O'Brien said, "Great, I'll pick up Carmen and her brother. We'll all meet at the restaurant around eight o'clock."

I had never said I would go but neither O'Brien nor my mom was going to let me off the hook.

By the time I got home, fed Wilbur, showered, fixed my hair, and changed, the car service was out front with my mom sitting in the rear seat.

I opened a back door and slid in next to her. We hit gridlock as soon as we entered Manhattan. The driver turned down a side street and then another trying to avoid the traffic. Eventually, he stopped at a red light and I realized that we were approaching 26 Federal Plaza, where the FBI field office was located. From our vantage point, I could see the skyscraper's main entrance, and as I watched, I saw two men walk outside the building. They stopped to talk, then shook hands and went in different directions. One of them was walking directly toward our car, which had tinted windows. As I watched him stroll by only inches away, I realized why he looked familiar.

It was Neal Kent, the defense attorney I'd just defeated in court. As the car moved through the intersection, it caught up with the other man who had come from FBI headquarters. He was FBI Special Agent Jack Longhorn.

"Dani, you're way too thin. You need to eat a good meal tonight instead of always snacking on those darn Junior Mints," Mom said.

But I wasn't paying attention. I was wondering why Carlos Gonzales's defense attorney and Agent Longhorn had been chatting like long-lost friends outside the FBI field office.

"Dani," my mom said loudly. "We're at the restaurant. Now let's go inside and have a good time. I know you are thinking about Bob, but you've got to move on with your life."

I hadn't been thinking of Bob. I suddenly felt the same feeling in my gut that I had felt earlier in the courtroom when I had noticed that neither Kent nor Gonzales seemed upset by the verdict. There was something going on.

38

T HE FIRST THING I DID WHEN I GOT TO work the next morning was find FBI Special Agent Longhorn's business card. I dialed his private line at the New York Field Office and his secretary put me right through.

"I've been meaning to give you a ring-a-ding," Longhorn said, sounding pleased to hear from me. "Congratulations on convicting Carlos Gonzales."

"Thank you," I replied, sounding equally cheery. "Actually, he's why I'm calling. I'm curious about the status of your federal drug and racketeering charges against him."

"They're progressing, but you know, young lady, a watched pot never boils."

I thought, We're in New York. Let's drop the folksy sayings. "Agent Longhorn, I'd like to read your investigative files about him if you don't mind."

Longhorn didn't instantly answer, and when he did, his voice sounded less jovial. "Why are you still interested in Carlos Gonzales?"

"He might have committed other crimes in our county," I said without elaborating.

"Is that so? Sorry, Ms. Fox, but I can't simply let you rummage through our INTEL files. After all, they contain confidential information about our informants. However, I can send you our original indictment."

Longhorn wasn't offering me anything special. Indictments were public record as soon as they were unsealed.

"That's great," I said, feigning enthusiasm.

"I'll get that indictment out to you as fast as a jack rabbit being chased by a coyote."

Really, enough already.

"One more thing," I said. "Have you had many dealings with Neal Kent? The Manhattan attorney who represented Carlos Gonzales?"

"Is Kent any good?" Longhorn asked, avoiding my question. And then, before I could reply, he said, "I guess that boy's not too good of a lawyer since you whupped his derrière. Sorry, young lady, but I got to go, someone's hollering at me, but I'll send you our indictment. Thanks for calling."

Clearly, he'd avoided my question about whether he knew Kent, which made me even more suspicious.

PART FOUR

AGAINST
ALL ODDS

You have to learn the rules of the game.
And then you have to play better than anyone else.

—*ALBERT EINSTEIN*

39

WILL HARRIS HAD WRITTEN ABOUT the Gonzales trial every day in the *Daily* and had done a good job of reporting the facts. Because Gonzales was a White Plains resident and a former prominent Hispanic leader, I knew Harris was also keeping tabs on the federal charges that the FBI had filed against Gonzales. I decided to call Harris. He answered on the third ring with a rushed voice.

"It's Dani Fox. Got a minute?"

"For you always, but I'm on a deadline. If it's going to take more than a minute, we'll have to talk later."

"What do you know about the FBI's case against Carlos Gonzales?"

Harris, who had been typing in the background, suddenly stopped. My question had gotten his attention. "What's going on here?" he asked. "I'm the one who calls you for information, remember?"

"Turning tables."

"Shall I assume Special Agent Longhorn isn't being forthcoming?"

"I'd rather you didn't assume anything."

"Let me finish this deadline piece. Then we can meet for a drink. In fact, let's meet around six thirty tonight, or are you afraid to be seen with me in public?"

Actually, I was. I didn't want rumors circulating through

the courthouse that I was one of his sources, especially since Whitaker was paranoid about anyone in our office talking to the media except for him.

"Let's just chat on the phone after your deadline."

"Not if you want to discuss Carlos Gonzales. I'm only doing that in person. Look, I'll buy the drinks. How about Elaine's restaurant over on Huguenot Street in New Rochelle? That should be discreet enough for both of us."

I agreed reluctantly.

Elaine's Supper Club sounded elegant, exclusive. It wasn't. The brown shag carpeting needed to be replaced and the knotty pine paneling gave it a tired, outdated feel. I arrived early and immediately regretted it. Entering a bar alone is never a problem for a man. Everyone assumes a man is there to blow off steam after work. But if a woman walks in alone, men assume she's on the prowl, looking for zipless sex. Three men were sitting at the bar, four others crowded into a booth were talking loudly. I didn't recognize any of them. I checked my watch. It was 6:25. There was no sign of Harris.

A waitress, who looked as worn out as Elaine's and called me "hon," asked what I wanted to drink. I replied, a bit louder than necessary, that I was waiting for someone but would take Dr Pepper.

"We don't have soda pop," she answered.

I ordered a draft beer. As the waitress made her way to the bar, one of the men who'd been sitting there sauntered over.

"Be happy to buy you that beer. You want some company?"

"Someone's joining me."

Harris arrived ten minutes late. "Got a new editor and he's a ballbuster, urr, sorry." He sat across from me in the booth. "Never met an editor yet who didn't want to put his mark on a story. Most make it worse."

Harris surveyed our dismal surroundings. "I didn't realize this place had gotten so run-down." He noticed the men at the bar watching us. "I hope waiting hasn't been too tough on you."

"Only one barfly buzzed me," I replied. "He must have noticed my *bee-stung* lips."

"You liked my story—or are you being sarcastic? I also said you were a real looker."

The waitress interrupted us. She called Harris "hon," too. He ordered a draft.

"Actually, I was pretty proud of that bee-stung line. I got several comments from other reporters about how clever it was. And accurate."

"It's always difficult to read something someone writes about your appearance. I also have to be careful because of my boss."

"Say no more. Everyone knows Whitaker is a news whore."

"Those are your words, not mine." His comment reminded me that this wasn't a social meeting. "Before I say anything more," I said, "I want to make sure we understand the ground rules."

"Sure thing."

"This conversation has got to be completely off the record. Just you and me talking. I don't want to read my name in the paper tomorrow. Got that?"

"No problem," he said. "You got my word. I know you want to talk about Gonzales, but before we get into that, I'd like to ask you what you have heard about Paul Pisani."

"What about him?" I asked, taking a sip from my beer. "The truth is that I've not seen him lately. He's been strangely absent from the courthouse but I don't have a clue why."

"You really don't?"

"No, should I?"

Harris looked at me intently and said, "I got wind that Pisani knocked up some young intern at the courthouse. She's still in college and was working in the county clerk's office. Her parents are supposedly close friends with Whitaker. They all go to the same country club and they're threatening to go public."

Based on the shocked look on my face, Harris knew I was hearing this for the first time.

"All I can tell you is that Pisani has a reputation. This wouldn't be the first time that he's seduced some young girl and broken her heart. He's a sleazeball."

I suddenly realized that I could get into big trouble talking so frankly.

"We are off the record, right?" I asked.

He looked hurt. "When you told me about your cousin and her abusive husband, I promised I wouldn't put it in the paper. And I didn't, did I?"

"No, you didn't and I really appreciated that."

"I think I've proven you can trust me."

Without thinking, I reached over and gently touched his hand. "I do trust you, Will."

I suddenly realized what I had done and pulled back my hand.

He looked confused and I felt embarrassed. We both ignored what had just happened.

"Listen," I said, "because of this trial and the fact that I work across the street from the courthouse, I don't hear all the gossip that I used to hear. But I will ask around if you want me to, and if I learn that Pisani got someone pregnant, I'll tell you."

"Thanks." He took a drink of beer and asked, "Can I ask you why you would tell me about Pisani—I mean, I appreciate it, but I'm also a bit surprised."

"Because I think Paul Pisani abuses women just like the Rudy Hitchinses and Juan Lopezes of society. He just does it without using his fists. He's a predator."

A serious look washed over his face. "Unfortunately, that's not something that just men do."

I realized Harris knew a lot about me because he had interviewed me for the newspaper, but I didn't know much about him.

"Have you always wanted to be a journalist?" I asked. "You're so good at it."

He looked pleased and said, "Yes, I have. It's in my blood. My dad and mom ran a small-town paper, and when I was a kid, I used to help them. I did everything from taking ads to answering the phone to setting type for the printing press. I edited the college newspaper later. I've been a journalist nearly all of my life."

"You never thought about doing anything else?"

"Actually, I considered going to law school."

"What happened?"

"Life. Not too many people know it, but I'll tell you my sad story. When I was in college, I fell in love and got married. I knew it was a mistake as soon as I said 'I do.' But we'd been going out for several years. We were childhood sweethearts and I didn't want to hurt her. Because we were both in school, I couldn't afford law school after I graduated, so I went right to work for the *Daily* and I've been working here ever since."

"You're still married?" I asked.

"Oh, no, no, no. That only lasted a year after graduation. We ended up hurting each other because I didn't have the guts to say no when I knew in my heart that I should have. Her parents were angry and mine were disappointed, but it was the best thing for us."

"Where's she now?"

"Somewhere out west. Last I heard, she was getting married again. I don't usually tell people that I've been married. It makes them think of me as damaged goods, especially women. They think I'm unreliable."

He'd finished his beer and signaled our waitress to bring him another one. I was only half done with mine but she brought me another mug without me asking.

"How about you?" he asked. "Since we're being personal. You got a boyfriend?"

"I had one. But I'd rather not talk about it. He broke my heart."

Harris took his glass and clinked it against my mug.

"Here's to mending broken hearts."

I decided to change our conversation. "Do you know why the U.S. Attorney hasn't prosecuted Carlos Gonzales yet on the FBI's drug and racketeering case?"

Harris glanced around the room to see if anyone was within earshot. Satisfied they weren't, he said, "I'm not sure, but I have a theory. That's one reason I suggested we talk in person. I thought maybe we could exchange ideas."

"So let's hear it."

"This is what I know. Carlos Gonzales was running drugs out of his jewelry store in Manhattan. You already know that, too, but did you know that Gonzales might be part of a Colombian drug cartel? Agent Longhorn told me. Could be a big case. Headline-making stuff."

"You're talking about Manuel Rodriquez, right?" I replied.

A look of disappointment appeared on his face.

"Longhorn told me the same thing," I explained. "He asked me to keep it top secret."

"That's interesting. He acts like a dumb hillbilly, but he's slick."

"Is that it—what you wanted to tell me?" I asked. "That Gonzales might be part of this cartel?"

"No, that's not my theory. But knowing Longhorn told you fits into my hypothesis. I got a tip last week that two cops in Manhattan were going to plead guilty to taking bribes. My tipster said the cops had a connection to the Gonzales case, so I drove into the city and attended their hearing. Both cops worked in the thirty-fourth precinct and they both admitted to taking drug payoffs. They only made brief appearances in court and there was nothing in the record that identified who was paying them. I couldn't get anything out of their lawyers or the U.S. Attorney's office, which prosecuted them."

"That probably happens a lot to reporters."

"No, it doesn't. And that's what made me suspicious. The U.S. Attorney's office in the Southern District and the FBI love to go after local cops and local politicians. They always hold press conferences and make a big deal out of the arrests because it makes them look good and the locals look like amateurs. But that didn't happen in this case. Everything was hush-hush about these two cops."

"Did you find a connection with Carlos Gonzales?"

"Not at first. Then I realized the thirty-fourth precinct covers the neighborhood where Gonzales owned his jewelry store."

Harris again checked the room to see if anyone was listening. He was clearly enjoying sharing his theory. "That coincidence made me wonder if Gonzales had been paying those cops bribes. But no one would talk to me—until I tracked down one of the cops' wives."

"You talked to the guy's wife?"

"Yeah, I went to the cop's house and I told his wife that I wanted to hear her side of the story. That's what we always tell people—we want to hear their side. She tells me her husband had no choice but to plead guilty because the FBI had tape recordings of him."

"Wiretaps? A snitch?"

"I don't know. I'm not sure how they got them and neither was she, but they had cops talking on tape about payoffs. And that's not all the FBI had. She said Carlos Gonzales was going to testify against them."

"Wait, Gonzales was going to testify for the FBI?"

"That's what the cop's wife told me. She said he had cut some sort of sweetheart deal with the FBI."

"Holy shit! Carlos Gonzales working for the FBI—I can't believe it," I said.

"I couldn't either at first, but now I think he is. In fact, I'm sure of it. Here's what I think happened. Somehow, the FBI got a strong case against Gonzales. He's a smart operator and he realizes that he's not going to beat it. He's going to prison. So what does he do? He starts telling Longhorn all about Manuel Rodriquez and the Colombian cartel. Whether it's true or not doesn't matter because Longhorn wants it to be true. He wants Gonzales to be a big fish because it will impress everyone in Washington. But before Longhorn can impress his bosses, he's got to prove that Gonzales is a credible witness and not just blowing smoke. So Longhorn pressures Gonzales to demonstrate that he's part of the team and Gonzales shows that he is by agreeing to flip over and testify against his buddies in the thirty-fourth precinct. The FBI had all three of them. Gonzales was simply the first rat to run off the ship."

"If that's true, Longhorn is protecting Gonzales by keeping him locked up in jail. If he hits the street, he's a dead man, especially if he is linked to the Colombian cartel."

"That's right," he said, "but all I got is a theory right now because no one will talk to me about it."

Harris wet his lips and then said, "Everything was going swell for Mr. Gonzales and Agent Longhorn until you came along."

"Me?"

"That's right, you. You come charging in with rape, sodomy, and all these other horrific charges. Suddenly, Longhorn has a major public-relations problem. It's bad enough that he's cut some sort of deal with a drug dealer. But now he discovers Gonzales raped and sodomized his own kid and beat the hell out of her with a belt. Then Whitaker makes the case into a big New York story, making Carlos Gonzales page-one news. So Longhorn decides to keep Gonzales buried and drag out the Feds' case as long as possible until you and Whitaker and the media go away. That's why the U.S. Attorney is keeping quiet about those two dirty cops. Longhorn is waiting for the spotlight to fade. What I don't know is what the FBI offered Gonzales in return for him becoming a snitch."

"I'd sure like to know what Gonzales is getting, too—assuming your theory is true," I replied.

"Want to hear another theory I have?"

I nodded.

"I think the FBI got Neal Kent and his big-shot law firm to defend Gonzales. Gonzales's financial assets have been frozen and Kent never works for free, but for some strange reason, he suddenly agreed to represent Gonzales pro bono. Now that would be a real headline: 'FBI Gets Lawyer to Defend Child Abuser-Rapist.' Why? Because they could control him."

I didn't say anything to Harris, but that would explain why I saw Kent and Longhorn talking. Those sneaky bastards, I thought.

Given our respective jobs, I couldn't buy for him and I didn't want him buying for me. I pulled out a ten and told Will to do the same. That would be more than enough to cover our tab and give our "hon"-calling waitress a hefty tip.

I said, "I got a lot more out of this conversation than you did. Thanks for sharing your theory with me."

I stood up to leave.

"Dani," Harris said, "I mean, Ms. Fox. How about we grab some dinner? I'm really having a good time."

I considered it but said no. "I've enjoyed talking to you, too, but not tonight. Sorry, I got to get home."

He looked disappointed as I walked out of Elaine's.

When I got to my car, I took a deep breath. I liked Harris but it was too soon for me to even consider going out with someone new. I was still grieving for my lost relationship with Bob. But for the first time, I felt hopeful.

I was actually smiling when I arrived home and reached the front porch with my door key in hand.

Suddenly, I froze. My front door was ajar. Someone had broken the door frame, splintering the wood on both sides of the dead bolt. Staying on the porch, I peered inside. Although it was dark, I could see that my living room was in shambles. A knife had been taken to the upholstery of my chairs and couch. They were ruined. Family photographs on my mantel had been thrown on the floor. Lamps and chairs were over-turned. It looked as if someone had turned a bull loose inside.

I thought about Wilbur. Racing down the porch steps, I ran into the backyard to his pen.

"Wilbur!" I yelled. "Wilbur, where are you?"

I couldn't see him.

"Wilbur!" I screamed.

I heard a grunt and then saw his snout emerge from under his wooden trough.

"You're safe!" I declared as he ambled toward me, grunting for food. I threw open the pen's gate and rubbed behind his ears with my left hand.

Within minutes, after I called from a neighbor's house, two White Plains patrol cars and O'Brien's unmarked Ford arrived. O'Brien emerged from his vehicle holding a flashlight and his newly issued Glock nine-millimeter semiautomatic.

"You haven't gone inside, have you?" he demanded, rushing forward.

"No way."

One of the officers positioned himself at the back door while O'Brien and the other patrolman gingerly made their way through the front. I waited anxiously with Wilbur near one of the squad cars. A good ten minutes later, O'Brien emerged still holding the flashlight but with his handgun holstered.

"Whoever did this is gone, but he's done a lot of damage," he said. "I'm glad you were out when he came calling."

"Was it Juan Lopez?"

"Well, someone used a knife on your upholstery and your mattress and he likes beds, but I don't think we should rule out Rudy Hitchins, either. Or maybe it was someone who Carlos Gonzales called from jail. All of them are capable of this."

"Great," I said.

O'Brien looked at me and snapped, "Where's your snub nose?"

"In my purse," I replied. In my haste to check on Wilbur, I'd forgotten that I had it.

He shook his head. "Dani, you didn't buy it to carry around. Next time, you need to have that gun in your hands when I come running in here to save you."

"Next time?"

40

"**YOUR REPORTER PAL IS RIGHT!**" DE-
tective O'Brien declared the following afternoon
when he came storming into my office. "Dani,
Longhorn fucked us."

O'Brien plopped down in a chair across from my desk and
continued his rant. "I told you those FBI bastards couldn't be
trusted."

"What'd you learn?"

Like a hound on a fresh scene, O'Brien had hit the ground
running as soon as I'd told him the theory that Will Harris had
shared with me over beers.

"I went to see some pals of mine in Manhattan," O'Brien
said, "and then I telephoned a buddy who works in Washington at the FBI."

"Wait, you actually have a buddy who's an FBI agent?"

"He used to be a real cop like me. Anyway, what this reporter told you is pretty accurate. Gonzales is quietly helping
the FBI build cases against corrupt cops in the thirty-fourth
precinct and he's also spinning out tales about the Colombians. Longhorn's got him buried in jail—not because he's afraid
Gonzales is going to run away, but for his own protection."

"What's Longhorn giving him for his cooperation?"

O'Brien replied in a disgusted voice, "You ain't gonna like
this, Dani. Not one bit."

"Just tell me what the hell Gonzales is getting in return for helping the Feds!"

"A clean slate. A free ride. The FBI is going to put Gonzales into the Federal Witness Protection Program. He'll get a new name, new identity, and be relocated in a new town—all courtesy of the Justice Department. He'll simply disappear. There's a chance he might even get to take his youngest two kids with him."

"They can't do that! What about those federal drug-trafficking and racketeering charges?"

"Like they never happened."

"But he's facing twenty-five years in prison here in New York for what he did to Carmen. He's been convicted and that's a state sentence. The FBI can't just ignore that sentence."

O'Brien said, "Actually, Dani, they can. And they will. You're talking about the Justice Department. They can pull all the strings they have to. My friend tells me Longhorn has promised Gonzales that he'll never have to serve a single day in prison for the rapes and the beatings that he gave his daughter."

I suddenly realized that was why Gonzales and Neal Kent hadn't seemed that upset in the courtroom after the jury found him guilty. Gonzales had known all along he was going to get a free pass into witness protection.

"I'm going to Federal Plaza," I said. "I want Longhorn to tell me to my face that he's letting a sadistic rapist walk."

"I'll drive," O'Brien volunteered.

41

F BI SPECIAL AGENT JACK LONGHORN
kept us waiting for thirty minutes. We hadn't called
ahead, his secretary explained. But I suspected Longhorn
was trying to discover if we had uncovered his secret arrangement with Gonzales.

When we were finally escorted inside his office, we discovered Longhorn had called in reinforcements. There were two other men with him seated at a conference table.

"I'd like to introduce you," Longhorn said in a matter-of-fact voice, "to Special Agent Ronnie Cart, who works with me and Jason Gilbert, who's an assistant U.S. Attorney for the Southern District of New York."

They didn't offer to shake hands and neither did we. As soon as we were seated at the table, Longhorn asked: "What brings you here unannounced this afternoon?"

I got right to the point. "I'd like to know if you're putting Carlos Gonzales into the Federal Witness Protection Program."

I was watching Longhorn's eyes, searching for some sign of surprise, but his years of training as a bureaucrat had taught him how to maintain a poker face.

"I'm afraid I can't comment one way or another about that. While it's our policy to be as cooperative as possible with local law enforcement, I don't think our drug and racketeering charges fall under the purview of the Westchester County

District Attorney's Office. Or to be blunt, Ms. Fox, you don't have a dog in this fight."

I noticed Longhorn's FBI buddy was fighting back a grin.

Now I was really angry. "Carlos Gonzales raped and tortured his daughter. If you put him into the witness program, I'm sure the New York media would enjoy exposing how the FBI has relocated him into some unsuspecting community."

For the first time, I saw a glint of reaction in Longhorn's face. He put his hands on the conference table and tapped his fingers—as if he were playing a piano. When he stopped, he said in a voice edged with anger, "Ms. Fox, you might want to consider a few things before you say anything more. First, I don't take kindly to threats. Gonzales is in the MCC awaiting trial on federal drug and racketeering charges that are still pending. Nothing has been officially resolved in that criminal matter and I know of no paperwork that suggests Mr. Gonzales has entered into any sort of arrangement with the FBI or anyone else. If you were to make your charge in public, you'd be putting his life in grave jeopardy and possibly be opening yourself up to federal criminal charges."

"What charges?" I said.

"Oh, I'm sure we could find something," he replied coldly. He wasn't finished lecturing me. "Second, you need to do some homework when it comes to the Federal Witness Protection Program. Start with the names: Joseph 'the Animal' Barboza and Vincent Charles Teresa, aka 'Fat Vinnie.' Between them, those two boys killed more than twenty men and stole at least one hundred fifty million dollars. Yet Uncle Sam opened his arms and gave them big hugs when they decided to come over to our side. That's the sort of critter this program was created to protect. Third, let's presume, for the sake of argument, that you are correct. Let's say Gonzales is a candidate for the program. If he can give the government the names of his Colombian connections and their mules who may be bringing millions of dollars' worth of dope into Manhattan each year and ruining thousands of lives and also hand us the heads of dirty NYPD cops—then that's a pretty sweet deal for the government—no matter what harm he did to his daughter. It's called a greater good. And it's none of your goddamn business."

We locked eyes.

Assistant U.S. Attorney Gilbert chimed in, "Ms. Fox, I'm not certain how familiar you might be with the rules and regulations that govern the Federal Witness Protection Program, but logic would dictate that it would be against the federal government's best interest for anyone in the FBI or the Justice Department to comment about whether an individual is, or may be, a candidate for that program. If we were to tell you that Mr. Gonzales was a candidate, it would defeat the very purpose of it, wouldn't it? I'd also like to point out that it is against the law for anyone involved in law enforcement, and that includes state officials such as you, to reveal information about someone who has been admitted into the program. We recently prosecuted and convicted a U.S. Marshal in Newark who revealed the identity of a protected witness."

Longhorn wanted the last word. "I think this meeting is over. Good-bye, Ms. Fox."

I WAS SO FURIOUS during the return ride to White Plains that I could barely speak. Surprisingly, O'Brien was dead calm.

"You wanna stop for some beers?" he asked when we hit the White Plains city limits. "Hell, let's go over to O'Toole's and kick back."

"Why aren't you angry?"

"Dani, I've been around the track a long time and you've got to learn that sometimes you lose."

"Not this time, not after what he did to his daughter!"

In a concerned voice, O'Brien said, "Listen, what Longhorn said is true: the FBI and the Justice Department can come down on you with a hammer."

"You afraid of them?"

"Longhorn, as a man, no. He's a punk. But I am afraid of the power he wields. And I sure as hell don't want the IRS or any other federal agency breathing down my neck—and neither should you. I told you those Hoover boys couldn't be trusted and they play rough. They can destroy careers and lives. You need to be careful. We both do."

I asked O'Brien to drop me at my office, even though it was now dark and after hours. There was something that Longhorn had said that I had taken to heart. I didn't know much about the Federal Witness Protection Program, and if I was going to prevent the FBI from making Gonzales disappear, I needed to do some late-night homework.

42

W ITSEC, THE ACRONYM FOR THE
Witness Protection Security Program, more
commonly known as the federal witness protection program, had been around for only a few years. The government officially created it on October 15, 1970, when the
Organized Crime Control Act became law. Buried deep inside
that massive bill was a short section entitled "Title V: Protected
Facilities for Housing Government Witnesses, Section 901(a)"
that said the Justice Department could cut deals with criminals
and give them new identities in return for their testimony. Another part of that same crime bill created a program called the
Racketeer Influenced and Corrupt Organizations Act (RICO).
It allowed the Justice Department to prosecute the heads of
crime syndicates for crimes they ordered but were carried out
by their underlings. The Justice Department was now using
the two programs—WITSEC and RICO—to decimate the
mob. FBI agents would catch a mobster, threaten him with life
in prison, and then get him to "flip" and testify against his
bosses.

I dug in and soon made some interesting discoveries investigating WITSEC. While the FBI could submit "candidates,"
the bureau actually didn't have the authority to guarantee a
witness that he would be accepted into the program. That decision was made by the Office of Enforcement Operations, a
tiny office buried inside the bowels of the Justice Department.

However, the FBI was not actually in charge of protecting witnesses once they were accepted into the program. That job fell to the U.S. Marshals Service. The marshals, who could trace their history back to the old Wild West days, were responsible for hiding and giving witnesses new identities.

Those two discoveries were important because they meant Longhorn didn't really have final say over Carlos Gonzales's future. He had to get the Justice Department to approve Gonzales and the U.S. Marshals to accept him. Put simply, Longhorn could be overruled.

All I needed to do was find a reason for the government to overrule him.

It took me hours and hours of digging, but I finally found what I'd been so desperately searching for: a legal loophole. I immediately dialed O'Brien's home number. As it was ringing, I checked the clock on my office wall. Wow. It was 3:45 a.m. I'd completely lost track of time.

"Hello?" a sleepy woman's voice answered.

I wasn't expecting a woman to answer because O'Brien had told me he was twice divorced. I said, "I work with Detective O'Brien and need to speak to him. Did I dial the wrong number?"

No sooner had the words left my mouth than I realized that I knew that woman's voice, or I thought I had. She was someone I had heard repeatedly on the telephone.

There was a muffled sound, probably caused by her putting her hand over the receiver. The next sound I heard was O'Brien's gruff "Hello."

"Hey. I'm still at the office but I had to call. I think I found a way to beat Longhorn. But it's going to depend on those records you are getting for me."

Still half asleep, O'Brien said, "What records?"

I reminded him that he'd promised to pull the autopsy and investigative files about Benita Gonzales's alleged suicide.

"I need to read about that case as soon as possible to see if she was, indeed, murdered by Carlos Gonzales."

"Sure, okay, I'll bring them to you this morning. Now why don't you go to bed?" he said. "Get some sleep and stop calling me."

"One more thing," I said.

"What," he replied in an irritating voice. "It's three forty-five in the morning."

"Is the woman who answered the phone who I think it is? It sounded just like her."

When O'Brien slammed down the receiver, I knew that I had hit pay dirt. One mystery was solved. The reason why O'Brien knew what Whitaker's pollster was telling him before the elections and other tidbits about Whitaker's private conversations inside the D.A.'s office was because he was sleeping with Whitaker's uptight and formidable secretary. O'Brien was sleeping with Hillary Potts!

43

B Y THE TIME I GOT HOME AND GOT TO bed, it was time for me to head back to work. Anne Marie greeted me as soon as I stepped into the Domestic Violence Unit. "Have you heard what's happening at the courthouse?" she asked.

"What?"

"Paul Pisani just resigned. Rumors are flying but he supposedly got some young intern pregnant and Whitaker forced him to resign."

The moment I reached my desk, I dialed Will Harris at the *Daily*. I'd promised to call him and I also wanted to thank him for the other night when we'd met for beers.

"Will Harris."

"Hi. It's Dani."

"You okay?" he asked. "Our police reporter told me there'd been a break-in at your house. He saw it on the police logs. Vandalism."

"Yeah, I seem to make men angry," I said, making a stab at humor. "But that's not why I called. Pisani just resigned. Rumor is that he got a girl pregnant, just like you said the other night."

"Paul Pisani caught with his fly open. Our editor is going to love this. Thanks for the tip. And thanks, too, for chatting the other night. I'd like to do it again, if you want, when you're ready."

"Let me think about it."

"Here's something else to think about. I'm going to talk to that cop's wife again. I'll see if I can find out any more about the FBI and Gonzales. I'll let you know if I do."

I considered telling him about my showdown with FBI Agent Longhorn, but I decided against it. Instead, I said, "I hope you find Paul Pisani today. I'd like to hear him talk his way out of this one."

"Can I quote you on that?" Harris said, quickly adding, "I'm joking!"

I thought, Maybe I need to mail that coffee mug with the word PRICK on it to Pisani. He'd earned it.

An hour later, O'Brien arrived in my office with a painfully thin yellow folder that contained two documents and a half-dozen photographs of Carmen Gonzales's stepmother, Benita Gonzales. The first document was the police department's report.

According to it, White Plains officer Whitey McLean had arrived at the Gonzaleses' two-story house in an upscale White Plains neighborhood shortly after two a.m. after getting a call from the police dispatcher. Carlos Gonzales had called the dispatcher seven minutes earlier and reported that he'd found his wife, Benita, dead in the couple's bedroom. Officer McLean had gone directly to the bedroom where he'd observed a woman lying on the bed with whitish vomit next to her mouth on the sheet. During an interview, Gonzales told McLean that Benita had been suffering from severe depression brought on by the Christmas holidays. He said Benita frequently used cocaine to help lift her out of her dark moods. Officer McLean noted in his report that Gonzales had admitted that he and his wife had argued earlier in the evening about her erratic mood swings. Because of their quarrel, Carlos had gone to sleep on the living-room sofa. He'd awakened later and went upstairs and found her dead on their bed. Carlos told the officer that

Benita did not snort cocaine but took it orally. Because of the white vomit next to his wife's mouth, Gonzales suspected Benita had either accidentally or intentionally taken an overdose. Gonzales further admitted that they both used the drug recreationally.

In his report, Officer McLean noted that he'd briefly spoken to two of the Gonzaleses' four children, Carmen and Hector, and both had told him that the Gonzales family was a "happy" one. The officer further wrote that Carlos Gonzales did not have a criminal record and that there were no signs in the bedroom that suggested foul play.

Having read the police report, I turned to the medical examiner's findings. This was the sheet that I was most interested in. It was routine practice in White Plains for the medical examiner to examine a body when someone died at home. Dr. S. A. Swante, an assistant M.E., had performed the autopsy that same night and had noted in his paperwork that he'd found large amounts of ingested cocaine in Benita's bloodstream, more than enough to kill her. I turned to the portion of his findings that identified the chemical contents inside Benita's stomach. Dr. Swante had found undigested food, including milk. He performed a series of toxicology tests and determined that the milk in her stomach had contained cocaine. He concluded that Benita had ingested a lethal dose of cocaine with milk.

That was exactly what I needed to read!

Carmen had told me that her father had awakened her during the night and instructed her to take a glass of milk to her stepmother. That's how Carlos had poisoned his wife. She might have been suspicious if *he'd* offered her anything, but not if Carmen brought her a glass of milk. Gonzales had sent his unknowing daughter into that bedroom with the lethal dose. I had goose bumps.

I now had the two pieces of evidence that I needed to begin

building a circumstantial murder case—Carmen's testimony
and Dr. Swante's findings.

Dr. Swante listed the cause of death as a cocaine overdose,
but because Gonzales had told Officer McLean that Benita
often ingested cocaine to combat her dark mood swings, the
coroner had decided that the manner of her death had been
suicide, either accidental or intentional. Benita's remains had
been cremated the next morning.

There were several photographs in the file. A half-dozen
black-and-white eight-by-ten photos of Benita had been taken
during the autopsy by Dr. Swante, who had carefully photo-
graphed her entire body before starting to dissect it. The photos showed a nude attractive thirty-four-year-old woman on a
steel table. Someone had also tucked another snapshot into the
file that was markedly different from the others. It was a Polaroid that I assumed Officer McLean had been given as evidence on the night Benita had killed herself. There was no
mention in McLean's report that explained why he had collected the Polaroid, but I assumed it was for identification
purposes.

In this photo, a beaming Benita was shown perched on the
knee of a fat Santa Claus. She was holding a small child. I
flipped over the Polaroid and read: "Adolpho, age 2, and me.
12-22-74."

December 22 was the same day that Benita had been found
dead. I remembered that Carmen had said Benita had taken all
the children to a shopping mall earlier that afternoon. Carmen,
her brother, Hector, and their stepsiblings, Angel and Adolpho, had gone on that outing. Obviously, this Polaroid had
been snapped that afternoon at the mall with Santa Claus.

In the Santa picture, Benita certainly didn't appear depressed.
She was smiling, holding her youngest child, and wearing a red
wool holiday sweater that had a big reindeer pin on it. I recog-

nized the pin because it was one of those that had a blinking red light on Rudolph's nose.

I called O'Brien into my office and briefed him. "I think we have enough to charge Gonzales with murder," I said, "and we've got to do it before the FBI makes him disappear. Let's go talk to Whitaker."

A S O'BRIEN AND I WERE WALKING across the street from the Domestic Violence Unit's offices to the courthouse, the detective slowed his pace and gently touched my arm. "Counselor," he said in a whisper, "you and I got to talk." We stopped on the sidewalk.

"About what you said when you called me earlier this morning?"

"The loophole that I found in the witness protection program?" I replied.

"No, c'mon, stop being coy. About me and you know who?"

"Ms. Potts?"

He grimaced and looked to see if anyone walking past us had overheard me.

"Yeah, her and me. It's personal, as in nobody's business. Are we square on that?"

I ran my fingers across my mouth, saying, "My lips are sealed." But I couldn't help myself from adding, "You and Hillary Potts. Damn, O'Brien, you know I own you for life now, right?" I popped a mint into my mouth, laughed, and as I walked by him, added, "I love seeing a big man with a gun now beholden to the counselor he called kid."

He bit down so hard on his ever-present toothpick that it broke and had to be replaced.

When we arrived at the D.A.'s office, Miss Hillary Potts

was as icy to me as always. She looked at O'Brien without the slightest hint that the two were sleeping together. She informed us that D.A. Whitaker and Chief of Staff Steinberg were in a meeting and had left orders not to be disturbed.

I thought, *I bet they don't want to be disturbed because they are doing Paul Pisani damage control.* Women voters were not going to be happy when they heard what he had done.

"Something big must have happened, huh?" I asked Miss Potts, but she didn't bite.

O'Brien said, "Miss Potts, this is important. It's about a murder charge that we'd like to file."

She rose from her desk without giving the slightest hint that she was romantically involved with O'Brien and quietly slipped inside Whitaker's office. A few minutes later, she returned and announced, "He'll give you five minutes. That's it."

O'Brien and I hurried by her. Whitaker and Steinberg were sitting in the lounge area, so I took a seat in the leather chair next to Whitaker's and O'Brien sat on the couch beside Steinberg. I'd already decided to put all of my cards on the table, so I quickly told Whitaker and Steinberg about our trip to the FBI's field office and my confrontation with Special Agent Longhorn. I explained that Longhorn intended to put Gonzales into witness protection, which meant he wouldn't have to serve a single day in a New York prison for raping and beating Carmen. I told them about my private conversation with Carmen and how her father had awakened her during the night to take Benita a glass of milk. I showed Whitaker the autopsy report, having marked the section where Dr. Swante had concluded that Benita had died from a cocaine overdose with milk in her stomach. It all fit. He had caused her to drink the milk laced with cocaine. This was not a suicide. It was murder.

Whitaker listened closely without interrupting and then asked: "Miss Fox, didn't you just tell us that Agent Longhorn is putting Carlos Gonzales into WITSEC?"

"Yes, sir. That's his plan."

"If that's what he's doing, then why does any of this matter? What's the point of putting Gonzales on trial for murder if the FBI is going to give him a new identity and make him disappear into WITSEC?"

"I've found a legal loophole that we can use to stop Agent Longhorn."

All three of them—Whitaker, Steinberg, and O'Brien—gave me a curious look.

"Agent Longhorn," I said, "is correct about WITSEC giving cold-blooded killers a clean slate and a new identity in return for their cooperation. But in its entire history, the Justice Department has never allowed anyone to enter WITSEC and go into hiding if he murdered a civilian."

"I'm not following you," Steinberg said.

"Those hit men—Joe 'the Animal' Barboza and 'Fat Vinnie' Teresa—they murdered other mobsters. They killed their own criminal associates. But WITSEC doesn't take criminals who murder innocent civilians. An FBI agent tried last year to get a gangster into WITSEC who'd set off a bomb that killed a small child and his parents. Both the Justice Department and U.S. Marshals said no. They drafted a specific regulation about this very issue. Benita Gonzales wasn't a criminal, and if I can convict Carlos Gonzales of murdering her, he won't be eligible to go into WITSEC. He'll have to go to prison here in New York and there's nothing Agent Longhorn can do to stop that. That's my loophole."

"I'll be damned," Whitaker said. "It seems you've caught Agent Longhorn with his pants down."

"I'd like to charge Gonzales with murder two to get the maximum—twenty-five to life."

"You've done a good job," Whitaker said. "But I need to think about it."

"Actually," Steinberg said, "the timing of murder charges against Carlos Gonzales might be a smart idea right now."

I realized what Steinberg was hinting. Filing murder charges against Carlos Gonzales would make Paul Pisani's actions old news.

"Carlos Gonzales," I volunteered, "is a monster. I'm sure the residents in Westchester County—especially women voters—will be grateful when he is charged."

"And what about the FBI and Agent Longhorn?" Whitaker asked.

"Sir, the last time I checked, he wasn't a registered voter here."

45

T WO DAYS AFTER OUR MEETING, Whitaker announced during a press conference that a grand jury had indicted Carlos Gonzales.

Whitaker said a few words at the beginning of the press conference and then let me take over and answer questions. I'd never seen him share the spotlight. I assumed he was keeping a low profile because he didn't want reporters peppering him with questions about Pisani's sudden resignation. By now, everyone in the courthouse and Westchester political circles had heard about his womanizing.

Later that afternoon after I got off work, I drove to Mom's so we could watch the local news together.

"Look! Look!" Mom said when my face appeared on the newscast. "There you are and you look so beautiful!"

I must admit that I did look good. My Janis Joplin days were over. I'd dropped by Bergdorf Goodman and Jane Criswell had helped me pick out a new dress. It was a long-sleeved, knee-length Halston with shoulder pads that was identical to one that a model had worn in a *New York Times* full-page advertisement. The Halston was a rich royal blue with a jagged, pencil-thin black line that curled around the arms and ran up the dress's high-necked collar. Across my waist was an ink-colored belt. The accessories Jane selected for the Halston were button earrings in the same color blue as my dress. As always, I wore a thin gold ankle bracelet. The shoes were Charles Jourdan with spiked heels.

The clip lasted only a few minutes.

"I'm going to call O'Brien," I said.

"Did you see me?" I asked when he answered.

"Yeah, you done good."

"If I done so good, why do you sound like you're going to a funeral?"

"Dani, you just spit in the face of Special Agent Jack Longhorn and the FBI. He's not going to take this lying down. You'd better prepare yourself for a few surprises."

46

A FEW DAYS AFTER OUR NEWS CON-
ference, an extremely hostile Carlos Gonzales was
brought into the Westchester County Courthouse
before a scowling Judge Morano for arraignment. The confident smirk Gonzales had exhibited during his first trial was
gone. He glared at me, and for the first time I felt as if I was
seeing the hate that Carmen and Benita had witnessed when he
was wielding his leather belt.

A young attorney, whom I'd never met, stepped forward to
stand next to Gonzales at the defense table. He looked barely
out of law school. Not recognizing him, Judge Morano said,
"Introduce yourself and please tell me you're licensed to practice in the State of New York. I hate wasting time."

"Your Honor," the young man said.

As if on cue, the doors to the courtroom opened and Paul
Pisani waltzed through the spectators' gallery.

"I apologize, Judge Morano, for being a few minutes late,"
Pisani said. "I'll be representing Carlos Gonzales in this matter. This young man is an associate of mine."

I noticed the courtroom door open again. This time, it was
Special Agent Longhorn who slipped inside, taking a seat on a
back row. Longhorn was too slick to leave a trail but I could
feel his cold fingers pulling strings. In my gut, I knew he'd arranged for Pisani to defend Gonzales. The significance of this

moment was not lost on me. Longhorn was hoping "Mr. Invincible" would be able to stop me from convicting Gonzales of murder so that the FBI could continue using him as a snitch, rewarding him with a new identity and a clean start. The FBI was protecting a murderer for what Longhorn called "a greater good"—but in reality it was to gain a position he coveted.

So much for all of us being on the same side, I thought.

From the bench, Judge Morano said, "Welcome back, Mr. Pisani, although it's a bit odd to see you on the defense side of the courtroom."

"Judge," Pisani said with a big smile, "I go where the innocent are, whether they're victims of a crime or have been falsely accused of committing one. All I care about is justice."

Judge Morano smirked and I felt my stomach churn.

The routine hearing took less than five minutes. As he was being taken away in handcuffs, Gonzales shot me another menacing look. But Pisani was all chuckles and grins as he made his way toward me, pausing to speak to the court clerk and bailiff.

"I seem to remember," Pisani said, "that you learned how to prosecute a case by studying my old trials. Now you'll get to see me in action firsthand. There's a reason for that 'Mr. Invincible' moniker."

What a pompous ass, I thought. I retorted, "Right, and if Jesus Christ had five thousand dollars and you were practicing law, things would be a lot different today."

He laughed.

"What strings did Agent Longhorn pull to get you involved in this case? Did he promise you a new identity, too, or maybe a box of condoms?"

Pisani's demeanor and voice changed. I'd hit him hard and he didn't appreciate it. "I'm looking forward to trying this case against you, Ms. Fox. What did you call the courtroom when we first met—a 'moral battleground'—yes, those were your words, 'where a war was being waged between good and evil every day.' Are you ready for some moral combat, my dear?"

"Do you also remember," I replied, "that you called me naive when I said that good lawyers don't leave their conscience outside the courtroom door?"

I glanced over my shoulder at Agent Longhorn, who was still in the courtroom talking to some spectators whom I didn't recognize. I wasn't going to let the FBI's backdoor involvement in this case drop.

"Tell me, what's it like being in bed with Longhorn?" I immediately regretted my poor choice of words.

Leaning close, Pisani whispered, "I can't imagine it's nearly as much fun as being in bed with you, Ms. Fox. But I guess I'll have to settle for only fucking you in court."

He walked away.

The *Daily* published a page-one story the next morning written by Will Harris under the headline:

Feisty Female Prosecutor vs. Mr. Invincible

Former all-star prosecutor Paul Pisani, known as "Mr. Invincible" when he tried cases for the Westchester County District Attorney's Office, will be going toe-to-toe against Assistant District Attorney Dani Fox in a sensational murder trial of a White Plains man. The first female prosecutor in Westchester County, Fox has emerged as a fiery advocate for battered women.

The matchup is causing courthouse tongues to wag and promises to be one of the most bitterly fought trials in recent memory.

Pisani and Fox once played on the same team, but

Pisani abruptly resigned recently from the prosecutor's office without explanation to join the Manhattan law firm of Hart, Hammerman and Kent.

Known for his eloquence and ability to sway jurors, Pisani is defending Carlos Gonzales, 47, of White Plains, on murder charges. In the indictment, a grand jury charges him with poisoning his second wife, Benita Gonzales.

Pisani said yesterday that his client is innocent. He claimed Fox had a personal grudge against Gonzales because of an earlier case. In that highly publicized trial held in White Plains only a few weeks ago, Gonzales was convicted of twenty-two criminal counts related to incest, rape, sodomy and physical abuse of his teenage daughter. He was sentenced to twenty-five years in prison.

Gonzales also is awaiting trial in Manhattan on drug-trafficking and racketeering charges. A spokesman for the Justice Department said no trial date has been set for those federal charges.

In an interview, Pisani pointed out that the Westchester County Medical Examiner's office originally ruled that Benita Gonzales's death at the couple's home on Dec. 22, 1974, was a suicide. But after Gonzales was convicted of brutalizing his daughter, Fox decided to reopen the matter.

"My client didn't commit a murder," Pisani said. "Mr. Gonzales did something far worse in Westchester County—he irritated Dani Fox. This case has all the bearings of a personal vendetta being waged by a radical feminist."

When asked for a comment, Fox replied that she didn't care if "Paul Pisani, Mickey Mouse, Daffy Duck or Goofy defended Carlos Gonzales. We are

confident we can convince twelve Westchester men
and women beyond a reasonable doubt that he murdered Benita Gonzales."

This time, Will Harris had not described me as having *bee-
stung lips.*

47

A S I EXPECTED, PISANI PAPERED THE court with motions, the most important being a change of venue, claiming it would be impossible for his client to get a fair trial in Westchester County because of adverse publicity stemming from his earlier conviction. Miserable Morano rejected all of Pisani's requests.

Our trial began with voir dire—the questioning of jurors. Pisani asked potential jurors if they'd read about his client in the newspapers or heard about him on the radio or television. Anyone who had was excused. The ones we settled on all claimed that they'd never heard of Gonzales. The fact that the defendant had been convicted of raping and beating his daughter and still faced federal charges in Manhattan could not be mentioned in court. This trial was about one thing and one thing only: Had Gonzales murdered his wife?

What the jurors, judge, and public didn't know was that it was actually about much, much more. It was about Agent Longhorn and stopping Gonzales from walking out of this courtroom a completely free man with a new face.

After picking seven men and five women jurors, along with two male alternates, we were ready to begin. I spoke first, giving what had become my standard opening. I offered jurors a summary of what the state would prove with testimony and evidence and I used my brief remarks to introduce the major witnesses. While laying out the case, I couldn't come across as emotional because I knew it would be held against me. When men showed emotion it often was viewed as passion. When women showed emotion in court, jurors viewed it as weak or histrionic.

Pisani did not walk to the podium to deliver his opening statement. Rising from his chair at the defense table, he stood next to his seated client and said, "When Ms. Fox read the indictment, I saw the looks of horror on your faces. My client has been accused of a despicable crime. He's accused of sending his teenage daughter into a bedroom carrying a glass of milk tainted with cocaine in order to kill his wife, Benita Gonzales. That is absolutely horrific—if it were true." Reaching over, Pisani placed his hand on Gonzales's shoulder and said, "I just want you to know that those charges are not true. Mr. Gonzales did not murder his wife. He loved his wife. He loved her very much. Mr. Gonzales is not guilty. And that brings us to what Judge Morano has given each of us twenty minutes to talk about—getting blamed for something you didn't do."

Our moral combat had begun.

48

"DOCTOR SWANTE," I SAID, "DURING your autopsy of Benita Gonzales, were you able to determine a cause of death?"

"Yes, I determined that she had died from an overdose of cocaine."

I'd called the assistant medical examiner as one of my first witnesses because he was my weakest one. It was better to get him out of the way early on.

An immigrant from India, middle-aged and wearing thick glasses, Dr. Swante looked uncomfortable in the witness chair. I'd already gotten his original autopsy report admitted into evidence. In that report, he'd concluded that Benita's death had been an intentional or unintentional suicide. I'd also submitted his most recent "amended report," where he had decided that her death was, in fact, "suspicious." In addition to the autopsy report, I'd gotten the photographs of Benita that he'd taken during his examination admitted as evidence without Pisani objecting.

Knowing he was understandably uncomfortable, I asked, "Doctor Swante, what is a lethal dose of cocaine?"

"A lethal dose by mouth is estimated at from zero-point-five to one-point-three grams per day of cocaine."

"Were you able during your autopsy to determine how much cocaine Benita Gonzales had in her system when she died?"

"Yes. She had ingested a minimum of five grams of cocaine. That would have been nearly four times more cocaine in her system than what was required for it to be fatal."

For several minutes, I asked Dr. Swante technical questions about how he had been able to determine the amount of cocaine in her body. Next, I asked him if he knew how the drug had been introduced into her system.

"I concluded this woman ingested the cocaine orally. My toxicology report and examination showed both cocaine and milk in her stomach, which she apparently drank that night."

"Doctor, I am going to ask you a hypothetical question: If cocaine were mixed with milk, would the person drinking the milk know it?"

"Objection."

"Your Honor, the hypothetical is based on facts already in evidence."

"I am going to allow it."

"Depending on the amount of cocaine," Dr. Swante said, "it could be tasteless in milk."

"So, Doctor, based upon your toxicology and the milk and cocaine in her stomach, you can state with a reasonable degree of certainty that she ingested the cocaine orally?"

"I can state the cocaine was in the milk when she drank it that night."

Because this was such a critical point, I went through another long series of technical questions that clarified how the assistant M.E. had been able to determine that Benita had ingested milk tainted with cocaine. Having provided jurors with sufficient scientific evidence, I moved on.

"Doctor Swante, can you tell us what happens when someone orally ingests a lethal amount of cocaine?"

"Acute ingestion and intoxication causes intense agitation, convulsions, hypertension, rhythm disturbance, and coronary insufficiency."

"So is it your testimony that a person who ingests cocaine would not simply drift off to sleep?"

For the first time, he smiled and said, "No, no. Benita Gonzales did not have pleasant, sleepy dreams. After she ingested cocaine, her entire body would have begun shaking, she would have vomited and become agitated and ultimately suffered a heart attack. It would have been an extremely painful way to die."

"It would not be your first choice if you wished to commit suicide?"

"Oh my, no."

"How long does it take someone who has ingested cocaine for the drug to reach a life-threatening stage?" I asked.

"Two-thirds of deaths occur within five hours after taking an overdose. One-third within one hour after absorption of the drug, depending on whether it was snorted, injected, or ingested. Based on my experience, I estimate Benita Gonzales, given the amount of cocaine that I found in her system, probably took at least fifty-five minutes to die."

"Nearly an hour, and during this hour, she would have been in intense pain, is that correct?"

"Yes," Dr. Swante said. "She would have been vomiting and having convulsions."

"Would someone watching her realize that she was sick and needed immediate medical attention?"

"Objection," Pisani said. "Calls for speculation."

"Sustained."

I didn't care. Jurors had gotten my point. Benita Gonzales had spent at least an hour in that bedroom thrashing about and being physically ill. If she wasn't being murdered, why hadn't her husband driven her to a doctor?

I asked Dr. Swante if he had found any evidence during the autopsy that suggested Benita Gonzales frequently used cocaine or was an addict. Carlos Gonzales had told the police that Benita often used cocaine to lift her out of her depression, and I wanted to use Dr. Swante's testimony to show that the defendant was a liar.

"A person who regularly uses cocaine would suffer considerable tooth damage. The inside of an addict's teeth shows decay from continued contact with rocks of cocaine. This would be similar to decay caused by prolonged sucking on a lollipop. I found no evidence of such tooth decay when I examined her teeth. Nor did I find needle marks from frequent drug injections. There was no damage to the interior of her nose—her nostrils—that happens from prolonged snorting of the drug. In my medical opinion, this woman was not a frequent user of cocaine because there were absolutely no signs of frequent cocaine use."

We'd reached the point where I needed to tackle the toughest question: Why had Dr. Swante initially ruled her death a suicide?

"Is it still your opinion that this woman committed suicide either intentionally or inadvertently?"

Removing his glasses and rubbing his eyes, Dr. Swante replied, "When we collected the body, this woman's husband told the police that she had been deeply depressed for many days and often used cocaine to lift her spirits. The police officer at the scene told me there was no evidence that suggested foul play. I had several autopsies to perform that night. We were shorthanded because another examiner had called in sick. Based on what the husband and the police reported, I decided this woman had committed suicide. But I now believe this death should be identified as undetermined."

"Why would you change the manner of death from suicide to undetermined?"

"Because from rereading my notes and the autopsy report, I now believe this woman was not a frequent cocaine user, as was reported to us by her husband. I also find it suspicious that she died at home and was not taken to a hospital when she first began showing signs of distress. This is why I have changed my opinion and now believe the death was suspicious."

IT WAS NOW PISANI'S TURN to cross-examine. I was about to see "Mr. Invincible" at work.

"Doctor Swante, are you aware that cocaine is a drug that requires higher and higher doses in order for an addict to get high?"

"Yes, that is indeed a medical fact. It becomes necessary for addicts to increase their use to achieve the feelings of elation that they crave."

"That being the case, if Benita Gonzales frequently used cocaine, she would have to take higher and higher doses to get a feeling of relief, if she were depressed, isn't that accurate?"

"That is a lot of 'ifs' but I would agree. If she used cocaine regularly, she would require higher and higher doses to lift her spirits."

"Isn't it true, Doctor Swante, that some addicts have been known to take up to five grams per day of cocaine without going into convulsions or dying?"

"Yes, indeed that is true. But as I testified earlier, there were no telltale signs that this woman was a frequent user or had in any way built up a tolerance to cocaine."

"By no signs, you mean no needle marks? No damage to her nostrils from sniffing the drug and, I believe you said, no tooth decay—is that right?"

"Yes, that is correct."

"Tell me, Doctor Swante, if someone wanted to hide their addiction, couldn't they simply brush their teeth after they took the drug orally—wouldn't that prevent the cocaine from causing tooth damage?"

"I suppose it would."

"And if they gargled with mouthwash, would that prevent tooth decay?"

"Yes, I suppose it would, too."

"And mixing it with milk? Wouldn't that keep the cocaine from rotting someone's teeth?"

"Yes, if cocaine were taken orally with milk over and over again, I suspect there would be little or no signs of tooth decay."

"If that is the case, then you really can't tell us if Benita Gonzales was or wasn't a frequent user of cocaine, based solely on a lack of tooth decay, can you?"

Pisani had boxed Dr. Swante into a corner, and the physician looked even more uncomfortable than he had been. Dr. Swante said, "There are other indicators besides tooth decay that suggest this woman was not a frequent user of cocaine."

"Oh really, such as what?"

"Addicts typically show signs of anorexia—massive weight loss—and there were no such signs with this lady."

"You said 'typically' but not always, isn't that correct?"

"Yes, I assume there are addicts who do not show weight loss," Dr. Swante said. He was digging himself in deeper and deeper.

"So, Doctor Swante, is it now your testimony that Benita Gonzales could have been an addict?"

"I still believe it is unlikely this woman was a frequent user."

"But you didn't answer my question. You said it was unlikely but possible—especially if she mixed cocaine with milk and ate lots of food. Then she could have been a frequent user without showing any traditional signs, isn't that correct?"

"Yes, I will acknowledge that she could have been a frequent user."

In a matter of minutes, Pisani had gotten Dr. Swante to completely reverse his earlier testimony.

Continuing, Pisani said, "Isn't it true, Doctor, that cocaine addicts experience physical exhaustion and depression—wild mood swings. Don't they exhibit what is known as 'cocaine blues' for several weeks after they come down from a high?"

"I object," I said. "If Mr. Pisani wants to offer testimony, he needs to be sworn in."

"I'll rephrase my question. Isn't it true, to a reasonable degree of medical certainty, that persons who frequently use cocaine often show signs of erratic swings in their moods, including signs of severe depression?"

"Yes," Dr. Swante said. "That is an accurate statement. Studies have shown that frequent users of cocaine suffer feelings of hopelessness and depression."

"Now, Doctor, isn't it also true, to a reasonable degree of medical certainty, that feelings of hopelessness and depression can lead to suicide?"

"I object," I said. "Doctor Swante is a forensic pathologist, not a psychiatrist."

"Sustained."

Pisani looked at me, smiled smugly, and said, "As a forensic pathologist, is there any scientific test that you can perform during an autopsy that would reveal if someone was depressed or hopeless when they died?"

"There is no such medical test," Dr. Swante testified. "I have no idea about what this woman's state of mind was when she died. I can only tell you that she died from an overdose of cocaine."

"Just to be clear. You cannot tell us if this woman was depressed. Also, your testimony now is that there is a possibility that Benita Gonzales was a frequent user of cocaine. Is that correct, sir?"

"I object. He's already been asked and answered that question."

"Overruled. Answer the question."

"In my medical opinion, I do not believe this woman was a frequent user of cocaine, but I will admit once again that there is a possibility that she was one, and I do not know if she was depressed."

During the next several minutes, Pisani grilled Dr. Swante about various notes that he'd taken during the autopsy. The shrewd defense attorney wasn't as interested in what Dr. Swante had written as much as he wanted to point out to jurors that Dr. Swante had been rushed and not as thorough as he should have been.

"In retrospect," the witness acknowledged, "I should have taken more time with this autopsy."

Satisfied, Pisani said, "You originally ruled that Benita Gonzales had committed suicide either intentionally or unintentionally. You have just testified that you now believe her death was suspicious. What new scientific evidence changed your mind?"

"There was no new scientific evidence. I changed my mind when I reread my notes."

"Notes that you just admitted had been rushed and were somewhat incomplete, is that correct?"

Pisani had Dr. Swante squirming and he was not about to ease up. "Doctor Swante, who asked you to take a second look at your notes?"

"The D.A.'s office."

"Because Ms. Fox asked you—that's why, is that your answer? She told you that she wanted to charge my client so you changed your mind."

"No, there was no mention of criminal charges."

"Please, Doctor Swante, are you asking this jury to believe that Ms. Fox would ask you to take a second look at your notes if she didn't plan on charging my client? After all, she is in the business of prosecuting people, is she not? And you told her what she wanted to hear, is that correct?"

"She asked me to take a second look. I did and I changed my mind."

Pisani said in a voice edged with disgust, "You looked and changed your mind, I see. I have no more questions."

In my redirect, I attempted to undo the damage that Pisani had done to Dr. Swante's credibility. But I knew it was too late. He'd come across as being sloppy and weak-kneed. Still I wasn't too concerned, because I'd managed to get a key piece of evidence into the record.

Benita Gonzales had drunk milk laced with cocaine. Pisani had not disputed that. My next challenge would be proving who had put that fatal dose of cocaine into her drink.

49

A FTER DR. SWANTE STEPPED DOWN, Judge Morano adjourned court for the day. I needed to prepare for tomorrow, so I walked across the street to my office. Everyone had gone home, which guaranteed me solitude. Just before eight p.m., I ordered a pizza, and twenty minutes later, I heard someone knock on our locked front door. Grabbing my purse, I started down the hallway.

My office is in the far rear corner of our suite. The front of our building has plate-glass windows from the waist up because it was formerly a store. We'd painted the glass to protect the privacy of our clients, but our front door was clear glass.

I expected to see the pizza boy waiting, but when I approached the door, no one was there. He must have given up, I decided. I'd been so engrossed in my work, I wasn't certain how much time had passed between his first knock and me hearing him.

I reached to unlock the door, thinking I would go outside to see if the delivery guy was still lingering around with my dinner. As I began turning the dead bolt, a man leaped in front of the door. He was wearing a black ski mask and he grabbed the door from the outside and jerked on it with his right hand.

Startled, I stepped back and screamed. Although the dead bolt was half turned, it held. The man raised both of his arms above his head and I saw that he had been carrying a baseball bat in his left hand. He swung the wooden bat down into the glass door, sending cracks in a thousand different directions but not breaking through the thick pane. He raised it again.

I remembered the pistol in my purse this time, and I fumbled to find it. The instant I raised the .357 snub nose, the attacker ducked sideways out of my sight.

Although I was armed, I wasn't going to risk unlocking the door and going out after him. With my pistol still aimed at the shattered door, I moved to the reception desk and, with my left hand, picked up the telephone, dialing 911.

"This is Assistant District Attorney Dani Fox," I said breathlessly. "I'm at the Domestic Violence Unit office across from the courthouse and someone has just smashed our front door with a baseball bat! He still might be outside!"

The dispatcher told me to stay on the line, so I continued to stand next to the reception desk with my left hand holding the phone to my ear and my right hand on the .357's trigger. Within seconds, I heard the sound of a siren, and then the shape of a figure appeared at the door. Because of its shattered glass, I couldn't make out who was outside, so I kept my finger on the trigger, resisting the urge to fire blindly.

Flashing red lights suddenly appeared. Someone yelled, "Drop it! Hands in the air!"

"The police have a suspect," the dispatcher told me over the phone. Lowering my handgun, I unbolted the half-locked door and stepped gingerly into the evening air.

Two White Plains police officers had a young man in handcuffs. Next to him on the sidewalk was a pizza box. He was not wearing a black ski mask or dark clothing. By the time O'Brien arrived, the frightened pizza boy had been freed and the officers were checking the area for the masked attacker.

"Glad you found your gun?" O'Brien said.

"Glad I didn't just shoot the pizza guy."

Examining the cracked door, I said, "Do you think he was just some angry husband or was he trying to break in because he knew I was here?"

"Did he look familiar?"

How did I know? I wasn't used to seeing men in black ski masks. Besides, it had happened so fast. I had a new appreciation for witnesses when they were asked in court to describe their assailant.

"He was dressed in black—black boots, black jeans, black jacket, black gloves, and black ski mask with two holes for the eyes and one for his mouth. Obviously, that means he'd planned this beforehand and didn't just show up with a bat. But I have no idea if I've ever seen him before."

"Height, weight?"

"I remember the bat. It was a Louisville Slugger."

"Did he look like Rudy Hitchins or Juan Lopez?"

"I wish I knew. If it had been one of them, I would have shot first and asked questions later."

O'Brien said, "Just wondering. When Hitchins was in high school, he played a lot of ball. In fact, he was a pretty decent player. His pals used to call him Slugger."

50

D AY TWO OF THE MURDER TRIAL BE-
gan precisely at nine a.m. on a Thursday with me
calling my second witness, Benita's stepson, Hector.
I called him because I needed to get the Polaroid photograph
of Benita Gonzales on the day that she'd died introduced into
evidence.

As required by New York law, the photograph of Benita
holding little Adolpho while sitting on the lap of a shopping
mall Santa Claus had been shown to Paul Pisani during pretrial
discovery.

Hector had taken the snapshot with the family's Polaroid
camera, so I asked him if he had seen the picture, where it had
come from, and whether it was the photo that he had taken of
his deceased stepmother. He correctly identified it. Hector
further testified that he was familiar with the scene depicted in
the photograph and that it was a fair and accurate representa-
tion of his stepmother at the time taken. These were all procedural steps that I had to undertake in order to get the snapshot
admitted.

When I offered the photograph into evidence, Pisani asked
the court for a voir dire examination of the young photogra-
pher to determine if there were any inaccuracies or misleading
features in the photograph. Pisani interrogated Hector, asking
if the photo had been magnified or reduced in size to create a
distortion. To a casual observer, these questions might have

seemed redundant and a waste of the court's time. But Pisani was doing a thorough job. He asked Hector whether Benita had put on makeup or combed her hair or otherwise "freshened up" for the photograph. Hector replied that she had not—it was taken spontaneously after hours of shopping.

When he finished, Pisani objected to the photograph's introduction on the grounds of relevance. But the judge overruled him and the photograph was admitted.

I then asked Hector a few questions about the night that his stepmother had died but didn't keep him on the stand long and neither did Pisani. He had been only twelve years old at the time. When Hector stepped down, I suspected the jurors didn't have a clue why we had made such a fuss about the Polaroid.

But I knew the photo would be significant later in the trial when I planned to take full advantage of the photograph's hidden importance.

My next witness was Dr. Susan Treater, a New York psychiatrist with an impressive background. A petite woman in her early forties, Dr. Treater had worked at the Menninger Clinic in Topeka, Kansas, before moving east to join the psychiatric staff at Bellevue Hospital. I quickly established her as an expert witness in matters regarding suicide, which was her specialty.

"What is depression, Doctor Treater?"

"Depression is a serious mental disorder. Any of us can suffer from occasional depression, such as sad feelings that happen when a relative or pet dies. But ninety percent of people who die by suicide have clinical depression or another diagnosable mental illness, such as manic depression or schizophrenia. That is much different from feeling badly because your dog Rover died."

"What are the signs, typically, of clinical depression?"

"Clinical depression negatively affects how you feel, the

way you think, and how you act. Individuals with clinical depression are unable to function as they once did. Often they have lost interest in activities that were once enjoyable to them, and they feel sad and hopeless for extended periods of time. It can change your eating habits, how you think, your ability to work, and how you interact with people."

I showed Dr. Treater the autopsy report, amended report, autopsy photographs, and the Polaroid that I'd already gotten introduced as evidence. "Have you seen each of these exhibits before, Doctor?"

"Yes, at your request, I read the autopsy report and examined the photographs. In addition, I conducted interviews with Benita Gonzales's children, her mother, and several neighbors of the Gonzales family who knew Benita before she died, and I spoke to the police officers who responded to the emergency call."

"Does a person have to be depressed in order to commit suicide?"

"Ninety percent of people who die by their own hands have clinical depression or another diagnosable mental illness. Suicide is not something a person just wakes up and decides to do one day. There are warning signs."

"What are these signs?"

"Traditional warning signs would be talking and always thinking about death, trouble sleeping and eating, loss of interest in things that a person once cared about, making comments about being hopeless, helpless, or worthless. Visiting or calling people to say good-bye."

"For the record, Benita Gonzales was not your patient, correct?"

"That's true, I never met her."

"But you did study the exhibits that I just introduced, plus you interviewed her children and her neighbors. Did you interview the defendant, Carlos Gonzales?"

"No, he declined to talk to me."

"Did you reach any conclusions based on your research?"

Turning and looking squarely at the jurors, Dr. Treater said, "Because of Benita Gonzales's personal appearance, her actions immediately prior to her death, and interviews I conducted as a mental health professional, I do not believe this woman was clinically depressed or suicidal on the day she died."

PISANI ATTACKED QUICKLY. Because he knew it would be difficult to undermine the facts that I'd presented, he went after Dr. Treater's credibility.

"Doctor Treater, does the name Randy Rollins mean anything to you?"

The psychiatrist, who had been poised, suddenly looked uncomfortable. "Mr. Rollins was a hospital patient of mine. But I am not at liberty to discuss his case, given doctor and patient confidentiality laws."

Pisani smiled and I knew why. Lawyers love it when nonlawyers try to hide behind the law. "Doctor Treater, I have not asked you to divulge confidential information. I merely asked if you knew him. Now, isn't it true that his parents filed a multimillion-dollar lawsuit against you and the hospital?"

I objected, claiming that such questions were not relevant, but I knew Judge Morano would overrule me because Pisani had a perfect right to attack her credibility and professional qualifications through a prior malpractice case.

Still trying to outmaneuver Pisani, Dr. Treater said, "I was sued but confidentiality agreements were signed so I can't discuss it."

Pisani smirked and said, "Those confidentiality statements only apply to the settlement. I have a copy of the original lawsuit if you would like to refresh your memory." He lifted up a four-inch-thick file.

"That won't be necessary."

"Why did this young man's parents sue you?"

"Their son committed suicide after being discharged from the hospital."

"And who signed his discharge papers?"

"I did."

"When you signed them, did you believe he was suicidal?"

"I did not."

"Did his parents try to stop him from being discharged?"

"They did."

"How long was it between the time when you discharged him and the moment when he stuck a twelve-gauge shotgun into his mouth and pulled the trigger?"

Dr. Treater looked as if she was about to become teary eyed. "Fifty-five minutes."

"This young man killed himself fifty-five minutes after you declared, in your professional opinion as an expert on depression and suicide, that it was safe for him to be discharged from the hospital because he was not depressed and not suicidal, even though his own parents said otherwise?"

"Yes," she said in a sad voice.

"Based on what you've just testified, I would conclude one or two things happened—either it is impossible to predict when someone is going to commit suicide or you are not very good at your job, wouldn't you agree?"

"He was not showing any traditional signs or symptoms of clinical depression and suicidal thinking when I discharged him."

"For the record, this young man was someone who you were treating and personally knew. You never met Benita Gonzales. And you were wrong about him, isn't that right?"

"Yes."

———

MY NEXT WITNESS was White Plains police officer Whitey McLean, the first patrolman to respond to the Gonzaleses' house. After I asked him some rudimentary questions, I had his official police report introduced as evidence. I then asked Officer McLean, "What was the defendant's demeanor when you got to his house?"

"To me, he didn't seem that upset. He seemed more nervous. I got the feeling he wanted us to hurry up and get her body out of there. He didn't want to leave his kids alone with us, which, at the time, I assumed was because he was protective of them."

I asked him if he had found an empty drinking glass in the room or any evidence of illegal drugs.

"No, the place was really tidy."

Had he questioned any of the Gonzaleses' children? He said that he'd talked to both Carmen and her brother, Hector.

"What did they tell you?"

"They said they had a good family."

"Was the defendant in the room when you questioned them?"

"Yeah, that was probably a mistake in retrospect, but he was standing right there with them. At the time, I didn't think anything of it."

"Did the defendant mention how his wife used cocaine?"

"Yeah, I remember exactly what he said because I thought most people snorted it or shot it in their veins, but he said she used to chew it like candy, like rock candy. That was a new one to me."

I considered that a crucial bit of testimony based on Dr. Swante's earlier testimony about a lack of any tooth decay in Benita's mouth. Satisfied, I sat down.

Pisani began his cross-examination by asking Officer McLean if either Carmen or Hector had seemed afraid of their father.

"The kids had both been crying, which was understandable, but no. I didn't think either of them was afraid of him. I asked them if they wanted to speak to a counselor and they both said no."

"If you would have suspected foul play, you would have called for a homicide detective, isn't that right?"

"Normally, one of them would have come that night. That's routine, but we were told it was a suicide and we had a bunch of other calls. There was a couple of shootings, so when the M.E. showed up, the body got taken away and, well, that was the end of it. I filed my report and the case was closed."

"The case was closed because no one suspected anything improper had happened, isn't that true?"

"Yeah, I figured the woman had killed herself."

"Did you ask Mr. Gonzales if his wife ever took cocaine some other way besides orally? For instance, in her milk at night to help her sleep?"

"No," Officer McLean said. "He told me that she used cocaine because she was depressed. That she sucked on it. That was all he said."

After Officer McLean stepped down, Judge Morano adjourned court for lunch. I noticed Agent Longhorn standing at the courtroom's double wooden doors. When Pisani reached him, they walked out together.

I hoped they both choked on a pastrami sandwich.

51

I BEGAN THE AFTERNOON WITH YOLANDA Torres. After the allegations in the rape trial, I didn't want to call her. O'Brien had interviewed her during Gonzales's first trial, but I wasn't comfortable calling her. Even now, I knew it was risky putting her on the stand but she had called O'Brien and shared a story with him that could help our case. Just to make sure that she'd show up sober, I had O'Brien pick her up that morning, buy her breakfast, and babysit her until I called her as a witness.

Yolanda Torres was from Guatemala. She had dark skin and long black hair that she'd woven into a single braid and coiled around the back of her head. She took the witness stand wearing a plain black cotton skirt and a pink, long-sleeved blouse. Both were well worn but, I suspected, were the best clothes that she owned. She was currently unemployed but worked sporadically cleaning houses.

I asked her a series of questions that established how she knew the defendant.

"Did you know Benita Gonzales?"

"Yes, I knew her for years, but then we lost touch. She called me one day and asked if I wanted to see Carmen and Hector. She brought them to the park and I saw them there. I hadn't seen them since their mother died and now they are much older."

"Why didn't you stay in touch with them?"

"I was afraid—of Carlos. He didn't want me near them. He'd never liked me because I didn't like how he had treated Rosita, who I loved like a sister. I was devastated when she died during childbirth."

"After Carlos Gonzales remarried and his second wife, Benita Gonzales, was found dead, did you have a conversation with him?"

We were moving into dangerous territory. I had warned Yolanda that she could not tell the jury about the earlier trial. She could not tell them that Carlos Gonzales had begun raping and abusing Carmen. She could not say that Gonzales had moved Carmen into his bedroom. Yolanda was supposed to keep her testimony short and answer only my direct questions. I didn't want Pisani asking for a mistrial because I had tainted the jurors.

"Yes," Yolanda said, "I spoke to Carlos about Carmen. She used to come see me after her own mother died because I was like another mother to her. Then, when her father remarried, she stopped coming. She liked her stepmother, Benita. They became close. Carmen was upset when she died. She had lost her own mother, Rosita, and now her stepmother, too. She asked me to talk to her father. She said the two of them were having *serious problems*. I went to see him and he got very angry and threatened me."

"The defendant threatened you? What did he say?"

"He told me to leave him and his family alone. He said, 'I killed that bitch I was married to and I will kill you, too.'"

"Do you know whom he was referring to when he said 'that bitch'?"

"He meant Benita, his second wife. He told me he'd poisoned her. He said the cops were stupid and believed she'd taken an overdose, but he'd killed her."

"Did you believe him?"

"I sure did."

"Did he tell you why he killed her?"

"He said she was going to call the cops on him and divorce him. He said it was because he was selling cocaine and Benita didn't want any part of it."

I had just established a motive for Gonzales wanting his wife dead. I'd also managed to get into the transcript that Gonzales was selling cocaine. As I sat down, I said a silent prayer. Yolanda Torres was going to need all the help she could get to withstand the harangue that was coming.

"ARE YOU AN ALCOHOLIC?" Pisani asked.

"I drink too much sometimes," Yolanda replied.

"Have you ever been arrested for being drunk in public?"

Yolanda looked at me for help, but Pisani was well within his rights. I knew the judge would override my objection.

"Yes, the police arrested me a few times."

Picking up a sheet of paper, Pisani said, "How many times in the past, say, four years, have you been arrested on disorderly conduct charges?"

"I don't understand the question."

In a belittling voice, Pisani said, "How many times have you been arrested by the *policia* for being *desordenado*?"

"*Quizás cuatro veces.*"

Judge Morano said, "You need to answer in English."

"Maybe four times."

"Four times?" Pisani said. "According to these police reports, the correct number would be more than ten times. Isn't that true?"

"If you say."

"Who is Romero Sanchez?"

I objected. "This witness is not on trial here. How is this relevant to her testimony?"

"It goes to her credibility," Pisani said.

"Objection overruled. Answer the question."

"We lived together for a while—him and me."

"Did you go to the police and swear out a complaint against Mr. Sanchez at one point?"

"Yes."

"What did you tell the police?"

"He was beating me. I told them to arrest him."

"Did you tell them anything else?"

"I said he had threatened to kill me."

"What happened after the police arrested him?"

"I told the police to let him go."

"Can you elaborate on that, please?"

Yolanda looked confused, so Pisani said, "I want you to tell us exactly what happened. Why did the police let Mr. Sanchez go?"

"Because I told the police I'd lied."

"About Mr. Sanchez hitting you? Or him threatening to kill you?"

"Both," she said softly.

"Romero Sanchez had never hit you, had he?"

"No."

"He'd never threatened to kill you, had he?"

"No."

"But you told the police that he had, is that correct?"

"Yes."

"You lied. When was the last time you had a drink of alcohol?"

"Do you mean beer?"

"Any alcoholic beverage."

"I had a few beers last night to calm my nerves."

"How many beers is a few? Give us a number."

"Two six-packs."

Pisani had effectively put Yolanda on trial. She came across as a drunk and a liar.

I STILL HAD TIME that afternoon for one more witness. I called Maria Hildago, the former stripper who'd been Gonzales's last girlfriend before he'd been arrested by the FBI. I watched a scowl appear on Judge Morano's face as Miss Hildago walked forward. She was wearing shiny knee-high, white patent-leather boots and a red patent-leather micro skirt. She was at least an E cup and both of her breasts were prominently on display in a V-neck madras blouse that matched a two-inch-wide headband that was holding her shoulder-length platinum-colored hair in place. She'd chosen silver lip gloss and eye shadow for her appearance.

Judge Morano called us to the bench. Covering his microphone, he said, "Miss Fox, your witness is not dressed appropriately to appear in my courtroom. This is not a disco or a bordello."

"Your Honor, I can't control what a witness chooses to wear to court."

"Well, you'd better if you wish for her to testify. We'll take a half-hour break."

A half hour was not enough time for Hildago to get to her Yonkers apartment and back to court, so I hustled her into a nearby JCPenney clothing store. She was not happy when court reconvened and she appeared in a modest three-button jacket and skirt. Out of spite, she kept her white patent-leather knee-high boots.

Judge Morano looked pleased.

I asked the witness if she knew Gonzales, how they'd met, and a quick series of other background questions. She had been dancing at a gentlemen's club and he'd bought her several drinks, she testified. A week later, when she needed a place to stay, Gonzales had taken her into his house and his bed.

I asked, "Did you ever have a conversation with the defendant about the death of his second wife, Benita?"

"Yeah, sure did. He said she'd OD'd on cocaine."

"By OD, you mean overdosed?"

"Well, of course, darling. We were in his bedroom and he asked me if I wanted to do some coke and I said—"

Judge Morano interrupted her.

"Miss," he said sternly, "do you realize you are under oath in a court of law?"

She looked up at him and said, "Well, of course I do."

"Do you understand that if you admit here that you engaged in a crime, you can be prosecuted? You are also entitled to plead the Fifth and not incriminate yourself."

A look of surprise came over her face. "Oh, you mean doing coke?"

"That's correct."

"Your Honor," I said, "Miss Hildago has not testified that she used cocaine. She said the defendant offered her the drug."

Judge Morano shot me an irritated look and said, "I know what she said."

"Perhaps I should rephrase my question."

"Go ahead," he said, "but the witness has been warned."

"What, if anything, did the defendant tell you about his wife's death?"

In a cautious voice, Hildago said, "He told me his wife took five grams of coke that was dissolved in milk and drank it. He said it killed her."

"He told you that she had put cocaine into her milk, dissolved it, and drank it voluntarily?"

"Yes, that's what he said. I looked at him and said, 'No wonder she's dead. She either wanted to get really high or she was really stupid.' And then he got this funny look on his face and he said, 'She never used drugs. She didn't know I put it there.' "

"So he told you that he was the one who actually put the cocaine in the milk?"

"That's right and it really upset me because that's a lot of coke for a newbie and I thought to myself, 'What the hell?' He realized I was upset and he said, 'It was an accident.' But I thought, 'How could it be an accident?' I mean, if you got five grams and a glass of milk and you put that in the glass and you give it to someone, what do you expect is going to happen?"

"Did you ask him why he put it in her milk?"

"No, that's all he said and I let it drop because we were sorta busy, if you know what I mean."

"Miss Hildago, how are you employed?" Pisani began.

"I'm a professional dancer in gentlemen's clubs."

"You testified that you moved into Mr. Gonzales's house. Did he ever mistreat you?"

"You mean like hit me? Heck no! I wouldn't stand for that."

"Were you afraid of him?"

"Heck no. He treated me real nice."

"Did you meet his children?"

"Yep, all four of them, but I didn't really spend any time with them. I'm not a real kid person."

"You testified that the defendant told you that he had put cocaine in milk for his wife, is that your testimony?"

"That's what he said."

"What was your condition when he told you this?"

Hildago glanced at the judge nervously.

"I'm not saying anyone took cocaine but I am saying we both were feeling, well, very happy."

"Were you high?"

Again she looked at the judge and then said, "Yes."

"When you get high, do you hallucinate?"

"Yes, oh, I have hallucinated, I don't think that's a crime."

"Did you hallucinate that night?"

She pondered the question and said, "As a matter of fact, I did."

"And when you had this conversation about his wife and the cocaine, were you hallucinating?"

"I don't think so. But maybe I was, like I said, we was busy."

"Busy?"

"We was having intimate male and female relations."

JUDGE MORANO ADJOURNED court for the day. As I was collecting my papers, O'Brien came up to me.

"Whew!" he said, letting out a sad sigh. "Rough day, Counselor. You putting Carmen on tomorrow?"

I nodded. Carmen Gonzales would probably be my last and most important witness.

"I hope she does as well at this trial as she did at the first one because we need help here. No offense, but Pisani is knocking the you know what out of our witnesses," O'Brien said.

I should have been furious with him. But I knew he was right.

52

HAVING CARMEN TESTIFY AGAINST her father the first time had been an ordeal. I thought of the way he'd glared at her when she'd testified in the first trial. I thought of the power and control over her that he represented. I could only imagine her terror. When I had told Carmen that her father might disappear into the Federal Witness Protection Program, the look on her face had been one of true horror. She knew that if he remained free, she would always be looking over her shoulder and live in fear of retribution. His freedom would mean constant captivity for her.

Friday morning would be hell for her.

Carmen Gonzales did not look at her father when she took the witness stand. I asked her to recall the day when her stepmother died.

"My stepmom took us to the shopping mall. It was almost Christmas and my stepmom had given me some money to buy presents for my brother and stepsister and stepbrother and my dad and her. We were happy when we got home. We put extra decorations on the tree that we'd bought and I told my stepmom that I loved Christmas. She told me, 'Carmen, I'm going to leave the lights on the tree burning all night from now until Christmas because I know you kids love seeing them.' And then my dad came in."

"What happened next?"

"My stepmom had made meatloaf for dinner. My dad took a taste of it and got really angry. He stood up and threw his plate on the floor and said, 'How dare you serve me this fucking garbage!' All of us kids ran up to our rooms to hide because we knew there was going to be a fight."

"They were going to argue?"

"No, my dad was going to beat her. That's what he did when he got angry. I heard them go into the bedroom and my father say, 'I'm going to keep hitting you, you fucking bitch, until you start bleeding.' I could hear her screaming. It was awful."

"Did anything else happen that night?"

"I was woke up by my father after midnight. He came into my bedroom and told me to get up because my stepmom was sick. He said I needed to get her a glass of milk in the kitchen. He said he'd poured one for her but she was angry at him, so he wanted me to get it from the kitchen and take it to her. I went downstairs and got the glass of milk on the counter and took it to my stepmom."

"Did she drink it?"

"When I went into her room she was crying. She took the milk and drank a sip of it and thanked me and told me to go back to bed."

"Did you tell her that your father had told you to bring her the milk?"

"No. I went back to bed, and about two hours later, he woke me up again and said, 'Something's wrong with your stepmom.' I went into the bedroom and she was lying on the bed and not moving; there was vomit near her mouth. It was whitish, not yellow like most vomit. And there was white powder all over the night table. The covers on the bed were all messed up, too."

"What was your father's state of emotion?"

"He was calm. He told me to get my brother, so I ran down

to his bedroom and got Hector. My father told us to clean up the room. He told me to sweep up all the white powder on the nightstand and floor. He told me to take the glass of milk to the kitchen and wash it out. When Hector and I were finished, he told us he was going to call the police, and if they asked any questions, he told us to tell them that we were a happy family and that my stepmom had been depressed and sad because it was the holidays."

"Is that what you did?"

"Yes, I was fourteen and I was afraid of him. I told the policeman that my stepmom had been sad and we were a happy family."

"Did your father ever tell you how your stepmother died?"

"After my stepmom's funeral, my father took my brother and me into his bedroom and he said that my stepmom had killed herself. He said she had committed suicide because she was sad and depressed."

"Did you believe him?"

"No. She'd been happy at the mall. I'd seen him use drugs, but never her. She was sweet to us."

"Was she a moody person?"

"No, she was always a happy person except when my father was around."

"When you were at the shopping mall, did you buy anything that afternoon?"

"I asked my stepmother what she wanted us kids to give her for Christmas and she told us she wanted Shalimar perfume, so I took the other kids because I was oldest and we put our money together and got her a bottle of Shalimar. I wrapped it and put it under the tree. After we got home that day, she went over to the tree and picked up the package and she told us, 'What did my darlings buy me?' She said she couldn't wait to open it Christmas morning. She said, 'I can't imagine what it is.' And then she smiled and said, 'But it's got to be special because it's from you all.' After she died, I took it from under the tree and hid it in my closet. It reminded me of her."

I kept Carmen on the stand the entire morning and felt good when we broke for lunch.

PISANI BEGAN HIS cross-examination as soon as court reconvened. "You testified this morning that your father fought with Benita and you heard your father say, 'I'm going to keep hitting you, you fucking bitch, until you start bleeding.' Is that correct?"

"Yes, that's exactly what he said."

"That's very dramatic," Pisani said. "Now is it your testimony that he was physically beating her?"

"Yes," she said, moving her eyes from Pisani to her father for the first time. "I know he was hitting her with a belt."

"Really?" Pisani said with a curious voice. "I wonder if you can explain to us why the autopsy report doesn't mention bruises or marks on your stepmother? How is that possible if your father was beating her the night that she died?"

Carmen looked puzzled and so was I. I'd not noticed that inconsistency. Was it possible that young Carmen had mixed up the dates in her memory? That she had remembered her father beating Benita and had merged that beating with the night's events by accident in her young mind? Regardless, Pisani had caught her in what appeared to be an exaggeration.

"I object," I said. "This witness is not the medical examiner. She had nothing to do with his report."

Having raised doubt in the jurors' minds about Carmen's credibility, Pisani said, "I'll withdraw the question."

He moved on. "Now, Miss Gonzales, did you see your father pour the glass of milk that you claim you took and gave to your mother?"

"No. He told me there was a glass of milk on the counter but I didn't see him actually pour it."

"So you don't know if your stepmother might have poured that milk earlier, do you?"

"I don't think she did."

"But you don't know, do you?"

"No."

"Now, you said your father told you that your mother had committed suicide. Is that correct?"

"Yes."

"You said that you'd never seen your stepmother take cocaine, but that you had seen your father take it, is that your testimony?"

"I saw him take it several months after my stepmom was dead. But not before that night. There was white powder on the nightstand that night, though, and the floor."

"But you don't know who put it there, do you? You weren't in the room when it was being used, isn't that correct?"

"Yes."

Pisani spent the next two hours quizzing Carmen, looking for the slightest contradictions. He got her to confirm that Benita had been alert and awake when Carmen had delivered the milk to her. Because Carmen had gone back to bed, she acknowledged that she had no idea what happened after that.

Pisani was skillfully planting seeds of doubt with each question. He was suggesting through his interrogation that Benita could have added cocaine to the milk after Carmen had returned to bed. It was also possible that Carlos and his wife had both taken drugs. He was carefully punching holes, creating uncertainties, sowing doubts. He was also trying to show that Carmen was either confused or was lying. He reminded jurors that she was only fourteen when Benita died.

"When the police came that night you told them that you

had a nice family and your mother was depressed, is that right?"

"That's what my father told us to say."

"You were fourteen; surely you knew telling the police a lie was wrong. Are you now testifying that you lied to the police?"

"Yes, I was frightened. I was more afraid of my father than of the police."

Finally, Pisani asked, "Do you hate your father?"

Carmen said in a calm voice, "Yes. I hate him."

"Do you hope he goes to prison?"

Without flinching, Carmen said, "Yes."

Pisani was finished.

Rising from my seat, I asked Judge Morano if we could approach the bench. He waved us forward.

"Mr. Pisani just asked this witness if she hated her father. I believe he has opened the door for me to ask her why she hates him."

"Your Honor, you know where she's going. She's trying to find a way to have this witness testify about her father's conviction for rape and abuse. If she does that, you'll have to declare a mistrial."

In his stern voice, Judge Morano said, "Mr. Pisani, I don't have to do anything that I don't want to do. And Miss Fox is correct, you did open the door, but I'm not going to allow this witness to talk about the defendant's earlier conviction. I'm going to handle it my way." He sent us back to our seats.

Addressing the jurors, Judge Morano said, "You just heard this witness say she hates her father. I'm going to have that stricken from the record and you are not to consider it when you deliberate."

I thought, *Thanks, Judge.* Pisani gets to make his point and I can't tell this jury why his daughter has a good reason for hating her father's guts. Meanwhile, you're covering your butt by deleting it from the jurors' minds. Right.

53

I COULDN'T SLEEP FRIDAY NIGHT. PISANI had done a good job cross-examining my witnesses. All it would take would be one juror having a single reasonable doubt. Just one juror.

At seven a.m., my phone rang and I silently cursed as I reached for it, assuming it was Mom. I was supposed to meet her for lunch and drive into the city to watch *The Best Little Whorehouse in Texas*, which had just opened at the 46th Street Theatre. I wasn't a big fan of musicals, but Mom was insisting that I take a night off from worrying about the trial.

"Sorry to call so early," Will Harris said, "but this is important."

"Don't reporters ever sleep?"

"Not ones who want to eventually get hired by the *New York Times*. I have ambitions, you know," he said in a painfully chipper voice.

Continuing, he said, "I told you that I was going to talk to the wife of one of those cops who got busted in the thirty-fourth precinct. I got hold of her Friday night and she said her husband's been reading my coverage of the Gonzales trial and he claims he can help you."

"How?"

"She won't tell me. Says her husband will only talk to you. But she said it's enough to guarantee a conviction."

I was wide awake now. "Where's this cop?"

"That's the bad and good news. He's doing time in Attica, which is a good six-hour drive from here."

"And the good news?"

"I can drive you there as soon as you're ready."

"You just said he wants to talk to me alone."

"That's right, but no harm in me tagging along. We can grab some breakfast and then make a day of it."

I wasn't sure if Harris was interested in spending time with me or was simply after an exclusive. Either way, I felt going together was not a good idea.

"Will, I really appreciate the tip, but this is something I need to do by myself."

"Dani, this would be a great chance for us to talk. Sorta like a date, actually."

I said I was uncomfortable mixing business and pleasure. "But I will let you know exclusively if it leads to something. I promise."

After I hung up the phone, I called O'Brien. I broke into a grin when a woman with a familiar voice answered.

"You know, Hillary," I said, "if you're going to sleep over and want to keep your romance a secret, you really shouldn't be answering the phone." I loved calling her Hillary for the first time. I laughed.

I could only imagine the look of horror on her uptight face as she handed O'Brien my call. I gave him the high points of my chat with Will Harris.

"I'm not riding in that damn sports car of yours," he said. "How soon before I can pick you up?"

"A half hour."

"You got fifteen minutes."

The prison was 343 miles from White Plains. O'Brien was not about to be chauffeured by a woman, so I knew once we started, he would keep the speedometer in his unmarked police car on 90 mph and he'd be reluctant to stop until we reached the prison gate. I don't know how a cop his age could drink a thermos full of coffee and not need to pee, but I watched him do it as we raced along Highway 17 to Interstate 390 through the picturesque communities of Goshen, Monticello, Liberty, and Binghamton.

Finally, I demanded he make a pit stop and he grumbled the entire time. I started seeing familiar sites as we approached Elmira and mentioned that this is where I'd lived as a child.

"My dad and grandfather are buried here," I said. Before I realized it, I had told O'Brien about my family. O'Brien chewed on his toothpick as he drove, without commenting. We were approaching the Elmira exit when he said, "You want to stop at the cemetery to pay your respects?"

"I'm not sure we have time."

"We'll make time. You're an assistant D.A. and my old man worked at Attica, remember? We don't have to worry about normal visiting hours. You do know where they're buried, don't you?"

"They're both World War Two vets so they're at Woodlawn National Cemetery. Some really important Americans are buried there."

"Oh yeah, anyone I've ever heard of?"

"Herman Melville, Thomas Nast, Irving Berlin?"

"Don't ring a bell."

"Okay, how about Ernie Davis—or Mark Twain?"

With a mischievous grin, O'Brien said, "Davis was the first black to ever win the Heisman Trophy. But that other character—Twain—not sure I've heard of him."

I smiled, knowing he was joking—or at least hoping he was.

I suddenly remembered that I'd forgotten to call Mom and cancel our Saturday-night theater date. I knew she would be disappointed, but I also knew that my mom was so independent and frugal that she would not let her tickets go to waste. She'd find a friend and a way to get to that show without me.

We drove to my grandfather's grave first and then to my dad's. I asked O'Brien to wait in the car when we were at my father's grave so that I could say a few words. Standing at the foot of his grave, I told him how much I loved him and regretted that he'd never seen me try a criminal case.

"Mom and I are fine but we miss you terribly."

When I got back into the car, I told O'Brien that I needed to find a pay phone so I could call Mom. O'Brien headed to a nearby gas station and finally went to relieve himself while I rang up Mom and explained.

Back on the interstate, O'Brien bumped the speed up to 95 mph and asked, "So how's your mom? You know, she's a real looker."

I looked at him with a horrified face and said, "Detective, don't you think you got enough on your plate with Miss Potts?"

"I was just teasing you. Giving you a bit back after that stunt you pulled this morning."

"Are you angry at me for talking to Hillary?" I relished calling her by her first name.

"She wasn't happy, that's for sure. In fact, she's damn mad that you know about us."

"I'm not going to say anything. I was just teasing her because she can be, how shall I say this? She's so prim and proper and I can only imagine the hoopla you two make," I said, intentionally staring at him to see his reaction.

O'Brien shot me a knowing glance and said, "Better to leave her alone or you'll have the both of us to deal with."

O'Brien was not the type to share personal information, so I was happy that he felt comfortable talking about Potts. I decided to push my luck. "You told me that retirement killed your dad. Is he buried in Attica—not at the prison, of course, but in the actual town?"

O'Brien kept his eyes on the road and didn't answer.

"I mean, if you want to pay your respects to your father, I'd be happy to wait."

"No need."

"I'm just saying since we stopped in Elmira, I'd be happy to return the courtesy."

"I said no need," O'Brien growled.

Neither of us spoke for several moments, but I just couldn't leave it alone.

"Maybe we could stop and see your mom then—if she still lives in Attica. I'd like to meet her."

"Give the touchy-feely family stuff a rest, okay?"

"I was just trying to make conversation. Besides, you asked me about my parents and told me my mom was good-looking."

O'Brien let out a sigh and said, "My mom is dead. Okay? She didn't have a happy life. Not everyone had a great childhood and wonderful parents."

"I'm sorry. I didn't know."

"Why would you? My father was from a different generation. He went to work, and when he came home, he had some beers, read the sports page, and expected my mom to raise the kids. The only time he got involved was when she needed backup. Then he'd come at us with his belt."

"Your father beat you?"

O'Brien turned and gave me an irked stare. "He gave me and my brothers whippings—not beatings. We deserved them, at least most the time. Like I said, it was different. It was about respect. When my old man asked you to do something, you didn't give him any lip or you got a fat lip. I remember going to school with two black eyes."

"None of your teachers said anything?"

"You joking? This was the thirties and I grew up in a tough blue-collar neighborhood. No one said nothing because no one considered it a problem. When kids got out of line, you smacked 'em. On good days, my old man might flip you a quarter so you could go to the Saturday matinee. On bad days, it was best you just stayed clear."

"How about your mom?"

"What about her?"

"Did he hit her, too?"

"What is this—some sort of domestic violence interview? Save it for work. Our clients need your help, I don't."

We rode in deafening silence for several miles. I watched the countryside passing by. Finally, he said, "Of course my old man hit my mother. It was just how he was. He was not a communicator. When I was little, there wasn't nothing I could do. But when I got big enough, I stood up to him one day."

"Wow, that was brave."

"My father looked at me differently when I did it. I was challenging him. It was as if he were sizing me up as a man. I think he'd always expected this day was coming. He knew I was going to take a swing at him and he said, 'You need to think about what you're about to try. 'Cause, boy, if we go at it—the free ride is over. This is my house and there can only be one man here. Even if you beat me, you're out on your butt.' "

"What happened?"

"I threw a punch. Caught him right in his jaw. But it didn't faze him as much as I thought. He was one tough bastard. He knocked me on my ass with one punch. I was sixteen and in good shape. He was probably forty. We went at it like two junkyard dogs. We beat each other until neither of us could lift an arm. My hands hurt for days. And that was the last night I ever spent living under his roof. The next day, I lied about my age and signed up for the Marines."

"Didn't your mom have a say?"

"Oh, she had plenty to say. She was furious. But her anger was all aimed at me. She told me I'd disrespected my old man and it wasn't up to me to fight her battles. She was worried about him when we were lying there both bloody. I remember her saying, 'Who's gonna pay the bills if he's laid up?' It was the damndest thing. I thought I was going to be her hero and she was angry at me for getting involved."

"She was wrong to do that."

"She was his wife. That's where her loyalty belonged."

I quietly realized that this was the reason why O'Brien had sought me out when he'd first learned about Rudy Hitchins beating Mary Margaret. It was the reason why he'd agreed to work with the Domestic Violence Unit. I looked at him driving, and in his tough face, I could see the small boy who had grown up being slapped around, who had tried to protect his mother, and who had been rejected emotionally by both when he'd tried to put an end to the violence.

54

THE ATTICA CORRECTIONAL FACILITY south of town looks like a medieval fortress. Constructed in the 1930s, it's surrounded by thick walls that rise more than thirty feet from the street. The entrance has a cupola fixed with two large search-lights. It is a forbidding place.

I'd never been inside the famed New York maximum-security penitentiary, and despite repairs after the 1971 riot, it remained gloomy and grim. Voices echoed off the cold gray walls, as did the sounds of cell doors opening and closing. We were greeted at the entrance by a beefy assistant warden. O'Brien had given me advice about how to act inside the walls.

"Don't refer to them as guards. It's disrespectful. They're correctional officers. They aren't knuckle-draggers. Don't describe the prisoners as convicts. That gives them too much respect. They're inmates."

I'd no idea terminology was so important, but O'Brien told me prisons were all about control, respect, and violence. Words mattered.

I'd come to interview Antonio Hernandez, one of the thirty-fourth precinct officers who'd pleaded guilty to accepting bribes from Carlos Gonzales. O'Brien stayed in the front lobby while I entered the prison through a sally port, which was a small passageway with bars at both ends. One gate opened,

I stepped inside, that gate closed, then the one in front of me opened. This way, there was always at least one set of bars between the interior of the prison and the exit.

A correctional officer escorted me to a visiting room that was more like a horse stall. It was divided into two separate areas by a brick half wall and wire mesh screen that rose from the bricks to the ceiling. There was a metal stool on each side of the screen. I stepped into my side and the door behind me was locked. A door on the other side of the wire screen opened and Hernandez was led in. The former police officer was wearing an orange jumpsuit, which meant that he was housed in the prison's protective custody—away from the general prison population for his own safety. There was a chain attached to his ankles that forced him to shuffle. He was handcuffed, and those cuffs were locked onto a belly belt, which kept him from extending his wrists more than a few inches from his waist.

O'Brien had told me that former cops had to be kept away from other prisoners because they would be murdered. The protective custody unit where Hernandez lived also was home to snitches and weaker inmates who would be easily preyed upon. Nothing like home sweet home.

Having never met Hernandez, I didn't know what to expect. He was in his early forties, about five feet ten inches tall and a mass of muscles. His forearms and biceps were huge from pumping iron. He had a Fu Manchu mustache and his head was shaved. I suspected his fierce look and weight-lifting regimen were born from necessity. He wanted to appear intimidating in prison. He did. At least to me.

"You wanted to talk to me about Carlos Gonzales."

"What I want is to cut a deal."

"I assume your attorney already has cut you the best deal possible with the U.S. Attorney. I'm an assistant county prosecutor. Your case doesn't fall under my jurisdiction."

"Look, I want my wife to get my police pension."

"I have no connections with the NYPD." There was no point in promising him what I couldn't deliver, even if he could help my case.

"Oh, you'll find a way. Talk to the U.S. Attorney and FBI, since they sent me here."

I decided not to mention that I wasn't exactly on good terms with the FBI right now.

"What do I get in return if I try to help your wife get your pension?"

"Carlos Gonzales's head on a silver platter."

"Tell me how you can do that."

"I'll testify to what I know."

"Okay, what do you know? How did you get involved with him?"

"My partner and me had been watching that piece of shit for months. We knew he was selling blow out of his jewelry business. One night, we see Gonzales ducking out the back door into the alley carrying a briefcase. My partner, Andy, says, 'Why does he have a briefcase?' I mean, it's not like he's a Wall Street tycoon. I pull our squad car into the alley and that stupid son of a bitch Gonzales starts running from us."

Hernandez grinned. He was enjoying himself. "Andy hops out of the squad car and goes after him on foot. While he's running, Gonzales tosses his briefcase into a trash Dumpster. Stupid. I mean, we'd seen him do it."

I didn't want to interrupt him, so I was just sitting there listening, but Hernandez suddenly paused. "All those years busting people, I never realized how uncomfortable being handcuffed is. Maybe you should have someone slap a pair on your wrists just to get the full experience, or maybe you already have been handcuffed a few times. Right?"

Great, I thought. I'd driven all the way to Attica with O'Brien and canceled a date with Mom to have a dishonest cop come on to me inside a prison interrogation room.

"Let's get on with this. You said Gonzales threw a briefcase into a Dumpster."

"Yeah, that's what I said. Normally my partner would have kept chasing Gonzales, but Andy had put on a few pounds and was winded, and besides, like I said, we knew who he was. Andy fishes the briefcase out of the Dumpster. He opens it and says, 'That shitbird's got a shitload of cash here.' I look and the entire case is filled with bills. My partner counts sixty-four large ones. Now at this point, we got no proof this is drug money. I mean the guy could have been on his way to make a deposit at the bank. Except he tosses the briefcase."

"It must have been a large briefcase to hold that much money."

"It's one like you lawyers like to carry. It doesn't open sideways like a suitcase. It opens from the top, so Andy reaches inside, touches the bottom, and says to me, 'There's something hidden down here.' He can tell because his hand should go another three or four inches deep but it don't. He takes out his knife and pries open the bottom and bingo, there's a packet of Charlie hidden there. We had him cold with dope."

"Can I assume you took the money and dope?"

"No," he said, appearing slightly offended as if I had insulted him, "you can't. Because neither of us had never done nothing wrong. We was good cops. But everyone has a price, lady. If I had sixty thousand bucks right now and I told you I'd give you the cash if you showed me your tits, you'd be pulling them out right now."

He was making me uncomfortable. "You and your partner had the money and were in the squad car, right?"

"Yeah, we were sitting there with this cash and this bag of dope, and instead of calling it in, like we should have, we began talking. Andy says, 'What if we take a few for ourselves? Maybe five grand each.' That's when I blew it. I got eighteen years on the force and instead of saying, 'I'm not risking my career for a lousy five grand,' I said, 'What about Gonzales?' I opened the door to the idea. I never should have done that."

For the first time, I detected regret in his voice. "Andy and me begin talking about how we could use the cash. About how we are risking our lives every day and we can't even afford to live in Manhattan. We talked about how the really big thieves are the ones who get elected to City Hall. They're stealing stuff and no one does nothing. And then Andy says, 'What the fuck is Gonzales going to do?' He don't want anything to do with this briefcase. We're the cops, no one would believe him if he ratted us out. And that's when I opened my big mouth and said, 'In for a dime, in for a dollar.'"

"What exactly did you mean?"

"I meant, why take five grand each? If we're going to take it, then let's take it all. Andy says, 'What about the blow?' I said, 'What if we take his cash and then we simply give him back the briefcase with the blow still in it. We're not dope dealers. We give it back and say something like, 'You dropped this.' Now, he's going to know we took the money, but so what? We got the cash, he gets the dope, and he can just mark it down as the cost of doing business. At the time, it sounded like a good plan."

"Only it didn't work, did it?"

"Oh, it worked just fine at first. The next day, Andy hands him the briefcase and says, 'You dropped this.' He just looks at us and says, 'I've never seen that before.' He thinks it's a trap, so Andy says to him, 'We ain't going to bust your ass.' Andy opens the case and shows Gonzales that it's empty. Gonzales knows we grabbed his money but he don't know if we found the dope. He takes the case and we walk out. I thought that was the end of it. But it was just the beginning."

Hernandez paused to catch his breath and then said, "For a lawyer, you got nice tits."

"Look, I came up here to hear your story. I didn't come up

here to talk about my anatomy. If you make another comment like that, I'm walking out."

"Hey, ease off, okay? You can't blame a guy for trying when you're locked up all the time."

"What about your wife?"

"She's got nice tits, too," he said, laughing.

I really didn't like him.

He got back to his story. "A week later, we're outside the jewelry store and out walks Gonzales all friendly. He says, real smart like, 'This briefcase looks like the one I owned, but it's not mine.' He hands us the very same briefcase and Andy looks inside and it's empty. Gonzales walks back into his business and I says, 'Check the fake bottom.' Andy pries it open, and sure enough, there's two stacks of cash. Five grand in each. I says, 'That little shit is trying to buy us off.' Andy gives me this disgusted look. He says, 'Partner, he already did.'"

I asked, "How long did you take bribes from Gonzales?"

"The gravy train ended six months later when we got busted."

"How'd the FBI get you on tape? Was Gonzales wearing a wire?"

"Lady, we ain't stupid. We always checked him for wires. No, as near as I can tell, Gonzales didn't start working for the Feds as a snitch until after they busted all of us. The way I figure it, the Feds got all three of us on a boom mike. You know what that is?"

I had no idea.

"A boom microphone is a directional listening device that the FBI can point at suspects and use to listen in on their conversations. It has a range of about a city block. The agents must have been following Gonzales, and when they saw him talking to us, they must have pointed a boom at us and tape-recorded our conversation."

"So that's how the FBI got you and Gonzales discussing bribes."

"Yeah, they got us talking about lots of things. My partner and me were running a scam on Gonzales. We was telling him that we needed more money—a bigger slice—because we had a lieutenant who wanted in on the action. We told Gonzales that this lieutenant could provide him with protection—you know—tips about who might be working as an undercover cop."

"Was there really a lieutenant willing to do that?"

"Naw, we was just feeding him bullshit to get more money. Of course, he didn't know that. Still, that little shitbird was suspicious, so he began telling us about how he was a real tough guy and how we shouldn't mess with him because he knew how to take care of business.

"I said to him, 'Oh really.' And he tells both of us—Andy and me—that he's a stone-cold killer. I says, 'Who'd you kill?' And this asshole comes right out and tells me that he poisoned his old lady. He told us he put cocaine in her glass of milk and had his little girl give it to her."

Hernandez certainly had my attention, but I was suspicious. "You could have read that information in the newspaper. You could be making all of this up. Do you really expect me to believe that Gonzales told two cops that he murdered his wife?"

"Two cops who was on his payroll, dear. It wasn't exactly like we was squeaky clean, and besides, Gonzales has a huge ego—he wanted to convince us that he was a tough guy."

I must have still looked skeptical because he said, "Listen, lady, I'm not a virgin here. You know the defense is going to attack me. But I can handle myself in court. I've testified plenty of times. I may be in prison, but I didn't kill nobody. I didn't break any arms. I can be a credible witness. But in return, you got to get the U.S. Attorney to give Andy and me our pensions for our families."

I'd heard enough. I said, "I need to think about this."

"Don't take too long," he said. "You know I can always call the other side and tell them that I'm willing to testify that Gonzales told us that his old lady killed herself. That she really did commit suicide."

"In other words, you're willing to testify for either side?"

"We earned them pensions. If you don't want to play ball, then I'm calling that other attorney, Pisani, and I'll tell him that I'll testify for Gonzales and so will Andy. We'll destroy your case unless you help us."

I rapped on the window at the officer stationed immediately outside my door and he opened it. "We're done here," I told him. As I started to exit, Hernandez gave me one parting comment. "Remember, if I don't get word from you in the next twenty-four hours, I'm talking to Pisani."

I removed the temporary visitor's pass that I'd been issued when I reached the sally port and slipped it into a drawer in the bulletproof control room. The officer compared my face to the photo on my assistant district attorney's ID badge that I had surrendered when I had gotten to the prison. Satisfied that I was, indeed, Dani Fox, he flipped a switch and the first row of bars in the sally port opened. Seconds later, I entered the lobby, where O'Brien was talking to the assistant warden. We said our good-byes. As we stepped outside, I felt like I needed a shower.

"What were you and the assistant warden talking about?" I asked O'Brien.

"We was talking about how women can be prosecutors and cops now, but that they'll never work in a prison like Attica. There's still a few jobs only a man can and should do."

"I think that place could use a woman's touch."

He chuckled and asked, "Did Hernandez tell you anything worthwhile?"

"He told me that Gonzales bragged to him and his partner about poisoning Benita with cocaine-tainted milk."

"Anyone who's been reading the newspapers knows that."

"Hernandez wants a deal. His pension for his testimony. And if we don't cooperate, then he's going to contact Pisani and offer to testify for Gonzales. He'll claim that Gonzales told him and his partner that Benita had committed suicide."

"What an asshole. Can you get him his pension?"

"I doubt it. Besides, I don't trust him and neither will jurors."

"So our trip today was a complete waste of a Saturday?"

"Not exactly. Mr. Hernandez may have helped me—without realizing it."

55

P ISANI WAS LEANING AGAINST THE
edge of the prosecutor's table with a smirk on his face
when I arrived in court Monday morning.

"I heard," Pisani said as I approached him, "that you and
Detective O'Brien made a little weekend jaunt."

I assumed Antonio Hernandez had contacted him, too,
from the prison. We'd gone up Saturday. Pisani had probably
been there on Sunday.

"Nothing like a trip upstate to help clear your mind," I
said.

"Ms. Fox, I know all about your conversation with Antonio Hernandez and I can only hope you're going to call him
today as a witness. I can't think of anything more pleasing at
this moment than to cross-examine that piece of shit."

Placing my briefcase on the table, I said, "If that's the most
pleasing thing that you can think of this morning, the clerk's
office must have run out of interns."

"Please don't concern yourself with what pleases me. Of
course, it would be easy to please you. But then, you're too
naive for my tastes and a bit of a bore. Like this trial's become
a bore. Despite all your bravado, you've not built a credible
circumstantial case and deep down you know it. You're going
to lose this case."

I realized that I shouldn't respond, but I couldn't help
myself. "Maybe I can liven up things today. As you just sug-

gested, I am planning on calling a witness who's not on my original list."

Pisani gave me a sickening smile and said, "Oh goody, you're going to bring Antonio Hernandez in as a surprise witness. I can't wait."

As soon as Judge Morano called court into session, he asked if I had any more witnesses.

"Your Honor, the prosecution wishes to call a witness who was not on our original list."

"And why wasn't this witness on your list?" the judge asked.

"Because until this weekend, I wasn't aware that he could provide important testimony in this matter."

I could practically see Pisani salivating.

Judge Morano asked Pisani, "Have you been informed that the prosecution intends to call a new witness?"

"Ms. Fox and I just spoke a few moments ago. If she wishes to call this witness, I will not object. In fact, I will be delighted!"

"Then call your witness, Miss Fox."

In a loud voice, I said, "The state calls FBI Special Agent Jack Longhorn."

Pisani's smug expression vanished. "Your Honor," he said, leaping to his feet, "this is not the witness Ms. Fox and I were discussing."

"You just told me that the two of you had talked about this," Judge Morano said, waving us forward for a sidebar conference. "Which one of you wants to tell me what's going on here?" he asked.

"The witness we discussed this morning is a prisoner at Attica prison," Pisani said.

"With all due respect to Mr. Pisani, I never said I was going to call that prisoner. Before court started, Mr. Pisani told me that he hoped I'd call him. He mentioned his name. I simply said I was going to call a witness who was not on the original list. I didn't say who."

In a weary voice, Judge Morano said, "I don't know what sort of semantic games you two are playing and quite frankly I don't care. Miss Fox, are you planning on calling a prisoner from Attica, because it will take time to get him here."

"Not at this time, Your Honor. FBI Agent Longhorn, who is seated in the back of the courtroom gallery, will suffice."

"You have any objections to Agent Longhorn testifying?" the judge asked Pisani.

Being cautious, Pisani said, "Quite frankly, I do. The FBI did not investigate this case so I don't see how having Agent Longhorn testify is relevant. Also, the FBI currently has criminal charges pending against my client. I suspect this is an attempt by Ms. Fox to prejudice my client's reputation by having Agent Longhorn testify."

"Miss Fox," the judge said, "are you trying to get information about those pending drug charges in through a back door?"

"No, Your Honor, the state wishes to call this witness because he has important testimony about this murder—not because of the federal charges."

"What the hell does he know about this murder?" Pisani said.

"Well, if I can get him on the witness stand, then we'll know, won't we?"

"Okay, Miss Fox," Judge Morano ruled, "you can call him, but you'll need to tie all this together in a nice bow for me rather quickly, and don't make me regret this by trying to get those federal charges into the record."

As Pisani and I were returning to our respective tables, I said, "You wanted some excitement, here it comes."

He didn't reply.

Agent Longhorn did not look pleased while he was being

sworn in. I began by asking him a quick series of questions that established who he was and his credentials as a federal agent. Then I got to the point.

"Agent Longhorn, do you know the defendant?"

"Yes."

"Have you ever heard the defendant talking about the death of his wife, Benita Gonzales?"

Longhorn looked directly at me and said, "I have never had a conversation with the defendant about his wife's death."

"That was not the question. I asked you if you'd ever heard the defendant talking about his wife's death."

Still trying to outmaneuver me, Longhorn reluctantly replied, "He may have talked about her death, but I was not present."

Pisani was on his feet. "Your Honor, Agent Longhorn is correct. If he did not personally have a conversation with my client, then anything that he might say is hearsay and not admissible."

Longhorn looked at me with a satisfied smile.

Judge Morano said, "Miss Fox, you know better than this. You can't ask Agent Longhorn to give hearsay testimony."

"I don't intend to, Your Honor. With the court's indulgence, I only have a few more questions for the witness and they will not pertain to hearsay."

Judge Morano let out a scowl and said, "A bow, Miss Fox. Tie it quickly, please."

"Special Agent Longhorn, do you have in your possession tape recordings of the defendant discussing the death of his wife?"

The boom microphone recordings. That is why I believed our trip to Attica had been worthwhile. Hernandez said that Gonzales had bragged about killing Benita during their last conversation before the FBI had arrested them. As soon as he'd said that, I'd known their conversation would be on tape recorded by the FBI with the boom microphone. I didn't need Hernandez to testify. If those tapes still existed, I had the killer himself being overheard discussing his wife's death on tape.

Longhorn twisted in the witness chair and said, "With all due respect, the tapes that you are citing are the property of the FBI and are covered by Rule 6 and federal grand jury secrecy. I can't discuss their contents."

I had no intention of letting him wiggle free.

"Your Honor, the state contends that Agent Longhorn has in his possession certain investigative materials that are relevant to this case. I would now ask that the court order Agent Longhorn to surrender either the original or certified copies of any materials that apply directly to this trial."

"We're going to take a short recess," Judge Morano said. "I want both counsel and Agent Longhorn to come into my chambers."

Judge Morano's office didn't look any cleaner since the last time that I'd entered it and he'd blown cigar smoke in my face. Removing his robe and hanging it on a hook, he said in an irked voice, "Exactly what is going on here, Miss Fox?"

"Your Honor, I believe the FBI used a boom microphone to listen to and tape-record a conversation that was held between the defendant and two NYPD officers who are now serving time in prison on corruption charges."

"What the hell is a boom microphone?" the judge asked.

"It's a directional microphone that can listen to conversations from a long distance away without suspects knowing that they are being observed and recorded," I said.

"And what makes you think the FBI tape-recorded the defendant in this matter?" the judge asked me.

"Both of the NYPD officers pleaded guilty after their attorneys were advised of the contents of the FBI tape recordings. I have been told that the FBI allowed these men's defense attorneys to listen to the tapes so they could fully advise their clients. Obviously, if the tapes already have been used in other criminal matters, then they do exist."

"Assuming these tapes exist," Judge Morano said, "exactly what do you expect to hear on them?"

"I have been told that Carlos Gonzales bragged about killing his wife while the FBI was secretly tape-recording him and the two officers. I believe it is within the prosecution's rights to have the portion of the tape-recorded conversations that are relevant to this case submitted in court and played to the jurors as evidence."

Judge Morano said, "Are you telling me the FBI has tape recordings of this defendant discussing a murder that he committed and the bureau did not surrender them to you as a prosecutor?"

"That's exactly what I'm telling you, Judge."

Judge Morano gave FBI Special Agent Longhorn a puzzled and angry look. "I've heard of prosecutors hiding statements from the defense, but never heard of the FBI hiding damning information from a prosecutor. Is what she's saying true, Agent Longhorn? Do you have information about this alleged murder that you are intentionally withholding?"

"Judge," Longhorn said, "as you noted, the law is clear that the state must provide evidence to the defense that might help prove his innocence. That's exculpatory evidence. But I do not believe there are any statutes that require the FBI to provide evidence, especially information protected by Rule 6(e) of the Federal Rules of Evidence, to a local prosecutor to help prove their case. That's not exculpatory; in fact, that's inculpatory."

I noticed that Agent Longhorn had dropped his habit of using folksy homilies.

"Special Agent Longhorn," the judge said, "that's one of

the worst excuses I've ever heard. If you have evidence that can help the prosecution, then why in the hell haven't you given it to Miss Fox? For godsakes, you're supposed to be on the same team."

"I'm not required by law to assist her," he said.

"Like hell you're not!" the judge snapped.

"Judge, these tapes are the property of the U.S. government," Agent Longhorn replied. "They involve sensitive investigative information and confidential informants. I would have to consult with the U.S. Attorney and the Justice Department and I am sure that they will oppose releasing this material."

If Judge Morano was irritated before, he was now fuming. "Miss Fox just said the FBI had turned over portions of those tape recordings to defense attorneys in another case. I'm going to issue a court order, demanding that you surrender those tapes to me by this afternoon so that I can listen to them, in the presence of a representative from your office and the U.S. Attorney's office. If I hear anything on those tapes that I believe is relevant to this trial, I will require those portions to be provided to Miss Fox and allow them to be submitted as evidence. If the tapes do not contain anything relevant, Miss Fox and I will have an unpleasant chat later."

"I'm sorry, Judge," Longhorn said, "but I'm not sure I can go along with your request."

Judge Morano rocked back in his seat and said, "Agent Longhorn, I don't seem to be making myself clear to you. This is not a request. You will either get those tapes to me by three p.m. today or you will be held in contempt of my court and jailed. Of course, you can attempt to get a higher court or a federal court to intervene and stay my order, but I've been on the bench a long time, son, and I know a lot of federal judges. If find out that you're intentionally withholding information that can aid the prosecution in a murder trial—you're going to run into legal skepticism and some extremely unfavorable publicity. You have until three p.m."

Agent Longhorn looked to Pisani for help, but for once in his life, Mr. Invincible was at a total loss for words.

56

THE FIRST TIME JURORS HEARD THE voice of Carlos Gonzales was when the clerk flipped on a reel-to-reel tape recorder that had been brought into the courtroom. It was Tuesday morning. Judge Morano had spent much of Monday night listening to FBI tapes and had ruled that exactly three minutes of a conversation that Gonzales had held with Antonio Hernandez and his fellow officer, Andy Bravero, was relevant to our trial and could be played. After Judge Morano called court into session, I quickly moved through the legal steps necessary to get the snippet admitted as evidence. Once that was done, the court clerk had turned on the player.

The first voice was Gonzales's.

"You don't think I got big enough cojones for murder? Is that right? Well, let me tell you both something that might surprise you. I snuffed my old lady, man. I did her. And the cops—they're so stupid they think she killed herself."

Judge Morano had decided that the person who spoke next did not need to be identified by name but rather would be referred to during the trial simply as voice one. I recognized him. It was Antonio Hernandez.

"Okay, Carlos, tell us, how'd you snuff your old lady?"

"I used blow, man. I mixed it with milk and then had my kid take the glass up to her in our bedroom. The dumb bitch didn't have a clue she'd been poisoned until it was way too late."

"Why'd you do her?"

That question came from a different voice. I assumed it was Hernandez's partner, Bravero.

"She was gonna take the kids and leave me. She threatened to go to the cops. I put five grams in that milk, man. It took forever to dissolve."

"She must have checked out higher than a kite," voice one could be heard saying.

"Naw, she started vomiting. I was with her in the bedroom to keep her from going for help. I held her down. Looked right into that bitch's eyes when she was dying. So don't tell me I don't have big cojones."

The tape came to an end.

I announced, "I'm done with Agent Longhorn as a witness."

Pisani knew he was in trouble. But he also knew that he had a friendly witness sitting in the chair who wanted to help him.

"Agent Longhorn, as an FBI agent, you could have charged my client with murder when you first heard his words on that tape. Isn't that correct?"

"I could have."

"But you didn't. Why?"

"Shucks," said Longhorn, falling back into his good ol' boy voice. "I thought he was exaggerating to impress the other men on that tape. I thought what he was saying was hogwash."

I stared at Longhorn with complete disgust. He was bending over backward to help Gonzales go free—and for what? He'd told me earlier it was for a "greater good," but I knew that the true greater good was that Gonzales was going to help Longhorn's career.

57

I RESTED MY CASE.

Pisani announced that his client would not testify. He also said the defense didn't need to call additional witnesses. "The defense rests," he announced in a confident voice. He immediately asked Judge Morano to dismiss the murder charge, claiming that I had failed to prove the elements of the crime of murder beyond a reasonable doubt. Judge Morano declined.

After a short break, we returned to court for our closing arguments.

HAVING STUDIED NEARLY all of Pisani's performances in earlier cases, I was well familiar with his tactics. I suspected he would begin with a personal story so he would appear to be just an average fellow, just like the jurors. He would attack the evidence, submit an alternative theory, and finally talk about "reasonable doubt."

Just as I'd thought, Pisani began with a short anecdote, hoping to touch jurors emotionally.

"I'm not married," he said, and then, looking at me, he added, "Of course, neither is Ms. Fox there. But I have many friends who are, and while it may be hard for you to believe it, these married couples actually get into arguments on occasion." He gave the jurors a smug smile and wink. "Sometimes these friends have dragged me into their arguments, and when I listen to them, I realize I am hearing two very different sides to a story. That is what we have here today."

Pisani took jurors through the testimony just as I had, but he led them down a completely different path. Dr. Swante had ruled Benita's death was a suicide until he was asked to change his opinion by the prosecution. There was no new evidence, no reason to switch, except for a request from Ms. Fox. Dr. Swante had testified that Benita wasn't a frequent user and then had admitted that she might have been one. How believable was he? Dr. Treater had never met Benita Gonzales so how did she know whether or not the deceased was depressed? Dr. Treater had thought one of her own patients, whom she'd known well, was not suicidal and he'd blown his head off fifty-five minutes later. So much for her credibility.

Officer Whitey McLean had not seen anything suspicious on the night when the victim's body had been found in her bedroom. He'd told the coroner that the death looked to him like a suicide. As for Yolanda Torres, she was an admitted alcoholic and proven liar who had once falsely accused her boyfriend, saying that he had beaten and threatened to kill her, only to admit later that she'd fabricated the charges. Maria Hildago had testified that she was high on drugs when she thought the defendant might have told her something about his wife's death. Chances are she was simply hallucinating.

Having undercut those witnesses, Pisani attacked Carmen's testimony. She'd told jurors that Carlos beat Benita that night, but the autopsy didn't show any evidence that Benita had been beaten. How did the prosecution explain that inconsistency?

Carmen also had admitted that she was bitter and angry at her father. "She is not a credible witness. She is an angry witness."

Finally, Pisani explained the tape recording of the defendant discussing his wife's death. It was braggadocio, a man trying to appear macho. "Agent Longhorn, himself, said he didn't believe Gonzales had murdered anyone."

Having done his best to undermine all the evidence and the witnesses' testimony, Pisani suggested an alternative theory about what had happened the night Benita died.

Benita was clearly unhappy in this marriage. That much was certain. Carmen had brought her a glass of milk. That much was certain. Depressed, unhappy Benita kissed her daughter good night, sent her to her bedroom, and then reached into the dresser where she and Carlos kept cocaine. It always had lifted her spirits before when she was feeling blue. Benita had always been careful to hide her cocaine use from her children and everyone else. She carefully sprinkled the particles into the milk and stirred it—perhaps with her own finger. She drank it. Her husband heard her cries later, raced upstairs, and saw her already dead on the bed. "This is not a murder. It is a tragedy. A suicide."

Pisani added, "This is not just the defense's theory about what happened that night. It is what the police and the coroner believed happened at the time. What changed their minds? Was it scientific evidence? No! It was an overzealous prosecutor named Dani Fox with an ax to grind."

Pisani was now making me the villain—a bitter, unmarried woman.

One of the first lessons that I'd learned as a prosecutor was that oftentimes a subtle bond is created between a defendant and jurors during a trial. Sitting together through tedious testimony, hearing intimate details about a person's life and personality, and knowing that another human being's fate is in your hands can create the impression that a defendant is not so different from the persons judging him. There was a tendency for jurors to think that defendants were just like them. That they shared the same values. It was difficult, I'd learned, for jurors to look at someone so ordinary, so seemingly respectable, and think of them violently poisoning their spouse. Jurors wanted to believe the good in a person. Sadly, jurors tended to empathize with defendants without even realizing it.

Pisani was using that to his full advantage.

Continuing his attack, he said, "Look at what sort of witnesses Ms. Fox is asking you to believe. An assistant medical examiner who is so weak-spined that he changes his ruling just because she asked him to. A psychiatrist who discharged a young patient only to have him kill himself. An alcoholic best friend who is an admitted liar. A hallucinating stripper and the defendant's own bitter daughter. Who would want their fate determined by such questionable testimony? If you look for cold, hard evidence, you will find that there is none. The only evidence is that this poor woman died from an overdose taken in milk. No one knows who put that cocaine there or why."

Pisani ended in his traditional manner: by discussing reasonable doubt. "Your job is to determine whether the evidence proves guilt beyond a reasonable doubt. This means you must decide if the evidence is truthful and compelling. I know you've all seen photos of Lady Justice. She is wearing a blindfold and holding a scale. As jurors, you are required to put guilt on one side of that scale. On the other side, you put reasonable doubt. Under our legal system, if there is even the slightest bit of reasonable doubt—even the weight of a feather—on those scales, then the law requires you—it doesn't really give you a choice—it demands that you to find the defendant not guilty regardless of what's on the other side—no matter how heavy that side is."

Continuing, Pisani said, "Every accused person in our society is presumed innocent until the state proves otherwise. The law demands that you begin your deliberations by recognizing that my client is innocent. It's up to the prosecutor to prove him guilty. The defense doesn't have to solve this case or explain loose ends. That is not our responsibility. The law says my client is innocent until the state presents such evidence that every one of you is convinced beyond a reasonable doubt that he committed this crime. When you retire, remember those scales, remember that if there is the slightest feather of doubt — and I promise you that there is plenty of reasonable doubt in this case — then you must acquit my client."

I had to hand it to Pisani. He'd used every trick in the book: equating reasonable doubt with a feather, yelling at times and whispering at others, making his closing a call to justice that any law-abiding citizen would acquit this murderer. He was good.

58

A S PISANI RETURNED TO HIS SEAT, I glanced at the notes I had been carefully scribbling during his closing, nervously reached into my pocket, and removed a Junior Mint that I had taken from my desk and stashed there. I waved my hand across my mouth to hide what I was doing and chewed it.

It was my job to counter his argument in my closing remarks. I took a deep breath and stood.

The prosecution goes last and I carefully and methodically went through the evidence that each witness had given. In doing so, I challenged each of the points that Pisani had just presented. Dr. Swante had testified the milk found in the victim's body had been laced with cocaine. He'd assured the jury that there was no evidence that Benita had been a frequent user of cocaine as her husband had claimed. "Carlos Gonzales lied about that," I said.

Dr. Treater had testified that in her opinion Benita had not appeared depressed or suicidal. "Carlos Gonzales lied about that." Officer McLean testified that Gonzales had appeared nervous that night and had told him that Benita frequently chewed rock cocaine. "Carlos Gonzales lied about that." The policeman also testified that the entire bedroom had been tidy. If Benita's death had been a suicide, why had Gonzales cleaned the room before notifying the police?

Yolanda Torres had testified that Gonzales had admitted

that he'd murdered Benita. Maria Hildago had testified that Gonzales had bragged about killing Benita. The defendant's daughter had described how her father had awakened her and sent her to get milk from the kitchen that he'd put there. And finally, the jurors had heard Carlos Gonzales's own voice on a tape recording describing how he had poisoned the milk and held his wife prisoner in their bedroom until she was dead.

I made no attempt to explain the inconsistency, nor could I, between Carmen's testimony about her stepmother being beaten and no record of injuries on Benita's back.

Having reviewed the evidence, I now spoke about the victim. "Benita was in the middle of Christmas; in the middle of raising a family; in the middle of her life when Carlos Gonzales—not God—decided he would end it. She had been Christmas shopping. She was in the midst of wrapping presents. She'd put up a tree. There were festive lights inside and outside her house. Mr. Pisani has called this a circumstantial case. Yes, there are no eyewitnesses. But come along with me and see if that circumstantial evidence is strong enough that you are unable to deny that this defendant killed his wife."

I stepped away from the podium and spoke without notes, while looking directly at the jurors. "Let's look at how Benita spends her last day alive. She takes her children to a shopping mall, she poses with Santa Claus with her baby boy. She gives her children money to buy presents, and when they get home, Benita tells her stepdaughter to leave the lights on the Christmas tree burning because the children love seeing them. If the children woke up, they'd see the lights and not be afraid. Benita tells her children that she can't wait to open the tiny present they had bought for her that day. Perfume. Benita was looking forward to Christmas. This was not a suicidal woman. Benita was enjoying her life as best she could."

I paused for a moment to let my words sink in. "Now let's talk about how that blissful day changed after Carlos Gonzales came home. We know there was a fight. The defendant's temper is immediate, it is urgent, it is unprovoked. We know this defendant knows cocaine. He buys it, he abuses it. We only bring that in to show you he has access to the instrument of death. He knows he can hide cocaine in milk. He knows how much to put into the milk to kill her. And that's exactly what he does. And then he wakes up his own daughter who is sleeping—dreaming about Christmas—and he sends her into the kitchen to get the poisoned milk for her mother. He sends a child to poison the mother of his children."

I hesitated again so that the jurors could picture the scene in the Gonzales's home that fatal evening. "What happens next? Does he call for help? Does he rush Benita to the hospital to get her stomach pumped? Of course not. Dr. Swante testified that it took about an hour for Benita to die. She died a painful death. What did the defendant do while she was dying? Maybe he smokes a cigarette. Maybe he has a glass of wine or snorts a line of cocaine. Who knows? But we do know that he was there in that bedroom, watching Benita, watching her go into convulsions. He was there, holding her down as she struggled, keeping her from getting help. He was there staring into her eyes as she frantically gasped for air and finally, painfully died."

I took a deep breath and said, "What does Carlos Gonzales do next? He wakes up Hector and Carmen and tells them to tidy up the room. He calls the cops and the paramedics but first he warns Hector and Carmen to keep quiet about the fights, about the beatings, and to tell everyone that theirs was a happy family. He orders them to lie."

By this point, I had covered all the evidence, reviewed all the testimony, and recounted the night of the murder. But there was still one final point that I needed to make. I was now ready to drop a hammer that I had been holding back for the entire trial.

Stepping briskly over to the table where the exhibits were on display, I picked up the Polaroid photograph of a smiling Benita Gonzales holding her young son while posing with a jolly-faced shopping-mall Santa.

"Before you go into the jury room to deliberate, you need to hear from one final witness: Benita Gonzales—the victim. Look at this photograph. Mr. Pisani would have you believe that Benita was suicidal. Look at her eyebrows in this photo. They are perfectly tweezed. You can see where she created an arch from the small stubs coming in. Look at her fingernails. They are perfectly manicured with bright red nail polish. Look at her hair. It is recently styled. This is not a woman winding down her affairs. This was a woman preparing for the holidays."

Still holding the photo in front of them, I said, "Does a woman who is going to kill herself that night worry about her eyebrows? Does she paint her fingernails? Does she go to her hairdresser? Does she take her children shopping and, when they get home that afternoon, reach under the Christmas tree and pick up the present that her children have just bought her and tease them by saying that she can't wait until Christmas morning, when she can open their precious gift?"

I looked into the faces of the women on the jury. These were the kinds of details a man may not have noticed or understood. The women jurors would.

Pointing at Gonzales, I said, "This man murdered Benita. She had every intention of celebrating the Christmas holidays with her children. She did not put cocaine in her own milk. She did not want to die. She did not accidentally or intentionally commit suicide. He poisoned her. You want hard evidence? Listen to what Benita Gonzales is telling you in this photo. She speaks to you from the grave. Look at her beaming smile, her manicured hands, her love of life, and her love for her children."

Lowering the photo, I said, "Ladies and gentlemen of the jury, while you are in the jury room deliberating, we will be waiting. Waiting for justice for Benita Gonzales."

I sat down.

Moments later, after the jurors had been escorted out and Judge Morano had left the room, my mom came up to me.

"Dear," she said, "that was a brilliant closing statement, but there's something on the edge of your mouth." I wiped my mouth. There was a smudge of chocolate on my lip.

59

TWO HOURS INTO JURY DELIBERA-
tions, the bailiff advised Judge Morano that the jury
had a question regarding one of the court's instructions and reading of the law. We all reconvened as the jury was
brought into the courtroom.

"I understand, Mr. Foreman, that the jury has a question,"
Judge Morano said.

"Yes, Your Honor," the foreman replied. "Please tell us
again about reasonable doubt."

I gulped and Mr. Invincible smirked. It wasn't a good sign
for me.

Judge Morano ordered his stenographer to reread the defi-
nition of reasonable doubt that he had given earlier to the jury.
For me, every word was painful and they were the last words
the jury heard as they again retired into the jury room.

Obviously a juror, or jurors, didn't believe I'd proven my
case beyond a reasonable doubt. I felt sick.

Every defense attorney knows time is on his side; the longer the wait the better the chance of acquittal. As each hour
passed, Mr. Invincible became evermore self-assured and I became less and less confident.

How could this be happening? I saw Carmen in the hallway and turned away from the teenager because I didn't want
her to see the self-doubt in my eyes.

Only the court officers who arranged for breakfast, lunch,

dinner, and travel knew what the jurors were doing in that room. They were close enough to hear the yelling and then the silence during the deliberations. If only I could be a fly on the wall. The wait was becoming unbearable. I couldn't think of anything else. I went through a painstaking analysis. Had I made my points, did I miss something in my summation, did they have enough common sense to connect the dots? Were they strong enough to render a verdict of guilty of murder without having heard from an eyewitness?

Finally, the knock on the jury door came. Was it another question for clarification, a read back of witness testimony, or a verdict? The court officer announced, "The jurors have reached a verdict."

I hurried inside the empty courtroom knowing it would take forever to get the judge, the defense, the stenographer, and the defendant from the bull pen. Mom was with me. The clerk waited patiently with the two of us. Word spread quickly through the halls. Spectators with reserved seats began filing into the courtroom.

Finally, the defendant appeared. His cuffs were unlocked as he stood at the defense table. I looked behind me and was surprised to see the courtroom, which had been empty only minutes before, packed. Carmen was there with her brother, Hector. And in the very back row, near the door, was FBI Agent Longhorn. I avoided his eyes and he avoided mine.

The unbearable silence was broken by a loud voice saying, "All rise," as Judge Morano walked directly into the room and took his seat. In his gruff voice, he told everyone to be seated and announced the obvious: that a verdict had been reached. My heart was pounding so loudly that I could barely hear him direct the court officers to bring in the jury.

They filed in slowly, one by one, without expression. I searched their faces for some sign—any sign—any clue—any indication of what they'd decided. Nothing. But wait, there

was one. It looked like one of the women jurors had been crying. One juror made eye contact with me and nodded as he
took his seat. Was that a good sign?

"Mr. Foreman, have you reached a verdict?" Judge Morano
asked.

The foreman stood and answered, "Yes, Your Honor, we
have."

"Please hand up the verdict sheet." A court officer fetched
it and gave it to the clerk, who passed it to Judge Morano. As I
had with the jurors, I now searched Judge Morano's face for a
clue as he silently read the verdict. I knew Mr. Invincible was
doing the same.

Without the slightest trace of emotion, Judge Morano
handed the sheet to his clerk and said: "There will be no out-
bursts in the courtroom when the verdict is announced."

He directed his clerk to "inquire of the foreman" and ordered Carlos Gonzales to rise from his seat.

The clerk said in a loud, clear voice, "In the matter of the
People of the State of New York versus Carlos Gonzales—"

My mind was racing. Had I done the right thing by indict-
ing Gonzales for murder in the second degree or had it been
too much to ask twelve people to agree unanimously, beyond
a reasonable doubt, without an eyewitness, without a confes-
sion, without even a clear manner of death, when even the
M.E. originally said it was suicide?

The clerk said: "On count one—murder in the second
degree—how do you find the defendant?"

Standing in the jury box, the foreman answered, "Guilty."

I breathed in, not realizing I had been holding my breath.
Gonzales glared at the foreman and each juror. Mr. Invincible
simply glanced down at the defense table.

As each juror was individually polled, their answers of
"yes" faded in the distance as I thought about how long it had
taken to get justice for Benita Gonzales. There would be no

escape into federal protection now. I glanced over my shoulder just in time to see Agent Longhorn duck from the courtroom.

While Judge Morano was thanking the jury and dismissing them, I noticed one of them staring at me. It was juror number five, a retired schoolteacher. She was in her midsixties and I had seen her eyeing the Polaroid with intensity when I was giving my closing statement. I wasn't able to give her any further thought, because as soon as Gonzales was taken away and Judge Morano had exited the courtroom, Carmen raced up to me and gave me a tight hug.

"You did it!" she said, smiling.

"He's going to prison. He'll never hurt you again."

My mother was standing next to Carmen.

"Your father would be so proud of you if he were here," she said.

"I feel as if he is here, Mom. Smiling down from heaven."

Paul Pisani left the courtroom without speaking to me. I didn't expect a compliment, but I thought he might make a snide remark or a sexual innuendo. In the end, he simply tucked his tail between his legs and ran away.

O'Brien was waiting to escort me from the courtroom.

As I stepped outside, Will Harris and other reporters came running up to me. I answered their questions and then, when all of them were leaving, I called Harris to the side.

"You're one of the reasons why I won this case. You told me about the cop in prison and he told me about the boom microphone and the damning tape recordings. I am willing to explain on the record for your readers the role that you played in this case. That way you can write an exclusive and claim credit for helping solve it."

Harris beamed. "I can see a headline in my head: 'Daily Reporter Helps Crack Murder Case.'"

"I like that a lot," I replied.

"But I think you may be giving me too much credit. I just interviewed juror number five and she said it wasn't the tape recording that convinced the jurors. It was your summation—you showing them Benita's photo and pointing out how well-groomed she was. That photo is what did it. As a woman, she understood."

O'BRIEN INVITED ME TO O'TOOLE'S to celebrate with the boys. But I declined. I also turned down an invitation from my mom. All I wanted to do was go home, take a hot bath, grill a steak, and eat a box of dark chocolates for dessert.

I let Wilbur into the kitchen and gave him a can of corn to tide him over until dinner. I stepped outside and lit some charcoal on my hibachi. It took several minutes for the coals to turn red, so I spent them making myself a salad and adding peanut butter to apples for Wilbur. The steak tasted great and Wilbur loved the apples.

By the time I had cleaned up the kitchen, it had turned dark and started raining. I led a reluctant Wilbur outside to his pen. There was no way that I was going to risk having him wake me up grunting in the morning. I was emotionally and physically exhausted and wanted to sleep late for once on a Saturday morning.

Lightning crackled and the rain felt good and cool on my skin as I dashed back inside. I locked the back door and crossed through the kitchen on my way to the bathroom to start a bath. As I entered the dining room, I noticed my front door was wide open.

I stopped in my tracks.

My purse with the .357 snub nose was on the dining-room table. I was taking a step toward it when I was smacked hard in my right shoulder by a baseball bat with such force that I was knocked to the floor. I heard a crack and knew my collarbone was broken. The pain was immediate and intense.

Looking up from the floor where I was lying on my back, I saw the masked face of a man dressed in black, towering above me with a wooden bat in his hand. There was no way I could get to my purse and pistol now because he was standing between me and the table.

He threw the baseball bat to one side, reached into the front pouch of his black sweatshirt, and withdrew a knife, which he flipped open with a twist of his wrist. Without warning, he kicked me in my abdomen, causing me to gasp for air. Stepping backward, he used his left hand to remove his ski mask.

Juan Lopez looked down at me.

"I told you that Maya was mine but you didn't listen."

He kicked me again, causing me to roll from my side completely over onto my stomach. As I was lying helpless and in pain on the floor watching him, Juan put his knife on the dining-room table and pulled his sweatshirt over his head. I could see the "MAYA" carved in his flabby stomach.

Retrieving his blade, he said, "I'm going to slit my own wrists and join Maya in heaven—right after I send you to hell."

Using my good arm, I pushed myself up and managed to bolt across the dining room. I was trying to get into my bedroom where my second gun, the .38 Wesson revolver, was on the nightstand.

"Run, run," he taunted me. "But you can't hide."

As I entered my bedroom, he caught up with me, grabbed my hair, and jerked me backward, causing my legs to fly out from under me. I landed hard on the floorboards and felt something warm flowing from my head. I was dazed but knew it was blood.

"Juan, hurting me isn't going to bring back Maya!"

"Oh, I'm going to hurt you. I'm going to hurt you bad. I'm going to carve a name into your chest. You know what name? BITCH. And then I'm going to put you in the oven just like I did Maya. The heat is going to purify your soul and burn away your sins."

He bent down, reaching for my blouse, but I was able to spin out of the way and roll into the hallway. Juan was now standing between me and my nightstand. I managed to get on my feet as he stepped forward swinging the knife at my face.

I ducked and ran faster than I thought imaginable toward the still-open front door.

He swung at me again as he chased me but missed as I dashed through the doorway out onto the front porch. The surface was wet and I started to slip backward. I immediately compensated by throwing my body forward—a move that caused me to lose my footing and tumble off the porch onto the wet front lawn. I hit so hard that the fall knocked the breath from my lungs. I spun over onto my back and looked up just in time to see Juan looming over me as the rain pelted both of us in the evening darkness. He raised the knife, which he was now holding with both hands, and was about to plunge the blade down into me when I heard a low boom and watched as a huge hole burst open in Juan's naked chest. His entire body flew backward. He hit the porch hard and didn't move.

O'Brien came running up to me holding a .12-gauge shotgun.

"You okay?"

I was soaked, my shoulder hurt like hell, and I'd been kicked in the gut and traumatized by a knife-wielding madman who wanted to cut my chest and stick me in an oven. "Yeah. I'm fine."

"I thought you might need a bit of watching tonight," he said. "I decided to skip going to O'Toole's with the boys."

He helped me to my feet and we walked over to where

Juan's body was lying motionless on my porch. O'Brien kicked Juan's foot.

"Huh. I thought it would be Rudy Hitchins lying here, not Juan Lopez," O'Brien said.

I felt a chill. Rudy Hitchins was still out there somewhere in the darkness, still seeking revenge.

O'Brien removed his toothpick and said to the corpse, "Let this be a lesson to you, punk. Never bring a knife to a gunfight." Inserting the toothpick back between his lips, he grinned and said, "God, I've always wanted to say that!"

EPILOGUE

A Week Later

I WAS LATE. AS USUAL. IT WAS MY FIRST day back after the shooting. As I made my way across the parking lot toward the front door of the Westchester County Courthouse, I saw a man walking several steps in front of me.

Oh crap, I thought. It was miserable Judge Morano. I intentionally slowed down. When he reached the front door, I expected him to hurry inside. But instead, he opened the door, turned, and looked at me.

"Hurry up, Miss Fox. We have serious cases waiting for us."

I walked with him into the lobby.

He was right.

ACKNOWLEDGMENTS

There are many to thank:

The countless men, women, and children who have crossed my path—those victims who demonstrated great courage and resolve in the face of enormous odds. They are the real heroes who give meaning to those of us who do the work of criminal justice.

Pete Earley, my collaborator, who comes to this effort with a background in reporting and writing as well as an intricate knowledge of the Federal Witness Protection Program. His assistance has been immeasurable. I am most grateful that he, like me, is willing to eat cold pizza during deadlines.

A special thank-you to Gretchen Young from Hyperion for her insight and intuition and her never-ending perseverance in the pursuit of the perfectly edited book. To her assistant, Allyson Rudolph, who works above and beyond to make sure the product is a good one. To Diane Aronson for her thorough work.

David Vigliano, who approached me when I was the sitting District Attorney of Westchester County, New York, to write a book such as this and who was steadfast in his effort to get me to put pen to paper. I thank him for his persistence.

My former District Attorney staff, including Chief Assistant Richard E. Weill; Executive Assistant David Hebert; Annemarie Corbalis, who fought in the trenches with me in the Domestic Violence Unit; and Roseanne Paniccia, my assistant and gatekeeper who always keeps me organized. Also, to Deborah Trevorah for putting in countless hours of transcribing and typing this manuscript.

To Al Pirro, who actually lived those years with me and whose recollection of the lunacy surrounding my early years in the district attorney's office is uncanny. His wisdom and brilliant mind never cease to amaze me. Thanks, Al, for your contributions to this book.

Finally, to my two children, Kiki and Alex, who have both chosen to follow their parents' footsteps into the legal profession. May they each find as much satisfaction and challenge in their pursuit of justice as I have found pursuing justice for society's underdogs.

If you enjoyed *Sly Fox*,
be sure to catch *Clever Fox*,
the new Dani Fox novel from
Judge Jeanine Pirro,
coming soon from Hyperion.

An excerpt, the Prologue and
Chapter One, follows.

PROLOGUE

THE GAG KEPT HER FROM SCREAMING and begging for her life. He didn't need to hear her cries or pleas to know how terrified she was. It showed in her dark eyes. Earlier, he'd bound her hands with an electrical cord that he'd cut from a bedside alarm clock and lassoed through an eye-hook that he'd screwed into the ceiling. She was now squirming helplessly in front of him on her tiptoes like an animal waiting to be killed and gutted.

He started with her clothing, savoring each twitch and tremble that she made as he cut through the expensive fabric. He wondered: Did she know what was about to happen? Fear was the ultimate rush. Better than crack cocaine. Better than sex. He took a step backward to admire her now-nude body.

This was the moment he'd been waiting for. The drawing of first blood is what he most enjoyed. There was no reason to hurry. He would inflict as much pain as humanly possible before she took her last breath.

As he reached forward with the knife blade extended, he felt true euphoria. He was God, only, rather than creating life, he was about to end one.

PART ONE

A NEW YEAR'S PROMISE

There will be killing till the score is paid.

—HOMER, THE ODYSSEY

Twelve minutes before midnight, December 31, 1979

"GET READY!" WILL HARRIS EXCLAIMED as he wrapped his left arm around my waist while hoisting a plastic cup of champagne to his lips with his other hand. "I can't think of anyone who I'd rather be spending New Year's Eve with."

He leaned down and gently kissed my cheek.

"I feel exactly the same way," I replied.

But his comment made me curious. It sounded as if he had done a mental inventory of all the women in his life before he'd decided that I was his best choice for the evening. Or maybe that was just the prosecutor in me coming out, reading too much into what was clearly supposed to be a compliment. Maybe it was because I had been hurt and lost at love before. My former boyfriend, Bob, had taken away my faith in men. Could I ever believe a guy again? How would I know if it was real?

Both of us looked upward at the glittering ball on the rooftop of One Times Square. It was a clear night, the stars visible in a dark blue sky.

Will had wanted to spend New Year's Eve at my house in suburban White Plains, New York, lounging in front of a cozy fire counting down the final seconds of 1979 along with Dick Clark.

But I'd insisted on escaping into Manhattan to watch the ball drop in Times Square.

My name is Dani Fox and I'm an assistant district attorney in Westchester County, a wealthy suburban enclave. I'm our county's only female prosecutor. Just 110 male assistant district attorneys and me. My specialties are crimes against women and children. Two years ago, I created one of the nation's first Domestic Violence Units and I often spend my days prosecuting husbands who believe their marriage vow gives them the right to beat their wives senseless.

These last few months have been especially difficult. My boyfriend, Will, is a reporter at the *White Plains Daily* and he chronicled several of the incidents that have turned my life topsy-turvy. My troubles began after I filed charges against Carlos Gonzales, a popular Hispanic businessman who'd beaten and raped his teenage daughter. It was a high-profile case and as soon as I got a jury to convict him, our esteemed Federal Bureau of Investigation rushed in to save him because they wanted Gonzales's help in a Manhattan drug case and that was considered more important than punishing a father for beating and raping his own daughter. The Justice Department offered Gonzales a free pass. In return for his testimony, he was told that he'd get a new identity and a fresh start in the Federal Witness Protection Program. Oh yeah, the Feds also were going to relocate his younger kids with him. I was horrified, did some digging, and discovered that this dirtbag also had murdered his wife. Her death had been considered a suicide. I got a jury to convict him again, which stopped the FBI from turning him loose. As you can imagine, that case hadn't made me any friends in the FBI.

On the same night that Gonzales was convicted, I was attacked in my own house by a deranged husband intent on carving the word *bitch* into my chest. Fortunately for me, Detective Tommy O'Brien, a big Irish cop who works with me at our unit, arrived just in time to stop the attack by firing a gut-ripping round of buckshot into my knife-wielding assailant.

Like I said, 1979 was a tough year.

There were some good things though. My pet pig, Wilbur, had survived a nasty encounter with pneumonia and nearly died. And I'd started dating Will, although I doubt Will would appreciate being lumped together with my pig's nearly fatal cold when it came to recalling the year's highlights.

Being with him—Will, not Wilbur—in Times Square tonight was exactly what I needed to take my mind off the pain and suffering that I witnessed every day in my office. It is heartbreaking to see the violence that men commit against the very women whom they'd promised to love and cherish as long as they both shall live.

"Five minutes!" Will said, sounding like an excited schoolboy.

I glanced at him. No one would mistake him for a fashion model, but Will was nice looking, tall, and fit. He had a strong jaw, a mop of sandy brown hair that always seemed to need a trim, and wore wire-rim glasses that he was constantly pushing up on his nose. It was his personality that first attracted me to him. Will was curious and smart, a workaholic—just like me—and passionate about his job. If you asked Will who he worked for, he wouldn't answer with the name of company that owned the *White Plains Daily*. A corporate official might have signed his paycheck, but Will said that he worked for the public.

The mob in Times Square crowded together more tightly. A tipsy, tall brunette bumped against me, spilling her champagne on my new black leather coat. I didn't complain. 'Tis the season. "Nineteen eighty is going to be our year," Will declared.

Our year? What, exactly had he meant? There were still parts of Will that remained a mystery; parts that I felt he was keeping hidden from me. Maybe he is just more private than I am. I say what's on my mind and rarely hold anything back when I'm in a relationship. Maybe Will is just more cautious about protecting himself from being hurt.

"Ten, nine, eight, seven," everyone began chanting in unison. Will and I joined in.

"Six, five, four."

I felt wonderful. It wasn't the cheap champagne that Will had brought with us. It was a feeling of anticipation, renewal, and saying goodbye to the one hell of an awful year!

"Three, two, one!"

A roar of "Happy New Year!" enveloped us as Will pulled me close and we kissed. I stood on my toes with my hands around his neck.

We held each other tightly for a minute and were about to kiss again when I felt the pager in my coat pocket shaking. The pager in his jacket began vibrating, too. We reached for them simultaneously. The only pages I get are emergencies so I knew it was not some New Year's Eve greeting from a friend. When the police call, they use a number code on my pager to tip me off. Will's newspaper does the same. We glanced at our codes and both said, "Shit!"

Without uttering another word, Will guided me through the sea of loud partygoers who were completely oblivious to the fact that someone had just been murdered. From a pay phone in a jammed bar on Forty-Third Street, I called the Yonkers police dispatcher who'd paged me.

"The vic's a woman," he said matter-of-factly. "Murdered and more."

"And more?"

"Some asshole cut pieces of her skin off."

"Butchered?"

"Tortured."

I handed Will the phone after I finished my call. He dialed the newspaper's city desk. After he finished, he said, "Sorry,

Dani, this isn't how I expected the first night of our new year together to end."

"Me, either," I replied, grabbing the lapel of his coat, pulling him close, and kissing him. But my mind was already miles away. Someone around us broke into a chorus of "Auld Lang Syne."

"How you getting there?" Will yelled above the singing.

"The usual. Squad car. Lights and sirens."

Will knew better than to ask for a ride. Arriving together would have crossed a line. "I got to go," he said. "It's going to take me much longer to get to Yonkers than you."

As he started to leave, I said, "See you at the homicide," and I thought: This is a hell of a way to welcome in the New Year!